OTHER BOOKS BY
JONATHAN STROUD

THE BARTIMAEUS TRILOGY:

The Amulet of Samarkand

The Golem's Eye

Ptolemy's Gate

The Leap

Buried Fire

HEROES
OF THE
VALLEY

JONATHAN STROUD

DISNEY · HYPERION BOOKS
NEW YORK

Printed in the United States of America

First Edition
10 9 8 7 6 5 4 3 2 1
Library of Congress Cataloging-in-Publication Data on file.

Designed by Elizabeth H. Clark

Reinforced binding
ISBN 978-1-4231-0966-2
Visit www.hyperionbooksforchildren.com

For Jill and John, with love

Main Characters

Svein's House

Arnkel	*Arbiter of the House*
Astrid	*Lawgiver of the House*
Leif	*Their elder son*
Gudny	*Their daughter*
Halli	*Their younger son*
Brodir	*Arnkel's brother*
Katla	*Halli's nurse*

Hakon's House

Hord	*Arbiter of the House*
Olaf	*His brother*
Ragnar	*Hord's son*

Arne's House

Ulfar	*Arbiter and Lawgiver of the House*
Aud	*His daughter*

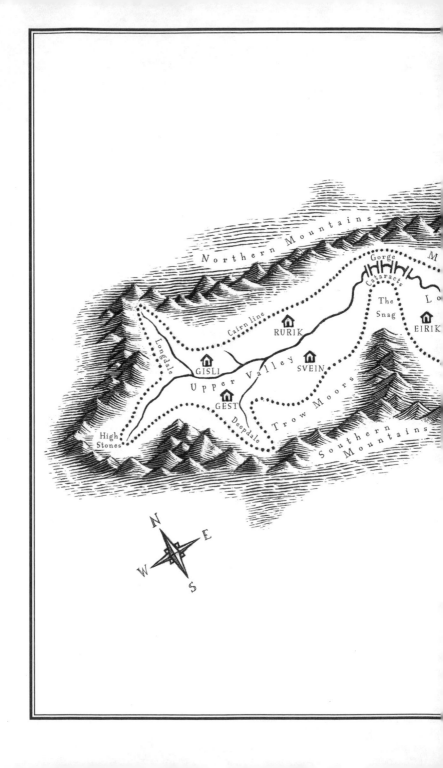

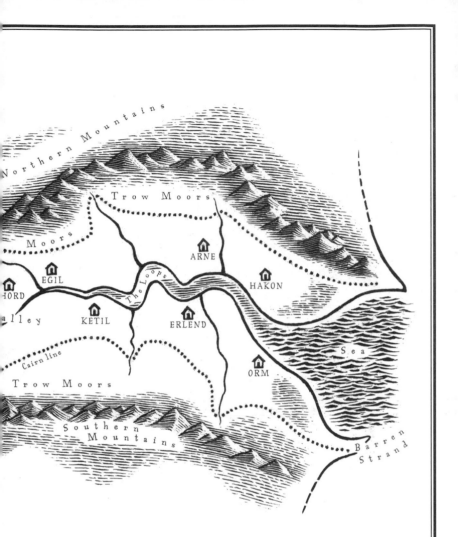

MAP of the VALLEY

SHOWING THE TWELVE HOUSES
OF THE HEROES

LISTEN THEN, and I'll tell you again of the Battle of the Rock. But none of your usual wriggling, or I'll stop before I've begun.

In those early years after the settlers came, the Trows infested the whole valley from Riversmouth to High Stones. After dark, not a home, not a byre, not a stable was safe from them. Their tunnels honeycombed the fields and went under the farmers' doors. Each night saw cows taken from the pastures and sheep from the slopes. Men walking late were snatched under within sight of home. Women and babies were dragged from their beds; in the morning, their blankets were found half buried in the earth. No one knew where the Trows' holes might open next, or what might be done.

To begin with, the people of each House paved their farms with heavy granite slabs—hall, stable, yards, and all, so that the Trows could not break through—and they circled the buildings with high stone walls, and posted guards upon them. This improved matters. But at night the fingers of the Trows could still be heard tap-tap-tapping below the floor stones, searching for weaknesses. It was not a pleasant situation.

Now for some years Svein had been in his prime, the greatest hero of the valley. He had slain many Trows in single combat, as well as ridding the roads of outlaws, wolves, and other menaces. But not everyone had his prowess, and he thought it was time to do something about the problem once and for all.

So he called the other heroes together one day in midsummer. All twelve met on a meadow midway along the valley—near where Eirik's House is now—and to begin with, there was much bristling of beards and flexing of shoulders, and every hand was on its sword hilt.

But Svein said: "Friends, it's no secret we've had our differences in the past. My leg is scarred, Ketil, where your spear point struck, and I fancy your backside still aches where I shot that arrow. But today I propose a truce. These Trows are getting out of hand. I suggest we stand together and drive them from the valley. What about it?"

As you'd expect, the others coughed and hummed and looked in every direction but at Svein. At last Egil stepped forward. "Svein," said he, "your words are like an arrow bolt in my heart. I'll stand with you." And one by one, motivated perhaps by shame as much as bravery, the others did likewise.

Then Thord said, "That's all very well, but what's in it for us?"

Svein said, "If we vow to protect the valley, it henceforth belongs to us forevermore. How's that sound?"

The others said that would do very nicely.

Then Orm said, "Where shall we make our stand?"

"I know the very place," said Svein, and he led the way to where a great rock rose from the meadow, tilted on its side in the wet earth. Heaven knows how it got there; it's half again as big as a farmhouse, as if a piece of the cliffs above the valley had been snapped off by a giant, and tossed into the field for fun. This stone lies aslant so that it rises like a ramp from the field. The lower portion is covered in grass and moss, but the higher parts are bare. A coppice of pine trees grows about it, and one or two trees are even balanced on the rock itself. It was called the Wedge then, but they call it Battle Rock now. Gatherings at Eirik's House are held there. You'll see it one day.

Svein then said, "Friends, let our next action, which summons the Trows, also bond us, so that we protect each other as best we can."

Then they drew their swords and each one cut another's forearm, so that their blood dripped upon the earth at the base of the great stone. The sun was just going down.

"That's good timing," Svein said. "Now we wait."

The men stood there, side by side along the rock's base, staring out across the fields.

It so happened that the stone walls around the Houses had been very successful at keeping the Trows out, so that famine gnawed in their bellies and made them desperate for the meat of men. When they smelled the spilled blood in the earth, they came hastening from far away. But to begin with, the men heard nothing.

After a while Svein said, "These Trows are getting sluggish. We'll catch our death of cold standing here all night."

And Rurik said, "The women will have drunk the kegs dry by the time we get home. This weighs on my mind."

And Gisli said, "This field of yours, Eirik, is really very bumpy. We should do you a favor and till it for you, once we've killed the Trows."

Just then they heard a faint, persistent noise, a scratchy sort of hum. It came from underground and all around them.

"That's good," Svein said. "I was getting bored."

While they were waiting, the moon had come out over Styr's Widow (which is the mountain with the hump-peak you can see from Gudny's window), and it shone its light full on the ground. And all across the field they could see the nettles and tussocks shaking as the Trows passed beneath them, tearing through the soil. Soon every inch of ground on that great field was settling and shifting back and forth as if it were water. But the men had their boots on solid rock and stood steady, though they did move back a pace.

Then Gisli said, "That's one job we don't have to do, after all. Eirik's field is going to be nicely tilled before the night's over."

But that was one comment too many for Gisli. Just as he spoke, the ground at his feet exploded with a shower of earth and a Trow rose up, grabbed Gisli by the neck with its long, thin hands, and pulled him down onto his knees in the mud of the field. Then it bit his throat out. Gisli was so surprised he didn't say anything.

With this, the moon went behind a cloud and the men were left blind.

They took another step back in the darkness, holding their swords in front of them, and listening to Gisli's body thrashing on the ground. A minute went by.

All at once, the sound of digging rose from a hum to a mutter to a roar, and along the base of the tilted rock the Trows burst forth, spattering the men with soil and reaching with their clasping fingers. Svein and the rest stepped back again, a little way up the rock, for they knew that Trows are weakened when they no longer touch the earth. And soon they heard the claws clicking on the stone.

Then—blinded as they were—they swung their

swords mightily and had the satisfaction of hearing several heads go bouncing down upon the rock. But as the dead Trows fell, new ones erupted from the churned muck of the field, and still more came pressing behind them, snapping their teeth and stretching out their thin, thin arms.

Little by little the line drew back up the slope, fighting all the way. The sides of that rock are steep and clifflike, yet the Trows clambered up them even so. The hero Gest, who was standing at one end of the line, stepped too close to the edge; the Trows grasped his ankle and pulled him down into the boiling horde. He wasn't seen again.

By now the remaining ten were weary, and most of them were wounded. They had retreated almost to the top of the rock, above where the pine trees grow, and they knew that somewhere close behind was a precipice dropping to the field. But still the Trows pressed at them, jaws gaping, claws slashing, crooning with hunger.

"Now," Svein said, "it would be pleasant to have a little light, if only so we could wake up and fight properly. I've been dozing all this time, and the rest has done me good."

Even as he spoke, the moon came out at last from behind the clouds and shone harshly on the scene. It did so as if in answer to Svein's words, which is why to this day we of his line all wear clothes of silver black.

And in that first flash of moonlight, all was revealed: the great rock rising, its slope choked black with the bodies of the Trows; the field itself, a waste of pits and holes through which the enemy still came; the summit of the rock, not ten paces from the precipice, where ten bloodied men still held their ground.

"Friends," Svein said then, "it is midsummer. The night will not last forever."

And with that, all ten gave a great cry and redoubled their efforts joyfully and not one of them took another step back toward the edge of that cliff.

Dawn came; the sun rose over the sea. With the light, the people of the nearby House, who had lain awake all night trembling in their beds, unlocked the gates and ventured into the fields. It was very silent now.

They picked their way across the field, among the pits and holes, and when they got to the base of the rock they found the Trows' bodies piled there like chaff.

Then they looked up and seemed to see twelve men standing high above them on the rock, though the dawn rays shone so strongly along the valley that it was hard to be sure. They climbed up eagerly, only to find, right at the very top, ten dead men lying slumped together in a line, their eyes unseeing, their hands still warm upon their swords.

So! That is the story, and the truth of it. Since that day no living Trow has dared enter the valley, though still they watch us hungrily from above.

Now pass me that ale and let me drink. My throat is parched.

PART

I

1

SVEIN WAS A BABY when he came to the valley with the settlers. They'd been so long in the mountains, the sun and snow had burned their faces black. When they came down at last among the sweet green forests, they stopped to rest in a quiet glade. Baby Svein sat in the grass and looked about him. What did he see? Sky, trees, his parents sleeping. Also a great black serpent, winding from behind a log, fangs drawn back to strike his mother's throat. What did he do? He reached out his chubby hands and caught the snake by its tail. When his parents woke they saw Svein grinning at them, a throttled serpent hanging like rope between his fists.

Svein's father said: "This portent's clear. Our son shall be a hero. When he's old enough, he shall have my sword and silver belt, and with them he shall never lose a battle."

Svein's mother said: "The valley will belong to him. Let's build our farm here. It's a place of luck for us."

So it was. Other settlers spread about the valley, but *our* House, first and greatest, was built right here.

HALLI SVEINSSON WAS BORN shortly after noon one Midwinter's Day, when snow clouds hung low over Svein's House and the skirts of the hills could not be seen. In the very hour of his birth the drifts piled so high against the old Trow walls that a portion of them collapsed. Some people said this was a portent of great good in the boy, others of great evil; the man whose pigs the wall had crushed had no opinion either way, but wanted recompense from the child's parents. He sought arbitration on the matter at the Gathering the following year, but the case was thrown out as unproven.

When Halli was older, Katla, his nurse, drew his attention to the date of his arrival in the world. She clucked and whistled through her nose at the sinister implications. "It is a dangerous day, Midwinter," she said, as she tucked him tight into his cot. "Brats born then have an affinity with dark and secret things, with witchcraft and the promptings of the moon. You must be careful not to listen to this side of your nature, else it will lead without fail to your death and the destruction of your loved ones. Aside from that, dear Halli, there is nothing to worry about. Sleep well."

Despite the raging snowstorm, Halli's father took the blood and bits from the midwife as soon as the cord was cut, and set out up the hill. After a climb that left him frostbitten in three fingers, he got to the cairns and threw the gift beyond the stones for the Trows to feed on. It was considered that they must have liked what they ate, because from the first, the baby drank lustily at the breast. He grew fat and thrived, and the black creep did not touch him all that winter. He was the first of Astrid's children to live since Gudny's birth three years before, and this was a matter for great rejoicing among the people of the House.

In the spring, Halli's parents held a feast to celebrate the latest in Svein's line. The cradle was set out upon the dais in the hall, and the people shuffled past to pay their respects. Arnkel and Astrid sat together on the Law Seats and accepted the birth gifts—the offerings of skins, cloth, carved toys, and pickled vegetables—while little Gudny stood stiff and silent at her mother's side, her blond hair immaculately braided into a dragon's tail. Halli's older brother, Leif, heir to the House and all its lands, ignored the proceedings; he played with the dogs under the table, fighting with them for scraps.

Cradleside comment was loudly complimentary, but at the corners of the hall, where Eyjolf and the servants had stacked the ale-kegs and the lantern smoke coiled thickly, opinions were less sure.

"The baby is a peculiar-looking creature."

"There is nothing of his mother in him."

"More to the point, nothing of his *father*. I see more of his uncle there."

"A Trow is more likely! Astrid cannot abide Brodir; that's no secret."

"Well, the boy has life in him, all the same. Listen to him cry!"

As Halli grew, his distinctiveness did not diminish. His father, black-maned Arnkel, was broad in shoulder and sinewy in limb, a tall, commanding presence in the hall and fields. His mother, Astrid, had fair tresses and the pinkish skin of her kin down-valley; she too was tall and slender, with a beauty strange and disquieting among the dark-haired people of Svein's House. Leif and Gudny mirrored their parents in miniature: both were considered slim, graceful, and easy on the eye.

By contrast, Halli was from the first short in leg and broad in back, a cumbersome stump of a boy, with hands like ham-joints, and a low, swinging gait. His skin was swarthy even by the standards of men bred among the mountains. With a small, snubbed nose, a defiant, protruding chin, and wide-spaced eyes alive with curiosity, he glared out at the world from under an unruly mess of thick black hair.

His father would sit the infant Halli on his lap at mealtimes and study him fondly, while chubby fingers explored the wiry bristle-comb of his beard and tugged it till the tears came. "The boy is strong, Astrid," he gasped, "and mettlesome. Did Eyjolf tell you he caught him toddling in the stables? Right between Hrafn's hooves he went, and began to tweak his tail!"

"And where was Katla while our child risked death? Oh, I shall pull her silly hair for negligence."

"Do not chide her. She is growing short of breath and is easily bewildered. Gudny can help guard her brother—eh,

Gudny?" Arnkel ruffled his daughter's hair, making her flinch and scowl up from her needlework.

"Not me. He went prying in my room and ate my cloudberries. Get Leif to do it."

But Leif was out in the moat-meadow, throwing stones at birds.

In those early years the demands of hall and House kept Astrid and Arnkel from active involvement with Halli's daily welfare. Instead it fell to Katla, his ancient, white-haired, bark-skinned crone of a nurse to tend to his needs, just as she had tended Leif's and Gudny's, and before them all, their father's also. Katla was stiff and bent as a gallows, a shuffling hedge-witch whose appearance sent the girls of Svein's House squealing to their doors. But her almond eyes were bright and her knowledge gushed unceasingly. Halli loved her without restraint.

In the mornings she brought the warm tub to Halli's room by candlelight and, after washing him, wrestled him into his tunic and leggings, combed his hair, and led him to the hall for breakfast. Then she sat nearby, head nodding in the sunlight, while he played with wood shards on the rushes of the floor. Most days, she dozed; most days Halli would promptly lever himself up and totter off to explore the private rooms behind the hall, or venture out into the yard, where the echo of Grim's anvil mingled with the whirring of the weavers' looms and he could watch the men working far off on the hill. From Svein's House it was possible to see the ridges on both sides of the valley, and the little dark uneven stubs that ran continuously along the tops. They reminded Halli of Katla's teeth. Behind the cairns, hazy with distance even on a clear day, were the mountains, white-crested, flanks dropping precipitously out of view.

Often Halli lost himself down the lanes and side alleys of the House, strolling happily with the dogs among the workshops, cottages, sties, and stables until hunger drove him back at last to Katla's anxious embrace. In the evening they ate apart from his family in the kitchen of the hall, a comfortable region full of hot, savorsome vapors, broad benches, and pitted tables, with the glow of the fire reflecting in a hundred hanging pots and dishes.

There Katla would talk and Halli would listen.

"Without question," she would say, "your features come from your father's side. You are the image of his uncle Onund, who farmed High Crag when I was a girl."

This was an unknowable gulf of time. Some people claimed Katla was more than sixty years old.

"Uncle Onund . . ." Halli repeated. "Was he *very* handsome, Katla?"

"He was the ugliest of men, and had a difficult temperament to boot. By day he was amenable enough and indeed something of a weakling, as you yourself may be. But after dark he gained greatly in strength, and was liable to ferocious rages in which he tossed men through windows and snapped benches in his hall."

This awoke Halli's interest. "Where did this magical strength come from?"

"Most probably drink. In the end, an aggrieved tenant smothered him in his sleep, and it is a measure of the dislike in which Onund was held that the Council merely fined his killer six sheep and a hen. Indeed, the fellow ended by marrying the widow."

"I do not think I am like my great-uncle Onund, Katla."

"Well, you certainly do not have his height. Ah! See how your face corrugates sensually when you frown! You are Onund to the life. It is clear enough to look at you that you are prone to evil just as he was. You must guard against his darker impulses. But in the meantime you must eat those sprouts."

It did not take Halli long to discover that—Onund possibly excepted—his lineage was a matter of importance to everyone at Svein's House. This was welcome to a degree, since every door was open to him: he could wander at will past the sour-smelling vats of Unn the tanner and lie beneath the drying racks, looking up at the skins flapping against the sky; he could stand in the hot blackness of Grim's forge, watching the sparks dance like demons beneath the crashing hammer; he could sit with the women washing clothes in the stream below the walls and listen to their talk of lawsuits, marriages, and other Houses far away down-valley by the sea.

There were some fifty persons at the farm; by age four Halli knew the names of all, together with most of their secrets and peculiarities. This valuable information came more readily to him than the other children of the House.

On the other hand his status resulted in much unwanted attention. As Arnkel's second son, Halli's life was valuable: should Leif succumb to creep or marsh-fever, Halli would be heir. It meant that he was frequently prevented from carrying out important activities at the most inconvenient moment. Vigilant bystanders plucked him from the Trow wall as he began to navigate its teetering brink; they stopped him sailing the goose pond on an upturned trough with a pitchfork for an oar. Most often they pulled him away from older, bigger boys just as they came to blows.

In such cases he was brought before his mother, where she sat sewing and reciting genealogies with Gudny in the hall.

"Why *this* time, Halli?"

"Brusi insulted me, Mother. I wished to fight him."

A sigh. "How precisely did he insult you?"

"I do not wish to say. It doesn't bear repeating."

"*Halli . . .*" This was spoken in a deeper, more dangerous voice.

"If you must know, he called me a fat-thighed marsh imp; I overheard him as he spoke with Ingirid! Why are you laughing, Gudny?"

"It's just that Brusi's description is so delightfully apt, little Halli. It amuses me."

"Halli," his mother said patiently, "Brusi is twice your age and size. Admittedly his wit is wearisome, but still, you must ignore it. Why? Because if you fight, he would hammer you into the ground like a short, squat tent peg, which would not be appropriate for a son of Svein."

"But how else am I to protect my honor, Mother? Or of those close to me? What about when Brusi calls Gudny a thin-lipped, preening little sow? Must I sit back and ignore this matter too?"

Gudny emitted an incoherent noise and put down her stitching. "Brusi said *that*?"

"Not yet. But it is surely only a matter of time."

"Mother!"

"Halli, do not be insolent. You have no need to protect your honor with violent acts. Look to the wall!" She pointed up into the shadows above the Law Seats, where Svein's weapons hung muffled in the dust of years. "The days are long past when men made fools of themselves for honor. You must set an example as Arnkel's son! What if something should happen to Leif? You would become Arbiter yourself, as—as what number in direct line from our Founder, Gudny?"

"Eighteenth," Gudny said instantly. She looked smug. Halli made a face at her.

"Good girl. As eighteenth in line, after Arnkel and Thorir and Flosi and the others going back in time, all of whom were great men. In your father's case he is so still.

Don't you aspire to be like your father, Halli?"

Halli shrugged. "I'm sure he digs excellent beet fields, and turns manure with a deft technique. In truth his example does not overthrill me. I prefer—" He stopped.

Gudny glanced up slyly from her work. "A man like Uncle Brodir. Isn't that so, Halli?"

Blood came to the face of Halli's mother then. She banged her fist upon the table. "That's enough! Gudny, not a word more! Halli, be gone! If you are troublesome again, I shall have your father beat you."

Halli and Gudny had learned early that mentioning their uncle Brodir was a reliable method of upsetting their mother deeply. She who as Lawgiver dealt imperturbably in the hall with the rankest murderers and thieves found the very name distasteful and hard to stomach. At some level her brother-in-law offended her, though she never spoke the reason.

For Halli, this curious power only added to Brodir's allure, a fascination that had begun in early childhood with his uncle's beard. Alone of all the men of Svein's House, Brodir did not shape the hair upon his face. Halli's father, for instance, in a ritual of great solemnity, regularly stood above a hot tub, staring through the steam at a polished reflective disc, methodically shaving his cheekbones and his lower neck before trimming the rest with a small bone-handled knife. His mustache was carefully curled, his beard kept to the length of the first knuckle on his forefinger. His example as Arbiter was followed by the other men of the House, save Kugi the sty-boy, who, though a man, was hairless on his chin—and Brodir. Brodir never touched his beard at all. It bloomed out like a gorse thicket, a nest for crows, an ivy entanglement strangling a tree. Halli was entranced by it.

"Shaping a beard is a down-valley tradition," Brodir advised him. "In these parts it has long been thought unmanly."

"But everyone apart from you does it."

"Oh, well, *they* follow your father, and *he* is influenced by dear Astrid, who comes from Erlend's House down among the Loops, where people's hair is so light-rooted it often blows off in the sea winds. It makes little difference if *they* clip and preen."

Beard aside, Brodir was unlike Halli's father in so many ways it was hard to imagine they had blood kinship at all. Where Arnkel was big-boned, Brodir was slight (though inclined to an ale-paunch around the belly), and with a somewhat pudgy, ill-formed face ("Onund's stock again," was Katla's verdict). Arnkel radiated a ponderous authority, but Brodir had none whatsoever and seemed the happier for it. Despite being a second son, he had never taken possession of one of the smaller farms dotted among the lands of Svein's House. It was said that in his youth he had traveled far along the valley; now he remained at the old hall, working in the fields among the men, and drinking with them after dark. Most evenings he was consequently raucous, humorous, and abrasive. Occasionally he absented himself on his horse, Brawler, and disappeared for days, returning wild-eyed with stories of what he'd seen.

And it was the stories that Halli loved him for above all.

On summer evenings, while Brodir was sober, and the westering sun still warmed the bench outside the hall, they sat together, looking up toward the southern ridge, and talked. Then Halli heard of the rich lands of the Loops, where the river was languorous and the cows and farmers both grew fat; he heard of the estuary beyond, where the Houses were built on great stone levees so that during the floods of spring they seemed to float upon the water, chimneys gently smoking, like scattered boats or islands. He heard, too, of the higher tributaries, where the valley petered out among places of waterfall and tumbled stone, where grass gave over to slate and no animals lived except the chits and chaffinches.

But always Brodir returned at last to the greatest of the Twelve Houses—Svein's—to its leaders, the Arbiters and Lawgivers, to their feuds and love affairs, and the positions of their cairns upon the hill. And above all, he told of Svein himself, of his countless startling adventures, of his escapades upon the moors when it was still permitted to go there, and of the great Battle of the Rock, when he and the lesser heroes held out against the Trows and drove them from the valley to the heights.

"See his cairn up there?" Brodir would say, pointing with his cup. "Well, it's more like a mound now, I suppose, with all the grass upon it. All the heroes were buried like that, up on the ridge above their Houses. Know how they positioned him inside?"

"No, Uncle."

"Sitting on a stone seat, facing toward the moors, with his sword upright in his hand. Know why?"

"To scare the Trows."

"Yes, and keep them scared. It's worked, too."

"Are there cairns *all* along the valley? Not just here?"

"From Riversmouth to High Stones, both sides. We all follow the heroes and reinforce the boundary like good children. There are as many piles of stones above the valley as there are leaves on a summer tree, and each pile sits atop a forgotten son or daughter of a House."

"I will one day be like Svein," Halli said stoutly, "and do great deeds that are long remembered. Though I do not much want to end up on the hill."

Brodir sat back on the bench. "You will find such deeds are difficult now. Where are the swords? Under the cairns or rusting on the walls! We are none of us allowed to be like Svein anymore. . . ." He took a sip of ale. "Save perhaps in our early deaths. All us Sveinssons die young. But no doubt your mother has told you this."

"She has not."

"Oh, and she a great one for the histories! So she did

not tell you of my elder brother, Leif? What happened to him?"

"No."

"Ah . . ." He looked contemplatively at his cup.

"*Uncle—*"

"Eaten by wolves up-valley, age sixteen." Brodir pulled at his nose and sniffed. "It had been a hard winter for the wolves, and proved harder still for Leif. The attack happened on Gestsson land, but the pack had come down from the Trow-moors, so our family could not prove negligence. . . . So it goes. Then there was Bjorn in the previous generation . . ."

"Wolves?"

"Bear. A single swipe while picking cloudberries up by Skafti's boulder. Mind you, that was better than *his* father, Flosi, your great-grandfather. A sad demise."

"How, Uncle? How?"

"Bee sting. Swelled to the most appalling size . . . Not one for the ballads, if truth be known . . . Cheer up, boy! Do not fear—these are unusual deaths."

"I am glad to hear it."

"Yes, most of us die of overindulgence." He raised his cup and tapped it. "Too much of this. We're fated that way."

Halli swung his legs back and forth beneath the bench. "Not me, Uncle."

"Your grandfather Thorir said exactly that. But he died

24

even so—at your parents' wedding as a matter of fact."

"Of drink?"

"In a way. He fell down the well while hunting for the piss-house. Well, it is a gloomy outlook. I think I will go to the keg for another draft to cheer me. But you, my boy, should go to bed."

For Halli in his early youth, bedtime was the most intimate moment of the day, when he could mull on events and what he had learned. He lay beneath his woolen blanket, staring up at the window at the end of the cot, through which the stars shone cold over the dark slabs of the mountains, and listened to the hum of voices from the hall, where his parents conducted the evening arbitrations. When Katla came in to snuff the light he would question her on whatever was on his mind.

"Tell me of the Trows, Katla."

His room would be dark, save for the flickering candle on the shelf. The wrinkles in the nurse's face stood out like furrows on a winter field; she was a carving from some black-grained wood. Her words drifted in and out of his sleep-fogged mind.

"Ah, the Trows . . . Their faces are dark as the mud under stones. . . . They smell of graves and they hide from the sun. . . . They wait inside the hill for an unwary soul to stray too high upon its slopes. Then they will *spring!* Set one foot beyond those cairns, Halli, and they will rise up and pull you screaming into the earth. . . . Well, I expect you are growing cozy now. I shall blow the candle out. . . . What was that, boy?"

"Have you ever seen a Trow, Katla?"

"No, thank Svein!"

"Oh . . . Is there anything wicked you *have* seen?"

"Never! At my age I consider it a miracle and a blessing to have been so spared. But note that my safety does not stem from good fortune alone. No, I have always carried strong charms on my person to ward off evil of all kinds. I scatter flowers on the cairns of my parents every spring; I leave offerings by the weeping willows to placate the wheer-folk. In addition, I avoid apple trees at noon, keep my eyes averted from the pointing shadows of the cairns, and never, ever relieve myself near a stream or berry bush for fear of offending its fairy resident. So you can see for yourself it is as much good sense and preparedness as anything. And if you wish to live long, you will follow my example. Not another word, dear Halli! This candle must go out."

It is not to be thought that Halli was a retiring, unassuming child; indeed, from the first, he was unusually confident and overbearing. But he knew when to be silent. Day on day, year on year, he listened quietly to the tales of Svein's House. And every night, as certainly as if played out upon his mother's loom, the threads of each story were woven into his life and dreams.

2

SVEIN'S QUALITIES WERE EVIDENT from the first. As a child he was stronger than any man, capable of breaking a bullock's neck in an armlock. He was proud and passionate, too, and, if his temper got the better of him, very hard to manage. Once he threw an insolent servant over a haystack; after that, when the anger was on him, he went out hunting Trows. When he was no older than you, he carried one of their claws home in his thigh after a fight out in the fields. The Trow had dragged him so deep into the earth that his armpits were filled with mud, but Svein caught hold of a tree root and held on all night till the sun rose over the Snag. Then the Trow's power was sapped and Svein broke free. He found the claw in his leg when he got home. "I was lucky," he said. "That was a young one, not at full strength."

No, I don't know where the claw is now. Don't ask so many questions.

AT FOURTEEN HALLI remained short, broad, and bandy in the leg. Though only two years from full manhood, he was a little over half the height of his brother Leif, while his head reached Gudny's shoulders only when he stood on tiptoe.

However, he had the luck of good health. He remained untouched by black creep, sow's fever, dank mottle, or any of the dozen other maladies that were endemic to the upper valley. This hardiness was aligned to a certain vitality of spirit that manifested itself in every thought and action, and that chafed at the daily restrictions of the House.

Most of Svein's people were taciturn and patient, weathered inside and out by exposure to the mountain seasons. For them the long, slow rhythms of farm and field held sway; they tended the animals, grew crops, and practiced their crafts just as their parents had done. Despite their status, Arnkel and Astrid made no exception for themselves or their children and threw themselves into every chore, but it was noticed by all that Halli had little interest in following their example.

"Anyone see Halli today?" Arnkel growled as the men, hot and straw-strewn, gathered in the yard for their day's-end ale. "He did not work my field."

"Nor mine," Leif said. "He should have been helping the women rake hay."

Bolli the bread maker came waddling across the flagstones. "I'll tell you exactly where he was! Back here, stealing my oatcakes!"

"You caught him at it?"

"I as good as saw him! As I labored at my oven, I heard

a horrid screeching outside my door. I hurried out to find a cat tied by the tail to the door latch; it took me much effort to work the string loose. When I returned inside, what did I see? A hook on the end of a pole retreating through my window, with five fine cakes impaled upon its point! I ran to the window, but too late! The villain was gone."

Arnkel scowled. "You're sure this was Halli?"

"Who else would it be?"

A murmur of weary agreement rose among the men. "All year it has been like this!" Grim the smith said. "A series of jokes and thefts and escapades at the expense of others! He contrives one after the other with the speed of someone possessed."

Unn the tanner nodded. "My goat stolen and tethered up beside the crags! Do you recall it? He said he wished to lure a wolf!"

"What about those snares he left in the orchard?" Leif said. "Allegedly so that he could 'catch an imp.' Who did he catch instead? Me! My ankles throb even now!"

"Remember those thistles wedged inside the privy?"

"My leggings hung upon the flagpole!"

"No punishment seems to bother him. He is impervious to threats!"

Arnkel's brother Brodir had been listening in silence. Now he put down his cup and wiped his hand across his ragged beard. "You take it all too seriously," he said. "Where is the harm in any of this? The boy is imaginative and

29

bored, that's all. He wants adventure—a little stimulation."

"Oh, stimulation I can help him with." Arnkel tapped his horse strap meaningfully against his palm. "Someone find Halli and bring him to me."

Despite repeated beatings, complaints about Halli's behavior continued through the summer. In desperation Arnkel put his son in the daily care of Eyjolf, head servant of the House.

One evening, when Katla was pulling the nightdress over Halli's head, he was summoned into the hall. His father, who had just finished the day's arbitrations, sat in his Law Seat, his horse strap in his hand. Halli blinked at it, and then at Eyjolf grinning beside the dais.

"Halli," Arnkel said slowly, "Eyjolf seeks arbitration on your behavior today."

Halli stared bleakly about him. The hall was empty; golden light drifted through the western window and glinted on the hero's treasures. The fire had not been lit and the air was growing chill. The Seat next to his father's was empty.

"Shouldn't Mother be here, if it's an arbitration?"

Arnkel's face darkened. "I feel sure I can make this judgment without her help. No detailed knowledge of the Law will be necessary to comprehend your deeds. So then, Eyjolf—make your charge."

The head servant was almost as old as Katla. Stooped, cadaverous, and of somewhat sour deportment, his eyes looked on Halli without affection. "Great Arnkel, as you requested, I have been putting Halli to good constructive work, mainly in the latrines, the middens, and the tanning vats. For three days he has been giving me the runaround, vexing me with impudence. At last, today, as I took him to muck out the stables, he gave me the slip and ran into the servants' quarters. As I followed, a set of booby traps way-laid me. I was tripped by a concealed wire, spread-eagled by butter on the flagstones, frightened by a makeshift ghost hidden round a corner, and finally, when I tottered into my own small room, soundly drenched by a bucket of slops bal-anced on the open door. I was forced to duck my head repeatedly in the horse trough, to the amusement of people in the yard. Then, when I looked up, what did I see? Halli, smirking down at me from atop the roof of Grim's forge! He claimed to be watching the ridge for signs of Trows."

As he pronounced the final word, Eyjolf made a com-plex series of careful signs. Halli, who had been listening with a show of unconcern, took sudden interest.

"What are you doing, old Eyjolf? Does *every* entrance to your body have to be protected when you talk of Trows?"

"Insolent child! I am stoppering myself against their unclean power. Be silent! Arnkel, it took me an age to get him down from that roof. He might have fallen and broken his neck, which would have been a shame for you, if not for me. These are the facts, and the truth of it. I request arbi-tration and a thrashing for Halli."

Arnkel spoke in the deep tones he used as Arbiter. "Halli," he said, "this is a grim catalogue. It sorrows me that you should display, in such short order, wanton disrespect to a valued servant, disregard for your own safety, and blithe irreverence to the supernatural dangers that surround us. Do you have anything to say?"

Halli nodded. "Father, I draw attention to Eyjolf's misconduct. He has neglected to mention that he gave his solemn word not to report any of this to you. In return for his oath I climbed down from the roof promptly and spent the whole day mucking out the stables."

Halli's father scratched at his beard. "Maybe, but that does not negate your crimes."

"Those are easily answered," Halli said. "As to my own well-being, I was in no danger. I am spry as a goat, as you have often observed. I made no damage to the fabric of Grim's roof. My interest in the Trows is born from a desire to more fully comprehend the dangers that beset us and is not in the least irreverent. As for my disrespect to Eyjolf, it appears well founded, since he is an oath-breaker and should be strung up by the heels from the flag mast in the yard."

At this, Eyjolf made a shrill interjection, but Halli's father shushed him.

Arnkel tapped the horse strap with his fingers and stared at his son. "Halli, your argument is tenuous, but since it hinges on a question of personal honor I feel I have to pause. Above all things we must maintain the honor of ourselves and of our House, and this extends to bargains made between men. Eyjolf, did you in fact agree to keep quiet about events today?"

The old man huffed and blew and sucked in his cheeks, but had to admit it was so.

"Then in all conscience I cannot beat Halli in this instance."

"Thank you, Father! Will Eyjolf be punished for his lack of faith?"

"His disappointment in your acquittal will suffice. See how his face sags. Wait! Do not leave so readily. I have said I will not punish you, but I have not yet finished."

Halli halted on his way to the door. "Oh?"

"It is clear that you are bored with your tasks here," Arnkel said. "Very well, I have another for you. The near flock needs moving to the high pastures above the House for the last few weeks of summer. Do you know the spot? It is a lonely place, close to the boundary where the Trows walk at night. There is danger of wolves, too, even this season. To protect the flock a shepherd must be quick-witted and nimble, brave and enterprising. . . . But you rejoice in such qualities, do you not?" Arnkel smiled thinly at his son. "Who knows? Perhaps you will at last see a Trow."

Halli hesitated, then shrugged as if the matter were of no consequence. "Shall I be back for the Gathering?"

"I will send someone for you in good time. Not another word! You may go."

The high pasture was little more than an hour's walk from Svein's House if a certain winding track was used to scale the ridge, but its location felt considerably more remote. It was a place of boulders, clefts, and deep blue shadow, where the only sound was the breeze and birdsong. The sheep wandered near and far, growing fat on grass and sedge. Halli found a ruined stone hut on a grass spur in the center of the pasture; he camped there, eating cloudberries, drinking ewe's milk, and taking water from a spring. Every few days a boy brought up cheese, bread, fruits, and meat. Otherwise he was alone.

Not for anything would Halli have admitted to his father any nervousness in the prospect of his solitude, but that nervousness existed, for the line of cairns loomed close upon the skyline.

Across the top end of the pasture, a stone wall had been built straddling the contour of the hill. It was there to prevent the sheep straying close to the summit of the ridge, where the cairns were. It was there to prevent people straying too. Halli stood at the wall often, gazing up toward the tooth-shaped stacks of stone that were just visible on the hump of the hill. Some were tall and thin, some broad, others sloughed or crooked. Each one hid the body of an ancestor; all were there to help Svein guard the boundary against the wicked Trows. Even in full sunlight they remained dark, a somber, watchful presence; on gray days their proximity cast a pall on Halli's mood. In late afternoons, he was careful lest their long low shadows should touch him and he be Trow-stricken.

Each night he lay in the hut's black silence, nostrils filled with the smell of earth and the sour wool of his blanket, and imagined the Trows shuffling on the moors above, straining against the boundary, hungry for his flesh. . . . At such times the boundary seemed scant protection. He whispered thanks to the ancestors for their vigilance and hid his head until sleep came.

If Halli's nights were troublesome, the days were pleasant and eased the frustrations of his heart. For the first time that he could remember he was free to do as he saw fit. No one gave him orders; no one beat him. His parents' disapproving eyes were far away. He was not required to carry out dull jobs in House or field.

Instead, he lay in the grass and dreamed great deeds— those that Svein had accomplished in the distant past, and those that *he* one day intended to perform.

While the sheep grazed peaceably, Halli would survey the scene below, following the brown-green slabs of Svein's fields as they fell toward the valley's central fold, where he had never been. Here, he knew, the great road ran beside the river, away east to the cataracts and beyond. On the opposite side of the river, the wooded slopes rose steeply. These belonged to Rurik's House. He could see smoke from its chimneys sometimes, hanging over distant trees. Rurik's ridge, like Svein's, was topped with cairns; beyond hung the gray slopes and white crests of the mountains, part of the great unbroken wall which swung round north, west, and south, hemming in the valley.

Long ago, great Svein had explored all this. Sword in hand he had journeyed up and down the valley from High Stones to the sea, fighting Trows, killing outlaws, gaining renown. . . . Each morning Halli would gaze toward the rising sun, to the jagged silhouette of the Snag, the granite spur that hid the lower valley. One day he too would go that way—below the Snag, down through the gorge, in search of adventure just as Svein had done.

In the meantime, he had some sheep to tend to.

Halli had nothing against the sheep, a hardy mountain breed with black faces and wiry wool. Most of the time they took care of themselves. Once a yearling lamb fell into a crack between two boulders and had to be pulled free. On another occasion a ewe broke a foreleg in a tumble from a crag —Halli fashioned a crude splint from a wood stave and the fabric of his tunic, and sent her hobbling on her way. But as the weeks went by their company began to pall and Halli grew tired of his duties. He spent more and more time staring uphill—toward the cairns.

No one he knew had ever seen a Trow. No one could tell him anything about them. How many of them were there? What did they eat, with humans out of reach? What would the moor look like, over the brow of the hill? Would he see their burrow-holes, the bones of their past victims?

Halli had many questions, but he never thought to approach the cairns.

At one end of the pasture, perhaps in the gales of the previous winter, a section of the guard wall had fallen down. Its stones littered the long grass over a wide area. On his arrival, Halli had realized that he should rebuild it, and had in fact made an attempt to do so, but had discovered the job to be arduous and backbreaking. He soon gave up, and since the sheep never ventured to that end of the meadow anyway, he quickly forgot about the matter.

The weeks passed. One afternoon, when the first tints of brown and amber were showing in the trees of the valley far below, Halli woke from a doze to discover that the flock, with ovine caprice, had for the first time migrated to the far end of the field. No fewer than eight sheep had strayed across the scattered stones of the fallen wall and were cropping the grass on the far side.

Uttering an exclamation of dismay, Halli seized his stick and hurried across the field. Shouting, waving, gesticulating, he drove the main flock away from the tumbled stretch; one of the stray sheep jumped back over the stones to join them, but the other seven made no move.

Halli returned to the hole in the wall and, making a protective gesture much as he had seen Eyjolf do, scrambled over the stones onto the forbidden slope.

The seven sheep regarded him narrowly from various positions near and far.

Halli employed all his shepherd's wiles. He moved slowly so as not to frighten the strays; he made a series of soothing chirrups in his throat; he kept the stick low, motioning gently in the direction of the wall, as he circled round to drive them steadily, subtly, inexorably toward the hole.

As one, the sheep bolted in seven different directions across the hill.

Halli cursed and swore; he charged after the nearest sheep and succeeded only in driving it a few yards farther up the slope. Scampering at another, he slipped, lost his balance, and tumbled head over heels to land upside down upon a muddy tussock. Such was the pattern of the afternoon.

After a long time and much exertion Halli had managed to coerce six of the sheep back through the hole. He was mud-stained, sweating, and out of breath; his stick had snapped in two.

One sheep only remained.

She was a young ewe, skittish, and swift, and she had climbed higher up the slope than any of the others. She was almost at the cairns.

Halli took a deep breath, moistened his lips, and began to climb, angling his path so as to approach the ewe tail-on. He kept a weather eye on the nearest cairns—tumbledown columns of mossy rock showing stark against the sky. Luck was with him in one sense: it was a cloudy day and the cairns projected no shadows. But the ewe was wary, turning and starting at every gust of wind. She saw him when he was still six feet from her.

Halli stopped dead. The sheep stared at him. She was in the lee of a cairn, right on the boundary of the valley, cropping the long grass that grew around the ancient stones. Behind her he glimpsed a green expanse—the high moors, where the heroes had walked long ago and only the Trows lived now. His mouth was dry, his eyes staring. He saw no movement; heard nothing but the wind.

Slowly, slowly, Halli tore up a long clutch of grass. Slowly he held it out toward the ewe. Slowly he backed away, with a smile of supplication.

The ewe turned her head, cropped grass. She was no longer looking in Halli's direction.

Halli hesitated. Then he made a desperate lunge.

The ewe's legs kicked: she was away, past the cairn, onto the moors.

Halli fell to his knees, tears breaking in his eyes. He watched the ewe dance away across the grass. She came to rest again, not too distant. Not far—but she was out of reach now. Gone. He could not follow her.

A few feet from him, the cairn rose dark and silent. If he had stretched out a hand he could have touched it. The thought made the hackles rise on the back of his neck.

Stumbling, gasping, he backed away down the slope toward the safety of the wall.

For the rest of the day he watched the skyline, but the ewe did not reappear. Dusk came; Halli crouched uneasily in the darkness of his hut. Sometime in the depths of the night he heard a high-pitched screaming, a sound of animal terror and pain. It ceased abruptly. Halli stared into blackness, every muscle cringing; he did not sleep until dawn.

Next morning he climbed the slope again and, from a wary distance, looked beyond the cairns.

The ewe was gone, but here and there, scattered in an out-flung arc, he saw red and tattered strips of wool, a bloody raggedness on the ground.

3

WHEN EGIL LIKENED Svein's old mother to a she-toad, Svein soon got to hear about it. He set straight off to Egil's hall and nailed a wolf pelt to the door. Egil came rushing out.

"What's this? A challenge? Where do you want to fight?"

"Right here, or anywhere, it's your decision."

"We'll do it on Dove Crag."

Up on high they wrestled, each trying to push the other off. Svein was confident; his iron limbs had never failed him. But Egil matched his strength. The sun went down, the sun came up; there they were, still locked together. Neither would budge. They were fixed so still that birds began roosting on their heads.

"They'll be nesting here soon," said Svein. "That one's brought a twig."

"One of yours is laying an egg."

With that they parleyed and became blood kinsmen. Years later, they stood together at the Battle of the Rock.

"IT WAS THE TROWS for sure," Uncle Brodir said. "They only emerge at night. Why do you doubt it?"

Halli shook his head. "I did not say I doubted it, just . . . What do they eat, most of the time, when no boys or sheep come their way?"

Uncle Brodir cuffed him good-naturedly around the head. "As always, you ask too many questions. Here is one in return. You're sure *you* did not pass the cairns?"

"No, Uncle. Certainly not!"

"Good. Because that would bring ruin upon us all, or so the stories have it. Now then, forget the ewe. Tell your father it broke its neck in a fall. We cannot move the flock tonight. Let's build up the fire. I have fresh meat with me."

A day after the loss of the sheep, Halli had seen Brodir, beard resplendent, stout staff in one hand, clambering up the hill to bring him home. They had made a joyful greeting.

Brodir said: "Your exile has done you good. I have never seen you look so hale and sinewy. No doubt you will cause even more trouble when you return home."

"Have I been missed?" Halli said.

"Not hugely, save for Katla and me. The rest seem to struggle on without you."

With a sigh, Halli rearranged the branches of the fire. "What is the news?"

"Little enough. Your parents grow harassed at the proximity of the Gathering."

"I am not too late for it, then? I was growing fearful."

"It is seven days away, and the House struggles to be ready. Low Meadow has been cleared and the grass scythed. The first booths have been constructed. Your brother, Leif, oversees preparations; he struts around in his cloak like a pompous goose, giving orders that everyone ignores. Meanwhile Gudny spends hours in her room preening before the mirror; she hopes to attract the notice of eligible men from down-valley Houses. So: you have missed nothing. Except that Eyjolf suffers a strange malady. Each morning his cheeks are red and swollen, and itchy like an imp kiss. He has tried numerous remedies, but the problem persists."

"He might check inside his pillow," Halli said blandly. "Perhaps someone put a strand of poison ivy there."

Brodir chuckled. "Ah. Perhaps! I will leave him to discover it for himself."

The meal was good and the companionship better. Brodir produced a wine sack and Halli shared it eagerly. As the unsteady warmth coursed through him, he listened to Brodir telling of Svein's adventures on the moors, of his killing of dragons, of his three journeys to the Trow-king's hall. As always the tales thrilled his heart; but tonight they hung heavy on it too.

At last he said bitterly: "Uncle, is it wrong to wish myself dead and buried with the heroes in their cairns? I would have been happier to have lived in their time, long ago, when a man could seek his fortune in the manner he saw fit. Today there's no opportunity to do anything. Even the Trows are out of bounds."

Brodir grunted. "Audacity was a virtue then. It is not so now. The women of the Council see to that. Mind you, even in Svein's time the heroes were considered reckless. They became respectable only through death."

"Death would be preferable to what my parents have planned for me!" Halli kicked a boot out savagely and sent a branch hissing deeper into the fire. "Father has told me more than once, I must apply myself to farming, learn every skill. Then, when I am numb with boredom, I shall be given a hovel of my own to manage till my hair goes gray and my life winks out! He didn't put it in quite those terms, admittedly."

Brodir's teeth glinted in the firelight. He took a sip of wine and patted Halli on the shoulder. "The thing is, boy," he said, "we are younger sons, you and I, and that makes us surplus to requirements. We do not inherit, like Arnkel has and that idiot Leif is bound to. Nor do we marry easily, as Gudny will, if anyone can stomach her cool nature. What are we to do? Where can we go? The boundary is set upon the ridges and the impassable ocean waits at river's end. Small wonder we are troublesome in our youth."

Halli looked up at his uncle. "You were as bad as me?"

"Oh, I was far worse." He chuckled. "Far worse. You cannot guess."

Halli waited hopefully, but Brodir said no more. "I will follow your example," Halli said, as soberly as he could. "I will travel the valley and see the world! And to hell with what my father thinks."

"The valley isn't as big as you suppose. Leastways, your exploration will soon be done. Eleven lesser Houses you'll find, all populated by dunces, scoundrels, and shysters. The sea-girt ones are the worst: blond-haired villains to a man. Only one good House and that's Svein's." Brodir spat into the fire. "You'll be back here soon enough. In the meantime do not judge your father harshly. He has responsibilities to his people, and has Astrid on his back. He means well for you."

"Even so, I wish I was free of his hopes and intentions." Halli's face felt hot; he threw himself back from the fire to lie in the soft, cold grass, gazing up at the stars.

When Halli arrived back at the House he found a great crowd working in the yard. After his month alone he was momentarily dazed by the intensity of noise and movement. His mother passed, carrying a basket piled high with colored cloth. She placed it on the ground and hugged him briefly. "Welcome, my son. Good to have you back. I will hear your account another time. Now, listen well. The Gathering is almost upon us and we are not yet ready! There is much to be done and you must work as hard as anyone. Be aware there is no time for tricks, frolics, deceitfulness, or any other form of nonsense, on pain of direst penalty. Do you understand me?"

"Yes, Mother."

"Very well. Run along to Grim; he needs help carrying griddles to the meadow."

There was palpable excitement in the air and Halli shared it. For the first time in his memory, the Autumn Gathering was coming to Svein's House, and it promised wonders that he had never seen. Soon the near meadows would witness the arrival of almost four hundred people, a number he could hardly comprehend. They would accommodate the representatives of all eleven other Houses— their leading families and tradespeople, their servants, horses, carts, and chattels, together with those from lesser farms. There would be feasting, storytelling, the thrill of horse fights, wrestling, and trials of strength; the Council would meet to debate the latest legal cases. . . . Halli thrilled at the possibilities. For once he would not feel trapped, cut off—he would see the whole valley without setting foot from home.

For two days he worked as hard as anyone, constructing the trade booths that would fringe the meadow. He held the posts steady while the men hammered them into the soft ground; he carried blocks of turf from the drying rooms and laid them out, row upon row, to form walls between the posts. He helped dig roasting pits and fix griddles into position; he gathered hay and straw for the visitors' animals.

On the third day the House was decorated. Svein's colors swung proudly from the flagpole in the yard; from every rooftop flags of black and silver flapped like seabirds. Threads of bunting lay upon the Trow wall; a great tent had been erected outside the hall, filled with ale casks ready to be broached. Trestle tables were set around, groaning with skins, cloths, bone implements and whistles, and other produce of the House. By evening, all neared readiness; people's efforts slowed. Halli's brother, Leif, strode vigorously about, resplendent in his silver-black cape, bestowing heavy compliments.

Halli grew tired of work; he gathered several like-minded children together in an alley behind the tannery.

"Who wants a game?" he asked. "Dead Crows or the Battle of the Rock?"

The Battle was chosen, as it usually was. Halli said he would be Svein.

"Shouldn't you be a Trow?" Ketil, Grim's son, asked. "It would give things added authenticity."

Halli scowled. "Who here is Sveinsson among us? *I* shall be Svein."

Ketil, Sturla, and Kugi, the squint-eyed youth who cleaned the piggery, were voted Trows. They were given broken sickles to represent their slashing claws. For helmets, Halli and the heroes used rusting buckets stolen from the smithy; for swords they took wood snags from the stables. The great battle was fought on a stretch of

Trow wall that had more or less collapsed, forming a scree of ancient stones, turfed and mossy. Upon the rock the heroes stood abreast, uttering wise, defiant comments. The Trow horde burst up from below, roaring and screaming. Birds flew from the roofs of Svein's House; cows started in the meadows. The women working in the tannery cursed and gesticulated. Battle was joined amid a hail of sticks and fists.

Leif Sveinsson strode from the yard, cape flapping. He watched the fight with a baleful eye. After a few moments his presence was detected; with abrupt finality the battle quietened. A few desultory coughs and gasps, then silence.

"This is a fine sight!" Leif said slowly. "The Gathering is almost upon us, and here are you urchins playing like dogs on a bone heap! Eyjolf and I have a hundred chores we can give you before dark. If you don't step to it, I'll lock you in the lumber rooms for the duration of the fair!"

Leif was eighteen, a big man, burly and thick-necked. He had the trick of keeping his head a trifle lowered, like a bull's, and staring abruptly up from under his brows, as if only self-restraint prevented him from acting with sudden appalling passion. The children were daunted and ashen-faced.

Halli spoke from the top of the Trow wall. "It wasn't long ago, brother, that you enjoyed these games yourself! Come and join in! I'll lend you my helmet."

Leif stepped closer. "Do you ardently wish for a clouting, Halli?"

"No."

"Then I suggest you remember my seniority and age." Leif drew himself up, chest swelling; he had his finest tunic on, tight black leggings, a pair of polished boots. "As one who will one day lead this House, I have responsibilities to maintain. I have no time for rolling in the dirt."

"That's not what Gudrun the goat girl told me," Halli said casually. "She said when you left her hut last night you were covered in straw."

Several noises coincided then: the laughter of the others, Leif's roar of wrath, the scrabbling of Halli's boots upon the Trow wall as he attempted to escape. But his legs were short and his brother's long. The outcome was swift and painful.

Leif nodded grimly. "Let that be a lesson to you all. I have a quick way with cheek like that. Now—here are your tasks . . ." Standing astride the Trow wall he issued orders to the children down below.

Behind him, Halli dabbed silently at the blood running from his nose. When he had finished, he wiped his face with his sleeve to remove the blood and tears. Then he stood, took careful aim, and kicked Leif squarely in the center of his buttocks.

With a high-pitched wail Leif toppled from the wall, arms flapping like a bird. Below was an extensive dunghill.

The fall was just long enough for Leif to roll forward in midair so that he met the brown soil of the mound head-first.

An emphatic squelch: Leif's head, shoulders, upper arms, and midriff disappeared from view. His legs stuck straight up, gyrating oddly; the tip of his silver-black cloak settled gently upon the dank slope of the mound.

The gasp of horror from the assembled children gave way to pop-eyed wonder.

Halli said: "Look how deep he's gone! I wouldn't have guessed it was so soft."

Kugi the sty-boy raised a hand. "I just added a fresh barrow-load."

"That would explain it. But how on earth does he remain so upright? Look at his legs a-waving! It is quite athletic. He should do this at the fair."

As they watched, however, the legs dropped down, the back bent swiftly; Leif was now in a kneeling position, head and shoulders still buried in the muck. His hands pushed, his muscles strained; with a protracted popping noise, his upper half emerged in a shower of debris. A violent stench spread rapidly.

As one, the children began edging toward the nearest cottage doors and alleys.

Halli thought it time to descend silently from the wall.

Hesitantly, precariously, Leif got to his feet, his boots slipping and sloughing in the mire. His back was to them;

his cape hung lank and limp. Slowly, he turned; with awful deliberation he raised his caked and matted head and gazed upon them. For an instant everyone froze; he held them all transfixed.

Then, like dandelion seeds upon the wind, they scattered.

Halli moved fastest of all. Obscured as his brother's face had been, the emotion in his eyes was painfully suggestive. Halli leaped from the Trow wall. As he landed, he heard a frantic clattering of stones as his brother scrambled up the other side.

Halli ran up the alley beside Unn's tannery. His legs fairly flew, but his strides were not large. He heard Leif roar, heard him spring down to the cobbles. Up ahead a woman carried washing; she blocked his route. He ducked sideways into the tannery, raced between the scrubbing racks, slipped on discarded sheep fat, and fell on his back to land heavily against a soaking vat.

Unn stood above him. Her face was pink, her hands stained. "Halli? What—"

In darted Leif; he saw Halli, lunged for him. Halli rolled to the side, between the legs of a rack. Leif swiped, missed him, and careered into the soaking vat, which toppled over, sending foul yellow curing fluid cascading to the floor. Unn cried out in woe. Brusi, her son, screamed and leaped to avoid the deluge; he grabbed a rafter, hung suspended. Leif paid them no heed; he charged toward the main door, through which Halli was busy fleeing. Leif seized a scrubbing brush, hurled it at Halli's head; it missed, bounced back off the jamb, and struck Leif in the eye.

In the central yard of Svein's House, preparations for the Assembly neared completion. Boys swept the cobbles; the tables were neatly stacked; flags flew merrily. Arnkel and Astrid stood at the hall porch, handing out refreshing ale.

Out into the yard ran Leif. Where was Halli? There—darting below a trestle! Leif sprang, vaulted the table, scattering pots around him. People lurched aside, fell back, knocking into each other; plates and produce fell crashing to the stones.

Halli evaded Leif's outstretched hand and hopped onto a table piled with cloth. Leif followed, trampling the cloth with his dung-caked boots. Halli jumped down, ran into the ale tent. In charged Leif, saw Halli clambering across the stack of ale casks. Pushing a woman aside, he sprang like a wolf and landed heavily on the barrels, dislodging several kegs from the stack. They rumbled out of the tent and away across the yard, sending onlookers flying like skittles before breaking on the cottage walls.

Now Leif closed in. He had Halli trapped at the top of the stack. Halli looked about, saw a rope hanging loose from the tent roof. He jumped, grabbed hold, swung wildly, and fell suddenly to earth as half the tent gave way. He landed heavily amid a gently settling mass of cloth

and bunting, stumbled forward from the capsized tent
—and stopped dead.

Leif loomed behind him. "Now then, *brother*—"

He too stopped. He looked around. Before them stood
Arnkel and Astrid, dark-eyed, stony-faced; on every side the
people of Svein's House steadily converged, men, women,
urchins from the gutter, all in utter silence.

Astrid's fair hair was coiled and braided tight to her
scalp; her exposed neck shone thin and white. Her expression reminded Halli of that she wore during judgments in
the hall, when felons were sent wailing to the gallows. Her
eyes flicked between Leif and Halli, and back again.

"You look like my sons," she said, "but by your actions
you are strangers to me." Neither spoke; the crowd watched,
listened. Somewhere at the back, a baby cried. "What,"
Astrid continued in the same calm tones, "is your explanation?"

Leif stepped forward. His account was rambling,
aggrieved, full of self-pity.

Their father, Arnkel, held up a hand. "Enough, my son.
Step back a little. Your stench makes my eyes water. What of
you, Halli?"

Halli gave a shrug. "Yes, I pushed him in the dung heap.
Why not? He had struck me and abused me and my companions, as they can easily confirm." He looked about, but
Sturla, Kugi, and the others had melted back among the
throng. Halli sighed. "The fact remains, I thought it a

matter of honor that I could not overlook."

His uncle Brodir was standing in the crowd. "This seems reasonable enough."

Astrid addressed him sharply. "Your contributions, Brodir, are not looked for. Halli, do not dare talk to me of honor! You are a wretch—you have none!"

Arnkel added: "If you felt Leif had wronged you, you should have challenged him fairly, not kicked his backside."

"But Leif is considerably stronger than I am, Father. If we fought fairly, he would have beaten me to a sorry pulp. Isn't that so, Leif?"

"Yes, as I will gladly prove."

"You see, Father? In all honesty, what good would that have done?"

"Well—"

"And didn't great Svein often ambush the other heroes in the days before their truce and the Battle of the Rock?" Halli cried. "*He* didn't utter an official challenge to Hakon when he saw him riding alone beside the cataract. He just threw a boulder down from the Snag. Think of my boot as Svein's boulder and Leif's arse as Hakon: the principle is the same! Only my aim was better."

Arnkel adjusted his feet uneasily. "You have a point, but—"

"Your *proper* conduct, Halli," his mother interrupted, in a voice like glass shards, "would have been to ignore Leif's actions altogether. Just as *he* should have ignored yours. Now you have both shamed me! It will take great effort to repair this destruction before our guests arrive. Yet it must be done; all must put down their ale cups and set to. Tonight's feast will be delayed." A murmur of discontent ran round the crowd. "But first, to your punishments. Leif—your appearance and behavior are a disgrace. I would bar you from the Gathering, but you are Arnkel's heir: you must attend. Let this public shame be sufficient. Go now and wash in the horse trough."

Leif slunk away. "Now," Astrid said, "Halli . . ."

"He is just a boy!" Uncle Brodir cried out. "With a boy's exuberance! This mess can easily be cleared—"

Astrid spoke in a cold, high voice. "We all know of *your* youthful exuberance, Brodir, and what you did. The House paid dearly for it."

She stared at him. Brodir flushed dark, his lips white and drawn. He opened his mouth, then closed it. A sudden movement—he was gone into the crowd.

Then Astrid addressed Halli. "In two days," she said, "the Gathering begins. It will be an occasion of great festivity, when even Gudrun the goat girl may make merry from dawn till dusk. Everyone here shall enjoy it, except for you. You are banned for the duration of the Gathering from the festival meadows, and shall take no part in formal feasting in this hall. You may not drink from the kegs, nor eat from the roasting pits; the cooks will serve you scraps in the kitchens. For four days it will be as if you are gone up to your cairn. Perhaps *this* will inspire you to restrain your behavior."

Halli said nothing. He looked at his mother with hot eyes.

As he exited the yard, Halli succeeded in maintaining a stiff, proud posture and a defiant expression. Once he got to the family apartments, his defenses slackened and his pace slowed. He lay quietly on his bed, staring at the ceiling. Up and down the corridor he heard the footsteps of his family and the servants. Each time he tensed in expectation of a visitor; he even hoped for it, however angry they might be. But whether out of rage, embarrassment, or plain indifference, no one came to see him.

He was on the point of attempting sleep when Katla opened the door and entered, carrying a plate of chicken, turnip, and purple sprouting. Without ceremony she plumped it down upon Halli's bed and blinked at him.

"Thought you'd be hungry, dear," Katla said.

"Yes."

"Eat, then."

Halli sat up and did so. While he ate, Katla bustled quietly about the room.

When he had finished, Halli set down his knife and said in a small voice: "That was very good. It tasted all the better because it's the last proper meal I shall have for a while, at least until after the Gathering." As he said this, he faltered; he put his hand over his eyes and kept them there.

Katla did not appear to have noticed. "There will be *other* Gatherings, dear," she said. "Next summer's is not far away. That is at Orm's House, I believe."

Halli said savagely, "All my life I've known nothing of the world. Now, when the world has finally come to me— I'm banned from seeing it! I've a good mind to run away, Katla. I'll not stay here."

"Yes, dear. Your legs are somewhat short. You will not get far. Do you want to put on your nightdress now?"

"No. Katla."

"Yes?"

"Are there roads beyond the cairns?"

The old woman blinked. "Roads? Whatever do you mean?"

"Old ones that the settlers took. To get to this valley in the days before Svein. To other valleys, other people."

Slowly, bemusedly, she shook her head. "If there were trails they will be lost. The settlement was long ago. Besides, there are no other valleys, no other people."

"How do you know that?"

"How *can* there be roads, where the Trows are? They devour all who go there."

Halli hunched his shoulders, thinking of the ewe. "What if we made swords again and went up to fight them? Maybe we could cross the moors, and—"

With a click of knees Katla sat upon the bed. "Halli,

Halli. There was a boy once, like you in a lot of ways, though taller, I expect. *He* disregarded the Trows."

"I didn't say *that*, only—"

"He was not of Svein's line, but from some House where they have less sense—Eirik's or Hakon's, most like. Well, that boy made it known he would go a-wandering up on the moors. He was mad, of course—they should have chained him in a hut—but they let him go. They watched him skip beyond the cairns, go prancing up onto the ridge; once or twice he waved at them in his insolence. Know what happened then?"

Halli sighed. "I assume something unpleasant?"

"You assume correctly. A thick hill-fog came down. The boy was lost from view; it grew so dark it seemed that night had fallen, though it was not yet afternoon. At the point when the fog was thickest, the people heard thin cries—not far off, but of course, they could not go to help. A wind sprang up and blew the fog higher up the moors, letting the sun in. The people saw the boy then, wedged in the ground up to his waist, not ten yards from the nearest cairn. He was still alive; he called and pleaded faintly. A brave man ran to a thicket, cut down a sapling, thrust it out beyond the stones. The boy grasped it; the people pulled . . . Well."

Halli said: "I think I guess the rest."

"Your imagination could not be so dreadful. The first thing they noticed was that he was *lighter* than expected. Then they saw he left a red trail on the ground behind him.

Then they saw that his bottom half was gone."

"Yes. I think—"

"Gone! Everything up to his navel. The rest had been eaten, or carried off into the hole. Of course he was dead before he reached the cairns. So that is the story of the boy who disbelieved in the Trows. I can tell you many others in similar vein."

"I know. I think I will sleep now."

"If nothing else it proves that your lot could be worse. Yes, your legs are short, but at least you have them still. Accept your situation with good grace, and all will soon be well." And with that Katla blew out the light and shuffled from the room.

4

SVEIN WAS FRIENDLY with Egil, but even as a youth the other heroes tried his nerves. There was never a fair or horse-meet when they weren't coming up and challenging him to some trial or other. As well as their temerity, he disliked their oddities of speech, their strange modes of dress, and in particular the way his down-valley rivals always smelled of fish. When Arne and Erlend suggested a boulder toss one time, Svein threw his out of the field altogether and into the middle of the river, to form a little island. Then, since their stench insulted him, he caught the heroes by the hind legs and lobbed them both midstream.

TWO DAYS LATER the Gathering began. Shortly after dawn the first riders were seen approaching along the road, slow gray shadows emerging from the beech wood; behind came carts, muddy and travel-stained. A horn was blown at the north gate, fires were lit in the meadow roasting-pits, and kegs broached in readiness. Wrapped in thick cloaks against the chill, Arnkel and Astrid walked down to make the greeting.

The sun rose over the Snag, striking the roof of the hall. Men and women rushed from the kitchens, bearing bread and cakes under fresh white linen down to the tables in the fields. The first arrivals worked to build their tents and hang the colors of their House upon their chosen booth. Children ran across the wet grass, shouting. Now the road was thick with traffic; it rang with hooves and squealing wheels. The air grew warm and cloaks were hurled aside; tunics and kirtles of a dozen colors mingled in the meadow. Hands were grasped, hugs exchanged; time and again the horns sounded against the babble of the throng. The excitement carried far upon the autumn winds.

From high on the Trow wall, Halli watched for as long as he could stomach, then retreated to his room where the happy sounds were mostly muffled.

The deep frustration that dwelled within him now flared into life and burned hotly in his breast. The whole valley had assembled for a joyous festival outside his gate, and he was denied the opportunity to taste its pleasures! His family had much to answer for.

Rising from his bed, he padded down the passage and passed through the drapes into the deserted hall. Outside in the yard laughter rang; here dust drifted through thin shards of sunlight extending from the windows in the western wall. The light hit the hero's treasures behind the Law Seats: his helmet, scarred and dented; his boar spear, black with centuries of smoke; his longbow, with its fragments of trailing gut string. Svein's shield was there too, a circle of pitted black wood, with metal rim and centerpiece; beside it hung his moldering quiver of arrows. Beneath it all, upon its shelf of stone, sat the little box in which Svein's lucky silver belt lay folded. Halli stood below, staring at the treasures, at the symbols of Svein's life of action.

All that was lacking was the sword. *That* was in Svein's hands, high on the hill.

Sudden rage rose through him and pressed against the inside of his teeth. Even in death, Svein had more zest and purpose than Halli did! *He* still warded off the Trows, while Halli was helpless, kicking his heels at his parents' orders, doomed to a life of restless boredom until he dropped dead and joined his ancestors under the stones.

He could bear it no longer. The hall stifled him. With swift steps, Halli left the building by the back door. He slipped between the stables to the Trow wall, scaled it, and set off on a circuitous route amid the cabbage fields. Before long he attained the road, not far from the meadows where the Gathering was in full swing.

Most of the booths were covered now and filled with wares for trading; a tangled knot of crowds undulated between the ale kegs and the mound where the storytellers sat. One field was already filled with tents of rainbow colors, and still more newcomers came trailing along the road to enter at a gaudily decorated gate.

Halli approached diffidently, tempted to enter, calculating

his chances. At the gate stood Grim the smith, muscular and watchful. Grim noticed Halli and made certain gestures that were at once brief and ornately threatening.

Halli's shoulders fell. He trudged back in the direction of the House, before suddenly veering down a narrow dirt path between the turnip fields.

Close to the eastern side of the House, where the Trow wall had crumbled into a gentle slope of grass and burdock, lay Svein's orchard. It was a field of perhaps thirty trees, mainly apple and wind pear, clustering together within a low turf wall. The crops were not extensive, and the orchard was usually unfrequented. Today it would be quite empty. In search of solitude and seclusion, Halli made his way there.

Two steps in and the dark green boughs closed over him, shutting out the world. The sounds of the Gathering seemed suddenly distant. Halli breathed more easily; he walked a few paces, stopped, and closed his eyes in silent contemplation.

At that moment there was a sudden complicated sound right over his head. It began with rasping bark, snapping twigs, and a single squeal, and finished with a hail of apples bouncing on his skull.

Halli leaped athletically aside too late to avoid a single apple. As he did so he heard a heavy thud at the base of the nearest tree. He turned and stared: a girl sprawled among the roots, hastily smoothing her skirts down over her out-stretched legs. A profusion of apples lay across her lap and in the grass beside her. Her feet were bare and black with dirt. Her kirtle—originally a pleasant purple, the color of ripe plums—was smeared with green. Her face was largely obscured by long, straw-colored hair that had escaped its clasp and fallen forward during the descent.

Used as Halli was to Gudny's immaculate composure, this was a sight to awaken wonder. He blinked at the girl uncertainly.

She blew hard through her mouth and brushed the strands of hair carelessly away.

"That'll teach me to try carrying twenty in my skirt," she said. "Did any fall on you?" She looked anxious.

"Nearly all."

"Damn. They'll be bruised and no good. If they'd hit the moss they'd have been all right." She patted the ground beside her. "It's pretty thick down here, luckily for my arse. Help me up, then."

Halli opened his mouth, but found he had nothing specific to say. He stretched out a hand and hoisted the girl to her feet.

"Thanks." She stood before him, brushing fragments of tree out of her clothes and inspecting some scratches on her bare brown arms. She was taller than he was by half a head, and perhaps a little older. She considered her kirtle sadly. "My aunt is going to kill me," she went on. "I'm meant to attend the debates in this tomorrow and of course this is the only formal one I've brought. I should have got changed, but the tent hasn't been put up, and I didn't fancy stripping in the middle of that meadow. Wouldn't have done my marriage prospects any good at all, I shouldn't think. Or maybe it would. Well, pick them up for me, there's a good boy. I suppose they'll have to do."

Halli had been staring at the girl in something of a daze. "Do what?"

"Pick them up. The apples." She waited, eyebrows raised. "For a servant you're a bit useless. My father would have knocked you into next week by now."

Halli cleared his throat, drew himself up to his full height, somewhere adjacent to her nape, and spoke in an assertive voice. "You make a mistake. I'm not a servant."

The girl rolled her eyes. "What do you call it then at Svein's House? 'Menial'? 'Attendant'? 'Drudge'? Drudge would do. We could split hairs all day, but the end's the same. Just pick up the apples."

"My name is Halli Sveinsson. I am—"

"Great Arne, you don't call yourself a 'retainer,' do you? They call them that at Hakon's, I believe. It's just like them for pomposity. At Arne's House we keep things simple and straightforward. A servant's a servant." She paused. "What?"

Halli was showing his teeth now; he spoke with pointed care. "My name is Halli Sveinsson, son of Arnkel, Arbiter of this House, and of Astrid, its Lawgiver. You, whoever you may be, are a guest at my House and are stealing my apples. Might I ask why, instead of treating me with appropriate respect, you demean my status by assuming I am a lowly servant? What explanation can you possibly offer?"

The girl pointed at his clothes. "No colors."

"Oh." Halli looked down. "Ah." It was true. Down at the Gathering, his family would be wearing formal cloth of silver-black—even now Leif no doubt pranced in his across the meadow; other important persons of the house, such as Grim, Unn, even Eyjolf, were allowed darker clothes with silver braids. But Halli had been forbidden any formal wear. His tunic was of plain brown cloth; it was worn and stained. On such an occasion it spoke "servant" loud and clear.

The girl coughed. "So . . . What explanation can you possibly offer?"

Halli scratched the back of his neck. "Well, I'm—I'm not wearing the colors."

"Ye-es. I know. I've just said that."

Halli felt blood come to his face. "I can assure you," he began, "that I am Halli—"

"No need to give the whole ancestry again," the girl said. "We're in an orchard, not a feast hall. I know who you are now. I know all about your lot. I've done your House in my aunt's lessons, more's the pity. Most of you die silly deaths."

Halli stiffened. "No, we don't."

"You do. Bears, wolves, wells, ant stings . . . What's that if not silly?"

"It was a bee actually. A bee sting."

"I'm surprised none of you've died from choking on a fly, though if you keep your jaw open like that you'll be the one to go." The girl's face, which had hitherto worn an expression of careless disdain, suddenly split with the broadest of grins. Her eyes creased and twinkled. Halli's stomach gave a lurch, which he attributed to indigestion.

"Anyway," the girl went on, "who cares about genealogies and the histories of each House? It's all nonsense. Bores me rigid. I'm Aud Ulfar's-daughter, of Arne's House." She stuck out a grubby hand, frowned at the palm, then hastily wiped it on her kirtle. "Don't know where *that* came from. Must have been living in the tree. Didn't think they came out this season. There—it's cleaner now."

With some hesitation Halli grasped her hand, struggling to remember what he knew of Arne's House far down-valley. He had an idea Ulfar Arnesson was his mother's cousin . . . certainly the man had visited on several occasions. Halli vaguely recalled his parents approving of Ulfar for his knowledge of the law.

"I have met your father," Halli ventured. "He is a wise and judicious man."

The girl wrinkled her nose. "Really? Stuffy and pompous, I'd say. *You're* not like that, I hope?"

Halli bridled instantly. "No."

"Good. So why aren't you at the Gathering, then, all decked out in the official colors? The rest of your family were lined up when we rode in. That sister of yours is a stiff piece of work. *Ve-ry* haughty. Looked me over like I was something gray washed up in the torrents. And I hadn't even got my kirtle dirty then." She ran her hand suddenly through her disordered hair. "And now the clasp's gone too, so that's the end of *that* braid." She shook her head. "My aunt really *is* going to kill me. . . . You were saying?"

Halli blinked. "I was?"

"About why you're skulking up here in your everyday rags."

"Um . . ." Halli ran through a range of lies and obfuscations, but none seemed credible. He shrugged. "I'm forbidden to attend."

"Why?"

"I took action against my brother on a matter of honor."

The girl raised her eyebrow. "Mm-hmm? Which means what, exactly?"

"He hit me. I pushed him into the dung-heap."

Aud Ulfar's-daughter gave an odd little laugh, short and sharp like a dog's bark. She said: "In truth, you're not missing much at the Gathering. Everyone's parading between tents, trying to outdo each other in displays of wealth. The Eirikssons have a bear tethered at their booth; the torque around its neck is gold, they claim." She uttered another abrupt little laugh. "Whether that's so or not, it peed on their reception rug just as the Ketilssons came calling. Old

68

Ljot Eiriksson had to sit there talking through his teeth while his leggings grew wet. Couldn't get up for loss of face."

Her glee made Halli laugh for the first time in days. Then he sighed. "You speak of these great folk with such familiarity," he said. "I wish I knew them as you do. I have never yet been to a Gathering." It did not occur to Halli to keep this matter secret; the girl's directness had awoken the same quality in him.

"Oh, the Founders' families are *very* tiresome," Aud said. "Present company excepted, of course. The worst are the marshsiders, the Ormssons and Hakonssons with their ridiculous hair and revolting swagger. The Hakonssons came smarming round our booth just now. Made my blood boil to see my father acting the lick-spittle, groveling and cowering as if he wasn't *also* descended from a hero! That's why I came away. Wandered up and found this place. You don't mind if I *take* some apples, do you, Halli Sveinsson? It's all stodge and ale down there."

Halli made an easy gesture. "Please. By all means. I'll help you."

They stooped to the ground, gathering the windfalls from the turf. Halli scrabbled a few together in his hands and stood again, waiting. He watched Aud crouching on her haunches, turning the apples over, setting a select few in the lap of her skirt. The air was warm in the orchard; he felt a little flushed. A cheer rose from the distant meadow beyond the House, making him blink and look away through the trees.

Aud straightened, brushing her hair from her face. "Well. I'd better get back."

Halli blew out a breath. "I'll escort you," he said abruptly. "If you like. I know a short way through the House. If you don't mind climbing the wall."

She grinned. "All right."

At the edge of the enclosure the trees gave way to the slope of tumbled Trow-stone. They climbed cautiously, feeling their way over the sharp snags of rock hidden among the long, dry grasses. Above them rose the blank walls of the outer cottages, windowless and covered with yellow lichen. At the top was a four-foot drop to a backyard of log stacks drying under awnings. Halli jumped to the slabs; he turned to help Aud, only to find she had already leaped down beside him.

"That's a lousy wall," she said. "A Trow with one leg could hop up backward."

"It was high in Svein's day," Halli said, shortly. "No need, now, is there?"

"At Arne's House the wall has been leveled. The buildings lie within gardens."

"What sort of a man *was* Arne?" Halli asked, as they walked up between the stables. From the central yard came the escalating murmur of voices, busyness, the sweet-sour mingling of bread and ale. "He doesn't figure much in the stories."

Aud glanced at him. "Why do you say that? He is the hero of the central cycle!"

Halli's brow corrugated. "Of some lesser tales, maybe."

"Of all the finest exploits! Who else stole the Trow-king's treasure? Who else killed Flori's brothers armed only with a pruning knife? Who else, above all, mustered the Founders together on Battle Rock?"

"What?" Halli stopped dead in his tracks. "Why, that was Svein!"

Aud Ulfar's-daughter gave a tinkling laugh. "You are a great wit, Halli. You make me smile. Well, perhaps *your* tellers have it so."

A certain condescension had reappeared in her tone. Halli was irritated; he spoke hotly. "If what you say is true, if Arne *was* so preeminent a figure, why then is Svein's House the greatest in the valley?"

They had passed the stables and Svein's hall, and were at the edge of the central yard. Silver-black flags flicked high above. The yard was thick with people carrying trays and tankards and rolling kegs to and fro. The House was busier than he had ever seen. Aud looked at it for a moment, then turned to him. Her mouth smiled, but her eyes were hot and angry. "Unlike you," she said, "I have traveled more than two paces from my door. I can tell you that Arne's House is twice the size of Svein's, and *Arne's* is small compared to some. Don't speak what you don't know."

Halli bit his lip; to his surprise her anger wounded him.

"I'm sorry," he faltered. "I spoke with a fool's tongue. I was . . . wrong to criticize your House and Founder. I would be grateful if you do not think the worse of me."

Hesitating, he forced himself to meet her gaze. The anger was still there, but Halli was relieved to see amusement too, unforced, unbitter. "That's all right," Aud said suddenly. "I don't really care. All this business about Houses is rubbish, when you look at it. Just based on silly stories. I don't believe any of it."

Halli stared. "What stories?"

"All that stuff about the heroes. Their great adventures."

"You don't believe it?"

Her laugh again. "No."

"But how else were the Trows—"

"Oh, I don't believe in *them* either. It's all—Oh no. That's *all* I need."

On the margins of the crowd a knot of youths strode toward them, resplendent in tunics of the brightest orange-red. Halli, despite his ignorance, knew immediately they were from far down-valley. All had his mother's coloring: pink-faced, blue-eyed, with hair the color of sandstone. Young as they were—midteens, he guessed, the cusp of manhood—one or two were attempting beards, shaved shorter even than his father's style. Their hair was drawn back and tied tight behind their skulls with circlets of polished bronze. It was a peculiar look, and Halli thought it unmanly. Their clothes were richly made, with fine brocade about the sleeves and collars.

The leader, the tallest boy, the blondest, with the squarest jaw, bowed his head. "Aud Ulfar's-daughter."

She inclined her head slowly in response. "Ragnar Hakonsson."

"I didn't expect to find you up here, associating with the retainers of Svein's House." His voice was high and nasal, with an inflection Halli had not heard before. "Why aren't you down in the meadow? There will be dances before long."

Aud spoke carelessly. "I was hungry for apples. You?"

"The crowd at the ale tent in the meadow is too thick. Father sent us to bring an ale keg to our booth. If the Sveinssons had any sense they'd have distributed kegs already—that's what Father did, three years ago. But what do you expect? That fool Leif Sveinsson is already drunk, careering round, ogling the girls like the bumpkin he is. I'm surprised he hasn't fixed on you."

Aud's eyes flicked uneasily to Halli; she cleared her throat. Before she could speak, Halli stepped forward with a deft touch of his forelock. "Lords, may I be of assistance? If you desire ale I can bring you a keg with all speed."

Until that moment none of the youths had so much as glanced Halli's way.

"At Hakon's House retainers are silent until spoken to," one said.

"And taller," said another.

"He deserves a clip round the ear for that," said a third,

a youth with a thin fox-face. "For his cheek, I mean, not his height. Though that's offensive too."

Ragnar Hakonsson said easily: "All right, boy, get us a keg of the best ale you can. Meanwhile, if the Lady Aud would accompany us back to the meadow for the dances, she can help enjoy the drinking of it."

Aud had been staring at Halli in some perplexity, but now she seemed to collect herself. "I'd be glad to." She smiled round at the youths, eyes creasing. Halli watched them shift and simper, basking in her attention. He felt an odd prickling in his belly.

"What are you waiting for?" Ragnar Hakonsson inquired. "Get going, boy."

Halli gave a smile in which his canines were prominent. "Of course, sir. I am sorry to have caused offense. If I might just give these apples to the Lady Aud. . . . Now, one cask of ale without delay! If you would wait by the main gate I will fetch it for you from the tent yonder."

Halli pattered away into the crowd. When he was out of sight his movements became slower, more deliberate. He entered the tent stealthily, keeping well away from the attendants, who busily trundled casks from the central pile to handcarts waiting in the yard. A hop, a skip; Halli was at the rear of the stack. Selecting a solitary keg with a tap at its end, he rolled it to a place where the tent fabric was flapped and torn. A moment later, he was back in the yard on the side opposite to the waiting Hakonssons.

He rolled the keg rapidly into the deserted workshop of Unn the tanner.

The process of curing skins to make strong leather was a messy and unpleasant business, and as always the bitter smells made him gasp and wrinkle his nose. He considered Unn's vats where the curing leather festered. Each contained solutions of—among other things—water, urine, chopped bark, decaying vegetation, sour milk, and animal fats—ideal substances for hardening the skins.

Now they would have another, more satisfying, purpose.

Halli found a jug and set it under the keg. He poured out a good quantity of ale, some of which he drank, some of which he transferred to an empty vat. Then, turning the keg upside down, he unscrewed and removed the tap, leaving its small round hole. Taking up the jug again, he scooped it full of foul black liquid from the nearest vat. Moving carefully to avoid getting any of the noxious substance on himself, he poured it into the keg, where it fizzed and steamed.

Halli considered. Enough?

He recalled Ragnar's haughty manner and the possessive way he talked to Aud.

Perhaps a little more.

Another jugful went into the keg, together with a scraping of white paste from a nearby bowl. From the smell Halli guessed this to be chicken dung, used for cleaning flesh from skins.

All was ready. Halli refixed the tap and went his way.

Ragnar Hakonsson and his friends waited at the gate, surrounding Aud in an admiring horseshoe ring. They regarded Halli impatiently as he approached.

"You took your time, boy."

Aud said: "Do not be hard on the lad. He means well, I believe."

Halli performed an ornate salute. "I found the finest ale I could, sirs, a special brew for the noblest guests. If I might be so bold, I would suggest it is too strong for the Lady Aud to sample." He looked at her pointedly, bowed, and withdrew.

Down to the meadow went the happy Hakonsson party, clustering close about Aud, each youth laughing louder than his fellows. Halli watched them from the shadows of the gate, then went back to the hall.

5

SVEIN'S YOUTHFUL PROWESS irritated the other heroes so much that several decided to kill him, but their ambushes never went to plan. One time Hakon lay in concealment and shot Svein with arrows. The first struck Svein's silver belt and bounced harmlessly away; the second narrowly missed his neck and pinned him to an oak tree by the tangle of his plaits. Svein was unable to pull free without plucking out half his hair, which he was unwilling to do. Seeing him standing helpless, Hakon drew his sword and sauntered up to make an end of him, but Svein pulled the oak up by the roots and—whirling it round like a fighting staff—gave Hakon the thrashing of his life. Svein made light of the incident afterward. "It was only a sapling," he said. "It was no great feat."

THE FIRST DAY OF the Gathering ended happily with festive revelry in the meadows, but with the mists of morning, news drifted up to Svein's House of a misfortune befalling the Hakonsson deputation. A violent cramp and sickness had overtaken the menfolk of the party;

they had spent all night leaping urgently into nearby bushes before returning groaning to their mats. Several neighboring parties had been forced to move their tents farther afield, while no less than six horses had shied and broken free of their tethers in their effort to move upwind of the Hakonssons.

Halli learned the particulars from Eyjolf, who was busy in the kitchen organizing herbal brews for the sufferers.

"It is a wretched inconvenience," the old man grumbled. "No crops will grow again in *that* corner of the meadow, take it from me."

Halli's expression was melancholy. "Does anyone know the cause?"

"No. *They* blame a keg of ale, which is ridiculous: no one else at the Gathering has complained. More likely it is their vile personal habits." Eyjolf looked left and right, spoke softly: "The sons of Hakon rarely wash, and I have heard it said that some of them cultivate the grime between their toes and crumble it on their salads as a garnish. So: they only have themselves to blame!"

Halli spent the day quietly; dusk found him behind the hall, throwing horseshoes round a hob stick in the flagstones. As he completed a cast, his father appeared beside him. Arnkel's face exhibited lines of weariness and care.

"My son," he said heavily, "I am glad to see you have been keeping out of trouble, as your mother and I requested. This is a small boon on such an unlucky day."

"What is the matter, Father?"

"It is those cursed Hakonssons! *Still* they vomit, without consideration for the general festivity; when they catch their breath, they vow to bring a legal case against me on a charge of poisoning! Oh, they would lose, of course, but the threat taints the atmosphere of the Gathering. There are no takers for our delicious giblet sausages and pigs' entrails in butter-sauce; worse still, some refuse to drink our ale! What is a Gathering without unseemly drunkenness?" He shook his head in wonder. "If matters continue, our visitors will disperse, bringing shame upon our House."

Halli said musingly, "Perhaps mention could be made of the Hakonssons' novel approach to hygiene, so that blame does not rest on us?"

His father grunted. "I have been spreading rumors to that very effect. Hopefully they will take root. Still, when the pompous fools recover I must appease them to forestall their legal action. They are a powerful House and are best kept on good terms." He took a horseshoe from Halli's arm and tossed it to spin elegantly round the stick. "I have taken the advice of Ulfar Arnesson, a well-known mediator of such troubles. He suggests a Friendship Feast held for the Hakonssons after the Gathering. Inevitably he intends to participate. Ulfar likes his food. Well, I must return below."

The idea of Ragnar Hakonsson coming to the hall gave Halli a gnawing worm of anxiety. At least he, Halli, would be elsewhere. A thought occurred to him. "Father, will Ulfar bring his daughter to the feast?"

"His daughter?" Arnkel frowned. "Is she a somewhat slatternly girl, with dirty kirtle and hair tied back without a jot of care? I thought her a servant of some kind. Then, yes—I presume she will attend. As will you."

Halli gave a jump. "But I am banned! Father—this is not a good idea!"

"The Gathering will be over then and your punishment complete. You will be a credit to the House, I'm sure. With luck you will entertain young Ragnar Hakonsson—if he recovers from his cramps, that is. He seems to have suffered most of all."

Two days later the Gathering was over, and Halli's restrictions were at an end. He dawdled about the House, observing from afar the dismantling of the tents, the clearing of booths, the loading of carts and horses. Most of the guests left that morning, passing in a stream along the road into the valley, but the knot of persons at the Hakonsson booth remained. Halli retreated to the hall where preparations were being made for the Friendship Feast. Beds were prepared for the overnight visitors, trestle tables drawn into the center of the hall, lanterns lit, bunches of sweet rosemary hung from the rafters, and fresh straw strewn upon the floor. Eyjolf and the servants located a cask of ale that had survived the Gathering. Cooks labored in the kitchens; a pig was killed and placed upon a spit; men returned from the river bearing fish.

Halli watched this all in agitation, trying to think of an excuse to avoid the feast. He approached his mother with a number of pretexts, but was rebuffed, and in due course found himself with Katla, being inserted at last into his formal clothes.

His mood was not improved by this outfit, which had once belonged to his brother. The tunic reached almost to his knees, while his leggings sagged beneath his buttocks. Katla did not heed his shrill complaints. Instead, she patted his face gently: "Halli, Halli, at every opportunity you scowl and knot your brows. Why do you think you aggravate people so? Like Midwinter's children everywhere, you spread a cloud of rancor."

"I am far less smelly than Leif, whose passing makes the pigs go pale."

"*That* is not what I meant, though you'll find it is a close-run thing. I speak of another effect you have. From the day you took your first steps on those fat little legs, you have spread division among even the mildest folk. Try to be sweet natured and innocent of expression! Especially with the Hakonssons, who are notoriously quick to take offense. Take care not to scowl at *them*. Feuds have begun with less."

As night fell Arnkel, Astrid, Leif, Gudny, and Halli gathered in the hall, waiting for the guests to arrive. They said little, wandering back and forth, fiddling with knives and dishes laid out on the table.

Halli's sister, Gudny, had piled her hair into a tower of intertwining braids; the process had taken her and her maid most of the afternoon. Now she stood making winsome faces into the polished silver dishes. As Halli wandered near she hailed him anxiously. "Tell me, brother, do you think my braids are tight enough? Look at these fine hair-grips I bought from a trader at the fair! They are antique—generations old!"

Halli was waiting with trepidation for Ragnar's arrival and did not wish to indulge his sister. Still, recalling Katla's advice, he bit back a sarcastic remark and arranged his features into an expression of sweet, wide-eyed benevolence.

His sister flinched. "If you want to sour the milk that is just the way to go about it. Oh no, Halli—here is Brodir! And Mother *begged* him to stay away."

With a flurry at the drapes, their uncle entered, looking very white and sour in the face. He went straight to the keg and filled a cup. Halli's mother, Astrid, hurried forward, pale with vexation and anxiety.

"Brodir! You *promised*! Please—you will not do us any good by being here! I will bring food to your room—you shall have the best cuts, the finest fruits. . . ."

It was clear to all that Brodir had been drinking, nevertheless his voice was calm. "Eyjolf! Lay an extra place here at the end. I will be attending after all. It seems to me, Astrid," he went on, "that tonight Svein's hall needs filling with those who hold his memory dear, not those who grovel before his enemies!"

"Do not be a fool, Brodir!" This was Arnkel, his voice high and strained. "Reconciliation has long been made—there is no bad blood between them and us."

Behind his beard, Brodir smiled blandly. "Why then object to my presence?"

Arnkel took a deep breath. "Because, brother, you live in the past."

"And because you have the skill of making the past *live*," Halli's mother hissed. "*Will* you be gone from here?"

"No, Astrid, I will not. What if the Hakonssons run true to form and try to steal Svein's treasures from the walls? *Someone* must be here to guard them." Brodir wheeled unsteadily around; his gaze fell on Halli. "Don't you agree, Halli? You're a true son of the House. *You* wouldn't cast me out."

Everyone looked at Halli. Everyone recoiled. Brodir said: "Is something wrong with your eyes, boy? If you want the privy, go now before the guests arrive."

As Halli abandoned his innocent, wide-eyed look, hooves sounded on the cobbles of the yard. Arnkel and Astrid cursed. Arnkel said: "If you love me, brother, do not rise to their bait." The family lined up inside the door.

A few moments later, handing their cloaks to Eyjolf and blinking in the warmth and light, the Hakonssons entered the hall.

There were fewer of them than Halli had expected—only three, in fact: two men and a youth. At the head of the line, Arnkel bowed stiffly. "Hord Hakonsson, we bid you and your family welcome and offer you friendship and service during your stay. Our House is yours." Beside him, Halli heard Brodir snort under his breath.

Hord Hakonsson spoke: "You do us honor with your generosity. I bring here my brother, Olaf, and my son, Ragnar, to share this fellowship in your great House. My wife will not be joining us."

Arnkel spoke anxiously. "I hope she is not still sick."

"No, indeed. She has left with the servants. As you know, our road is long."

At Halli's side, Brodir muttered: "That's insult number one; look at Astrid's face."

But Halli was gazing straight ahead, toward the fire, dry-mouthed at the prospect of Ragnar Hakonsson's approach. When he recognized Halli, what would he do? Strike him? Shout out? Call down a curse on his head? Anything was possible.

The three guests moved along the line, murmuring greetings to his family; Halli heard Leif's gruff salute, his sister simpering . . . then Hord Hakonsson came to Brodir.

There was a silence. Neither man said anything. They did not clasp hands.

Hord moved on. Now he stood before Halli, looking down at him from a great height. His beard was reddish, and shaved low and squared upon the cheeks. Like Ragnar and his companions, he wore his hair drawn back tightly behind the head. He was burly about the neck and shoulders, a very powerful man. Heaviness hung about his jowls and eyes; he looked at Halli with little interest. Halli cleared his throat, gave his name; his hand was enclosed in a giant meaty fist. Hord was gone.

Next came Olaf Hakonsson, Hord's younger brother. He was leaner about the face, with a nose somewhat like a blade, narrow and tapered at the tip, with lips drawn tight within his beard. He too ignored Brodir, nodded at Halli, moved away.

And now came Ragnar, pale and blotchy skinned, still evidently recovering from sickness. He arrived at Halli, looked at him, and paused. Halli tensed and cleared his throat. He waited for the explosive fury, the accusations. . . . Instead, Ragnar's eyes betrayed first boredom, then a certain faint perplexity. He looked Halli up and down; he frowned. . . . He seemed like a person waking from a dream, struggling to recall its details. . . . Then he shrugged, shook his head minutely, nodded blankly to Halli, and stepped away toward where servants proffered the ale cups and the fire licked high.

Halli was still gazing after him in astonishment when more guests came prancing down the line. Here was Ulfar Arnesson, the mediator, a slight man, gray of hair and beard, with darting, sparkling eyes. He clasped everyone's hands with generous urgency, as if by doing so he saved them from a nasty fall. Quiet, in his wake, came a slim, attractive girl plainly dressed in a clean plum kirtle, her pale hair drawn back and ornately braided. She walked straight-backed down the line, nodding politely. Halli noticed Leif and Gudny staring after her.

The corners of Aud's mouth flickered as she passed him, and her eyes gleamed bright. Then Eyjolf and his helpers came scurrying in with piled platters and the line dissolved to the table.

To begin with, the feast went well. They dined on goose and duck, brought steaming from the kitchen, together with salmon caught in the Deepdale streams, onion sauces, vegetables, and salad. Ale flowed freely from the cask and conversation was light and inconsequential. Seating was in order of precedence, so Halli found himself wedged at the far end, among the plates of scraps. If Gudrun the goat girl had been present she might have been positioned farther out, but it would have been a marginal decision.

To Halli's respective relief and satisfaction he was seated far from Ragnar and close to Aud. With fleeting, furtive glances he noted the grace of her movements, the delicacy with which she ate. She bore scant resemblance to the tousled, leaf-stained girl he had met in the orchard, except for the amusement in her eyes when she looked his way. He leaned close: "I'm glad you had none of the ale."

"I smelled it. Only a fool would have drunk it." She grinned pleasingly at him.

"The strangest thing," Halli whispered, "is that Ragnar hasn't recognized me. I can't understand it!"

She tore a strip of goose from a bone. "*That's* easily explained. When you met him, you wore servant's clothes. He would have looked straight through you, if at all. Now that you're in a Founder's colors and so an approximate equal, he deigns to look at you. Simple. For him it is as if it is the first time."

Halli shook his head. "I am glad *I* am not so blind."

The meal progressed. Halli's suspicions about Hord Hakonsson were immediately confirmed: he had a prodigious capacity for the joys of table. He talked and ate and drank unceasingly, tossing bones upon the floor with one hand while the other waved his empty cup for filling.

It was a different matter with Olaf, who was slight, with a frame almost womanish and no fine belly on him. Where his brother feasted like a bear, Olaf picked at his plate fastidiously, in the manner of some drab bird, toying with each morsel in his fingers so long that Halli became mesmerized and had to drink deep from his ale cup to forget it. He did not think him an impressive guest. But Olaf's eyes were quick and never still, and he spoke pleasant things to Halli's brother in an undertone, so that Leif laughed foolishly and choked upon his goose.

To Halli's disgust, his mother Astrid spent a good deal

of time talking with Ragnar, as if he were a person of great consequence. Halli's mood worsened further when he noticed that Ragnar's responses, far from making his mother bored or impatient as he would have assumed, provoked her regularly to peals of laughter.

Arnkel spoke politely with Hord and Ulfar. Brodir sat at the end of the table, next to Halli. He didn't have much to say at all.

The spit-roasted pig was brought in and the old dishes cleared away. Then Hord Hakonsson banged his cup upon the table and said: "Arnkel, the food is more than adequate. It easily makes up for the curious poisoning we suffered in your care. I say suffered: in truth Olaf and I were hardly affected; it was this delicate fawn who nearly died." He leaned forward and ruffled Ragnar's hair roughly. Ragnar said nothing, but stared at his plate.

"So," Hord went on, "we shall say no more about it and enjoy your hospitality. I particularly enjoy the coziness of this little room, which, after the lofty expanse of our hall at Hakon's House, is intimate indeed. So many quaint features—the carvings on the roof arches, for instance."

"Do you not have such carvings?" Gudny asked politely.

"Possibly so, my dear," Hord said, "but in Hakon's hall they are too high to see."

His brother Olaf said heartily: "It makes a change to have hot food; in our hall the distance to the kitchens is such that meals are often cold when they arrive at table."

Halli watched his parents' faces: both wore fixed smiles.

Hord said musingly: "Yes, this fellowship between our Houses is a fine thing! It puts me to mind of that time our two dear Founders, Hakon and Svein, undertook that adventure in the estuary, the year before the Battle of the Rock. Doubtless you will know the story. You'll recall that sea raiders had been burning settlements on the shore, and that no one knew how to deal with them. But Hakon and Svein . . ."

Aud leaned close to Halli. "Here we go. Wake me when it's over."

"But this is a fine tale!" Halli whispered back. "Though I thought it was Svein and Egil who did the deed."

"Tales warp to suit the teller," Aud said. "*I* heard it was Arne and Ketil."

Hord was already into his stride, slapping the table with great ham fists to emphasize his points. ". . . then the raiders' ship rammed the heroes' boat, causing a great gash in the stern. What did brave Svein do? He promptly stuck his backside in the hole and plugged the leak! This selfless action saved the day, allowing Hakon to fight the pirates off at odds of ten to one, until . . ."

Halli frowned and nudged his uncle's arm. "This is somewhat different from the version you told me!" But Brodir drank steadily from his cup and did not look at him.

". . . then Hakon said to the raiders: 'Your hospitality

has been pleasant, but now we must depart your hall.' And he threw his sword as if it were a boar spear, so that he skewered the raiders' iron-hearted leader through the mouth and fixed him twitching to the mast. Then he grasped Svein by the hair and plucked him from his plug hole with a great popping noise, so that the black water gushed in. Together they jumped into the waves. Svein's leggings had ripped; his bottom smiled up at the moon as he splashed and gasped. Of course, he could not swim, but . . ."

Halli watched his parents' faces: his mother had a dull, glazed look; her cheeks were flushed bright red; his father laughed loudly at Hord's tale, louder than anyone, as if he could not contain the mirth within him; he drank heavily between guffaws.

Hord finished his story with Hakon dragging Svein to the shore insensible. He raised his cup to the table and drained it.

Arnkel said heavily: "Well, well, that was pleasant hearing indeed. I am the happiest of men that our Houses continue such ancient amity. Let past misunderstandings be cast aside and buried with our fathers on the hill." He drank again. Hord chewed smilingly upon a piece of meat.

"Fine words indeed," Ulfar Arnesson, the mediator, said. "Now if I might—"

From the opposite end of the table, Brodir spoke for the first time: "I too enjoyed the tale. Almost as much as that fine old one about the Trow-king's bride. Do you recall it?

It seems that when Hakon was walking in the hills—as one could in those days—he was met by a group of Trows who mistook him for a female of their kind—though whether because of Hakon's essential girlishness or the brutish quality of his features (or both) was never quite determined. Well, he was spirited away to the Trow-king's bed, where—"

Gray-bearded Ulfar cleared his throat hastily. "That story is not well known."

Brodir blinked at him. "No? Then you will doubtless wish to hear it now."

"No, no. Thank you. Did I mention that I am fearful of the black creep this winter down at Arne's House? After a good hot summer it was ever thus. It claimed my poor dear wife last winter, leaving little Aud here motherless."

Hord and Olaf Hakonsson had both been regarding Brodir closely. With reluctance, they pulled their eyes away and glanced at Aud. "I am sorry to hear this, Ulfar," Olaf said.

"As am I," Arnkel said.

"Yes, yes, it is a sore affliction. I lost many of my farmhands also in the scourge, so that I fear for next year's harvest if more go to the hill."

Hord made a negligent gesture. "We can always spare a few helpers from our many farms. Creep is rare beside the sea."

Brodir spoke loudly: "If Ulfar is in need, why should he not come to us?"

"Perhaps he knows you have not many men to spare," Hord said agreeably. "Also, your farm is hellishly remote."

"Eyjolf!" Halli's mother said in a hearty voice. "I believe we have finished with the birds and fish. You may bring us the pudding now."

The old man stacked up a vast pile of plates and tottered from the hall.

"It is cloudberry pie," Astrid said. "With custard. I hope you like cloudberries."

"Oh, very much," Hord said, and he patted his belly.

"We do not get good cloudberries down-valley," Olaf remarked. "The soil is rather too rich. Up here, where the land is practically waste, they are delectable."

Brodir said: "Your boy there should be wary of eating many, since he evidently has the constitution of a shrew. A single berry might do him a mischief."

There was a silence. Hord looked at his son as if waiting for a response. Ragnar stared at his plate of meat. Slowly, Hord's face stained deep red. He half rose from his seat. "If anyone wishes to impugn the honor of my son, let them address their remarks to me."

Brodir smiled. "I would not dream of speaking to him personally, even to ask his name, for fear he collapses and dies from nervous tension. Just to look at him one can see he is a true son of Hakon, well-known as a sword dodger and hedge lurker."

Arnkel stood abruptly; his chair squealed backward on

the floor. "Brodir!" he cried. "Leave this table now! I order you! Without another word!"

Halli's uncle's eyes were glazed; moisture trickled down his face, his beard gleamed with it. "Gladly," he said. "I have no stomach for this company." He stood, tossed his cup upon the table, and strode unsteadily to the drapes. He hurled them aside. They fell back into place, swung once, hung still.

Silence in the hall.

Halli's mother said, in a faint voice: "Cousin Ulfar, if Aud is at risk from creep this winter at your House, perhaps you will honor us by letting her stay with us?"

Ulfar's reply was fainter. "Thank you, Astrid. I will consider it."

They fell quiet again. Everyone stared at their plates. After an unknown time, with a triumphant rushing and an eruption of fragrant steam, Eyjolf and the servants bustled hot cloudberries into the hall.

6

ONE HARSH WINTER Svein and his companions went hunting in the hills. Svein had his bow, but had left his sword at home. In the pinewoods they were attacked by starving wolves. Svein killed three with arrows, but then the wolves closed in; he could no longer use the bow. A great gray she-wolf snapped her jaws upon his forearm; at the same moment, he saw another dragging his friend Bork into the bushes by a leg. With a bound Svein leaped after them, seized Bork's wolf under his free arm, and snapped its neck like a twig. Only then did he think to do the same with the she-wolf gnawing on him.

The wolf's jaws were locked and they had to saw the head off the body. Svein went home with the head still clamped fast upon his arm.

"What do you think of my bracelet, Mother?"

She pried it off with a crowbar, boiled away the skin, and fixed it with his other trophies on the wall above the gate.

As SOON AS WAS decently acceptable, the Friendship Feast came to an end. The guests retired to their rooms and the family dispersed gloomily to bed. Halli took a candle and passed down the private corridor. At Brodir's door he paused. From beyond the wood came sporadic sounds: muffled thuds, bangs, and pottery breaking.

With heavy tread he went on to his room and composed himself for sleep.

Brodir's behavior had been abusive and a breach of hospitality, but Halli found the cause of it perplexing. The rage within his uncle, his vehement dislike for the visitors, had clearly existed well before Hord and Olaf Hakonsson displayed their arrogance at table. His mother had known of this enmity—she had even asked Brodir to stay away—and from their frosty greeting, it seemed Hord knew Brodir of old.

What was their association? Halli could not recall hearing his uncle talk much of the Hakonssons when he recounted his youthful travels.

It was a mystery, but Halli felt sure that if he knew the details it would justify the extent of Brodir's fury, if not the way in which it was expressed. Lying in the dark he stared toward the ceiling, fingernails clenched into his palms as he rehearsed the numberless boasts and condescensions that Hord and Olaf had employed during the meal. Oh, Svein's House was small, was it? Meager, remote, and poorly manned? And great Svein himself a girlish buffoon, scarcely able to get up in the morning without his leggings falling round his ankles? The travesty made Halli grind his teeth.

True, he could take some pleasure that his tampered ale had laid the Hakonssons low, but what was this but just a trick, subtle and unmanly? How much better it would have been to have lived in the age when the heroes walked with swords at their belts, able to challenge one another when their honor was questioned. Ah, *then* Halli would have walked tall. Or at least moderately so. He would have sent Hord and Olaf packing quickly enough had they dared impugn his House!

His eyes closed; he saw himself elsewhere. His sword twinkled in sunlight, the Hakonssons yelped in fear. Aud was smiling at him as he strode along. Up on the hill the Trows prepared to flee his coming.

Visions of prowess enveloped him in pleasant warmth. Halli slept.

Above was a dark sky. Somewhere close was danger; Halli turned round and round, looking on all sides, but whatever it was remained consistently behind him, and his sword was nowhere to be found. His attempts grew frantic. At last, with a cry, he woke to find that he had threshed half the straw from his mattress and was entangled in his blanket like a rabbit in a net.

He lay still a moment, trying to recall the dream and its significance. All he could tell was that he had a fearful headache and needed urgently to pee. This wasn't especially significant. It was always thus when he had taken too much ale.

A pale light shone at the window. Slowly, stiffly, Halli got out of bed.

To his annoyance his pot was missing. Katla must have taken it for emptying and forgot to bring it back. The alternative, the privy, was out in the yard behind the hall, and Halli had to leave by the back door to get to it. It was very early yet; the sky was just beginning to lighten, and a gray haze hung over everything, motionless and silent. Halli's bare feet plashed lightly on the old Trow-stones; he felt the dew on the grass that grew between the flags. A light cold breeze blew against his bare legs and up his nightshirt.

His business in the privy took some time and brought to mind the torrents of springtime that so frequently caused loss of life. But it was over at last and he was much relieved, though his head still hurt.

As he pushed past the door out into the yard, he heard voices from the stables.

The words were spoken too low to be distinguished, but he thought them angry. From where he stood he could see that the stable doors had been pulled open, but the interior was hidden. The voices continued: three men arguing, talking over one another, alongside little separate sounds—clinks of harness, the chap of hooves—that told Halli that horses were being readied for the road.

He scratched the back of his neck, considering. Then he crossed the yard on soundless feet, climbed upon an upturned water butt beside the stable wall, selected a knothole in the wood, and peered through.

There was Ragnar Hakonsson, immaculately cloaked and ready for travel, sitting on a fine gray mare. Ragnar's face was taut and drawn, still sickly; he watched an altercation between three men standing deeper in the stable.

The men were lit firstly by the dawn light filtering through the slats in the wooden wall, so that it seemed as if a dozen gray and ghostly spears pierced them where they stood; secondly, by the pale radiance of two lanterns, one placed upon the straw beside the nearest stall, the other swinging in Olaf Hakonsson's fist. He and his brother Hord had been preparing for departure; their horses, handsome specimens, sleeker than the up-valley breed, were saddled and bridled, breakfasting quietly from their nosebags. Hord held their reins loosely in one hand. Both he and Olaf wore traveling cloaks wrapped tight about the necks against the morning chill; their boots had been cleaned and polished. As at the dinner it was clear they were richly appareled, important men.

By contrast, Halli's uncle Brodir wore the same clothes as the night before, his tunic stained and disheveled, his sleeves hanging loose, his leggings runkled, his hair disordered. It did not seem as if he had been to sleep at all. He stood in a foolish posture, with his head on one side and one thumb hooked into his belt, pointing and gesticulating insolently at the Hakonssons.

Exactly what Brodir said was hard to make out, for his

voice was incoherent and muffled by the furious retorts of Hord and Olaf. But Halli guessed his words held little wisdom. He had no doubt the three were continuing the dispute begun at Astrid's table the night before. Olaf Hakonsson in particular seemed incensed—he spoke almost as much as Brodir, with impassioned swings of his arms; the lantern in his hand cast eerie loops upon the stalls and made the household horses start and shy.

Much as Halli loved his uncle, Halli devoutly wished his father or mother—even Eyjolf—would come to lead him away. But the House was silent still: evidently the Hakonssons planned to leave as early as they could, before their hosts had risen.

It occurred to Halli that he should hurry away to rouse his parents, but his eye was fixed at the knothole as if nailed there.

Then Brodir lurched forward, jabbing a finger, and for the first time Halli heard him clearly. "Go ride then and find your women. In all likelihood they will have roosted for the night in trees, like so many carrion crows." He smiled toward them stupidly and stumbled in the straw.

Now Olaf spoke, in a voice distorted with rage: "Svein's House is renowned as a nest of inbred drunkards, who can scarcely cross a yard without tripping on their six-toed feet. Additionally—as you might know, Brodir—it is famous in our parts for its *lack of land*." At this Brodir uttered a curse, but Olaf continued on. "Still, now we have new things to report: we shall proclaim your vile hospitality from the rooftops, and also sing songs of your dwarfish nephew, so ugly that the mountains turn their backs on him and rivers burst their banks when he kneels to drink."

Hord Hakonsson reached forward, clapped his brother on his narrow back, and gestured to the horses. "This gains us nothing. Leave this sot to his folly."

With reluctance, Olaf nodded, but he spoke once more. "You are a notable traveler, Brodir Sveinsson. We will perhaps meet you one evening on a lonely road and continue this discussion. Know that the Council may have proclaimed an end to the old matter, but in our parts your deeds are not forgotten." He turned and took his reins. Then he set his lantern on the floor and, in an easy movement, mounted his horse. Hord did likewise; they nudged their horses forward until they were level with Ragnar's. Brodir took a stagger and a half-step backward to let them pass.

As they reached the open door of the stables, Brodir called after them.

"If we meet again be sure to bring men from other Houses to do your fighting for you. Yes, my nephew may be ugly enough to scare the scales off fish, but he is certainly no coward, while your boy there would hide his face if a mouse passed by. It is clear enough from this that Hakon's blood runs strongly in his veins. Oh, and I haven't forgotten what happened either. I don't regret it—nor its consequence."

So he spoke; and no sooner were the words out of his mouth than Olaf had leaped from his horse, taken two strides back into the stable, and struck Brodir across the face with the flat of his hand. Halli felt the blow as if it had been his own cheek: the shock of it made him jerk up; he cut the bridge of his nose against a splinter in the knothole.

Brodir's head snapped sideways, but drunk as he was—and caught by surprise—he did not fall, or even step back, though blood came from his nose.

Olaf intended this to be the end of the matter; he turned away to remount his horse, but as he did so Brodir gave a roar of rage and grappled him from behind, clasping him around the neck and dragging him backward so that he lost his balance and nearly fell. Despite his slenderness, Brodir proved himself no weakling; his arm circled Olaf's neck as if it were a band of iron; with his other hand he struck repeated blows against his side so that Olaf's eyes popped and his tongue lolled from his mouth.

But now Hord came rushing, cloak aflap behind him. He had descended swiftly from his horse; now he flung himself at Brodir, striking out with his great ham fists. Brodir dodged the first blow; the second fell against his beard and made him reel, but he held fast to Olaf, and kicked out with a boot, making Hord gasp and fall back against the nearest stall.

Halli had seen enough; without thought he leaped down from the water butt, nightshirt billowing about him, slapping at his legs. He ran round the side of the stable, past where Ragnar sat like a statue upon his horse, staring at the fight with puffy eyes; past the other horses standing still and placid, in and across the straw toward where his uncle and Olaf grappled. Hord saw him coming; as Halli darted close he stretched out a hand and grasped him tight across the arm, then with little effort swung him up so that Halli's feet left the ground. Halli felt a hot and wrenching pain across his shoulder; he lashed out frantically with arms and legs, but Hord's arm was too long and his grip too tight. Hord flexed his arm once and let go his hold. Halli flew across the stable into an empty stall, crashing down against the wooden wall so that his breath was driven from him and white lights swirled against his eyes.

He lay on his side in a mess of straw, tasting blood upon his tongue. The stable seemed to spin, then slowed and stopped. Halli looked. He saw Olaf Hakonsson lying slumped against the ground, his fingers clawing at his throat. Hord had broken Brodir's grip; now the two of them were wrestling close, arms locked tight against the other. They fought first one way, then the other, in grunting, gasping silence, colliding with the stalls so that the wood split, stirring the stable floor with their shuffling feet until the spears of dawn light coming through the slats about them were thick with whirling dust.

Brodir fought hard, but Hord had a bull's strength. The match was not long; all at once Hord wrenched Brodir round and pinned his arms from behind, holding him fast.

Olaf was struggling to his feet, very white-faced and bubbling at the lips.

Halli moved; a pain flared in his shoulder. He ignored it, sought to rise.

Something heavy crushed against his neck. A boot sole, pressing hard.

Ragnar Hakonsson's voice said: "No, Trow-face—you wait there."

Halli choked and scrabbled with his fingers at the boot. With bulging eyes he saw Olaf Hakonsson stand contemplatively before Brodir, who waited helplessly in Hord's grip.

He saw Olaf Hakonsson move away, slowly, deliberately, out of view toward the horses. He heard a rasp of leather— a pannier being opened—and the briefest of rummaging. Olaf stepped back into sight, his face expressionless, its pain and anger replaced with calm intention. In his hand he held a little knife, the kind used to cut cheese, pare hooves, pit fruit—daily tasks of a hundred kinds.

Halli watched him, his fingers clamped tight upon the leather of the boot upon his neck.

He saw Olaf Hakonsson step across to Brodir, draw back the knife, and stab him once in the heart, so that he died.

Olaf tossed the knife onto the straw. Then he turned and went to his horse.

Hord Hakonsson let Brodir's body drop upon the

ground. He too went to his horse. As he did so he looked at Ragnar, spoke a word. For a moment the boot pressed harder still on Halli's throat, then it was lifted away. A swirl of cloak, boots scuffing through straw—Ragnar was gone.

Halli lay motionless in the straw, eyes staring.

He heard Hakonssons' horses go slowly off across the yard. All the other horses in the stable were now neighing and shifting, and one or two kicked out against their stalls, because they smelled the blood and did not like it.

Halli lay motionless. Presently he heard the sudden spurring of the horses and the eager hoof-fall as they galloped out of Svein's House and away into the valley.

In those days, with the Trows still troublesome, few people dared climb up onto the moors. But Svein was keen to see what was up there, despite his mother's pleading. "No Trows will be out by day," he told her, "and I'll be home before dark. Make my favorite supper, for I'll be hungry when I get back." And with that he strapped on his silver belt, took his sword, and set out.

He climbed the ridge and came to the moors, all heathery and desolate, and looked about him. In the distance was a low round hill, and in the hill he spied a door. Svein walked until he came to the door. It was very large and painted black.

"This is a Trow-door sure enough," he said to himself, "and I can either leave it alone or open it and look inside. The first would be safe, but the second brings me honor." So he opened the door. When he looked in he saw a hall hung about with men's bones. There was a fire burning in the far distance. With infinite caution, Svein stole through the hall until he drew near the fire. There upon a rock sat a great fat Trow, busily fashioning a human skull into a drinking cup. When he saw this, Svein boiled with rage. "I can either go back," he said to himself, "or pay out this devil for his crimes. The first would be safe, but the second brings honor to my House." So he crept up behind the Trow and lopped off its head with one swing of his sword.

Svein was tempted to go on, but he looked back and saw that the light from the door was growing blue and dim. Evening was coming. So he went back down the hill and was home in time for supper.

And that was Svein's first visit to the Trowking's hall.

PART

II

7

SVEIN'S BROTHER HORKEL was killed by a neighbor in a dispute about land. When Svein heard, he said little, but took his sword and belt and went out. The neighbor had fled to a hut on a remote crag. It could only be reached by ladders two hundred rungs long, and they had been taken away. When Svein reached the crag foot, he considered the sheer cliff, while the killer shouted abusive remarks from the summit. Without words, Svein began to climb. The rock was loose and broke under his hands; the wind was strong and tore him from his footholds. Eagles pecked his ears. Night fell and Svein climbed on. At dawn the killer began throwing rocks, which Svein dodged by swinging out one-handed. He got to the top and slew his brother's killer with a single sword thrust, then climbed back down and returned to his House, where he took up his plow as if nothing had happened. "I have had a walk around," he told his mother. "Now I am back."

THE MEN ARNKEL SENT after the killers returned before dark, dust-stained and despondent. They had ridden hard all the way to the cataracts, but down-valley horses are light and swift, and the Hakonssons had long since passed the Snag. This set Arnkel raging until he frothed at the mouth. He picked up a trestle table and threw it against the wall, so it broke in two; he took the knife that had killed his brother and stabbed it into his own hand, into the palm that had clasped the hands of Brodir's murderers. Even Astrid fled from him and Arnkel remained all night alone in the hall.

Morning came again. Bright sunlight shone through Halli's window and across his counterpane. There was a smell of fresh air and wildflowers. When he woke from deep sleep, Halli lay still a while, staring at the triangles of light upon the plaster wall, at the black beams in the ceiling, at old Katla snoring in her corner chair. When he moved, his shoulder ached, but the poultices his nurse had given him had soothed the damaged muscles, and he could move his arm freely once more.

His memories of the previous day were fragmentary— little more than shards of shock, confusion, and pain. He had raised the alarm, yes: after that—what had he done? Little enough. Just stood by as the House sprang into action. He had been a bystander, ignored by all save Katla, who fussed and cosseted him and confined him to his bed.

Time to change all that. Halli rose, dressed slowly, winc- ing at certain movements, and went to the hall. The sun was already high, but a hush lay on the House. His father was sitting in his Law Seat, head on his breast. His wounded hand was black with dried blood. He had not bandaged it. Around his shoulders hung his formal cloak, a somber, crumpled silver-black. He was very still and silent. At his side stood Halli's mother, speaking softly in his ear.

A few people worked in remote corners of the hall, preparing flowers for Brodir's vigil, but no one dared approach where Arnkel sat.

Halli marched right up. "Father, I wish to have a sword."

Arnkel did not raise his head. His voice was low and quiet. "Why?"

"Simple enough. I intend to avenge my uncle."

For a long while Arnkel did not speak. At last he said, "My son, there *are* no swords. All were melted down. Save the ones the heroes hold, up on the hill."

"Grim could make a blade."

"Oh, Grim will do that, all right!" His mother's voice was shrill and furious; it cut across the muted hubbub of the room so that all activity stopped. "Even now he makes the sword that Brodir will take into his cairn, to help guard us from the Trows. But there are no swords for the *living*, as well you know! The Council forbids it, as is right, just as the Council will resolve this matter peacefully, to our eventual satisfaction. Let there be no further talk of avenging, you stupid boy."

Halli shrugged. "It is well known you never cared for Brodir, Mother. Father—what of you? Your rage and grief echo my own."

Arnkel stirred then; he sat a little higher. "Halli," he said wearily, "treat your mother with more respect, or I will beat you here and now." He pulled at his nose and looked toward the fire. "And I ask you not to speak to me again of vengeance, or swords, or the honor of Svein's House. Your impulses are good—I understand them, I share them! We all do." (At this there was a snort from Halli's mother.) "You have already done what you could—your bravery in the stable was admirable. It is not your fault you are no warrior. But the way to proceed now"—he took a deep breath—"is by mediation and settlement. Your mother is right. The old ways lead to feuding and more cairns on the hill. None of us want that."

"Brodir liked the old ways," Astrid said, "and sought to act on them. Where is he now? Under a white sheet, with a cold house waiting." She smiled palely at her son. "Halli, Halli, I know you loved his tales, I know you even admired him. But his values were those of the past. We do not follow them. The Lawgivers of each House will gather as soon as can be arranged. Indeed Ulfar Arnesson rides today to alert the down-valley Houses, and Leif goes to the upper ones, so with luck the Council will meet before winter falls. To them you will state what you saw. They will pass judgment. And you will be chief witness, Halli! Think of that! It is a *very* important role for someone so young."

Halli said blandly, "But what will happen to the Hakonssons then?"

"They will be forced to give us a very good settlement."

"You mean *land*? That's it? They give us a bit of land?"

"Land is not to be sniffed at, boy. It is where our wealth lies."

Arnkel Sveinsson sat staring toward the fire, a gaunt and ageing man. He spoke softly, as if to himself. "Mediation is the only way, and even here we may be forced to settle for less than we desire. Hakon's is a powerful House."

"Mediation has taken lands from us before," Astrid said, her lips compressed. "This time, at least, it will work in our favor. Ah, here is Leif, all ready to depart!"

Leif wore his traveling cloak, and his beard was newly trimmed. He bounded onto the dais and began discussions with his parents about his exact route to the upland farms. He was exuberant, eager to be off; he displayed no great grief at the circumstances of his mission.

Astrid patted Leif's arm fondly. "You look most handsome, my son! A fine emissary of the House. Do you not think so, Halli?"

But Halli had left the hall.

In the passage beyond the drapes he slowed his pace and came to a standstill, breathing deeply, willing his anger to subside.

"Halli."

Aud Ulfar's-daughter had appeared from the guest room. It would not be true to say that Halli had forgotten her existence, but recent events had pushed her from the forefront of his mind. She wore traveling clothes in a state of some disorder, and was doing something with her hair. Two bone hairpins protruded from between her lips. Amid the flow of his emotions it was hard for Halli to adjust to sudden conversation. "Oh. Hello."

"Sorry about your uncle." Her arms were behind her head, fiddling. The hairpins bobbed and quivered as she spoke.

"Thanks."

"Those bloody Hakonssons. They don't give a damn about anyone. First time they've killed someone like that, though—a free man from another House, I mean. I expect they kill their own people all the time. What had your uncle *done?*"

Halli's face was expressionless. "Nothing. He was drunk."

"Yes, wasn't he? Seems a bit harsh, though. Think yourself lucky they're not *your* neighbors. They're always shifting the boundary posts to their advantage, and of course my father never does anything about it, just bows and scrapes and kisses the ground beneath their boots. He's in a dilemma *now*, of course—his cousin, Astrid, on one side and Hord Hakonsson on the other . . . he'll have to tread carefully in the mediation. Still Father never does *anything* that isn't careful. Does anyone?" With a quick movement she plucked the pins from her lips and inserted them into her hair somewhere behind her head. "Damn, nearly lost it

114

there . . . No, it's fine . . . We're off to inform the Lawgivers now on our way home."

"I know. My parents just told me. They're eager for the settlement." His voice was bitter.

Aud turned her head, pointed to her hair. "How does it look?"

"Sort of lopsided."

"It'll do. So you were fond of him? Your uncle."

"Yes."

"I'm sorry. You know my mother died last winter. So I know how it feels to lose the only person who . . . Well." She ran her hands down her kirtle, looked away. "I've got to get ready. My father will be waiting."

Halli said: "Listen, I'm sorry too. About your loss."

She smiled then, her eyes glistening. "Oh, I go up the hill and talk to her all the time. Sit by the cairn, bring her flowers. Better than being at home with Father and my aunt, talking endlessly about marriage. Still—"

But Halli was frowning now. "Up at the cairn? What about the Trows?"

Aud blew her cheeks out in disdain. "Well, I don't cross over, and I don't go up at night. But even so . . . Who do you know, Halli Sveinsson, who has ever actually seen a Trow?"

"Well, *I* have, more or less."

"Yes, by 'seen' I mean *really* set eyes on one, not just wet your leggings when the wind howled through the cairns or a hare ran from a thicket."

Halli drew himself up. "Not two weeks ago I was high on the ridge, doing far-herding. There's a place where the wall's crumbled. A ewe got lost, strayed beyond the cairns. In the night"—his voice fell to a whisper; his round eyes stared left and right into the dim regions of the passage—"in the night, I heard her screaming. At dawn, there it was—her carcass lying! Torn to pieces, it was."

Aud yawned rudely. "I can barely breathe for sheer terror, Halli. You're a born storyteller. What happened then?"

"Er, that was it."

"What? That's your story? I've one word for you: wolves."

Halli sniffed. "But this was the *Trow*-moors."

Aud rolled her eyes. "During your stay up there, did you see wolves?"

"Yes, far off."

"Eagles?"

"Yes."

"Then why assume Trows killed your sheep when the other options are there in front of you? Why make things more complicated than they are?" Aud's voice grew animated. "When I get an itch on my bum I don't imagine a Trow's crept up and put it there, do I? I go for the simple explanation. Oh, Arne's blood, that's my father." Ulfar Arnesson's voice could be heard loudly calling in the hall. "I've got to go, and I'm still not packed. I'll see you before long anyhow, with luck—since your mother's invited me to stay this winter. But if you're passing Arne's House in the meantime, come and visit. We've got better ale down there than *you* serve, that's for sure." She grinned at him a final time, waved, and disappeared through her door, leaving Halli blinking after her in the silence of the passage.

For two days Brodir's body lay upon a wicker pallet in the center of the hall. Halli did not go to pay his respects. He had already seen his uncle dead, and the image was seared into his mind.

On the third morning, when mists still hung upon the ground, the burial party assembled in the yard. As with every funeral it was Arnkel's duty to lead them to the ridge; now he stood at the hall porch, fumbling with the clasps on his coat. Behind him, Halli, Leif, and Gudny watched as men emerged from cottages across the House. Each man carried a pick, a mattock, or a spade. Grim the smith walked among them, taking stock of the blades' quality and removing some to his forge for hasty whetting; the rasp of his stone fell muffled on the ear.

On the flagstones before the door, Brodir lay in his winding sheet upon a pallet suspended between poles. Another pallet supported the capstone for his cairn.

The men talked in whispers, hoods shadowing their faces, breath pluming in the air. They held their hands inside their fleeces and stamped their boots on the stones like horses straining to be off. Arnkel waited; now Halli's mother, followed by Eyjolf and another servant, came slowly from the direction of the killing shed, where a year-old ram had been led the night before. Each carried a parcel of meat wrapped in skin; these were passed to the burial party, who secured them on the pallet beside the stone.

At last Grim came from the forge, carrying a small piece of shaped iron, no longer than his forearm. This was Brodir's sword, to help him defend the valley. It would be placed upon his breast before the stones were piled on. Arnkel tucked it in his pack.

From their windows and doorways the people of Svein's House watched silently as Arnkel and Grim hoisted the first pallet between them. The line of men began shuffling out of the yard toward the hill gate. They did not waste words; the hole had to be dug and the cairn constructed on the ridge before nightfall. It was no small job.

As Halli washed and dressed soon after, he questioned Katla closely.

"What was the meat for?"

"You know this. Raise your arms. It is thrown onto the moor, to gain permission from the Trows to step across the boundary during the digging. Don't stint with your washing—these days you must scrub *there* too."

Halli wielded the cloth without interest. "And do the Trows come straight out to take it? Will the men see them?"

"Indeed not! The Trows do not come forth by day. They wait for dusk, by which time the men will be gone."

"What if no meat was left them?"

"That would give the Trows power to break through Svein's boundary in *their* turn, to the ruin of us all."

"It would be interesting to see a Trow," Halli remarked in a casual voice.

Katla instantly performed a number of wards and hexes. "Go to the trough right now and wash your mouth with oil and water."

Halli remained put, wrestling with his leggings. "What is so bad about that? I could go up to help with the burial, then wait and watch. I would not cross the boundary, like that boy you told me of, but only spy from the other side of the stones when the Trows came out to eat."

Katla made a little whimper and placed a gnarled hand on his arm. "Three reasons why that is a bad idea, Halli. Firstly it would be dark—you would see nothing. Secondly if you saw so much as a clawed toe, your eyes would drop out in horror and roll upon the floor. Thirdly, such an act of disobedience would annoy our blessed ancestors, who might chastize you."

"It's the *Trows* who are our enemies, Katla! What would our ancestors do?"

"Best not to test them. They are harsh with their judgments and a little inflexible, possibly on account of being dead."

"I think you are growing addled, old nurse. No—not the slippers. I would like my outdoor boots today."

The old woman looked at him narrowly. "I hope you are not fretting any longer about your uncle. He is with Svein now. And, if I might be bold, this tragedy is in some ways for the best. Brodir encouraged your recklessness, I believe."

"So my parents often assured me. Where is my fleece, Katla? The thickest one?"

"On the peg by the door. Halli, don't forget that your parents love you! They care about your fate! The last thing they want is to see you swinging from the gallows."

Halli paused. "What? How likely is that?"

"Your recklessness so far has resulted in minor crimes, I grant you, but larger ones will follow if you are not corrected." Katla sighed, her eyes misty with the past. "You won't remember Rorik of Slees Farm. He began stealing eggs from his neighbors' coops. Just fourteen, like you. But his father didn't beat him sufficiently, so what was he to think?" She shook her head. "Next thing we heard he'd killed a man in a fight over a milk cow and was strung up at the summer Gathering."

Halli stared at her. "And him only fourteen years old!"

"Oh no, he was thirty-odd by that time. The rot sets in early, that's my point."

Halli scowled. "Thank you for the advice. I am going out now."

As he walked to the door Katla spoke in some alarm. "Halli, my dear, I hope—I hope you are not thinking of going up the hill? Only grown men can take part in a burial, as you well know. And if you think to see the Trows—"

He laughed. "Don't worry about me. Good-bye, old nurse."

Then he went out, leaving her frowning after the closing door.

In the kitchen he stole a loaf of new bread, a whole round of goat's cheese and a hunk of bacon wrapped in cloth. He took two hip flasks also, filling one with wine, the other with water from the well. All these he placed in his backpack. Then, with a wolf's stealth, he went to his father's room.

On the bench in the corner sat Arnkel's chest, of old black wood, bound tight with iron. Halli had looked in many times from early boyhood and knew what it contained. His father's field tools: a sickle for harvesting, a billhook for working on the hedges, crop knives and sheep shears—some forged by Grim, others handed down across the years.

But there at the bottom was another knife, used only at formal banquets and at sacrifices. It was slender, long-handled, very sharp.

Halli took it, closed the chest again, and went to the hall.

All was still; on this melancholy day, most of the men were on the ridge, and the women worked elsewhere. There, behind the dais, was the wall of treasures—Svein's armor, Svein's weapons. Halli gazed up at the rotting bow and quiver, the broken shield, the dented helmet on its hook. The helmet transfixed him for a moment: sunlight glimmered on the scarred crown, the neck guards and the nosepiece, but the eyeholes were black, cold, expressionless.

Halli looked away; his eyes went to the stone shelf and the little box that rested there. He looked around. The hall was empty.

Halli reached up on tiptoe and pulled down the box. It was heavier than he expected and he almost dropped it. The wood was dark, pitted with age. Heart pounding, eyes darting, he pulled at the lid, feeling its resistance and the splintering of grain as it suddenly came away.

Inside the box something gleamed.

Halli glanced across the hall. He listened: somewhere close he heard Eyjolf scolding a servant, the hum of the looms from his sister's room, the laughter of children in the yard. For a moment he felt the pull of the familiar, the safety of his childhood home.

His gaze drifted to a trestle standing in the center of the room. It had a rumpled white cloth upon it and was surrounded by dying flowers.

Halli stared at the bier that had borne his uncle's body. Then he tilted the box and let Svein's silver belt fall into his hand. It was cold, heavy, and tightly folded. Without pause Halli put it in his pack. Then he replaced the box upon the shelf so that all was as before, set his pack upon his shoulders, and hurried from the hall.

Halli left Svein's House by a back route, scrambling down the wall and splashing through silted mud and bristling reeds to reach the lower meadow.

For a moment he glanced up toward the heights, where even now the digging would have begun. Then he turned his back, and without further regard for the ridge or the House nestled cozily beneath it, set off to kill the Hakonssons.

8

IN THOSE LAWLESS days traveling the valley was perilous. Not many men attempted it. Yet sometimes, when Svein grew bored of farming, he would take to the road, wandering where he would. Once he left home and went east by the cataracts to Eirik's lands. That year there were so many dangers abroad that the way was considered impassable, but Svein went alone with his sword tucked in his belt and a net in his hand. He entered the forest at a stroll, looking at butterflies and flowers. For three days distant watchers saw birds erupting from the trees in fright; they heard strange cries and bestial howls. On the fourth morning, Svein emerged near Eirik's House, strolling peaceably, dragging a heavy net. In the net were eleven heads, belonging to five robbers, three wolves, two Trows, and a hermit who had made an impertinent comment while Svein was bathing in a stream.

THE SUN WAS BRIGHT, the sky the color of eggshells. High clouds like twists of lamb's wool hung over the northern mountains, where pennants of windblown snow fluttered gently from the shimmering peaks. Every detail of the valley slopes was visible, everything gleamed: sheep backs, stone walls, the milk white waterfalls on the crags above Rurik's House. Even the pine trees on the slopes of the Snag shone with dark luster, mirroring the intentions of Halli's heart.

When he was safely away from the House, and had built up something of a sweat, he paused in the shadows of a meadow beech to inspect the hero's belt.

Daylight flashed on it as he drew it from the pack and let it unfurl between his fingers. The sight made him catch his breath: a chain of slender, silver links, ornate and interfolded. Metal whorls looped like fern fronds, in places thickening to suggest sleek shapes of animals and birds. It was craft far superior to anything Halli had ever seen. He wondered briefly at the workmanship, at who had made it long ago. But that was not as important as the effect it had. Great Svein had worn it and, according to the tales, it had brought him luck.

Halli took off his fleece and sleeveless jerkin and passed the belt around his waist. Slightly to his annoyance he found it was much too long. It appeared Svein had been a big man, as the legends said. Halli scratched his neck and pondered. Then he draped the belt over one shoulder, strapping it diagonally across his chest. Success—the belt was secure. When he put on his jerkin again, it was hidden from view.

Halli set off again, trotting through a sea of long, sweet

grass. A clot of scrawny cattle moved slowly across the field, tails flicking patiently at flies. A buzzard passed high above, soaring on the winds. Whether it was the hero's belt he wore or the brightness of the day, with every step Halli's exhilaration grew. At *last* he had thrown off the stifling confinement he had endured for so many years! His House and family were left behind. He was alone, an adventurer in the world.

In just such a way Svein had set out on journeys of his own. Halli smiled grimly as he strolled along. One day perhaps his story would be told just as Svein's were, recounted after feasting in the hall. Perhaps the very knife that he carried at his back would be up there, on display, or taken down to be passed wonderingly from hand to hand. . . .

With such pleasant conjectures to encourage him Halli walked throughout the morning, taking an undulating course northeast across the lonely meadows. Ahead of him the Snag rose in the distance, gray and sheer. He saw no one, which was as he wished. It was likely, following his conversation with Katla, that people might guess he had climbed the ridge, drawn by his interest in the burial and the Trows. If they thought that, so much the better. The hunt would begin up there, on the slopes of the ridge. By the time they guessed the truth—if they ever did—he would be halfway to Hakon's House, and the avenging of his uncle.

Brodir had not been the easiest of men, and in the last days Halli had sourly noted that his loss did not hang heavy on many hearts. The murder had caused outrage, but most people shared his mother's view that an advantageous settlement would soon be won.

For Halli the matter was quite different, his sorrow aggravated by a surreptitious guilt. Without his trick upon the Hakonssons he knew they would not have attended the Friendship Feast and so come into conflict with his uncle. True, it was Brodir's taunting and Hord's arrogance that had precipitated the fight, but Halli's original actions had played their part too. He could not deny the connection.

Back at the House this knowledge had tortured him through several sleepless nights. Now, out in the open air, with grass underfoot and the mountains beckoning him on, his shame lifted a little. It was still there, though, just enough to motivate him.

How exactly he would kill Olaf he didn't know, but it would soon be done. Halli's brows steepened darkly as he walked down the sunny hill. The killer, back within his House, would consider himself safe now; no doubt he was lounging in his hall, drinking deeply, and laughing at his escape. So what if he was fined a field or two? He was a wealthy man; this was a small price, and no claim on his honor. Let the Lawgivers do their worst—he cared not, secure in the greatness of his House. No doubt Ragnar and Hord laughed with him, heads back, eyes glinting, whiskered mouths agape. Well . . . perhaps they would die too.

Giddy with an upsurge of rage, Halli continued on his way amid the upland silence, across fields, through copses, circling out of his way to avoid small tenant farms, following the gradient ever downward toward the valley's central fold. He took lunch on a rocky outcrop in the center of a meadow, then, his legs a little weary, lay back under the pleasant sun. He awoke from sleep to find the afternoon much older, with banks of dark cloud building up above the summits to the north; without further dawdling he hastened onward to come at last in sight of the valley road.

It was a broad dirt track, laid with uneven flags of stone, but rutted and in mild disrepair. Halli was faintly surprised by the state of it: he had imagined something grander connecting his House with the lower valley. Still, it was exotic enough not to disappoint him: it would take him beyond the cataracts all the way to Hakon's and the distant sea. With a spring and a jump he scrambled down the last grass slope onto the stones.

For the first time in his life, he had left Svein's land. The road marked the boundary. To the north, beyond the hollow where he could hear the river running, rose the fields of Rurik's House. Halli stood still a moment feeling the imminence of new things. Then he withdrew his father's knife from his pack and tucked it in the waist strap of his tunic, just below the silver belt. Let his enemies beware! Halli Sveinsson was coming! With swaggering stride, Halli set off east along the road.

As evening drew in, gray clouds gathered overhead and it began to rain—a dreary insistent drizzle that pattered lightly on the roadside ferns and down the back of Halli's hood. Two oaks beside the way offered reasonable shelter. The ground beneath was dry. Halli halted, considering, then shook his head. Would Svein have let a little rain delay a quest? Hardly! He could do miles more before dark. Halli set his chin at a defiant angle and strode onward, swinging his arms purposefully, daring the rain to do its worst.

Now the road entered a treeless waste of beet fields and riverside scrub, without shelter of any kind. The drizzle intensified to heavy rain, then to a mountain downpour. Halli was drenched in seconds. Water buffeted his face; it ran across the road and collected in between the broken stones. Abandoning his easy stride, he scurried on like a rat, hopping and leaping to avoid the gathering puddles, until, in the half-light, he saw a yellow glimmering ahead.

Halli splashed closer, to discover a dilapidated hut set back from the side of the road. A single flame guttered dimly at a window.

He stumbled up the path and banged upon the door.

A pause. In the hope of escaping the worst of the torrent Halli pressed close against the door. He knocked again, harder. The reverberations dislodged a roof slate, which dropped in a nearby puddle, dousing him still further. A moment later the door swung abruptly open and Halli fell forward to collide against the silhouetted figure of a bent old man, dressed in a ragged tunic. He was quite bald save for a jutting pair of bone white eyebrows, tufted like thistles. Beneath these, two staring eyes looked on Halli with dumb horror.

Halli collected himself. "Good evening."

The old man said nothing. His gaze held a thousand accusations.

"I am traveling down the valley road," Halli continued brightly, "and still have far to go. You will see that it is raining a little. . . ." He gestured about him at the downpour. The old man's expression did not soften; if anything it grew more intense, more numbly aghast at what it saw.

"I was wondering," Halli went on, "whether, since it *is* raining quite heavily, and since it *is* something of a lonely district in which to spend the night outdoors, I might perhaps . . . perhaps . . ." The implacable gaze befuddled him; he faltered, then finished in a sudden rush. ". . . I was wondering if I might shelter here for the night."

There was a long silence during which the rain trickled deeper down the back of Halli's neck. The old man scratched his nose, sucked in his cheeks and, with due consideration, spoke. "You wish to come in?"

"That's right."

The old man grunted. "A meadow sprite desired entry to a wedding once," he said slowly. "It had been invited by the bride. She thought the honor would keep it sweet, bring them good luck. It came wearing smart boots and a moleskin coat; all fine 'how-d'ye-dos' and 'please-marms.' But when the time came for the feasting, it grew affronted—it wished to sit beside the bride. This pleasure was denied it— in a flash, it tore off its coat, vaulted the trestle, punched the husband, slapped the bride, pissed into the marriage cup and away with it up the chimney, lewd curses ringing through the rafters." He resumed staring at Halli from under his bristling brows.

Halli wiped rain from his face and cleared his throat. "I'll take that as a 'no,' then."

To his surprise, the old man shook his head. "Oh no, you can come in, much against my better judgment. You seem human enough, though no doubt you'll cut my throat as soon as I look away." He turned back into the hut with a fatalistic shrug.

"I assure you I shall do no such thing," Halli said, following hastily after and closing the door against the storm. "I am only too grateful for your kindness. This is a fine place you have here," he added, blinking round in the gloom at the dusty floor, the flickering dung-fire, the miserable straw mattress, the three-legged table balanced precariously against the corner of the room.

"It is a hovel, no more, no less. A blind man could see as much." The old man gestured. "Sit wherever you will, save on the mattress, where I shall squat. If you see something big as a mouse, moving sluggishly, crush it with your heel. The lice here are very large."

With due caution, Halli sat in the least unpleasant quarter of the hut, as close to the fire as he could, while the old man stirred the contents of a black pot suspended in the hearth. The atmosphere was warm and close; acrid dung-smoke tickled Halli's eyes. Small pools of water collected around his feet.

"May I place my fleece and boots by the fire?"

"You may, but be warned that if you seek to remove all your clothing I shall hurl you out into the night. For supper we have beet soup with dried ham. If I can cut the cursed thing, that is—it has been hanging from its hook for months, and is as tough as Trow-hide. I suppose *you* have no food with you?" the old man added, eyeing Halli's bag shrewdly.

"Bread and wine, which I'll gladly share," Halli said, kicking off his boots.

"Oh? Wine?" This news seemed to instill his host with new energy. He bustled around the hut, retrieving from crevices bowls, cups, and spoons, and all the while muttering under his breath, "Wine? Wine? That *is* good."

The contents of the pot began to bubble, and spat a rich, sweet scent into the room. Halli's cloak steamed by the fire. His spirits rose once more; *this* was how a day's quest should end—with safety, warmth, nourishment, even merry conversation.

"You are a Ruriksson tenant, I assume?" he said pleasantly.

The old man stopped short; his eyebrows bristled. With a jerk of the head he spat into the fire, narrowly avoiding the cooking pot. "Ruriksson? Do I *seem* a dribbling imbecile? Do I *have* six webbed fingers on each hand? No! Certainly not! I have nothing to do with *that* breed."

Halli was taken aback. "I'm sorry. I only assumed it because your hov—your house is on the northern side of the road. So you are tenant to the Sveinssons, then?"

The old man rolled his eyes and spat into the fire, so that it hissed and fizzed. "The *Sveinssons!* How *dare* you, boy! They are worse than the Rurikssons by far! They are penny-pinching, violent, and depraved. Their women, I have heard, suckle piglets for the pure enjoyment of it, and as for the men—"

Halli tapped a stockinged foot upon the floor. "Indeed. *I* am a Sveinsson."

The old man stared. "Surely not. I see no tail."

"Tail or not, that is my House."

"I assumed you were a boy from the high valleys, where life is hard and children are regularly born stunted."

"Yes, it seems we were both in error in our assumptions," Halli said briskly. "Now, perhaps the soup is ready?"

The old man grunted. "You mentioned wine, I believe?"

Soup was served, wine was poured, all in dour, resentful silence. Halli dunked dry bread in his soup and discovered it to be excellent; meanwhile the old man drew down from a roof beam a misshapen brown object of uncertain nature.

This was the ham. He proceeded to hack at it for some minutes with a rusted hasp-knife, without success.

Halli said: "Your knife is blunt. I have a better one." Reaching under his jerkin he took his father's knife from his belt and with it sliced easy strips of meat. The old man's eyes widened to see the knife. He watched the blade's deft motions, his body tense with longing.

At last, as if emerging from a dream, he gave a cry. "Stop, stop! That ham must last me months yet. Give it here." He seized it and bustled it back to its hiding place, all the time casting envious looks back at the knife balanced on Halli's knee.

Halli considered the old man's rags and the dingy, lonely hut around them. On sudden impulse he said, "Look, if you want the knife, you can have it. As payment for the night, I mean, and for this fine soup."

He handed it across carelessly; the old man took it in a trembling hand, his eyes round with disbelief, looking first to the knife, then at Halli, then to the knife again. "Well, now," he said, "that *is* good. And wine too!"

After that, and with the warming action of the wine, it was easier between them. They shared their names. The old man, Snorri, had no family or kin. The fields that ran between the road and the river were farmed by him, their beets traded to travelers passing. "This boundary strip was fought over long ago by the Houses of Svein and Rurik," he added. "Murders and massacres took place here—you will see the burial mounds a half-mile farther on—and both families committed atrocities, but no advantage was gained. In the end they agreed to leave the boundary waste. When I was a lad I wandered up here from Ketil's lands, found the fields empty and took them to my use."

Halli frowned at him over his cup. "Atrocities? By the *Sveinssons*? What nonsense is this? We are a noble, peaceful House."

"Like I say, it was long ago." Snorri scraped a strip of bread crust round his bowl. "Perhaps your habits—and other attributes—have changed since then." He squinted at Halli's rump. "You *seem* to sit quite comfortably."

"I *assure* you I have no tail. So you are quite alone here? Do you not feel lonely, without allegiance to a House?"

The old man grunted. "I am vulnerable, yes, but I can look after myself. Not six days ago, for instance, I was nearly killed by three horsemen going at pace along the road. I had to throw myself aside to escape the flying hooves."

Halli sat upright then. Firelight gleamed on his bared teeth. "Ah, really? Tell me more."

"What more is there to say? I turned a cartwheel, landed in the thistles, and suffered a number of intimate abrasions, which I will not show anyone on such short acquaintance." Snorri drank his wine stiffly. "Frankly I am surprised you ask."

"I meant about the horsemen."

"Oh, well, aside from the fact that they were two men and a youth and wore Hakonsson colors, I can tell you nothing." The old man's eyes grew speculating. "You seem unduly interested."

Halli said blandly, "I notice that you do not criticize the House of Hakon, as you did my House and the Rurikssons. Perhaps you favor them?"

"Not at all. I took it for granted that as uplanders we both share the same opinion."

Halli was still cautious. "Which is . . . ?"

"That they are arrogant, insufferable, and, on occasion, have been known to breed with fish. Now, if I may ask—what is your business with them?"

By now the wine flowed freely in Halli's veins and his warm weariness enfolded him like a cushioned bed. He saw no need for silence or evasion. Without further qualms he told Snorri his grievance and his purpose.

The old man's eyes bored into his. He nodded slowly. "You speak much of honor and the justice of your cause, but in short you seek to kill the man who killed your uncle. Am I right?"

Halli shrugged. "It must be done."

"Why? Then you will be as bad as he is."

"Not at all! He is a criminal and must pay for his deeds!"

"I imagine the men in the mounds along the road thought the exact same thing. Where are they now? Tangled in each other's bones. So, where will you do this? What is your plan?"

"At Hakon's House, I suppose. As for a plan, I will improvise when I get there."

"Interesting . . ." Snorri nodded sagely. "I have a further comment to make."

"Well?"

"You are an idiot. Have you any more wine?"

"No." Halli was scowling now, struggling to his feet. "If *that's* the way you feel, I shall impose upon you no longer! I will leave right now."

"Oh hush, do you want to drown in the storm? Sit down. Sit *down!*" Snorri's eyes flashed. Halli stared back as long as he could, then slumped to the ground with ill grace. The old man chuckled hoarsely. "Have you not *heard* of the size of Hakon's House, boy? They say its Trow walls still stand twenty feet high, bordered by a moat, deep and black. They have perhaps two hundred men within those walls, each one sturdy, strapping, and considerably bigger than you. Make one aggressive step toward your enemy and you will be seized and dandled from their gallows so fast you would see yourself below you as you swing. You are no warrior to fight them all, and no clever assassin to act by stealth—I can vouch for that, as with one swill of wine you've blabbed your secrets out to me!" He thrust his bowl away and lay back on his mattress with a sigh of contentment. "Take my advice, go back to your mother's skirts tomorrow. Time, I think, for sleep."

Halli could barely speak for rage. At last he calmed himself. "Do you have spare straw?"

"Yes, out the back, in a side shed. You are going to fetch it? Take the bludgeon in the corner—it will fend off the smaller rats. Throw a stone to distract the big ones, and scarper with what you can. That's what I do."

Halli slept on the bare earth floor.

9

AMONG THE DREADFUL beasts that Svein encountered in his youthful travels were: the Deepdale dragon, which darted from its cleft and swallowed its victims whole; the Old Trow of the Snag, sitting potbellied by its cauldron full of human meat; the carnivorous Marsh Imps of the Loops, which paddled about by night in little coracles made from children's skin. For variety's sake, Svein did not destroy them with his sword. He used a sharpened pine trunk to spear the dragon in its hole; he tricked the Old Trow into clambering into its own cauldron of boiling oil; he made a great fan of calf-hide and struck the Imps' coracles with a sudden squall, so that they all capsized and drowned.

NEXT MORNING, Halli was stiff in back and sore in head. His leggings seemed to have new holes in the toes, as if something had nibbled them in the night. His mood was not improved by discovering that Snorri had removed the remnants of his bread from his pack and eaten them for breakfast.

The old man listened to Halli's protests equably. "It was

stale and dry and tasteless," he said. "If you had eaten it, you would have had a dismal meal. If you had kept it, it would only have weighed you down. Really, you should thank me. Well, the rain has passed. You will no doubt want to be on your way back to your House."

Wordlessly, Halli laced his boots and put on his fleece. He pushed open the hovel door and went out into the sharp, pale light. White clouds hung low over the plateau, obscuring the mountains, and the air was fresh and wet. Rain could come again at any time. Coughing slightly, he hitched his pack higher on his shoulders.

"I do *not* return to Svein's House," he said. "I follow my quest down-valley, by way of the gorge and the cataracts. If you can tell me anything of that route, I will be grateful to hear it—any dangers a man might face, for instance?"

"Dangers . . ." Snorri sucked in his cheeks. "Well, it is an isolated path, for certain. For many miles a traveler is quite alone. But as for dangers . . ."

"None, I take it?"

"Well, there are the rockfalls, frequent this season. Even a small boulder could carry you into the torrents. Then there is the close proximity of the cairns. The wind rips up the gorge, carrying a traveler's scent straight up to the moors above the cliffs, so the Trows will clamor for you during the night. And don't forget the ghosts of the dead in the battle mounds beside the way. Do not let on to *them* you are a Sveinsson, by word or deed! Then they will pursue you in your dreams—the Rurikssons because you are an enemy of their House, the Sveinssons since they have been denied proper cairn burial and will hold you accountable. Best not to fall asleep in the higher reaches of the gorge, that's my advice."

Halli's face had grown a little slack. He looked with regret at his father's knife, now cradled securely in Snorri's belt. His foolish generosity had left him without a weapon of any kind, and there was nowhere to find one before he reached the gorge. . . .

He took a deep breath. Calm down. Would *Svein* have jumped at an old man's babbling? No! Besides, what good would a knife have been against ghosts?

"I can cope with all that," he said easily. "How long is the descent?"

"As the crow flies, not far, but the road zigzags above the cataracts. It will take the best part of two days to reach the pleasant fields of Eirik's House." The old man made a gesture of farewell. "Good luck with your insane quest. And thank you for the knife. Now I shall lop my beets with gay abandon. It is a fine gift and I won't forget it. In the unlikely event that you return up-valley, I may do *you* a good turn one day."

Halli smiled politely. Waving a cursory farewell, he splashed off down Snorri's path and onto the road. Before long the hut and its watching occupant were lost round the curve of the hill.

The road followed the plashing sound of the river ever

downward between dark fields hung about with mist and cloud. Halli made steady stumping progress, staring at the ground a few steps ahead, lost in introspection. Of course, it would not do to criticize the old fellow *too* harshly: his lonely life, without the bonds of friendship or allegiance that a House might give, had clearly warped his mind over long, hard years. Even so, his comments rankled. True, Halli did not have the *outward* appearance of a warrior, but his inner mettle was what counted, as Olaf Hakonsson would soon find out.

Before too long, by dour and gloomy effort, Halli reinforced his sense of purpose and thoroughly discounted every last thing that Snorri said. He was therefore surprised to discover the truth of one of the old man's assertions, as, through the mists beside the road, three long low mounds now came in sight. Two were set back in a field, one— smaller, shabbier, eroded at its margins by the wheels of carts upon the road—close by. Grass grew thickly upon it, lusher and darker than that around, as if its roots enjoyed rich soil. A crow of considerable size, with a single livid eye, perched at its top, inspecting Halli as he passed. Halli made a protective sign, cursing his gullibility even as he did so. This was a bird, no more, no less.

There was nothing to confirm Snorri's claim that Sveinsson bones lay here and Halli considered the story dubious. He had heard nothing of the matter from Brodir, Katla or anyone else. But to find a burial site without a single cairn unnerved him. What a melancholy fate, to lie so far from the ridges and your fellow men! He could well imagine uneasy spirits drifting here among the long wet grasses when night fell on the valley. . . . Even now, the mists seemed oddly active, as if strange forms—

Enough! Was he a fool, to be dismayed by figments? Pulling his hood close about his face, Halli hurried on along the road.

All morning the gradient steepened and the noise of the nearby river grew ever more eager, thrilled, insistent. The fields petered out and pine trees appeared, dotted here and there among scattered boulders and piles of scree. Halli knew that the lands of Svein and Rurik were left behind; he was drawing close to the gorge. Among the mists to the south, he glimpsed steep slopes rising: this was where the upper valley narrowed almost to nothing. Above, lost in cloud somewhere, rose the Snag, its summit almost as tall as the ridges either side. At its base, not far ahead, both river and road would fall suddenly away into the curling, precipitous gorge that led to the lower valley. When he stopped and listened, he could hear the booming of the falls.

Another noise sounded, this time behind him. Halli stiffened, listening hard. No doubt about it: hooves were approaching along the road—not fast, but quickly enough to overtake him before long.

Halli looked left and right: he saw boulders, brushwood, several pines. Without hesitation he sprang from the road, through the wet grasses, and secreted himself behind the nearest tree.

He waited. The sound of hooves grew louder. Perhaps it was his father, or someone else from Svein's House hunting him. Perhaps not. Best be cautious. Halli kept his eyes fixed on the road.

A knot of mist grew grayer, darker, then took expected form: a horse and rider.

Halli pressed himself against the trunk.

The horse's neck was lowered; it moved as if tired. The rider sat erect in the saddle, a bulky mass, cloak swathed tight about him, hood drawn up against the chill. His face was hidden, but Halli had already noted the horse's coloring—dark brown spots on a white coat—and knew that it did not come from Svein's House.

His first instinct was to let the stranger pass by, but then the loneliness of the place, and the proximity of the haunted mounds, returned to him. It would not hurt to have a companion for a time. It would make the gorge descent go quicker. What harm could it do, if he was cautious with his confidences? Certainly he would never again be as open as he had been with Snorri.

Halli stepped out from behind the tree and hailed the traveler, who pulled sharply on his reins. The horse halted and, without raising its head, immediately settled down to cropping the weeds growing through gaps in the flagstones. Traces of steam rose from its flank into the cool air. The rider pushed back his hood, revealing the face of a fat man, with a florid down-valley complexion and a short crop of sandy hair. He had no beard; his eyes were bright currants encased in swollen, doughy flesh. He wore an expression of mild concern.

"For an outlaw, you're on the small side," he remarked. "Where are the others?"

Halli looked about him. "What others?"

"I thought it was customary when waylaying someone to surround them, or at least outnumber them three to one. This is a poor show."

"I'm not ambushing you."

"Really? *Are* you an outlaw at all?"

"No."

"Then what were you doing behind the tree?"

Halli hesitated. He made an embarrassed gesture. "Oh, *you* know—"

The fat man's mouth puckered. "Caught short, eh? Needed a little solitude?"

"Why else would I hide?"

The currant eyes twinkled. "Guilty conscience, perhaps? What's your name?"

Halli cleared his throat. "I'm . . . Leif, son of a farmer on Gest's lands high up-valley. I'm going to Hakon's House to visit an uncle of mine. If you are heading that way I shall be glad to go with you for a while." He broke off abruptly; the fat man was watching him with an amused, ironical expression he didn't much like. "Or perhaps I would hold you up," he went on, "as I have no horse. Go on without me if you wish."

"Oh, no," the man said. "I wouldn't *dream* of being so rude. In truth, this nag can scarcely trot these days"—he slapped the horse's withers roughly—"so you will stroll beside us easily enough. Let's go on together and find somewhere dry for lunch."

The party proceeded down the road, the fat man whistling a merry tune that set his jowls swaying. The old horse struggled on; Halli marched silently alongside.

"So, Leif," the fat man said, after a time, "you are from Gest's House?"

He spoke casually, but Halli scented danger. "Well, from one of its tenant farms."

"Ah, I *thought* I did not see you when I was there last week. That would explain it. And you go to see a relative? At which House was it?"

"Hakon's."

"Ah! You must tell me the fellow's name. I travel widely, and have been there often. My name is Bjorn," the man went on, "and trading is my business. I go to and fro between the Houses, and roam the valley generally. What do I do? I buy, barter, exchange, and sell most things that women need. It is women"—he leaned swayingly outward from the saddle and winked at Halli, so that one eye disappeared into a fold of flesh—"women who are my best clients, eager to buy what they don't need. At a recent Gathering at Svein's House, I sold a dozen antique hair-grips to the Arbiter's vain daughter, and in return received an exquisite little tapestry that will bring me much gold down-valley. The joke is that each one of those hair-grips was carved a month back by a simpleton, and given to me in exchange for bread!" His laughter was a drawn-out wheeze; his shuddering sent quivers running through the bent back of the horse and made the panniers slung behind his thighs clank and jingle.

Halli, who by now thoroughly wished he had remained behind the tree, made an appreciative grunt and stepped aside, ostensibly to give the horse more space to negotiate the road. The terrain was difficult now, the way steep and covered with loose stones. The river, fleetingly visible to the north, rushed frothing over a series of little falls; the air was cold and wet with spray. Rising high on either side of them, thick bare-sided pine trees perched on terraces of rock and scree, forming a dark and somber skirt to the cliffs above. Here and there was evidence of vast rocks that had fallen from the height above, splitting trees and gouging scars in the tumbled waste.

"A cheerful spot," Bjorn called. "Let us eat before we enter the gorge and it becomes more dismal still."

They halted beside a great split boulder and shared a meal. Bjorn the trader contributed portions of smoked fish and cheese, and Halli supplied a little bacon. They each drank wine and water. The noise of the cataracts was very loud now and it was difficult to talk. Each sat staring out into the pines and mist, lost in his own thoughts.

During the halt a small incident occurred. While reaching over for his water flask, Halli's jerkin, which he had half unbuttoned, fell suddenly open, briefly exposing a portion of the hero's belt, still fastened across his chest. A flash of silver, a hasty fumble: Halli closed the jerkin, and buttoned it up tight. Glancing quickly across at his companion, he noticed Bjorn the trader's little black eyes fixed upon him with sudden intentness. At that moment, down among the pines, a crow cawed harshly—the sound made Halli's head jerk round. When he looked back, Bjorn's expression was placid once more; he seemed intent upon his bacon.

That afternoon they began their descent into the gorge. The cliffs closed in; pine trees pressed close about the road. The air grew cold, the light dim. They zigzagged precipitously down between walls of deep blue shadow, shrouded in hanging mist, a place of moss and water, numb with the crashing of the falls. The river was never far away, hurtling down beside them, first to the left, then the right, rushing beneath their feet under old stone bridges, roaring and foaming and dousing them with spray.

When the cliffs allowed, the road veered away from the tumbling river to follow a more gradual slope. Here speech was possible, allowing Bjorn to question Halli repeatedly about his background, his family, and his visit to his uncle. Halli's lies were as bland as he could fashion them, but he grew uncomfortable with the persistence of the man's attention. He wished for some means of leaving his company, but there was nowhere for him to go.

Sunlight receded from the gorge and evening drew in. They walked in dappled shadows, greenish gray and black. Several times the old horse lost its footing and stumbled, causing the trader to lurch forward in his saddle.

"You bag of bones!" he cried, slapping the horse's neck. "I shall sell you to the tanner for glue and gut strings! The beast is hungry," he shouted to Halli. "It has not fed well today. I tried negotiating for beet stalks with a mad old man in a hut this morning, but he refused. When I tried to take some anyway, he chased me off with a knife. Ah, it is a selfish world, where each man guards his possessions so jealously." He glanced sidelong at Halli. "My friend, it will soon be dark. Let us make camp for the night. There is a place I know not far ahead, where we can sit in comfort."

Halli frowned. "Can we not make it down today?"

"Impossible. We would fall over a crag and perish. Why so impetuous? I have tales to tell, and much good wine to drink. Have you a head for it, lad?"

Halli had less tolerance for wine than Katla, who after two cups would caper about the kitchens, bony heels kicking high as her chin. He shrugged. "Of course."

"Good, good. And here we are. . . ."

Among the pines to the left of the road was a small expanse of grass, scarred black by campfires at its center. It

149

was big enough for horses to be tethered, and for several travelers to lie in moderate comfort, provided they did not go too close to the far side. Here the grass ran down in a gentle slope, which suddenly steepened and opened out upon a void. While Bjorn tied his horse, Halli went to investigate, and was rewarded by a plunging view along the gorge, over forested cliffs, and out toward the lower valley. Far away, where the light still sparkled, he caught a glimpse of golden fields. Below him, however, was a precipice. Halli inched close to the lip and peered over, only to recoil quickly with a lurching stomach, and a confused impression of raging water, tumbled rocks, and splintered branches swathed in mist.

"Take care, Leif!" Bjorn the trader called. "That is a horrid drop! Come sit snug beside me, and let us talk of nicer things."

Wood was found, a blaze was lit; snippets of raw meat were toasted on the fire. During the meal Bjorn plied Halli with many cups of wine, most of which Halli poured into the grass when the trader's back was turned. Bjorn also made great show of bringing from his bags several curious objects. "See, my boy, here is a bone flute carved by Eirik himself: if played, it is said to wake the hero in his cairn! Oh yes, I have tried, but it is blocked and made no sound. Now, here, this oddly patterned skin. What do you think it is, eh? Nothing less than the hide of a sea beast washed up on Barren Strand! Yes, take it between your fingers." He watched Halli examine it for a time. "Is that not priceless? I would not swap it for

150

anything, except something of the *rarest* quality." He smiled at Halli, small eyes blinking, head slightly on one side. "And see here, perhaps this is my greatest prize of all. . . ."

He took from his pack a jet-black object, curved as a crescent moon, sharp as a sickle-blade, twice as long as the fingers on Halli's hand. "Here, Leif my lad, you see before you nothing less than a Trow's claw, taken from the ashes of Thord's House, when the Ketilssons burned it down. I believe it is the very one Thord brought back in his thigh. Certainly it is the only one I know of in the valley. To get another, you will have to go beyond the cairns and ask a Trow politely for the privilege!" He wheezed gently. "What do you think of *that*, eh?"

"It looks to me very much like hardwood, stained with dye," Halli said. "I should think a simpleton might have knocked it out a month ago, in return for bread."

Bjorn the trader concealed a scowl with difficulty. "Well, well, you are an upland boy, you have no eye for these things." He was silent for a time. "All I lack," he said at last, staring mournfully up into the dark trees, "are objects made of the rarest metals. Silver, say. Such treasures have not been made since the heroes' days—there are very few left now. Ah, but I would pay handsomely for such an item!"

Halli was toasting a piece of cheese on the end of a twig, turning it round and round so no drips were lost. He seemed intent upon his work; he made no answer.

Bjorn spoke softly, as if to himself. "There is a silver

goblet in the treasure room at Egil's House, so I am told, and I have heard a silver belt sits in a box at Svein's. If there are others, I do not know of them. Well, it is unlikely either of these would come into my hands. Their owners would not sell them, and a thief would find them hard to dispose of. Hard and perilous, for while he carried such a thing the shadow of the gallows would hang over his head every moment! Only someone like me, with contacts in every House, might successfully take it off his hands. . . . And certainly I would pay well for doing so, in thick gold coins. . . ." His little black eyes gleamed in the firelight. "What do you say to that, Leif?"

Halli drew the twig back and popped the molten cheese whole into his mouth. He chewed contemplatively, with Bjorn's attention fixed upon him. Several times he seemed about to speak, only to suddenly resume chewing, leaving Bjorn in a frenzy of impatience. At last he wiped his mouth on his sleeve, belched and said, "In an abstract sort of way, it is fascinating to hear your tales of business. Be sure that if I meet someone with such a silver item, I will direct him to you. But for now, I think I shall turn in; all that wine has gone to my head."

He got up and went round the fire, to where a natural bank offered a comfortable spot; here he lay down beneath his cloak and, with a number of grunts and sighs, composed himself for sleep.

Bjorn the trader stayed sitting where he was, staring into

the flames. For a long while he remained motionless, the firelight flickering against the contours of his great, impassive face. He drained his cup at last, and sat hunched and thoughtful as the fire slowly died, and the shadows closed in upon the little clearing in the middle of the gorge. Close by, the bony horse cropped grass; overhead, between invisible boughs, cold stars shone.

The fire burned low. Halli lay still. Bjorn was a dark hunched form.

Far below, the river chuntered over its bed of tumbled rocks. Somewhere in the forest that clung against the cliffs, an owl called. A branch snapped and shifted in the fire. Still Bjorn sat silent. And now Halli's breathing sounded out across the clearing, slow and heavy with the rhythm of deep sleep.

Outlined dimly by the firelight, Bjorn's shoulders shifted and dropped a little, as if with a release of tension. After some minutes, he leaned slowly to one side. Gentle noises followed as he foraged quietly in his bag. The noises stopped. Silence returned.

A tendon cracked as Bjorn got slowly, stiffly to his feet. Halli, watching from between his half-closed lids, saw him standing motionless for a moment, his head bowed. Then Bjorn began treading softly round beside the dying fire, using its last remaining light to guide his way. Despite his bulk, his boots were almost silent on the grass. He held something in his hand.

When Bjorn reached the bank, he slowed and stopped. He stood above Halli—a hulking shadow without face or features, outlined against the fire. Beneath his cloak, Halli lay quite still, every muscle in his body tensed with terror, struggling to maintain the nonchalant sounds of sleep. His throat was tight, constricted; his breath rasped in his open mouth. His chest rose and fell raggedly. He heard blood pulsing in his ears.

Still the dark shape did not move. Then it lifted an arm.

The pressure in Halli's throat became unbearable: he cried out loud and violently,

The shadow jerked back. Halli's shout echoed across the black gulf of the gorge.

Halli flung his cloak aside.

A sudden rush: the shadow swooped, one arm outstretched. A black, curved sickle shape flashed down. Halli rolled, sensed the impact as something drove deep into grass and soil behind his head. Now he was on all fours, springing away and up the bank—but his boot slipped in his cloak, made him stagger, fall—

Something caught his ankle. It pulled savagely, dragging him back down.

With a moan of fear, Halli rolled onto his back; he lashed out with his free boot, kicking up and outwards into the darkness. He felt it collide with something soft and yielding; he heard an incoherent sound of pain.

The grip on his ankle loosened. Against the firelight

Halli saw the shadow reeling, clutching at its stomach. He sprang up and away into the darkness of the clearing.

After a few steps he turned again, looked. There in the dying firelight: Bjorn, stumbling after him, one half in darkness, one half lit red. His hand clawed at his belly. His voice called softly. "Little Leif, you have hurt me, you have ruptured something in my guts. Oh, I shall pay you out for that."

Halli backed away, slowly, slowly. Behind him sounded the distant roaring of the river; he felt the stirring of air, of immense regions of emptiness. The precipice was close—he could go no farther safely. With crawling skin and eyes wide and staring, he stopped dead, watching the trader's lumbering approach.

Bjorn's mouth hung open; moisture gleamed on his lips and chin. "Little Leif, little Leif, give me the belt, or—to be frank, as one thief to another—I shall slice your throat open on a stone."

Halli bared his teeth. "Here is another option. Sling your buttocks onto your cringing nag and ride away in shame, for you shall never have the belt."

Bjorn tittered; even as he did so he leaped forward, faster than Halli had been expecting. Halli darted aside, too late. A great weight fell crushingly upon him; a stench of sweat, wine, and body odor burst against his face. A blow fell on his upper arm, making him cry out. Hot fingers clutched at his throat; his legs buckled, he toppled backward in the darkness, twisting as he did so, feeling the man's weight roll up and over him.

Halli fell heavily onto his back. He heard the impact as Bjorn struck the ground beyond him, felt the clasping fingers torn away. With desperate speed he struggled to his feet, knowing that Bjorn in the darkness was doing the same.

Something clutched at his back. Halli struck out blindly with a fist. The shock of the contact jarred his arm. There was a cry of rage, a retreating scuffle in the grass—then nothing.

Halli stumbled a few steps away, expecting Bjorn to launch himself upon him.

Nothing happened.

Weeping, gasping, Halli waited, half-crouched in the grass.

From far below, scarcely audible above the rushing of the distant river, came the faintest of impacts, a brief clattering of stones. It ceased. The river's roar continued undiminished. Wind moved the pine branches overhead. Otherwise the night was quiet, newly empty.

Across the clearing, the campfire dwindled to a narrow band of glowing embers.

Halli huddled where he was, staring wide-eyed at the dark.

10

WHEREVER HE WENT, people sung of Svein's deeds. House elders thrust gold and gifts into his hands, while pretty maidens waited for him every few yards along the road in states of disarray. Consumed by jealousy, the other young heroes of the valley sought to emulate him. Ketil marched into the forest to fight the outlaws, but was put to flight by a midget wielding a penknife. Eirik climbed Dove Crag to slay a man-eating bear, only to be chased by its cub for miles across the ridgetops.

Svein made no comment on any of this; he was not much one for words. By now he was fully grown: a tall, stern, barrel-chested mountain of a man, swift-moving, sure, and confident—quick to judge and act upon his judgments. Few people cared to challenge his opinions in the hall.

A T SOME POINT in the blackest hours before dawn, Halli had regained his cloak and taken shelter, but the morning found him cold and feverish. With shaking hands he built a new fire and ate the remnants of the meat beside it, taking long gulps from the wine flask as he did so. The old horse watched him from under a pine. Beyond the cliff edge, thin streaks of mist hung upon the distant trees.

Perhaps, Halli told himself, Svein too had found it hard, the first time he killed a man. The tales did not record his feelings, the softer emotions he must have felt, but it stood to reason he too would have been unnerved, even terrified by the experience.

It was a good sign, surely, to know such fear. *Not* to feel it would make you a lesser man. By overcoming it, and still triumphing, you showed your mettle.

So Halli told himself. But he remained by the fire a long time, and when at last he went to investigate Bjorn's bags, his legs still trembled under him.

The panniers contained a good deal that Halli rejected instantly: wooden hair-grips and carvings of assorted heroes, all crudely done; beads, necklaces of amber, bone brooch pins; a number of soiled linens. The treasures that Bjorn had shown him the evening before were no more tempting, since Halli did not believe any of them were genuine. But at the bottom of the second bag he found a better prize: a soft cloth wallet, heavy with coins.

Halli took the wallet and all of Bjorn's remaining food and wine. He flung the panniers away among the pines. Then he stamped out the fire and went over to the old horse, still tethered on the margins of the glade.

"I haven't the heart to ride you," he told it. "For what

it's worth, you're free of him. Go where you will."

He slapped its rump gently; after some consideration, the horse trotted away and down the cliff road. Soon it was lost among the trees.

As Halli followed it out of the clearing, his eye caught sight of something black sticking out from the grassy bank: the supposed Trow claw, driven into the earth with vicious force. With difficulty he prized it free and, on examination, found to his surprise that the craftsmanship was excellent—the wood smoothed to a polish, harder and heavier than he had imagined. It was sharp too, ripping the cloth of his pack as he pushed it in. Well, that was all to the good. It would do for protection until he bought a knife.

The remainder of his journey down the gorge was un-eventful. Steadily the cliffs drew back and the gradient lessened. The road broke out of the pinewoods into a land-scape of broken rocks and scattered debris—the beginning of the lower valley. The river returned to meet it with a succession of rapid loops and turns. Already it was broader than on the heights above; in places it raced down shallow terraces of stone before tumbling over into deep, dark pools. Halli began to see cattle on the slopes below the cliffs; goats too, penned in stony fields. Little by little the soil grew noticeably better, the grass a richer green. The numbers of cattle increased. The walls of the valley drew away from him; there was a sense of space and air. The sun burned the mists away and far off he saw a gap between the hills—a curious flatness of horizon, where he knew the sea must be.

Warmed by the sun, free of the dour seclusion of the gorge, Halli's spirits rose with every step. The horrors of the night receded, and he began to view his actions as less desperate and more considered than they had seemed before. He chuckled as he went. How cleverly he had led that villain to the cliff edge!

Beside the road, a wooden hero post—an ancient figure, worn and shapeless, but daubed with bright blue dye—marked a boundary. Away across the fields, beyond a band of trees, a number of curious red-tiled roofs showed. Flags flew from the gable ends, a sure mark of a great House. Good—there he could buy food, a knife, and other things, and—why not?—spread word of his recent victory. No doubt Bjorn had robbed many folk on the lonely roads. News of his death would be welcomed: with luck Halli would not even need to pay for his provisions.

Lost in pleasant reveries, Halli arrived at a place where the road forked around a pillar of stone; the right-hand way led along a broad path lined with fruit trees toward the distant House. Here and there about the orchard, women stood on ladders, collecting plums. A small sandy-haired, brown-limbed brat, wearing nothing but a long twill shirt, sat beneath the pillar in the dust of the road. He eyed Halli with listless curiosity.

"Good day, my boy," Halli said. "What are those roofs away among the trees?"

"Eirik's House, as everyone knows," the boy replied. "Shouldn't your legs be longer? Did a tree fall on you?"

Halli said: "Would you prefer a gold coin or a slap about the head? Think hard."

The urchin considered, picking his nose the while. "The coin."

"Then refrain from rude comments and run at speed to your House. Alert the people. Tell them a hero has arrived."

The boy looked in awe to the four points of the compass. "Where?"

"Here." Halli spoke with some asperity. "No—here. Me. I'm the hero."

The boy's face fell. "Give me the coin before I go. In fact give me two. I get a beating whenever I tell palpable untruths, so this must be made worth my while."

Halli stepped closer. "Do you dare to doubt my word? I have just slain a foul robber in the vastness of the gorge, while you dawdle purposelessly in the dirt. You should be leaping to my bidding!"

The boy slouched to his feet. "As to my purpose, I am waiting for my father. As to leaping, I have no energy for that. My mother and I have had little to eat these last few weeks, while Papa has been away. If he does not come soon, with money from his travels, we both shall surely starve."

Halli took the cloth wallet from his bag and selected a

coin. "There, there! A nice gold piece to ease your woes. Now then, stop gawping at my wallet. Hobble off as best you can and spread the word. I will follow on behind."

The boy moved off, slowly at first and with many backward glances. To Halli's displeasure he did not head up the road, but scampered over to one of the nearby trees, where a scrawny red-haired woman stood with a basket, collecting plums passed down from above. An animated conversation ensued, the boy pointing in Halli's direction. It ended with the woman hurrying forward, her colleagues watching from among the trees.

Halli drew himself up. "Now then, good woman, I bring important news—"

The woman spoke anxiously: "My son here says you have come down from the upper valley."

Halli bowed. "I have."

"You are brave indeed to travel alone through those desolate wastes."

"Well, they're not *that* desolate. Except the gorge, of course, where—"

"I wonder," the woman went on, "whether you met with anyone on your way? Please, my lad and I are worried sick about my husband, who—"

Halli raised a gentle hand. "Madam, I regret I have seen no other travelers. However, I *did* fall foul of a wicked trader, who attempted to rob and kill me. Ah, he was vile— a vast, corpulent beast of a man, utterly without virtue.

Fortunately I am not easily cowed—in the loneliest portion of the gorge, in the blackest hour of night, we fought. Suffice it to say, I slew him. Your people need fear his crimes no longer. Now, I am weary and wish to enjoy the refreshments of your House. One of those plums will do to begin with." With a wink and a grin, he bit into it dashingly.

The woman stared at him, slack-jawed. "A trader, you say?"

"That's what he *claimed*. In reality he was a peddler of sham artifacts and curios, wooden hair-grips and the like. And a hedge-thief, also. Shall we go?"

"Wooden hair-grips, you say?"

"Yes, yes." Halli smiled round at the other women, now steadily approaching from all directions. "Dear me. I hope not everyone at Eirik's House is so dense!"

The urchin was hopping at the woman's skirts, plucking at her sleeve. "The wallet, Ma, take a look at the wallet!"

Halli scowled. "You have had one coin already. Must I pay for this interrogation too? The wicked Bjorn was scarcely any greedier than you."

The woman gave a little gasp, echoed by several of the women roundabout. "Bjorn, you say?"

Halli rolled his eyes. "Yes! Bjorn!" He hesitated, suddenly cautious. "What of it? It is a common name."

With a wail, the woman dashed her palms against her forehead. "My husband! You have killed my husband."

"He had Papa's wallet, Ma! He did, he did!"

"My poor, fat Bjorn!"

Halli noticed the women of the orchard pressing close on every side, hefting gleaming fruit-knives in their hands. He spoke with agitation: "Are all you lowlanders hysterical? There is not a shred of proof that the man I killed has anything to do with this Bjorn of yours. Your husband is probably drunk under a hedge. Now—"

The boy gave a cry of woe and recognition. "Look! There! Grettir!"

Everyone looked back along the road. The old horse, having no doubt eaten its fill of roadside grass all day, had completed its descent of the gorge and now appeared, trotting homeward with a clear sense of purpose and familiarity. Amid dead silence it ambled past Halli, straight up to the boy, and nuzzled his hand fondly.

Everyone stared at the riderless horse. Everyone stared back at Halli.

Retreating slowly, he raised his hands in protest. "He was a robber! An outlaw!"

"No! Bjorn Eiriksson was a respected man!"

"A pillar of our House!"

Halli backed away along the road. "But ladies—he tried to rob me, kill me!"

"Why should he do that? What could he want with a vagabond like you? You lie!"

"Murderer!"

"Killer!"

"Catch him! Blow the Trow-horn! String him up!"

Halli abandoned all attempts at suavity and persuasion and ran away at speed along the high road, with the women of Eirik's House hard at his heels. They proved fleet of foot and looked set to bring him down until he dropped the contents of the wallet on the ground. Gold coins spun and rolled in all directions, causing the bulk of the pursuit to halt. Even so, Bjorn's wife remained close behind, screaming and clawing at him with long fingernails until he was obliged to push her into a ditch. After that he drew clear, but was pelted with plums and other fruits until he rounded a corner in the road.

The following days did not go well for Halli. The search parties from Eirik's House proved diligent, and he was forced to hide in a festering reed bed, nose deep among the thick black mud, until they at last gave up the hunt. Trudging forth again upon the road, he seemed more like a limping vagrant than an avenging hero: his food waterlogged, his skin flasks punctured by leeches, his coins lost, his clothes ragged and soiled.

Without provisions, without the money to pay for them, Halli was forced to resort to behavior he had not anticipated when he began his journey. Instead of a stately procession through the lower valley, stopping at every House he passed for shelter and gentle conversation, his days became filled with surreptitious skulking in ditches, with acts of thievery at lonely farmsteads, by constant evasion, concealment, and close pursuit. Hungry and exhausted, he was forced to steal food to keep alive, and while his spoils were drearily uniform—stale bread, cheese, a little fruit—the consequences had uncomfortable variety. He was chased by farmers with pitchforks and old men with sticks; by washerwomen with flailing flannels and by children with spinning discs of cow dung. On one occasion a band of infants put him to flight with stones after he tried to spear their cakes from a distant bush using the Trow's claw fixed to the end of a pole. There was little time any longer to dream about fame or the honor he would win. He concentrated on mere survival.

Yet always his determination drove him on. It would have been possible, at any moment, for Halli to turn round and head back on the long journey to Svein's House, to the old life he had left behind. But despite his troubles his desire to avenge his uncle remained steadfast, constant. Little by little, painful day by painful day, he drew closer to the House of Hakon and the sea.

Eirik's lands fell behind; the road took him through rich meadows belonging to Thord's and Egil's Houses. By now the valley was broad and generous; the river, a glimmering ribbon, wound back and forth across the plain. The ridges on either side were lower now than Halli had ever imagined, the mountains beyond them reduced to brown-gray foothills. But still, particularly when the sun was low, it was possible to see the cairn lines running unbroken, marking the edge of the habitable land.

From time to time, in his lonely evenings in the woods, chewing on a pilfered chicken bone or scrap of meat, Halli mulled on what he saw. Despite his many days of traveling, despite the strangeness of the buildings he passed, with their steeply arched gables, their bright red tiles, their white-washed plaster walls; despite the oddly dyed clothes that people wore, and the obvious bounty of the lowland fields, Halli was struck by the essential familiarity of it all. Houses, fields, livestock—and the cairns upon the hill. Trows above, people below.

As if from long ago, he heard his Uncle Brodir speaking. *The valley isn't as big as you suppose. . . .*

Still, there were some new wonders to be absorbed. He saw Battle Rock from a distance in the center of the plain— a jutting black pyramid set among dark trees—but owing to a local hue and cry involving a missing piglet and a leg of pork later spotted on his person, was unable to spare the time to visit.

Then there was the prospect of the sea. All his life Halli had wished to glimpse it. Now, as the miles passed steadily under his boots and he neared his destination, he noticed a salt tang on the air, borne by a fresh new wind. It whipped about his face and deep into his lungs, invigorating him even in his weariness. He began to spy white birds far out above the flat center of the valley, banking and gliding, spiraling down out of sight. The river now was separated from the road by marsh-flats and reed beds; he glimpsed it only occasionally beyond—a great white-blue expanse, dappled with specks of sunlight. Once or twice he saw things on it: low, flattened crescents, with poles and sails drifting upriver with the tide—the first true boats he had ever seen.

For days the way had been heavy with traffic: carts, riders, men and women going about their business; every field seemed to have its cottage, every mile its farm. Presently Halli came to a crossroads where the road—now twice as broad as in the upper valley, and in excellent repair—split decisively in two. A pair of hero posts stood facing each other, freshly carved. Wooden beards jutted, sightless eyes gazed fiercely, hands stayed frozen on the pommel of their swords. One post was dyed a warm, rich purple, the other a livid orange-red. Halli thought he knew both Houses.

"Yes, this is the boundary of Arne's and Hakon's," a young woman said. She had stopped her oxcart at the junction and was sipping water. "Two miles through woods to Arne's House; three miles beside the river to Hakon's. Which do you make for?"

Halli did not reply at first. In his mind's eye he saw the face of Aud Ulfar's-daughter, and in his weariness and hunger felt a strong temptation to seek her out. . . . He sighed; his jaw tightened. No. His quest was not complete. Much as he might wish it, it could not be done.

"Hakon's," he said firmly. "I go to Hakon's."

"Be warned," the woman advised, surveying Halli shrewdly, "they don't welcome beggars there. Wastrels, tramps, and other misfits are tied bare-bottomed to the market post and soundly whipped. Hord's orders. He is a strong, hard man."

"Oh, I know he is," Halli said. "Incidentally, I am not a beggar."

But the woman had already flicked her switch and headed on her way.

Three miles to Hakon's. A little farther on, with darkness falling, Halli camped for the night in a copse beside the road. As he lay shivering beneath his meager blanket of fallen leaves, fierce excitement surged within him.

Tomorrow, at long, long last, the murderer Olaf would be within his reach. Halli needed to spy out the land, of course, but the basic strategy was clear. Reach the House, find a crumbled bit of Trow wall, hop over it, and hide. At night, raid the smithy or one of the workrooms for a knife, then locate Olaf's room. Probably it would be at the back of the hall: perhaps there would be a window. . . . If not he would be forced to wait, kill him at dawn when he came out to use the privy or wash in the yard. When it was done, a quick departure—back over the wall and away across the fields. Above all, he must not be seen.

Whether it was his agitation, the cold, or the hunger in his belly, Halli did not sleep well. Toward dawn he fell into fitful slumber, and when he awoke, the sun was fully risen. Brushing himself down, he hurried on, impatient to see his destination.

And, shortly afterward, he saw it.

The road, which had topped a little rise, ran down toward the House of Hakon as if reaching it had been the sole aim and purpose of all its distance. On one side, patch-work fields of wheat rolled away, golden brown and silent, shimmering in the breeze. On the other, green meadows declined into gray-black mudflats spanned by a maze of brightly colored jetties; these reached out into the margins of the river, now so broad it stretched almost to the horizon. Halli saw huts lining the jetties, boats moored below them, and people, people everywhere—on jetties, in fields, working with hook and net, with winnow and scythe: more people than he ever dreamed could belong to a single House.

And beyond it all rose a great stone stockade, girt by a broad black saltwater moat, fed by channels from the estuary. The walls were more than twice as high as a man, windowless, close-fitting, dour and gray near the water, whitewashed higher up. At no point were they even remotely crumbled. The road climbed an earthwork ramp toward the House and crossed the moat by way of a broad wooden bridge. Above the walls the tops of many buildings could be seen, most of them two stories or more, their roofs arched and gabled. Chief among them stood a soaring hall, painted white and shining in the sun. From every gable orange-red flags fluttered with imperious splendor.

Hot-eyed, dry-mouthed, Halli stood motionless in the dust of the road. For the first time he understood the utter remoteness and true insignificance of Svein's House. The knowledge wedged like a stone in his throat.

His shoulders slumped, his pack slipped to the ground. In silent weariness, Halli flopped down onto the grass and rested his head in his hands.

11

THESE WERE SVEIN'S treasures: his drinking cup, hollowed from a dragon's tooth, which gave his ale a smoky quality; his necklace strung with a Trow-girl's finger bones, which rattled and tugged against his neck when Svein stooped near the earth; the silver belt that brought him luck in battle; his chain-mail armor, its loops as delicate as snakeskin; and above all else, above any of the wonders that he gathered in his years of greatness: his peerless sword.

This sword was given to Svein when he was six years old. It was an ancient blade. Some said that five strips of metal, each one flexible as sinew and hard as hill rock, had been melded together to make it. The sword's edge was thin as a grass-stem, sharp as a wolf's tooth; there was a serpent pattern down one side, thinly incised, so that blood ran into it and made the serpent glisten whenever Svein made a killing. The mere sight of it struck terror into Svein's enemies and unmanned them.

MANY TIMES DURING his journey Halli had imagined ways in which he might kill the Hakonssons. He had swung on ropes from pine trees as they passed on horseback, decapitating Olaf during the outward pass and Hord and Ragnar on the return. He had run down their hall as they sat drinking, plucked a boar spear from the wall and, without breaking stride, impaled all three with a single cast. He had shot them with arrows, crushed them with boulders and, in an entertaining sequence dreamed up in the hazy moments between wakefulness and sleep, drowned them side by side in a giant keg of ale.

Now, with the hard reality of Hakon's House laid out before him, all such fancies turned vaporous and vanished. So too did his blithe assumptions of the night before. He could not scale walls of that size; he could not cross the moat. The gate was the only entrance, but that meant crossing the bridge in full view of all. Not just ordinary people, either—he saw guards or lookouts stationed on the wall. At night the gates might well be closed; he had to do it in the day.

Halli did his best to suppress the hunger gnawing in his stomach and the leaden feeling in his limbs. Yes, it was a formidable obstacle. Yes, the place was bigger than he'd guessed. So what? Would Svein have balked at it and scurried home? No. He would have found a way.

He thought hard. Down-valley folk were fair-haired, pale-skinned; as a rule they were tall and slender too. A short, squat, black-maned stranger would stand out a mile if he tried waltzing to the door. Somehow he would have to hide as he passed the gate. In a cart, perhaps—under corn, vegetables, even manure . . . Halli set his jaw, grim-faced. Whatever it took, it must be done. Hakon's people were violent, aggressive, and suspicious; one sight of him and he would be seized and dragged to the whipping post, even before they guessed his mission. Halli clenched his fists at the thought of their cruel vindictiveness. No matter: soon he would slay Olaf and there would be wailing in their hall!

"You all right there?" a cheery voice said. "Anything I can do?"

Halli looked up: a man had appeared over the brow of the hill. He was tall and strapping, in early middle age. His fair hair was tied back, his beard shaved short and squared under the cheeks. His tunic had orange-red slashes on the shoulder, indicating his House affiliation. The bronze circlet in his hair shone in the morning sun. He had an open, pleasant face, flushed with walking.

Halli cleared his throat. "Er, no, no—I'm fine."

"Thought you looked a little worried about something. Can't have that on Hakon's day!" The man slung a bag down from his back and wiped his brow with a sleeve. "It's a hot one, this late in the year! How far've you come, then?"

Halli hesitated. "Well—"

"You're not from these parts, I can tell."

"No . . ."

The man smiled. "Ketil's, is it? Egil's maybe? We get a

few beggars coming down from Ketil's after the floods they had in spring."

"Egil's House," Halli said, at random. "And excuse me, but I'm not a beggar."

"No?" The man stepped back a little. "I hope you haven't got a plague. If it's dank mottle, you shouldn't be out of your pen."

"I'm not a beggar, not ill, just a little jaded." Halli gestured irritably at his filthy, ragged clothes. "It's been a long journey, that's all."

"Well, welcome to Hakon's lands!" The man patted Halli's shoulder in a friendly manner. "I'm Einar. Hungry? You look as if you could do with something."

"Oh. Yes, please." Halli watched agog as the man produced bread, cheese, and a skin of wine from his bag. He tried hard not to snatch them from his hand; as it was he ate and drank with unseemly haste.

"You're in rough shape," Einar observed. "They ought to treat you better up at Egil's. Here at Hakon's, our Arbiter Hord distributes grain to all when times are hard. Even in bad years, we get on fine."

Halli nodded, grunted, sucked at the wineskin.

"Yes, great Hord is a fine leader," Einar went on. "A hard, strong man, brave and resolute. He's brought wealth back to this House, as you can see just by looking. He's got big ideas, has Hord, and the energy of the heroes!" He glanced pleasantly at Halli. "But, still, we can't all be great men, can we? Each of us must travel his own small path. What brings you down this way, then?"

Halli stuffed the last of the cheese into this mouth and swallowed. He was a little out of breath. "I . . . I just wanted to see this famous House, maybe find work."

"Well, I don't know about work, but if you want to see Hakon's you've come on the right day. It's the anniversary of our Founder's triumph at Battle Rock! There'll be Trowshies and drinking and—" The man waved a hand in the direction of the House. "Look, come on with me and see it for yourself."

Halli blinked. "Will I be allowed in?"

"Of course. Why not? All friends are welcome. Even ones as ragged and pitiful as you. Besides, it is a day for charity. Would you like me to help you with your pack?"

"No. No, thank you."

Down the road they went together, toward the looming House. Up the long earth ramp, high above the fields and salt flats.

Halli said: "It is an impressive place."

"Isn't it? Hord has had the walls raised and reenforced. He has men patrolling them night and day. It was lax in his father's time."

"Who does he fear?"

Einar the lowlander laughed. "No one! But this is how it was in Hakon's day, and Hord wishes to emulate him! Many of us menfolk practice the old skills—we play with staff and arrow, we go hunting on the heights."

"Past the cairns?"

Einar's eyes were wide; he made a protective sign. "What? Are you mad? Now, see here—the new House gates, made of oak and iron!"

They had crossed the bridge, following a steady flow of people. Under a great arched gate they went, into a narrow street. Instantly the light was dimmer, all blue-gray shadow, with narrow triangles of brightness on the flagstones where the sharp blue sky showed through. The buildings hugged close together, white plaster on wood, flowers hanging from the eaves. Halli walked up a little rise, cool now, out of the sun, where the stones were smooth and curved with the feet of years. The food and wine had done their work: he felt newly eager, strong with purpose. Even so, the scale of it all astonished him. He passed open shop-fronts—a cooper, a leatherworker, a man making toys, a potter, a weaver, a stall with necklaces and brooches glinting in the shade. At Svein's House all this was done too, but only in the cottage back-rooms when men came in from the fields; goods were exchanged informally in the central yard, not presented so splendidly for sale.

The way opened out, the buildings drew back. Ahead of them stretched a wide space, as filled with people as a spring meadow is with flowers. At its far end, sheer and tall as the bluffs above the gorge, rose Hakon's hall. The doors at its center, sheltered beneath a gabled porch held up by great wood pillars, were themselves almost as high as the hall at Svein's. Halli's neck ached as he gazed up at the distant roof.

He blew his cheeks out, scowling. Yes, it was big. Yes, it was imposing! But none of that mattered. He would do what he had come to do.

So far all was well. He had gained the House with unexpected ease. Now for the next stage. He scanned the yard, narrowed eyes passing across the crowd, noting with surprise the mix of folk within it—there were plenty of wiry, dark-haired upland men and women dotted amid the taller, fleshier local throng.

Here and there about the yard stood booths with scarlet awnings, where people played games of chance and skill, took drinks, or listened to storytellers and balladeers. Everywhere was laughter, faces flushed and merry. Halli watched it all, unsmiling. It would be easy enough to detach himself from Einar, disappear among the crowds: but what then? Find somewhere to hide till dark?

Einar nudged him with his elbow. "How's *this* for a House, friend? Free ale and entertainment! As people finish their work, they gather. And tonight those of us who are invited will toast our Founder in the hall!"

"A feast?"

"You won't see it, I'm afraid. No foreigners in the House after dark. They'll have closed the gates by then."

"Will Hord and Olaf be there?" Halli asked carelessly. "And Ragnar Hakonsson?"

"Hord and Ragnar, for sure. Not Olaf, though. He's sick."

Halli looked at him, heart pounding. "Sick?"

"Trow-stricken. His horse stumbled near the boundary and Olaf was touched by the shadow of a cairn." Einar made another sign. "May Hakon help him recover! Like his brother, he is a noble man."

"Poor, poor fellow." Halli ran his tongue across his lips. "I suppose he will be in bed. Where would his room be, do you think? In the hall?"

But Einar was suddenly distracted. His eyes sparkled, he craned to see above the crowd. "My friend, you are in luck! Here comes our Arbiter now!"

Halli's eyes widened; he turned and saw, far off among the thickest mass of merrymakers, the figure of Hord Hakonsson. His head was easily visible, for he was taller than the rest. His broad, bearlike shoulders swung side to side. All gave way wherever he went, clapping backs, clasping hands, roaring out greetings to acquaintances he spied.

Einar said: "Is he not an impressive man?"

Halli spoke uneasily. "Very." He pulled the hood of his fleece over his head.

"Perhaps you'll get to meet him for yourself. He is heading our way."

Halli stepped back a few paces, gaze flicking left and right in search of escape. What Einar said was true: Hord was approaching. He wore a fur-rimmed cloak, held at the neck by a gold swan clasp. His voice, his swagger, the very drift of the cloak—all were heavy with latent power.

"Hey, friend," Einar said. "Where are you going? He'll speak with you."

"No, no, I am not worthy."

"Oh, don't say that. On Hakon's day even great Hord will look kindly upon your wretchedness. Here, I'll draw his attention to you." He raised his voice, "Arbiter—!"

"No, please—"

"Arbiter!"

Peering out frantically from deep within his hood, Halli saw Hord look up toward Einar and raise a hand in greeting. He began to approach, only to be intercepted by three squealing women of the House.

Einar grinned at Halli. "Don't fret. He will be over in a moment." He grasped Halli's cringing arm. "Do not be so shy. I hunt with him and know him well. Do not be abashed, despite your squalor. He is honorable to his friends."

Halli pulled desperately at the hand upon his sleeve. "No, listen! I must not go near him!"

Einar's smile flickered. "But why?"

"I—I—You were right before, I *do* have several curious ailments that should not be spread around, least of all to a great man such as Hord." Halli was retreating as he spoke. "Suppurating sores, that sort of thing. You won't want to hear the details. So I should stay well clear."

Now the smile was gone. "Wait! You were happy enough to be intimate with me."

"Ah, yes, but I—I took good care to remain downwind of you as we walked. The breeze blew the corrosive stench of my afflictions out to sea. Here, where it is so close and humid, I can promise nothing. But what do we care? Let's get some ale, link arms together, and drink to our friendship from each other's cups."

Einar's face had become a trifle pale. "Thank you, no. Perhaps it would be best if you left our House."

"Yes, yes. I will." Halli backed away. "Thank you for your help! Good-bye." Einar was lost to him amid the crowd.

There was no time to waste. With Hord—and perhaps Ragnar—prowling about the yard, it was not a place to linger. Halli angled his way amid the fair booths toward the corner of the hall. Somewhere in that great white building Olaf would be abed. A sickly, helpless, Trow-stricken Olaf. Halli smiled thinly. It sounded as if his job was more than half done.

Still it was no small matter to get inside the hall, carry out the killing, and escape unseen. He reached up a hand and touched the silver belt beneath his jerkin. As always its cold weight reassured him, and at that very moment he saw, a short way off along the side of the hall, another, smaller, porch and door.

Halli flitted closer, weaving his way among the crowd. He saw a man in servant's wear rolling a small barrel in through the door. Now it was empty, left ajar.

181

Halli paused beside a Trow-shy and watched the porch. Near him boys and girls stood hurling pebbles toward a set of slender poles, on each of which was balanced a turnip, painted with a black, leering, many-fanged face. A girl's stone hit directly: a head went flying amid a chorus of cheers.

Still the porch was quiet. No one passed in or out.

Halli darted forward. As he did so, two servant women bustled out, faces red and sweating, and hurried away down the side of the hall. Halli, who had veered off and taken up a posture of extreme attention at a sweetmeat booth, wheeled round, took a swift look all about, and strode purposefully, unhurriedly, in through the porch door.

Darkness, shadows, a pleasant mustiness: an immense storeroom filled with boxes, barrels, and sacks of grain. From ceiling hooks hung onions, chard, herbs and carrot bunches; smoked meats in long rows vanishing into the gloom. Halli took a deep breath—the room was almost the size of Svein's own hall—and hurried along the main aisle toward a distant flight of steps.

Footsteps. Halli crouched and skittered sideways like a crab behind a pile of flour sacks. He ducked his head low between his knees and held his breath.

A few feet from him the two servant women passed; he heard the rustle of their kirtles, the whisper of their breathing.

All was still; Halli straightened, shouldered his pack, stole silently along the aisle.

The steps were whitewashed, broad and worn; the light of day shone down on them. Halli peered up; he glimpsed soaring roof beams, the haze of vast space. Pressing close against the wall he climbed swiftly, fearing at any moment to meet someone hurrying down.

With each step more of Hakon's hall was revealed to him. Roof beams became joined to slender arches, which sat upon great columns. Between the columns shone brilliant panels of light—slender windows through which the autumn sun blazed fiercely. Now the walls beneath the windows came into view: they hung with stags' antlers and the skulls of beasts; fan-arrays of ancient spears; an endless row of black-stained braziers; tapestries and scarlet flags.

Halli's head broke level with the hall floor. He saw great rows of tables stretching away left and right; a central roasting pit, with an ox already spitted; servants on all sides, setting cups and knives upon the tables, bringing empty plates from somewhere out of view.

No one looked his way. Without hesitation, he scrambled up the last two steps and, bent double, scurried to the nearest table. Under it he went, among the trestle legs and rushes, and crouched still.

Time passed. Servants bustled, bringing supplies up from the stores. Men climbed into the roasting pit and turned the ox upon its spit. A bell rang, perhaps within the kitchens, perhaps a call to lunch. One by one the servants flitted from the hall.

A small dark shape emerged from beneath the table, stood quiet, hunched like a hunting wolf. It looked to the left: saw the great hall doors standing closed—from beyond came the hubbub of the crowds. To the right, at the far end of the hall, a steep, straight staircase ran up beneath the windows to an upper balcony. There were doors leading from the balcony—two doors, maybe three. Below, behind the raised dais and the Law Seats, Halli saw other arches, some curtained, others bare and empty.

A fire burned strongly in an open hearth halfway along the hall. The tables were laid now, ready for the evening feast. The smell of roast meat filled the air.

So, where would Olaf be?

Halli's head tilted. He stared toward the balcony.

Up there.

His hand reached out to the table beside him, picked up a long thin carving knife. He walked between the tables toward the stairs.

Somewhere behind, a rattling, a sudden flare of noise from outside the hall. The great doors had opened. Halli cursed, ducked away, pressed himself behind a column. He heard Hord's voice then, loud, imperious; boots echoing on the flagstones.

"I don't care!" Hord said. "Go see your uncle first and get him anything he wants. *Then* eat. You can stuff yourself stupid later anyhow."

The boots passed by; Halli peered out, saw Hord

striding away toward the drapes behind the dais. Up the staircase went Ragnar Hakonsson, blond, pale-faced, and sour of expression. Halli saw him reach the balcony, open a door, and disappear inside.

From a distance he heard Hord shouting, and the resulting sounds of high activity. Halli guessed the servants would soon be back. His eyes darted around, looking for a hiding place: there, close by his column, he saw a group of kegs and barrels, some upturned, others on their sides. All were empty; their contents transferred to kitchen or table. Could he—?

He heard hurrying from the passages.

A jump, a wriggle; Halli was gone. A large barrel in the center of the group rocked gently and was still. Its lid, which had been resting on the top of an adjoining cask, made surreptitious jerking movement sideways, and at last fell into place.

Twenty servants scampered into the hall. Preparations for the feast went on.

Afternoon became evening; evening became night. The hall was filled with revelers. Hakon's name was cheered to the rooftops, men drank to Hord, his wife and son, his brother Olaf, and the greatness of the House. From a barrel in a corner of the hall gentle snoring noises sounded. No one heard, no one came near. The feast came to its end.

The men of Hakon's House departed, some to their

rooms within the hall, others dispersing to the streets and countryside beyond. Down at the Trow wall a horn was blown and the House gates shut. The doors to the hall swung to; an elderly retainer drew its bolts. Others threw dirt on the hearth fire, dampening it down to a low red flicker. The last of the servants retired to their cots.

The hall was filled with shadows. The torches on the walls had dwindled and the light was a low, churning mix of orange-red.

Hord and Ragnar Hakonsson sat together at the central table, amid the debris of the feast.

Despite many hours' vigorous consumption, Hord appeared no different than he had that morning, save for a slight redness in the eyes. He cradled a wine cup in his hand and stared long at his son. On Ragnar the cares of the festival hung heavier; in the hall's light his face gleamed white as mutton bone.

For the first time in many hours the barrel lid moved. It tilted. Two eyes blinked out impatiently.

Halli was growing cramped.

He had slept long and soundly, for the barrel was warmer than the bushes of his travels. But now, on waking, he was conscious of many creeping aches, and of pins and needles in his extremities. He wished to move, to shift inside the barrel, but he feared what the noise might do.

Ragnar was saying, "I do not think she wants me, Father."

Hord snorted like a bull. "Did your mother want to marry me? Our fathers made agreement at a single meeting; next thing she knew my beard was tickling her face. Did she truly wish it? Who can say? She got on with it, as women do, and became a fine and devious Lawgiver. Do not be a milksop, boy! *Want* is not the issue—for her or you."

"I know," Ragnar said irritably. "But still . . ."

"You will be Arbiter here," Hord said, "when I drop dead. If she is your wife, then you rule two Houses. It is a match worth making." He made a stirring motion with his hand, staring at the liquid moving in the cup. "All things go around," he went on. "Our gains through your marriage will offset what we lose from Olaf's action."

Ragnar looked pained. "You think we will lose land? How much?"

"It depends how strongly the Sveinssons press the Council. Ulfar Arnesson has talked with them. He says they are set on making stringent demands, particularly the woman, though *she* never loved Brodir, Hakon knows." He picked at his teeth with a fingernail.

Halli's back was a slab of pain. He grimaced beneath the barrel lid. If he could just transfer the weight to his legs a little, squat instead of sit . . .

"Olaf shouldn't have done it," Ragnar remarked testily. "It was a reckless killing."

Hord's face colored; he cracked his cup hard down on the table so that the dishes hopped and rang. "By rights

Brodir should have been strung up years ago! You don't deny that, I hope?"

Ragnar looked down at his lap. "No."

"The only pity is that tree frog of a nephew saw it. He'll be primary witness, come the trial."

Halli had been adjusting his posture within the barrel, trying to take the pressure off his back; at Hord's words he froze.

"We should have cut *his* throat too," Ragnar said. "Saved us some acres."

"Well, *you* had your boot on his neck," Hord growled. "The chance was there. Still, it makes little difference now. He's beyond our reach. But this brings me to a separate matter. Regardless of the Council's ruling, I—"

Pain flared up Halli's back in a sudden spasm. He jerked forward slightly, knocking his palms against the barrel's sides.

The barrel shook.

Its lid, balanced precariously on its brim, wobbled.

Halli sensed the wobble. He reached up a hasty hand.

The lid slipped away from his brushing fingertips, revolved against the barrel brim, and crashed down upon the floor.

12

KOL KIN-KILLER had performed atrocities up and down the valley and was known to be a hard fighter. He gave allegiance to no House and counted a number of seasoned outlaws among his men. After Kol's band attacked Gest's place in the high valley, they traveled east again through Svein's lands. There was a farmstead up there, near Deepdale, where Svein's cousins lived. One day Svein saw black smoke rising above the hill. He rode to investigate, and found the farm burned and his cousins impaled on stakes of wood. Svein was so angry then that his followers fled from him. When he calmed down, he looked around and found the outlaws' trail going into the forest.

Svein said to his men: "You lot head home. I'm going hunting."

THE ECHOES OF THE CRASH reverberated between the columns, up and down the midnight hall. Ragnar and Hord sat rigid in their seats. Ragnar whispered: "Father . . ."

"Over by those casks," Hord said. "Get up and see."

Ragnar's chair scraped back harshly on the floor.

Halli, in his barrel, cringed down low as he could. He could sense the open space above him; cool air tickled the back of his neck.

"Here, boy," Hord said carelessly. "Take the knife."

A scrape of metal; Ragnar's footsteps drew close across the hall. Halli felt beside him in the barrel's darkness for his own knife, and grasped it tightly by the hilt.

"In one of these, you think, Father?" Ragnar's voice was not entirely steady.

"Hakon's blood, you mooncalf!" Hord roared. "Have a look and see!"

Hesitant movements, rasps of wood: barrel lids lifted and cast aside.

Halli heard Ragnar's breathing now, short and quick. He was very near. Halli tensed himself, ready to spring. . . .

"Ah! There!"

Ragnar's cry rang out—but it sounded almost eager and relieved. Halli, who had jolted upward, checked his movement. Something thudded against the wall. Ragnar's boots moved swiftly along the hall away from him. He called again: "See—there! Rats!"

Hord uttered a long, low groan.

Now Ragnar was returning to the table. "Big fat one, it was, Father! I almost got it with a lid. Would've sliced it in two."

"I can hear the ballads being written as we speak. Come

here, boy, and listen to me." Hord put his cup to his mouth and sucked wine in ruefully through his teeth. *"Rats!"* he said. "What a son of Hakon you are. Well, one last thing. I spoke with the head smith this afternoon. They are almost ready. You understand me?"

"Yes, Father."

"It is probable that the Council will rule against us in the Brodir case. They have a long history of setting politics ahead of justice; they want 'balance' in the valley, they want no one House to gain undue influence. This is all well known."

"Yes, Father."

"Well, great Hakon wouldn't have stood for it, and neither shall we. If things turn out as I hope, we'll have a way of taking matters into our own hands next year. It's too early to say how—but we'll be practicing this winter. I'll want you to practice too."

"Oh, I will, Father."

"Very good. Totter off to bed then, before you collapse with exhaustion. We don't want you sickening as well."

Ragnar spoke musingly. "Will Olaf die, you think?"

"Not he."

"But he is Trow-stricken."

"He has fever, that is all. Don't be a superstitious fool."

"The cairn shadow touched him! I saw it."

"So he rode too close! Is his horse sick? No! Why not, since the shadow fell across it too?" Hord set his cup upon the table and rose. "A real man does not pay heed to old wives' tales of Trows and curses! Olaf has had fever before; he overcame it then, and he will do so now. Right, off to bed, milksop, before you faint."

Each took candles from the table; they climbed the stairs to the balcony and parted. Doors closed abruptly. Silence descended on the hall.

For almost a minute, nothing happened.

Out from the barrel rose Halli, face contorted with pain. He swung himself out and dropped to the floor, where for some moments he hopped in silent agony until the cramps departed from his legs.

At last his steps grew steadier. He limped over to the tables, found a jug of ale, and drained it. Then he wiped his mouth, slung his bag upon his back and took up the knife once more.

So, to business. Now was the time.

Across the hall he went, trailing a long black shadow that slipped like a phantom over the fiery reflections on the floor. The knife glinted softly in his hand.

Onto the staircase, slowly, steadily. His feet made no sound. He kept his eyes fixed on the balcony above.

Halli neither hurried nor dawdled. He crossed a short half-landing and went on and upward to the top. In just such a manner Svein would have hunted Kol Kin-killer through the woods, or pursued the giant Deepdale boar.

He reached the balcony and passed across it to the door he had seen Ragnar enter long ago that afternoon.

He hesitated, listened. . . . Nothing stirred anywhere within the House.

With murder in his heart, he unlatched the door, stepped inside, and pushed it swiftly shut behind him.

Halli stood in darkness, but somewhere ahead of him a single light burned strongly. It was hard to tell how far away it was, for it blurred and shifted against his vision like a living thing, and he could not look directly at it. He closed his eyes and counted slowly under his breath, willing his eyesight to adjust, wrinkling his nose in the meantime at the room's foul air, at its taint of sickness.

He opened his eyes once more. Better: now the light had resolved itself. At its heart was a clear white core, suspended about a candle's wick; round this extended a soft yellow halo, bright near the core, fading outward to a haze that only brushed the surface of the dark. The illuminated circle was not large. It hung at an uncertain distance, disembodied and shimmering, like the moon's reflection in a winter lake.

There was a face in it.

Despite himself, Halli flinched back against the door, feeling the skin crawl upon his spine. It was a sinister spirit, something out of Katla's nursery tales, a disembodied horror, a glowing, floating head—

He shook himself savagely. Don't be a fool! This was Olaf! It was nothing but a man. A sick man with his head upon a pillow.

Olaf's eyes were closed, his mouth slightly agape; his thin nose jutted at the ceiling. His translucent skin stretched tight upon his features: everything beneath—cheekbones, nose cartilage, and jaw—all seemed close to breaking through. The hair of the beard curled sparsely on the chin like thorns around a stone.

Halli listened carefully, but heard no breath.

He stood in darkness by the door, gazing at the sleeping face. He did not move.

With careful deliberation Halli recalled to mind that moment in the stable: Brodir's body falling, the jerk of Olaf's arm, the implacable intention on that selfsame sleeping face as the knife was carried to his uncle. . . .

Halli closed his eyes and rubbed them with his free hand.

At about this time, with his enemy within his reach, he had expected to feel the surge of anger, the burst of adrenaline required to commit the necessary act. He had *not* expected the nausea that had suddenly come upon him. His legs shook beneath him; he felt as he had in the moments after his uncle's killing, helpless, stricken, physically sick.

It was *not* the appropriate reaction.

He breathed out silently, cursing himself in the name of Svein.

Just a few feet to walk, a single stab, and the journey would be over. His uncle would be avenged, his killer killed. It was simplicity itself. All he had to do was *move*.

With the hesitant, heavy motions of a sleepwalker, Halli stepped toward the circle of light. Its gleam reflected on the long knife in his hand, which suddenly seemed to carry extra weight, dragging his arm down.

He passed the margins of a clothes chest, open, spilling out rich linens; a low-backed chair, carved to a sinuous design; a table with wine cup, bread, and meats; a cold fireplace with a poker lying amid the ashes.

That was all. Before he knew it he was at the bedside.

Olaf Hakonsson's slender body lay beneath a thick fur quilt that had half fallen to the floor. His arms lay visible and outstretched, palms upward as if pleading. Now Halli saw a pulse beating in the scrawny throat, and the barest movement of the blanket across the chest.

One blow was all he needed. To where—the throat or chest? The heart would be proper, as Olaf had killed Brodir that way. But the throat was simpler. . . . Halli's lips were dry; his limbs felt oddly weak, his vision spun. Food and rest were what he needed, before he could do anything. Maybe he should go back to the hall, revive himself, come back when—

Halli snarled soundlessly in the dark. Stop delaying! *This* was the moment! It would never come again.

Halli shifted the knife so that the point was facing

down. He grasped it in both hands and, stepping close so that he leaned out a little over the trestle bed, raised it high over the naked throat.

He took a deep breath, paused—

From nowhere, an image came to him. Back in the gorge: Bjorn the trader's silhouette, his arm raised ready to murder Halli in his sleep. The terror that Halli had felt then, as he lay waiting for the blow, collided with the terror that he felt *now*, as he stood ready to deliver just such a blow himself. And they were the same terror.

Halli's arm shook; he almost dropped the knife. Tears welled in his eyes and blinded him. Suppressing the urge to sniffle loudly, he stumbled back a pace, lowered his arms and, with misery engulfing him, wiped his face clear with a sleeve.

When he looked back at the bed, Olaf Hakonsson's eyes were open, watching him.

Stone weights hung on Halli's spine: he was fixed, immovable. He felt as if at any moment he might plummet through the floor.

He stared at the figure in the bed as if a Trow had appeared before him.

Olaf Hakonsson's mouth moved a little. His voice was the barest whisper.

"Couldn't do it, eh?"

Halli's tongue had frozen against the inside of his teeth. He could not answer.

The whisper came again. "Why not?"

Numbly Halli shook his head.

Lids flickered; the yellow eyes grew hooded like an owl's. "What? Speak up."

With an effort of will Halli said, "I don't know. It isn't lack of hatred."

There was the faintest of hissing between the open lips; the sick man might have been laughing. "I'm sure! I'm sure! Your presence makes *that* clear enough." The whisper faltered, the eyes closed. "Tell me, are the House gates locked, the doors to the hall barred?"

"Yes."

"Are the men of Hakon's House gathered in their rooms below?"

"Yes."

"Does my brother sleep beyond this very wall?"

"I imagine he does."

Olaf's eyes remained closed; his murmur was almost respectful. "Yet despite all these obstacles you have reached me—like a diminutive, dark-eyed ghost risen from its cairn. I'm impressed. You're a brave and resourceful youth."

Halli said nothing.

"I only have one question."

"Which is?"

"Who the devil are you?"

Halli stepped back in shock. "*What?* You don't recognize me?"

Olaf Hakonsson's eyes gazed on Halli with a dull light. "Should I?"

"Of *course!*"

"Sorry."

"But—but you must."

A considered pause. "No."

"Just a few short weeks since you killed my uncle before my eyes and you don't know who I am! I don't believe this." Halli stepped close. "What, was it that forgettable for you? Here, take a good long look."

A weak hand was raised from the bed. "Say no more. I have it."

"It's about time."

"You're the nephew of that cheating farmer we hung out on Far Shingle. You share his physique. Shortest gallows I ever built."

Halli made an incoherent noise. "No. No—you're wrong."

"What, store-barns crammed with grain, and no tithe given to the House? He was a cheat and you're blind not to see it. What are you doing here on *his* behalf? You're not even his son! It's a *son's* job to honor a dead man."

Halli's rage swelled; he took a step forward, raising the knife a little. "Be silent! I am not one of those tenants you treat so shamefully, but a man of noble blood."

The whisper from the bed was harsh and mocking. "Close. In fact you are a child who attacks an invalid in his sleep. It isn't quite the same thing."

"I didn't *know* you were ill when I——" Halli broke off. His head spun. Candlelight danced in his eyes; darkness pressed in on every side. He moved the knife so that the point drew near to Olaf's throat. "Clearly the fever has destroyed your memory. Let me make things plain for you. I am Halli Sveinsson, son of Arnkel, nephew of brave Brodir, whom you murdered not four weeks past. I watched you kill him as he stood helpless, like an animal led to the block, when all he had done was speak out against your arrogance." Halli let the point press upon the yellow skin. "You are the worst of murderers, to slay a man for a few drunken words, and I suggest you do not dare speak to me again of nobility, since it is a subject you know nothing of."

The hooded eyes were almost closed now; only a glitter shone beneath the lids. The thinnest of breaths eased out between the parted lips. "Ah," Olaf whispered.

"You recognize me now?"

"I do. You have traveled a long way to fail at the last, Halli Sveinsson."

Halli bared his teeth; the knife pressed harder on the neck. "I have not failed."

"Kill me, then."

Halli stood motionless.

"Well?"

Halli stared unseeingly at the point of the weapon, at the whitening knuckles on his hand, at the exposed throat waiting. He did not move. Then slowly, as if from deep within him, his outstretched arm began to shake.

Olaf Hakonsson raised a hand from the coverlet and gently pushed the knife aside. "I'd call that failure, wouldn't you? Wait! Don't run away! That makes it even worse."

Dizzy with shame, hardly knowing what he did, Halli had taken several steps back into the shadows. It was true. He'd failed. He'd failed his uncle, lying far away beneath his cairn—he had *failed* poor Brodir. He'd disgraced his House too, and the memory of Svein. What kind of avenger couldn't make the kill? What kind of hero shook with fear like that? Halli wasn't fit to carry the family name, let alone wear the silver belt. His fingers loosened; the knife dropped to the ground.

Olaf had not moved his head; in his cocoon of light he gazed up at the ceiling. "You know what the problem is?" he whispered. "Here's my guess. You do not care as much for your uncle as you thought."

Halli's voice echoed hoarsely in the darkness. "No! That is not the reason!"

"Why else would you falter? You're no coward. I saw that with my own eyes, back in the stable. But you cannot avenge him, even so. Clearly you do not love him."

"No. I do. I did."

"You do not love him." With hesitant, uneven movements, Olaf raised his head from the pillow; his shoulders bent forward, his elbows back. Now he was propped a little on his arms, at the edge of the circle of light, gazing blindly out toward where Halli stood in the darkness. "And I'll tell you why. Because you know what your uncle was. Not an honorable man. Not a peaceful man. Not a man of virtue and the quiet fields. He was a drinker, a braggart, a brawling fool who brought shame upon your family. He was a man of violence."

"Oh, yes?" Derision entered Halli's voice. "When it was *you* who—"

"Can it be that your parents have never told you?" Skin shifted over the bones of the face; Olaf's eyes crinkled with sudden merriment. "Oh, dear me. I don't believe they *did*." He pushed himself a little higher on the bed. "Halli, my boy—what did Brodir tell you of his youth? Did *he* give you hints and clues, perhaps? Did *he* tell you what he did one night, how he lost a thousand acres of your House's land?" He waited; no sound came from the darkness. "You may as well speak," Olaf said. "I know you're there. I can see your eyes gleaming in the corner like a wolf's. No word for me? Would you like me to tell you Brodir's tale? You'll have to listen hard—the fever's stolen my voice."

"You know I won't believe you," Halli said.

"No, well. I don't believe most stories myself." Olaf was sitting up now. The blankets had fallen from him. He wore a long nightgown that shimmered on the margins of the candlelight; his limbs were very thin. "But you'll find there's truth in this one." He swung his legs round and out from beneath the blankets; his feet touched the rug below the bed. "Ah, it's cold! By rights I shouldn't stir, but I feel an obligation"—he coughed, drew his nightshirt close about his neck—"to open your eyes at last. Did Brodir not tell you how he killed a man? Not honorably, I mean—not in some man-to-man duel, as it was in Hakon's day, not in the heat of battle, but slyly, treacherously, and unprovoked?"

He stretched out a hand into the darkness and drew the wine cup from the table. Halli's heart beat against his chest. He wished to block his ears, to leave now before another word was said, but found himself transfixed. He neither moved nor answered.

Olaf took a long sip from the cup, making hideous gulping, smacking sounds deep in his throat. He set the cup down. "Well, it won't surprise you to hear that your uncle Brodir traveled far in his younger days, visited most Houses at one time or another, sometimes on family business, sometimes on a whim. He came here often, Halli—a wiry little mountain man, dark-eyed and serious in pursuit of pleasure. We knew him well enough—too well, when the ale was in him. You know how he always became . . . *boisterous* at such times?"

Halli said sullenly, "*That* is no crime."

"True. It's a way of life for squalid upland Houses such as yours." Olaf sat forward on the edge of the bed, his face in shadow. "In those days Hord and I had a younger sister. Her name was Thora. She could have married anyone she

chose, being a daughter of Hakon's House and very beautiful, and many men tried their luck with her, your uncle
Brodir included. But Thora refused them all. Brodir wasn't
so keen on that. He pestered her whenever he came here, and
several times Hord and I had to step in and calm things
down. Poor Thora—she disliked all the attention, and anyway, she loved another." Olaf coughed again, slumping over,
hands clasped between his knees, gazing at the floor. "She
loved a boy from this very House, a carpenter, handsome
and golden haired—I can see his face now, though I forget
his name. It came about, little Halli, that your uncle was
here on business one feast night, and news of Thora's carpenter came to his ears. This displeased him—his drunken
pride was wounded. Know what he did?"

Halli said softly, "You're lying."

"He stepped over to the lad, where he stood talking, and
without further ado struck him so hard that he fell to the
floor. What happened? His skull struck the hearthstone and
cracked like a snail shell. Nothing could be done—he died
soon after. But when everyone stood back and looked for
the man who'd killed him, your uncle was gone."

"Lies," Halli whispered. "Lies."

"Not at all. Ask your mother."

There was a silence. "The Council—in their wisdom, in
their desire for peace and harmony—didn't want to hang an
Arbiter's son," Olaf went on. "They called it manslaughter,
not outright murder. So your uncle lived."

"If true," Halli said huskily, "if true, it was a wicked act, but also an accident. An accident," he repeated, "and you got land for it. Yet you killed Brodir, long years later, to avenge someone whose name you can't recall!"

"Not *him*," Olaf whispered. "I avenged my sister. Poor Thora, who loved that boy so fervently she hung herself the night he died. My sister, who died because of Brodir. Your uncle was owed his death." His head hung low, his voice barely carried to Halli's burning ears.

For a time neither said anything. At last Halli stirred. "You wouldn't have let her marry the carpenter."

Olaf looked at him.

"Some common lad? I don't think so. She'd have been fixed up with the son of another House. Wouldn't she?"

Olaf gave the slightest perceptible shrug.

"There's no doubt of it," Halli said. "She'd have had her heart broken one way or the other." He moved backward toward the door. "But thank you for the story. I'd been wondering why I failed to kill you and now perhaps I see the reason. There have been too many futile deaths already, and there's no honor in any of it. Well, if the fever doesn't take you, I'll speak against you at the trial and you'll lose land and face. There the matter will end. Good-bye." He turned to go, but the back of the room was black, and he could not see the door.

Behind him, Olaf's whisper was amused. "What an odd little fellow you are. Hasn't it occurred to you that without your testimony the case will fall apart? I'm hardly likely to let you go alive, am I?"

Halli inched forward, feeling with his hands. "Fine words, but you're a sick old man."

"Oh, well, you know—I'm not as bad as all that."

Halli heard a movement, the faintest rustling, as if a weight had suddenly been released from the mattress, letting the straw expand.

He looked over his shoulder.

And saw the candle guttering violently, its halo of light distorting and spinning above the empty bed.

13

FOR THREE DAYS Svein followed Kol's trail, neither eating nor sleeping, until he came to the outlaws' camp on a bluff close to the Snag. There were twenty men there, but Svein didn't hesitate—he leaped in, sword swinging, and the battle began. Soon eight outlaws lay dead, but now Svein was hard-pressed. He retreated up the track, still fighting, until he came to a little shepherd's hut. He ran inside and barred the door.

Kol and his men took up position outside the hut waiting for Svein to come out.

Inside the hut Svein found flints, a candle, and lumps of wood for the fire. He thought a bit, then set about whittling the wood into the rough shape of a man's head.

That night the outlaws saw a light at the hut's window and Svein's shadow framed upon the wall beyond. They set a man to watch, and the rest lay down to sleep.

Leaving the dummy where it was, Svein broke a hole in the back of the hut and crawled out. Then he crept round and struck off the heads of Kol and his outlaws, one by one by one. He set them on stakes beside the valley road to discourage further nuisance.

HALLI LURCHED FORWARD and his hands collided with the rough, cold plaster wall. Where was the door? As he scrabbled side to side, he heard behind him the briefest scraping on the floor.

The poker in the hearth.

Halli's fingers met with wood, felt furiously for the latch.

A waft of air. Halli ducked instinctively. With a cracking thud something crashed into the plaster above his head. Unseen fragments rained into his hair.

A whisper in the darkness. "Damn. I forgot you were so short."

Rattles, wrenching sounds: the poker being pried free. Halli found the latch and pulled at the door. Dim light burst on his eyes; he glimpsed the shadowed balcony and, beyond the balustrade, the hall's great emptiness, faintly glowing red. Halli sprang: as he did so, something struck him on the thigh with venomous force. An explosion of pain; Halli's leg gave way. He collided with the door frame, and collapsed upon the balcony.

Halli looked up. Out from the darkness of the door came Olaf Hakonsson, slowly, slowly, a gaunt specter in a woolen nightgown. In his hands was a long black poker. His face was white, his eyes staring; the loose skin on his arms flapped as he raised them high to strike.

Halli rolled sideways, pushed with his good leg, and clawed his way forward along the floor. Behind came the steady padding of a sick man's feet.

Halli bent his back; on hands and knees, he strove to stand. One leg was numb, thin threads of pain playing upon his thigh; placing his weight upon the other he staggered upright, fell forward to lean against the balustrade.

A glance behind: a livid face, a poker swinging.

Halli lurched aside, toward the stair head.

The balustrade splintered. Pieces of wood fell spinning to the hall below.

His leg was stiff and tender with each tread; hopping, limping, he reached the stairs and, grasping the banisters with both hands to prevent a fall, flung himself down. Something swished above him through the air.

Olaf's cry was a wheezing whisper, swallowed by the vastness of the hall. "Hord! Hord! Ragnar! Wake up! An enemy is here! Ah, curse it—where is my *voice?*"

Down the staircase Halli hobbled, leaning on the banisters, swinging his bad leg out to the side, wincing whenever it touched down. He could not go fast, but neither could Olaf: he heard his pursuer's heels land heavily on each step, heard the rasp and rattle of his throat, the rustle of the nightgown.

On to the half-landing. Below and to the left opened the

cavernous space—black save for the glowing hearth and the hot coals of the roasting pit. The braziers on the walls were pinpoints of redness; a hundred cups and plates glinted sullenly across the tables of the empty hall.

To his right, upon the wall, five spears in a fan. Halli stumbled across and seized one, sought to pull it free. He needed a weapon to defend himself—*why* had he dropped the knife? What a fool he was! He pulled, tugged, nearly plucked his arm out of his socket. No good—the spear was tightly fixed—and here came Olaf, eyes like gray hollows, shuffling over the landing with his weapon at the ready.

Down the final flight of steps, careering, half tumbling, out into the belly of the hall. Halli veered slowly toward the central tables. Far to his right, at the end of the hazy line of columns, he saw the great doors to the yard. Even from here he could see the bar drawn fast across them.

"Hord! Ragnar! Wake!" Again the tortured whisper. Halli, turning his head, saw Olaf negotiating the final step. His face was shimmering with sweat, matted hair half covered his eyes, his chest rose and fell in spasms.

"Let's face it," Halli said. "They're asleep and snoring like the drunken hogs they are. Go back to bed while you still can. This chase will be the death of you."

Olaf grinned horribly. "But Halli, Halli, how will you get out? All the doors are locked."

"I'll think of something." Halli turned his head in the rough direction of the storeroom steps by which he had entered. Too risky: the outer door would be locked for sure, and he'd be trapped down there. . . . The only option was to try the arches behind the Law Seats—look for a window, perhaps, or—

A gasp of effort, a blur of movement on the fringes of his vision. Halli lurched aside; the poker stirred the air beside his shoulder and cracked into the flagstones. Olaf swore.

Halli said: "That was a good try, but you're getting weaker. And *my* leg seems to be improving." It was, too; it felt marginally less numb as he limped away, toward the roasting pit, where the carcass of the ox—a ruined, glistening mass of bones and meat—still hung above the burning coals. The floor by the pit was drenched in fat; Halli slipped and nearly lost his balance. As he righted himself he saw two iron skewers resting against the lip; he bent, seized them, and turned again as Olaf staggered near.

Halli took one skewer in his right hand, one in his left. He waved them menacingly in Olaf's direction.

Olaf hissed derisively. "Hakon's ghost, how terrifying! If I were a roast chicken, I'd be running for the door!"

"Beware," Halli growled. "Up-valley, men fight with two blades."

"You look as if you're swatting flies," Olaf said. "It amazes me more and more that you came here at all. You cannot kill, you cannot fight—you're the most deluded youth I have ever met!" He swiped with the poker, knocked one of the skewers clean from Halli's hand; it whipped through the air and stuck, quivering, between the rib bones of the ox.

Halli, blanching, stepped back around the edge of the pit and hurled the second skewer like a spear at Olaf, who ducked aside; it struck the side of his face and clattered to the floor. Olaf straightened, fingering his cheek.

"You *dare* strike a son of Hakon in his hall? If I was well . . ."

"I'd still run rings around you, since I am a son of Svein, who incidentally threw *your* forefather arse-first into a thornbush. Do you know the story? I only hope Hakon was wearing a longer nightshirt than *you* seem to favor." Halli backed away across the hall, faster than before, his bad leg protesting.

Whether it was rage or the pain in his cheek, Olaf too had put on speed. "Ah, you coward! Look at you, running."

"Actually, it's called improvising." Halli came abreast of a table, piled high with debris from the feast. He caught up a cup and threw it at Olaf, who dodged. Next he seized a plate, hurled that, and then a greasy ham bone. Olaf evaded the plate, but was struck on the head by the bone, drawing forth hoarse curses.

Down beside the table came Olaf, with Halli backing steadily away, casting everything he could reach in the direction of his enemy. Cups, fruit, bowls, spittoons, chicken carcasses, table knives, certain spherical vegetables that had been cooked but left uneaten—all went flying in Olaf's face. He dodged some, swatted away others, but was knocked and battered even so.

Halli finished with a medley of soft plums.

"Open your mouth a little wider," he called. "I'll try to get one in."

For the first time since entering Olaf's room he felt exhilaration. Yes, he had failed to do what he had come for, and probably all was lost. But fighting for his life was a different thing from trying to kill a helpless enemy, and Halli found he much preferred it. Particularly since the numbness in his leg was definitely fading now.

He glanced off down the hall: he was halfway to the dais and the arches. But Olaf was still close and would soon awaken others if allowed to leave the room. Which meant Halli had to somehow stop him.

Here came Olaf at his hobbling run, poker raised high.

Halli darted to the nearby hearth in search of other metal implements, but discovered nothing. Sweat broke out instantly on his face, for the central logs still burned beneath the dirt and the bone white ash beneath his feet was hot.

Olaf approached at speed. Halli scuffed his boots through the ashes on the stones and kicked a shower of it onto Olaf's bare legs, causing him to prance about in pain.

Projecting from the edges of the fire were several unburned branches. Halli pulled free the nearest, a long bent stick. Its end glowed white and red. Holding it in both hands he swung it to and fro, eliciting a series of elaborate whistling sounds. For a moment Olaf hung back, daunted, then with an oath darted in, swinging the poker down wildly. Halli held up the branch to block the blow; the impact made the teeth jangle in his jaw and his knees give way. He dropped the branch, fell down among the hot white ashes, which plumed up in a mist around him.

Olaf's face was dreadful, a death mask, grinning madly. His lips were drawn so wide it seemed his skin must crack. He stepped over Halli and raised his arms.

Halli sought to scramble free, but his legs were caught between his enemy's. He thrashed back and forth in a panic, writhing like an eel, knocking the inside of Olaf's knees even as the he drove the poker down. Olaf lost his balance; the poker struck the flagstones beside Halli's head with a ring that echoed to the rafters of the hall. Olaf fell beside Halli among the ashes, nearer the fire, where they were very hot.

A moment more and both were on their feet again, their bodies white with ash. Halli's leg betrayed him: before he could escape, Olaf's hand jerked out and caught him by the throat.

The grip was like iron; Halli's eyes bulged. He struggled feebly.

Olaf said: "You surely know better than to hope for mercy." He raised his arm so that Halli's boots departed from the floor. He hung suspended by the neck.

Halli gurgled and kicked. He could not breathe. His fingers tore at Olaf's wrist. Olaf chuckled. "No good doing that, my lad. I may be sick, but I won't let go. I've strangled bigger men than you this way."

Quite suddenly Halli stopped wriggling. He went completely limp. He raised a hand slowly and pointed—first at Olaf, then at the floor, the hearth and back to Olaf. After a pause, he did it again.

Olaf narrowed his eyes. "What? I don't understand you. What are you saying?"

Halli, now purple in the face, repeated the performance with the same deliberate care.

Olaf shook his head. "Sorry. Makes no sense to me."

This time the gestures were accompanied by a prolonged and enigmatic gurgle and an ambiguous twitching of the eyebrows.

Olaf scowled. "Ah! This is hopeless! If you can't be clear, don't try."

Rather pointedly, Halli indicated the fingers throttling his throat. Olaf rolled his eyes and slackened his grip a little.

"Well?"

A feeble croak: "You're on fire."

Olaf stared at Halli. Then he gazed down to see long yellow ribbons of flame licking up from the fringes of his nightshirt. Even as he looked the flames grew and spread eagerly, the wool strands within them flaring white, then black.

Olaf gave a whispered howl of fear, flung Halli aside, and danced away across the hall, patting desperately at his burning flanks.

Rubbing at his neck, Halli stumbled in the opposite direction, pausing only to snatch up the smoldering branch from where it lay. He limped past the dais and underneath the balcony. Looking back he saw Olaf blundering about— a thin, black figure silhouetted in a fiery haze. Olaf fell against a wall tapestry, clawing at it, seeking, perhaps, some cloth to snuff the flames. Instead the dry threads of the tapestry ignited, sending yellow-orange spurts of fire licking up the wall.

This seemed like a good idea to Halli. He set his branch to some nearby drapes, and watched the fabric take and burn.

With a sudden whoof, the burning tapestry fell from the wall. It collapsed on Olaf and he was lost to view.

From directly above him, on the balcony, came sudden shouts and running feet.

Halli imagined Hord and Ragnar running down the stairs. After Olaf's sickly pursuit, their speed and urgency unnerved him. At a limping run, Halli exited the hall.

The passage that he took was long, dark, and many cornered, with several doors that opened onto quarters for the servants. He glimpsed hunched forms in bunks, and shadowed, sleeping faces. Soon all would be awake. Halli redoubled his speed, urging his body on, hunting for some method of leaving Hakon's hall.

His headlong flight had stimulated the fire within his branch and now the wood was burning nicely. To delay pursuit Halli set fire to things where he could: a drape here, a basket of clothing there. The passage behind was wreathed in smoke.

At last a window: tall, slender, shuttered. Halli threw the casement wide and clambered onto the ledge. He crouched there, blinking into darkness. Cold rain hit his face and made the sweat on his brow itch.

A few feet ahead, and some way below him, he glimpsed a broad band of stones—the top of the great Trow wall that encircled the House. Beyond he could see nothing. Directly under the window hung an abyss of black; he sensed a drop that would break his bones.

Halli cocked his head back toward the passage, where footsteps could be heard approaching, and behind *that* the noise of distant shouts and screams. Somewhere far away, around the dark mass of the hall, a bell began to ring.

There was little time to waste. Halli threw his stick over his shoulder into the passage, stepped back as far as he could upon the ledge, and jumping from his good leg, leaped high and hard out into the night.

For an instant all sounds cut out. Rain pattered on his face. His legs bent ready.

Halli crashed down upon the wall, rolled, sprang upright, conscious of a sudden flaring pain. The bad leg:

jarred, or something. No time. The bell's noise was loud outside. Other bells now rang out, here and there about the House.

The stones on the Trow wall were worn and smooth and slippery with rain. Halli loped along the parapet like an injured beast, glancing this way and that—over his shoulder; across the parapet and out into the night; down on the jumbled cottages that crowded all round Hakon's hall, where lights now woke in windows and the bells rang ever louder. He was caught in indecision: he did not like the thought of what lay beyond the parapet—he recalled the height of the Trow walls and their deep black moat too well.

But neither did remaining in Hakon's House have much to favor it.

Away along the curve of the wall, somewhere near the gate, he saw the lights of torches shifting, congregating, separating. They multiplied with ominous purpose. A great and angry glow swelled silently around them, illuminating the sides of cottages and, in an unpleasant coincidence that Halli didn't fail to notice, a jutting gallows set upon the wall. The lights fragmented: some broke off one way, some another. He heard voices raised in command, boots on flagstones, and the querulous howls of dogs.

Halli blew out his cheeks and glanced behind him. Far off along the parapet he spied lights and hurrying forms.

Raising his hood to shield his face from view he stepped to the edge of the wall and looked over speculatively. Utter blackness. Far below he heard rain thrashing on water. He hesitated, biting his lip.

A fragment of stone in the wall beside him leaped up and struck his cheek close to his eye. A broken arrow shaft skidded away along the parapet.

Halli closed his eyes, ran three steps forward, and jumped.

The fall was quick enough, but oddly fractured, so that there seemed an infinity of moments in which he hung suspended, legs pumping, arms spread wide, wind striking him from below, with his stomach lurching upward against his teeth, and his bag and hair whipping out above him, and yet no time or space to come to terms with any of this before he hit the surface and the rushing dark exploded all around.

The air was ripped away and icy blackness swallowed him.

Everything ceased: rain, lights, bell, noise.

Eyes staring, hands aloft, Halli dropped silently into the moat's black space.

A FARMER UP IN DEEPDALE had three daughters and Svein went along to visit them with a view to taking a wife. He found them all to be handsome enough, with long, sweet-smelling hair and sturdy hams. It was hard to choose between them.

Svein said: "I am going up to the Trow-king's hall. What shall I bring you?"

"Gold and silver," said the eldest, "so that I can wear it about my neck."

"A cooking pot and ladle," said the second. "For mine have broken."

The youngest smiled. "Oh, just a pretty little flower from the moorside to gaze at while I think of you."

Svein went off up to the hall. It was his second visit. This time he went in deeper than before, past the burning fire and the hanging bones, to the Trows' living quarters. They were all asleep in pores and fissures and he was able to kill a good many without difficulty. He saw a staircase leading down into the earth, but it was getting late, so he hunted about, found gold and silver, and a cooking pot and ladle, and left. On the moor he picked a flower. Then he came back and gave the daughters what they'd asked for.

"Have you made up your mind between us?" they said.

"Yes," said Svein. "You, the eldest, are clearly

a vain sort of trollop, while you, the youngest, are appallingly fey. I'll pick you, the middle one, for your commonsense request." So he went home with the middle sister, and she made him a very fine wife.

And that was Svein's second visit to the Trow-king's hall.

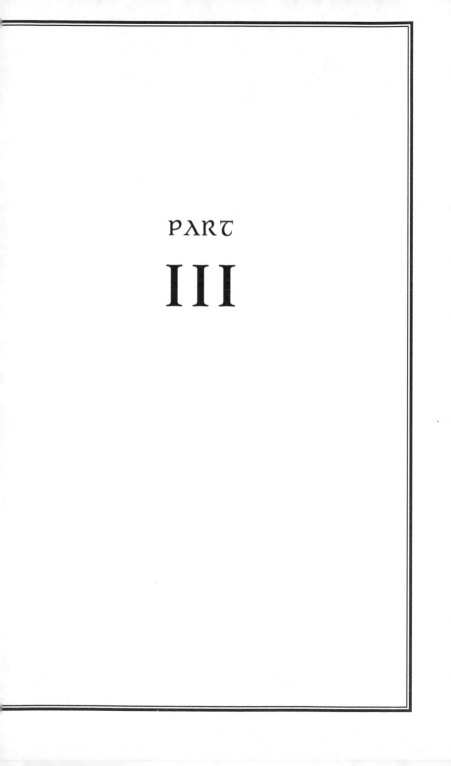

PART

III

14

SVEIN WASN'T QUITE sixteen when his father died, but when he took charge people knew about it. The first thing he did was gather everyone in the yard.

"Take a look around you," Svein said. "What do you see? Cottages and cabbage fields, mud and manure. All that's going to change. I intend our House to be the greatest in the valley, and for that we need more lands. There are lots of other farms nearby, and we need to get them under our control. We'll take our swords now and go and persuade them."

One of his men said: "But we're not used to battle. All we know is farming."

"That's another thing," Svein said. "Every night, when the Trows come prowling, you all cower under your beds. We'll have no more of that now I'm your leader. It's time for our enemies to fear our House." He drew his sword. "Any objections?"

No one had any objections. They went to get their weapons.

HIS RUSE HAD NOT fooled them. Crouching low in the shadows of the gully he heard the many-throated wail welling up beneath the rain, rolling over the wet slopes of the hillside and breaking on the crags above, as the dogs came bounding and splashing up the stream. Turning his head, he pressed his face into the grass for a moment, willing himself to move. If he did not climb up and out of the gully now, they would very soon clear the rise and see him. He imagined the pack's speed, its hunger for the chase; he imagined the men following on behind, grim faced, with their flails and scythes, their knifes and the lengths of rope. They would not go to the effort of bringing him back to the House now, not when they had come so far. They'd pick the first tree with a strong enough branch and have done with it.

He closed his eyes, pressing his head hard into the grass and mud, smelling its dark, sour smell. It would be easier not to run. They had been following him all day and now his knee was swollen; it had stiffened even in this short delay, as he waited here under the leaden skies, hoping they would follow the false trail, the loop downstream. But they'd got the scent even through the water; now they were right on his heels again. Even if he ran it could not be long before they brought him down. It would be easier to stay put.

Just below the rise, where the stream descended into a little series of waterfalls, a fresh volley of barks erupted. That would be where he'd gashed his arm; they'd found the blood on the rock. The sound tore through fatigue, gave Halli purpose. He wrenched his head back, forcing himself to look up the gully side. It wasn't steep. He could do it, even with his knee. Grasping the grass with both hands, he hauled himself upward. His bare feet slipped in wetness, his fingers stubbed against stones; he fell back a little way. Then his toes found purchase and he pushed up with greater force. The knee complained, but no worse than expected. Hand over hand, digging his fingers into the turf, Halli climbed the slope. A few moments later, oblivious to the scratches, he was pulling himself through hanging spirals of briar and bramble and out onto horizontal ground.

Ahead of him the ridge slope fell away to the west in a lumpen mess of dips and protruding rocks. Beyond rose a blue-gray mass, a blanket of trees draped, half-folded, on the bones of the hill. A forest. A forest meant shelter. Better try for it than remain out in the open and be torn apart.

Stumbling, limping, Halli flung himself forward onto the open hillside.

A darker gray than the clouds behind, smoke threads from the burning House spread silently against the sky.

He had lost the first boot in the black stillness of the moat, somewhere between his touching down on the soft, yielding mud and the final panicked kick that brought him upward into air. It was already gone when his head broke surface into rain, as he flapped and floundered toward the edge, protected by darkness from the arrows. Away to his left, on the surface of the water, he saw a dancing square of reflected fire.

To begin with he thought he had evaded them, that they had stayed to fight the blaze. He had crossed several fields with that hope swelling in his breast, until he had climbed a little way and could properly look behind him. Then, from the lower slopes of the ridge, with gray dawn blooming above the sea and Hakon's House aflame, he saw the lights of the search party shifting and congregating beside the black disc of the moat and heard the hounds take up their cry.

Cairns up above, sea to the east: inevitably he would be driven west, back up the valley—and they had known this too. They had moved swiftly on the lower ground to cut him off, going by paths unknown to him. He had only recently crossed the shepherds' track into the bracken when the first outriders of the pack came rushing up and flung themselves, twisting and slavering, upon his scent. And that would have been the end, right there, if he hadn't stuffed his remaining boot deep between two rocks, far down as he could push it, and splashed away across a stream. The respite saved him. While they worried away at the hole, howling, snarling, he climbed on, wading whenever he could through the little streams that ran like veins down to the sea.

But the day had worn on, and they had never lost his trail. And now Halli's resources were almost at an end.

Shortly before he reached the forest the pack burst out upon the hill. He knew from the frenzy in their barks that they had seen him. Trees or no trees, it was not long now.

He fell down a bank, under the spreading eaves of the edgemost oaks, to discover the first dry ground he had felt that day and—away to his right—a wooden post, marking a House boundary. The hero's features were lost beneath a covering of thick green moss, but part of the body was still free of it, and Halli thought to see the faintest trace of purple dye upon the pitted wood as he stumbled by.

Purple meant Arne's lands, which meant—

No. The House would be far away. He would never reach it in time.

Halli ran blindly into the wood's dimness, ducking under branches, ripping through tangled wastes of dead brown ferns. His feet plowed up gouts of fallen leaves, plunged into unexpected hollows, caught against root and thorn. He fell, rose, and plunged on—only to fall again soon after. His weariness could no longer be overcome: soon, when he fell, he would not rise. Grasping a bough for support, he righted himself once more and started to negotiate another mass of bracken. On the third step, his leg gave way. He tumbled forward, hands outstretched—and found the ground falling away steeply before him. Head over heels down the slope he went, ferns splintering, soil flying, over and over—

And out suddenly, painfully, upon the level dirt and pebbles of a forest road.

Stones settled, ferns subsided. Halli no longer moved.

He lay where he was—on his back, legs sprawled, one knee bent—staring up at the net of branches above the road. The sky beyond was darkening to night. This made him smile a little: he had kept them going all day, which wasn't such a bad effort. But it was ending now. There was no point trying to prolong the inevitable. Get it over with. Have done.

He closed his eyes, waiting, listening . . .

Yes. Here they came.

Halli didn't bother to move or stir, or even pay much attention to the noise, so it was only when it was very close that he realized its distinctiveness. It wasn't dogs or a company of men, but a crisper, more solitary sound.

In a spirit of listless curiosity, Halli raised his head a little and saw a single horse and rider trotting swiftly along the track through the gathering gloom.

There were purple sashes on the bridle.

With a guttural cry, Halli lifted a bloodied hand.

The rider squealed, the horse reared; its hooves made anxious patterns in the mud, not overly far from Halli's head.

Something in the squeal made Halli open his eyes wide. He stared up at the rider, at the slender silhouette outlined against the sky, and felt hope course sickeningly through him.

"Aud?" His voice was cracked, unrecognizable.

Rain began to patter on leaves. The horse shifted. Away in the forest the dogs were silent, but they would be close; they would not take long to find him.

The rider had given him the briefest of glances, then looked away. She flicked the reins; the horse moved forward, its forehooves stepping delicately over Halli's legs.

"*Aud!* It's *me.* Halli Sveinsson!" In despair he levered himself onto an elbow and tried to rise. *"Please!"*

"Halli—?" The horse stopped. The girl gave a sudden laugh, short and sharp like a fox's bark. "Great Arne, it is! What are you *doing?*" The voice was amused, but artificially so, with wariness and bafflement underlying.

He got slowly to his feet. "I'm sorry to startle you."

"The horse was startled. Not me. I squealed to calm it down." Her hair was loose and damp with rain, her face paler than he remembered it, though perhaps it was the light. She sat rigid in the saddle, holding the reins ready. He sensed her thoughts racing. "Great Arne," she said abruptly, "you look terrible. You're so *thin.*"

"Yes, well recently I haven't eaten much." A sound in the undergrowth, somewhere up the slope; he spun round, staring back into the forest shades. "Listen—"

"By the smell of it you haven't *washed* either," the girl said. "Not for a long time. Did you see how the horse reared when she caught your scent? Last time she did that, there was a dead bear in the path, and it didn't smell half as bad as you, though it must have been there a week at least. It was all swollen and sticky and covered in flies."

"Yes. Aud—"

"What are you *doing*, Halli?" She spoke with something of the tart detachment he remembered from their first meeting in the orchard.

Halli looked behind him again. No time to waste, no time at all. Yet he knew he couldn't hurry her. He did not know her well enough to plead outright—if she was frightened or unnerved, she'd just ride off and leave him. "Listen, Aud, it's hard to explain right now, but you remember you said I could come and visit you sometime? Well, I—I thought I'd take you up on the offer. But perhaps first we could—"

Aud stared suddenly up into the woods. "What was that?"

Halli took a deep breath. "Dogs. Hunting hounds. They're after me."

"Who are?"

He hesitated. "Some people."

Aud Ulfar's-daughter considered him coolly, adjusting her hood, pulling her cloak tighter against the late afternoon chill. "Some people?"

"That's right."

A flick of fair hair had escaped a braid and fallen over the side of her face. She blew it aside and looked at him. "You wouldn't care to be more specific?"

Halli hopped with agitation from one foot to another, staring back repeatedly behind him. "In truth it is something of a personal matter, which I would rather keep to myself than bandy to the four winds, but notwithstanding that I would be so *extremely* grateful if you could just help me out by—"

"How delightful for you," Aud said abruptly. "Well, I mustn't hold you up. No doubt you've many hours yet to run. May I suggest you limp away east again, out of Arnesson territory? I don't want blood spilled here. Goodbye."

Again the horse moved forward; this time Halli flung himself bodily in front of it, speaking at great speed. "It's the Hakonssons!" he cried. "All of them, or most! If they catch me, they'll string me from the highest tree! Aud, help me now and I vow I'll be forever in your debt!"

She raised her eyebrows then; a grin flickered on her face. "I must say I'm intrigued. What did you do *this* time to make them quite so angry?"

Somewhere in the trees at the top of the rise a cacophony of barking erupted, peaked and fragmented as the hounds rushed on. Halli clasped his hands together in what he hoped was a decisive, manly, and yet subtly imploring gesture. "*Please*, I'll tell you everything, only not right now . . ."

Down the slope the pack ran, slipping, tumbling, snapping at fresh scent.

Aud scratched her chin. "Well . . ."

The leaders were hustling through the ferns.

". . . All right, then. Hop on." She reached out a hand and swung him up. With a tug of the reins the horse was away and galloping, just as the first dogs fell out onto the road.

Night fell; the moon rose, softly illuminating the rushing trees. The side of Halli's head bounced repeatedly against Aud's shoulder, and her hair flicked back and forth against his face. He bore it well.

At last the horse's canter slowed. Halli looked up. Ahead, amid a dark circlet of trees, rose the outlines of a House—smaller than Hakon's, bigger, he thought, than Svein's, though without the surrounding wall. A cluster of buildings, lit with merry colored lights, bright, joyful, and welcoming. In the center rose an elegant hall, illuminated windows running down its length. Faintly on the air, Halli smelled good things to eat, and his heart leaped at the thought of feather pillows, hot water, and well-stocked banquet tables.

At which Aud turned aside up an ill-made track to a dilapidated barn, whose doors hung open to the elements. The horse displayed a marked reluctance to enter, but was coerced inside; the black interior was rank and sour, featuring a complex variety of farmyard odors.

Halli spoke carefully. "Where is this?"

"This is the old hay barn."

"Thank you, but I shall do the tour tomorrow. Oughtn't we to step onto the hall for supper?"

"*This* shall be your hall tonight," Aud said. "Do you think my father will welcome a ragged beggar like you with open arms?"

Halli made an affronted noise. "There's such a thing as charity."

"Also such things as suspicion and disgust. The last vagrant who came was rolled in the mill wheel, and *he* would have run in shock from *you*. Even if my father restrained himself, he would be sure to ask some searching questions. About that silver belt beneath your fleece, for one."

"What silver belt?"

Aud shook her head. "Oh, dear. If you wish me to ride back to Hakon's House, I *can*. I know the way."

"Yes, yes, the silver belt. We can talk about that tomorrow."

"All right. It would be best for now if your feet do not touch the ground. We should leave no scent here just in case. Somewhere close is a hatch to the hayloft. Raise your hands and feel the ceiling. Since you are so pitifully short, you may need to stand on the saddle."

She motioned the horse forward slowly, slowly, down the center of the barn. With grim resignation and extreme care, Halli stood on the saddle, holding on to Aud's shoulder with one hand. He reached out teeteringly left and right until a sudden sharp blow to his forehead made lights flare against his eyes. With a cry of woe he toppled to the side.

"Yes, it's beside a low beam," Aud said, grasping him by his arm. "Found it?"

Halli righted himself with difficulty. His voice was faint. "I think so."

"Good. Up you get then. I'll come back tomorrow, when I can."

"With food?"

"If I can. Well, get on. I'm famished and late for dinner. If I don't hurry I'll miss the meats and wine."

Halli made no audible response. He reached up, located an unseen aperture, took hold of its lip. Muscles flaring, body shaking, he pulled himself up and through the hole, rolling over at last to lie spread-eagled on his back. Beneath him, hooves clinked on stone and away along the track. Even before they left the barn, Halli was asleep.

15

SVEIN'S RAIDS ON THE upland farms lasted a couple of months. A few stubborn farmers resisted to begin with, but when they were killed and their buildings burned, the rest swore undying loyalty to the House. Soon Svein controlled all the land south of the river.

"Good," Svein said. "We've got a bit of order in these parts at last."

During the campaign, Svein trained his men in many of the arts of battle, practicing with sword and spear, staff and bow, until they were proficient with them all. Then he turned his attention to the Trows. Traps were set in the fields and lanes between the cottages, so that the monsters were set aflame with tar arrows, crushed with boulders, and harried by the sudden screaming ambush of his camouflaged men.

"This is more like it," said Svein.

A SHARP KICK ON THE backside woke Halli from the soundest of slumbers. His eyes snapped open and gazed stupidly upward at a lattice of beams and rafters, at spiders' webs and hanging flecks of straw. And a girl's face looking at him.

"Rise and shine," it said. "Did you know you're dribbling?"

It ducked away from his field of vision. There followed scuffles, the rasp of cloth and random thuds and clanks. Halli didn't move at first. Consciousness seeped back. He saw shards of daylight glinting between the roof beams. The air was warm and hazy, filled with drifting motes of dust. Doves called beyond the thatch.

"You're *still* dribbling," the voice said. "Try closing your mouth. It helps."

In a sudden flurry of activity Halli coughed, wiped his chin, and struggled to rise—a difficult task, as every inch of his body ached or stung and every muscle pained him. Several joints could barely move at all. When he was more or less upright, he looked across to see Aud Ulfar's-daughter sitting imperturbably on a ceiling beam, watching his progress. She wore a slightly rumpled blue kirtle. It was stained dark at the skirt's base where she had walked through grass. Her fair hair was drawn back behind her head in a single cursory braid.

"Morning, fugitive," she said, and grinned.

Halli looked at her. His face felt bruised and swollen. He rubbed at it with the palms of his hands. "Where's the sun?" he asked. His voice was thick and hesitant.

"Scarcely above the sea. It's early yet, but I thought I'd

check on you. Good job I did, or someone would have come by and heard your snores."

"I was snoring?"

"Like a hog on heat—whole barn shaking, birds wheeling about, dust coming from the rafters and everything. Surprised it didn't collapse on you." She looked him sympathetically up and down. "How are you feeling, anyway?"

"Well, not so—"

"Because you *look* bloody dreadful. I didn't quite realize last night because the light was going, but your face is like *death*, Halli. Your clothes are rags. And I'm not going to ask about those stains are on your leggings. To think I let you press up against my riding cloak last night; I'm going to have to burn it. Your poor feet, too—all scratched and bloodied. I've never *seen* a Founder's son look anything like you, Halli. I bet there's never been anything quite like this in the history of the valley. There'll be corpses under cairns in better nick than you right now."

She took a breath. Halli said: "Well, aside from that I'm in perfect shape, thanks for asking."

"I suppose you want something to eat?"

Halli's hunger was a knife scratching at the inside of his belly—he had not eaten since Hakon's hall, a day and a half before. "Please, if you've got some."

She gestured carelessly at a large cloth bag lying on the hay beside her. "There's food here. Bread, ale, pies, a little meat. I raided the kitchens at the end of the meal last night.

The skin bottle has willow tea to help ease any pain. Have what you want."

In moments Halli was across the intervening space and bending at the bag.

Aud Ulfar's-daughter uttered a squeal. "Arne's ghost."

Halli looked up with a mouthful of pie. "Sorry. I'm just so hungry."

"It's not that. I hadn't realized quite how ragged your tunic was."

"Oh."

Adjusting his posture hurriedly, Halli went on eating. The willow tea was, as expected, horribly bitter. The ale and pies had a better taste and brought on the full fury of his thirst and hunger.

Aud had retreated to a safe distance. "It's like feeding the pigs. Listen, I'm going. I want to hunt out some old clothes of Father's. They won't fit you but it'll be amusing to watch you try them. I'll be back in a bit. Stay here."

Halli looked up, pastry flaking at his mouth. "Aud, I—I haven't thanked you yet for what you've done. It's really . . . Well, that is, I don't know how to—"

She had reached the loft hatch, where the top of a ladder protruded, and leaped down onto it gracefully, long braid swinging. "Oh, please. It's not often I have an outlaw in my barn. It's an honor. Also, last night you groveled in the dirt and vowed to be in my debt forever—remember? I can't let an opportunity like that slip, can I? I have to keep you alive. Speaking of which, don't go out. I heard horses coming into the yard just as I went out the back. It's probably nothing, but I'd better find out what's going on. Then I'm coming back—to hear it all from you. I want the full story—nothing left out. Better get your strength up."

She winked at him and waved. Light from the open barn below lit up her face as she dropped from view. Halli returned to the bag.

Afterward, his belly aching, he waited for Aud's return. In the far corner of the loft there was a place where the thatch had broken open, allowing a thin oval of sunlight to spill onto the hay. Halli went to look out of the hole—he saw vegetable fields, trim lines of autumn crops, low walls, the margins of the Arnesson forest. Craning his neck through he could just see some of the outbuildings of the House away to his left—long, low, red-roofed—distant cottages and solitary trees. The scene was peaceful, ordinary, pleasant: he felt utterly detached from it. Abruptly, he drew his head inside.

Halli went to sit on the opposite side of the hayloft, where the shadows were brown and dim. More than once he heard the people of Arne's House going about their unknown business. He heard women passing, laughing together softly; the noise made him think suddenly of his mother. He heard men's voices at a distance, too far for clarity. Once hooves went past the barn at speed.

He let the sounds flow in and out of him; he did not stir, but sat staring into space. Thanks to the willow tea, the pain of his body was lessening, but the numbness he felt was more than that. Likewise, with his stomach full he became aware of an utter emptiness inside—no longer a lack of food, but the absence of any kind of passion. Anger, hatred, grief, and fear—the emotions that had swirled unceasingly within him, that had driven him ever onward through these recent weeks, that had so filled and shaped his mind—had all utterly drained away, leaving only their shape, their mold, behind them.

For an entire day he had not had space to consider their loss, but he saw now that they were gone even before he fled from Olaf's room. The revelation that he could not kill, that his entire journey was based on an utterly false premise, had turned his emotions inside out. His lack of self-knowledge shocked him, and all the ideals he had held so close, for so long, were knocked spinning into the air. He had been physically unable to avenge his kinsman, unable to do the necessary thing that the heroes' creed demanded. True, Olaf had afterward met his death, more or less accidentally—Halli had no doubt that the fiery tapestry had done its work—but what of that? Halli, reflecting on it, felt not even the dullest satisfaction.

Other certainties had been damaged in that room, foremost among them his worship of his uncle. Loath as Halli was to believe the story Olaf told, he could not deny it chimed with things he had heard at home. Brodir had been reckless in his youth and had forfeited them much land . . . so much he had heard from his family's own lips. Had he been a killer also? Halli didn't know. But that he had disgraced Svein's House long ago—and awoken the wrath of the men of Hakon—seemed all too clear.

Now Halli, by his actions, had followed in Brodir and Olaf's footsteps too. Another man was dead, a House aflame. . . . And all for what? Sitting alone in the dimness of the loft, Halli had no answer.

What could he do now? Where could he go? The only good thing about the matter was that his pursuers did not know him. He had stayed too far ahead throughout the chase. But if he was caught, if they found him in his current state . . . He blew out his cheeks. Well, Aud had saved him. It was thanks to her he was still alive.

He thought of her face at the ladder, lit by excitement and the morning sun. She had no idea. No idea what he had done. And she *shouldn't* know either—he straightened abruptly, setting his chin resolutely upward—she shouldn't be drawn in. When she got back, if she gave him clothes, he would thank her and depart. He wouldn't endanger her any further. No story, nothing.

A fleeting sensation of noble melancholy was still washing through him when he heard a sudden scraping on the ladder below and saw Aud's fair head and ragged pigtail rise into view. She hopped off the ladder and crouched down by the hole, breathing hard, her face purple with exertion. Her shoulders were high and tense, her face impassive, but her eyes were bright and shining. She looked at Halli. She looked at him in a way that she hadn't looked at him before. It was more of a gaze.

After a time Halli said, "So, er, no luck with the clothes?"

She shook her head minutely, still gazing at him.

Halli cleared his throat. "Look, you know how grateful I am. Clothes aside, I was wondering—do you think you could find me a horse? Well, it would need to be more of a pony actually. A smallish one. Not overly round in the belly. I have stirrup issues. The thing is I think I should leave here as soon as I can, so as not to . . . not to get you into trouble."

"You want to leave?"

"It would be best."

Aud gave a little laugh. She moved away from the hatch to a place where a crack of sunlight warmed the hay and sat cross-legged, smoothing her kirtle over her knees. Then she said: "I'm not sure that's a good idea right now."

"No?"

"No. You remember I heard hooves arriving at the House a while ago?"

Halli sighed. "Someone from Hakon's?"

"Not someone. *Thirty* men, all on horseback, all with

knives and ropes and hunting spears and I don't know what else. Hord Hakonsson himself leads them; when I got back he was in conference with my father, bearing news." Aud regarded Halli steadily. "It is some news. Perhaps you'd like to hear it. It seems that two nights ago an unknown intruder broke into Hakon's hall, killed Hord's brother Olaf, and set the place alight before diving into the moat and fleeing. They tracked him yesterday to the eastern edges of our forest where, if the trail marks are to be believed, he was picked up by a horseman and spirited away. The tracks were lost, but Hord intends to search far and wide until the killer and his accomplice are found."

Halli spoke haltingly. "Aud, look—I didn't intend you to get into—"

"Here's another thing," Aud went on. "The moment I arrived I was called in to speak with Hord. My father knew I'd been riding in the forest last night, you see. They questioned me closely about where I'd been and what I'd seen. They were very persistent. It was hard for a girl. In the end I told them—" She hesitated, watching Halli's face, which shone rather taut and pale in the dimness of the loft. "I told them I'd seen no one. Of *course* I didn't tell them anything! Why should I? Like I give a dung-straw for the Hakonssons! It's bad enough my stupid, spineless father should agree to Hord's every demand—he's already given them permission to conduct a thorough search of Arnesson lands. *Our* lands, like it belonged to *them!* They'll be rummaging in every barn and byre from here to the valley road for days." She scuffed a toe irritably in the straw. "So in short I'd stay put, if I were you."

Halli wiped a bead of sweat from his temple. "You know, this loft *is* cozy," he said. "Maybe I *will* stay here a while." A thought struck him. "Wait, won't they check here too?"

"Oh, they won't search the buildings of our *House*. That would be too dishonorable even for Father." She scowled to herself, then folded her arms. "There's no suggestion we're mixed up in the affair, just that the criminal has fled onto our lands. Speaking of which, Halli Sveinsson, isn't it time you told me all?"

He looked away from her. "No. It's best if I don't drag you in any deeper. I've endangered you enough as it is. Besides the story is not particularly interesting and I'm not sure I care to tell it. Not that I'm ungrateful for your help, you understand."

"Of course, of course." Aud tapped her fingers together briskly and rose to leave. "I'm going now. I feel an urge to sing up and down the House. It shall be a ballad of my own devising, entitled 'The Boy You Want Is in the Hay-barn.' Here's a sample couplet: 'Come, men, bring your axes, Halli's hiding here/See, in that straw, his bottom shaking; jab it with a spear.' What do you think?"

Halli stared at her. "You wouldn't do that."

"Wouldn't I? Better get talking."

It was not pride that made Halli reluctant to speak of his experiences, nor fear of the consequences of telling Aud, for he trusted her completely. Rather, it was the hollowness inside him. Already that day, as he had sat alone in the silence of the loft, a deadening emptiness had seemed about to swallow him. Now he dreaded what talking about it all might do. But there was no help for it.

"All right," he said. "Though I don't know where to begin."

"How about your uncle's death?" Aud said sweetly. "I was there, remember? Would that have anything to do with this?"

"It might."

Slowly at first, hesitantly, hauling the words up from deep within him, he told her everything. Of his family's indifference and his silent fury; of his taking of the hero's belt and his father's knife. Of Snorri's hut and Bjorn the trader and his tribulations in the lower valley. He did not embellish or exaggerate; he left nothing out. As he went on, and the telling grew easier, he found himself talking frankly about each setback, culminating in his bleak revelation in Olaf's room. Curiously, the more he spoke, the better he felt. As it had been in the orchard, long ago, so it was now—Aud seemed to draw truth from him. The great weight that had borne him down since Brodir's death shifted a little; fresh air stirred it and lifted it off his back. His head felt clearer than it had done for a long while.

Aud didn't interrupt or comment once, until the tale was done.

"So you *didn't* kill him then," she said. "Not purposefully, anyhow."

"No. I couldn't do it. I just couldn't." He shook his head miserably. "Right at the beginning that mad old man, Snorri, told me that I'd be no better than Olaf Hakonsson myself if I did what I set out to do. And I laughed at him. But then, when I had my uncle's killer there before me, I felt, I felt . . ." He made a helpless gesture. "Aud, I don't know what my weakness was, but I just felt physically . . . I couldn't bring myself to use the knife."

"Oh, but it wasn't weakness," Aud Ulfar's-daughter began. "Halli, listen—"

"It was like everything I believed just turned upside-down. And that wasn't the only time it happened. That man in the gorge. He tried to murder me. I thought he was an out-law, like the ones in the tales. But no! He was a respected man of Eirik's House! And I killed him."

Aud made a scornful noise through her nose. "Oh, come *on*. He attacked *you* and *he* stepped off the edge. Didn't he? You didn't push him. And the same applies to Olaf too. You didn't strike him down. It was his own fault he died, chasing you."

Halli grunted. "I suppose. Your argument sounds a bit technical. I'm not sure the Council would agree."

"Listen to me, Halli," Aud said. She shuffled forward,

stretched out her hand to touch him, and withdrew it abruptly. "Actually I *won't* if you don't mind. I must get you some water. Listen, Halli—when I heard what the Hakonssons said I didn't know what to think. It sounded . . . Well, I needed to hear it from you, what happened. It's just that if you *had* killed Olaf like you planned, I would have—" She shrugged, her face suddenly quiet, serious. "But you didn't. I didn't think you had. And I'm glad of it, that's all."

For a brief silence they looked at one another, then Halli found himself staring at portions of the loft floor. He cleared his throat. "You're very kind, but it's just that—"

"Shh." She had a finger to her lips.

Halli frowned. "Well, don't you think it's my turn—"

She shook her head furiously and got to her feet, pointing behind him at the slanting lattice roof. Pinpricks of light showed through the old thatch and between the beams. Down there was the road they had come in on, the way to Arne's hall. He heard horses, metal jingling, the coughing of weary men approaching.

Halli was on his feet in an instant, his aches and stiffness forgotten.

He stood beside Aud, silent and wary in the darkness of the loft.

Surely they would go past. They were on their way back to the forest. Surely—

The noises slowed, halted. A voice sounded—a deep

voice, a familiar voice, abrupt and condescending. "And *this*, Ulfar?"

In his mind's eye, Halli saw Aud's white-haired father, emollient, placating, scuttling up the track, keeping pace behind Hord's steed. "It is the old hay-barn, not much used, except in years of plenty which, Arne save us, we shall shortly have again." Ulfar sounded anxious, strained.

"We can look here too?" Hord said. It was more a statement than a question.

Halli and Aud stared at one other, faces white as ghosts. They stared across at the open loft hatch, at the haze of light spilling up from below.

"Of course! Check the loft, check its darkest corners! If he is here you may hang him in my yard outside my window! And if anyone of my House has helped him, they shall dance alongside! Yes, they will indeed! I will string them up myself."

"Yes, yes, Ulfar. You are very good. All right. Bork, Einar—take a look inside."

Bits rattled, leather creaked, heavy boots landed on the road. They crunched across stones toward the doors below.

16

SVEIN BECAME DISSATISFIED with the appearance of his House, which was little more than a few dilapidated cottages set amid the fields. "We can do better than this," said Svein.

He had his men drag pine trees down from the forests and set them quarrying stone, but when they began the hall, they ran into problems. The walls kept tumbling down.

There was an old woman up by Lank Mere who was said to be a witch. Most people avoided her, but Svein got on with her well enough. He went to ask about the walls.

"That's easy," she said. "You need someone to guard the foundations."

"Anyone in particular?"

"Young, handsome, strong. That sort of thing."

So Svein went back and chose a youth from the prisoners taken during the raids. He was killed and buried in the foundations, and after that the hall rose high and strong.

FOR SEVERAL HEARTBEATS Halli and Aud stood utterly transfixed, as—separated from them by only a few feet of air and a narrow thickness of wood—two men entered the barn. They listened to the scrabbling of footsteps on the earthen floor, to other indefinable fragments of sound that told of steady, purposeful movement to left and right across the space below.

The men would be checking the stalls, the old animal partitions; looking in hay piles too, if such there were. It wouldn't take them long to exhaust the possibilities.

Then they would climb the ladder.

Halli cast his eyes wildly about the loft space, at the sparse clumps and rills of straw that covered the flooring, at the sloping roof beams choked with webs.

Blank. Bare. Nowhere to go.

Except—

He grasped Aud's sleeve, distantly surprised at the slimness of the arm beneath the wool; when she looked up he jerked his head, pointed away to the rear of the barn, to where a ragged oval of light shone through.

The hole in the thatch.

Her face showed no acknowledgment, but she must have understood, because she was away from him instantly, moving across the loft with rapid steps that were at the same time soundless. Halli, following, found he could not go at anything like her speed without risking fatal noise. With ponderous care he negotiated the beams, thinking at any moment to hear a shouted challenge from the hatch behind him.

At the far corner Aud waited with an expression of aghast impatience; ignoring this as best he could, Halli leaned through the hole as he had done earlier that day. He scanned the fields cursorily, saw no one near and, grasping the rough dry thatch on either side, pulled himself forward and out into the open air.

The roof was layered with thick straw sheaves, originally tightly bound, but now old, worn and ragged. Its pitch was steep, and not far below the hole ended altogether with a long drop to a pile of building stones, wood spars, and tangled thorn.

Breathing hard, Halli drew himself out until his knees rested on the lip of the hole. His fingers scrabbled for purchase on either side. To his consternation the straw was loose; rough hanks came free in his grasp.

A frantic whisper came from behind. "For Arne's sake don't make such a meal of it. Shift your bum."

Halli twisted, seized straw above and to the right of the hole, and swung himself out. His toes found a hold; now he clung safely to the outside of the roof.

Somewhere distant, away and below in the barn's lower space, a voice spoke. He couldn't hear what it said.

Aud plunged forward through the hole. Halli stretched out a hand.

As she grasped it, a look of horror spread across her

face. The two actions were unconnected; she mouthed something and at the selfsame instant Halli realized what they had forgotten.

They had left the bags.

Before Halli could react she had ripped her hand from his, and ducked back out of sight.

Halli cursed under his breath. Clinging to the thatch one-handed, he craned his head over the hole, squinting in at the darkness.

There was Aud flitting away across the loft. There was the ladder. Its ends were shaking. Boots sounded on rungs.

With rapid steps Aud passed close behind the loft hatch. She scooped up Halli's bag from the straw, then crossed to where her cloth bag lay, open and empty. Taking it in one hand, she turned to go, then bent, and with the flat palm of the other, made violent brushing motions among the straw.

Halli stared in disbelief. Then he recalled the speed and ferocity of his meal—all the crumbs he'd scattered.

The ladder quivered. Aud looked up.

Halli gesticulated furiously at her. *Come on.*

Aud stopped brushing; without straightening, back bent low, she sped across the loft space, hopping between beams. Still she made no noise.

Now she was at the hole again, shoving the bags into Halli's waiting hand. Grasping the straw on both sides, she raised a knee, wedged a foot into the gap and thrust herself through, up and out—onto the roof. She was significantly faster than Halli had been, her momentum much greater. And she had not secured a handhold.

Out onto the lip of the hole she sprang, reached for the straw, lost her balance, fell forward—

Halli shot out a hand, grabbed her passing pigtail, and swung her around so she fell against him. Flailing arms scratched at his tunic; fingers found Svein's belt. Halli clung one-handed to the roof. Bracing her feet against the bottom of the roof thatch, Aud hung from Halli, suspended by hair and belt.

Someone jumped from the ladder into the hayloft.

Floorboards squeaked, boots scuffed through straw. A cough sounded, followed by a loud thud, possibly of head on beam, and a vehement curse. The noises moved close, then retreated. Above them, in the autumn sunlight, pink-white doves fluttered on the roof crest. Aud swung gently to and fro. Halli didn't move. His fingers, locked into the straw, grew slippery with sweat.

The search was neither long nor rigorous, but for Halli it seemed to go on forever—an endless sequence of silences and sudden footfalls, seemingly right beside the hole. His arm ached, his shoulder shook. His teeth pressed hard against his bottom lip.

Then: steps once more upon the ladder. Distant voices. Hooves moving away down the track on the other side of the barn.

Halli let out his pent-up breath. Aud pulled herself forward to grip the thatch beside him. They perched a while in silence.

"Close," Halli said.

"Yes." A grin. Then, "Halli?"

"What?"

"You can let go of my hair now."

Back in the safety of the loft, the exertion of the event caught up with Halli. His legs shook, his heart beat fast; he sat abruptly and rubbed his face with his hands.

Aud, by contrast, seemed energized by her experience. If she had been excited before, she was now almost radiant with agitation. She paced about the loft, arms swinging, feet kicking at the straw, marveling at the closeness of their escape.

"You'll be all right now," she said. "Safe. No one'll come back here now. No one ever does usually. My bloody father! Can you *believe* him? 'Oh yes, great Hord, I'll do anything you ask. I'll kill my own people if you tell me too. Look anywhere you like, trample our crops, pry into every corner of our House.' Ah! I'm surprised he didn't put on a saddle and bit and invite Hord to ride him across the fields. I *hate* my father! I hate him."

Halli, suddenly weary, shrugged. "Maybe he has no choice. They're his neighbors. He knows how powerful they are. How can he refuse them?"

"Huh." Aud was scathing. "My *mother* would have had no truck with Hord. One step out of place, she'd have sent him packing with a broom handle up—" Her voice was lost as she rounded a roof strut. "I reckon he'd have had trouble with his swagger then."

"She sounds a fine woman," Halli said.

"She was of Ketil's House. They're bluntly spoken."

"You take after your mother, at a guess."

"I have nothing of my father in me, that's for sure. We have little joy in each other's company." For a moment the light went out of her face. "In fact he's made no secret of his intention to marry me off as quickly as possible. Every chance he gets he touts me as if I were a nice plump bullock at the fair. But enough of boring stuff like that." She grinned again. "Halli—that was such a *close* one! You were *so clever* to think of the roof—I'd never have *dared* on my own. Now I understand how you survived everything you did."

Halli gave a short, humorless laugh. "Survived, yes. Achieved, nothing. What was it all for? Brodir's still dead and I'm no better off than when I started. Worse off, in fact, since I suppose I'll have to go back to my House now to the usual round of beatings and abuse. Svein knows what my parents'll do to me when I reappear."

Aud flopped down in the straw beside him. "You'll go back home?"

"Well, what else can I do? Wander about as a man without a House? No one would welcome me. I've seen enough of the valley to know that. I'll be treated as a beggar or a thief. Admittedly it doesn't help that I *did* actually rob people in half the Houses between here and the gorge. The Eirikssons in particular would delight in finding the man who killed their trader." He sighed. "No, I'll be going home."

"At least you won't have to make some marriage of convenience to satisfy your father," Aud said bitterly. "Being a second son you're spared all that. I'll be hitched to some fool to shore up the fortunes of this House, then have to sit beside him on Arne's Law Seats for years, deliberating about who stole which sheep, who put the dark eye on whose pig, and how many chickens they get in compensation. A world of fascinating adventure. My aunt's been teaching me the Law for six months now, and I've already nearly throttled her with boredom."

"Sorry, that's better than what's in store for me," Halli said. "You get the Law Seats. I get the remote farm up in the hills, where I'll work as tenant to my brother all my life."

"Oh, come *on*. That can't be too bad."

"You reckon? Know the farm's name? Far Bogside. The last incumbent died of marsh foot. You don't get any wolves round there, but only because they drown."

Aud let out her short, barking laugh. Halli laughed too. It was the first time he had done so in weeks.

"I didn't hurt you, did I?" he said. "When I got you by the hair?"

"Oh, yes. It was excruciating. Thanks for that, by the way."

"Well done on getting the bags."

"Yes, that nearly did for us. What's *in* yours? Felt light."

"Nothing much, anymore. That fake Trow claw the trader tried to kill me with."

"You know, Halli," Aud said, "I knew you were different when we met that day at your House. When you tricked Ragnar with that foul keg of ale. . . . You're not afraid of things, are you?"

Halli's brow furrowed. "Not in the way my parents are—or your father is, maybe. But I *do* get afraid. It's just that fear makes me sort of . . . angry and resentful, and I bite back at it. It's hard to describe."

"It isn't hard to describe, you idiot," Aud said. "It's called courage."

"No." He frowned then. "No. I told you what happened when I got to Olaf. That was the key moment, and I failed."

Aud threw back her head and groaned. "Not *this* again! Your mistake, Halli Sveinsson, is that you aspire to the wrong thing. You did a hundred brave acts during your trip down here, but they weren't the ones you were expecting. You kept waiting to find a sword somewhere so you could fight outlaws and monsters, and finally lop off Olaf's head. None of that happened, did it? So you're disappointed. But you shouldn't be, Halli, because it's nonsense, all of that. It's just stuff that happens in the stories. None of it's real."

Halli looked at her in some perplexity. "'Stories?' You've said this before. You mean the heroes?"

"The heroes, the Trows—the stories that bind us, Halli. The stories we all live by, that dictate what we do and where we go. The stories that give us our names, our identities, the places we belong, the people we hate. All of it."

"You don't believe them?"

"No. Do you?"

"Well, yes, I mean . . ." He pulled at his nose, looked all about him. "You don't think the heroes lived? Or fought the Trows? What about the Battle of the Rock? Do you deny all that?"

"Oh, *something* happened maybe. Men with the names Arne and Svein and Hakon and the rest lived, I don't doubt. Their bones are in the cairns, unless they've rotted all away. But did they do everything the stories say? No."

"But—"

"*Think* about it, Halli," she said. "Think how the stories overlap and contradict each other, how they're told differently up and down the valley. Think of what the heroes are supposed to have done. Take Arne, dear Founder of this House. He could throw boulders the size of cowsheds and leap over rivers in full spate. He once climbed the cataracts holding a baby in one hand, though precisely *why* he did so I forget."

"Perhaps there's *some* exaggeration that's crept in over the years," Halli began, "but—"

"What else? He took on ten men with his hands tied

behind his back, though what he fought with in that instance I don't dare guess. Oh, and he went into the hill and killed the Trow-king before coming home for breakfast."

"No," Halli put in, "it was supper. And I think you'll find *Svein* did that."

Aud gave a cry of frustration. "No, he *didn't*, Halli. Svein *didn't* do it, and neither did Arne. You, above everyone, should be able to vouch for this. What have you tried to be, these last few weeks? Well? You've tried to be like Svein, haven't you? How did it work out? How many boulders did you toss? How many rivers did you leap? How many outlaws' heads did you bring home in a little string bag?"

"A little string bag?" Halli frowned. "Sounds a bit girly. Who did that? Arne?"

Aud had flushed slightly. "No, no, I think it was Gest, or one of the other rubbish ones. Concentrate on what I'm saying. You went on this journey because you believed all those old wives'-tales and wanted to spin one about yourself. Didn't you?"

"No, it was my uncle—"

"Only in part. Admit it."

"Well—"

"It's true you're a bit extreme, but you're not the only one at it. Everyone's fixated with the tales. Remember Brodir and Hord swapping insults about each other's heroes during the feast? Say something rude about someone's Founder and it's like you've struck them in the face. It's pathetic. And you know what? Deep down it's all about rules, all about keeping everyone in their place."

Aud had got to her feet while saying this, and was circling the loft space, taking small, delicate steps over raised beams and ducking swiftly round the struts and jambs, talking animatedly, indifferent to the webs that caught in her hair and the must and grime that rubbed upon her kirtle. Her eyes burned bright in the darkened space, her face shone. Halli found he was staring at her open-mouthed.

"Are you all right?" she asked suddenly, swinging outward from a post. Her braid had come undone, and her hair hung loose.

"Yes. Yes. I was just going to say . . . I don't know what I was going to say."

"The worst of it is the cairns," Aud went on. "That stuff about the Trows. We suckle in our dread of them with our mothers' milk. But no one ever sees them. No one ever hears them. No one—"

"Well, that's because no one crosses the boundary."

"Exactly! No one dares. Because the heroes set the boundaries, and their old rules still apply. Even though there's good grazing up there! And who knows what else. When I sit by Mother's cairn, it gets me so angry. Arne's House could do with that extra land, as I expect Svein's could. But no. A Trow will eat you. The heroes made the rules and that's that."

"You know what I don't like about the cairns?" Halli

said, watching the patterns of her movement across the far side of the loft. "It's the look of them. The look of them up on the brow of the hill. It's like they get between me and the sun."

"Yes! They supposed to protect us, but it feels like the reverse. The way you can always see them. It's like they pen us in."

"But it wasn't always that way," Halli went on. "The heroes went up there. And the settlers too, of course. They came from somewhere beyond. Where was that? How did they get over the mountains? What's the other place like? I often wonder about that. They crossed into the valley up near Svein's House—or so the story goes. I suppose your people say the same about Arne's."

Aud turned then, and he sensed her scrutiny, though her face was now in shadow. "No," she said slowly. "They don't say that about Arne's. What, is there a path above Svein's, or something?"

"I don't know. I'd have to ask Katla." He sighed. "If she ever speaks to me again after what I did. If any of them do."

"Well, you won't be entirely alone. Don't forget I'm coming to stay with you over winter, so that I avoid the next outbreak of creep. Father wouldn't want me dead before he gets me safely . . . married off. . . ." Her voice trailed away; it was as if her mind was suddenly elsewhere. She was still now, almost for the first time.

Halli was saying, "I don't know what I think about the

Trows, really. It's true not everyone believes in them. Hord Hakonsson doesn't, for one—I heard him say as much to Ragnar. But what irritates me is that no one dares challenge the old edicts! Surely swords could be made again, and an expedition could go up to see if—what?" Aud was approaching him through the loft, eyes shining. Halli drew back with sudden caution. "What?"

"I've got it!" Her grin was broad, decisive, and welcoming: it made Halli feel as if he'd already agreed to whatever it was she was about to say. The sensation was troubling, but not entirely unpleasant. "I've got it!" she said again. "That's what we'll do."

"And what's 'that,' exactly?"

"Halli," she said, crouching by him, "you've wanted to do something worthy of the heroes, haven't you? Well, now you can, and I'll do it with you. I say that the Trows don't exist and never have, and you think it too, though you're loath to admit it. So let's see, shall we? This winter, when the snows have cleared, we'll cross the boundary. We'll test the tales. And when we've done that we'll go up beyond the cairns and find the path across the mountains. The one the settlers took." She laughed at the expression on his face. "Don't you see? It'll solve everything! We can forget Far Bogside and Father's marriage plans and just get out. Escape all the rules and restrictions, and the influence of men like Hord. We'll cross the boundary and leave the valley for good. You and me together. What do you say?"

17

Svein's House had its great new hall, but each night the Trows still came snuffling about the doors. This angered Svein. He began building protective walls around the perimeter of the site. He worked his people hard, but after a year the job still wasn't half done.

"This is no good," Svein said. "I need more hands."

The valley north of the river was controlled by the hero Rurik. It seemed to Svein that Rurik had able-bodied men to spare. Svein took a cudgel and a length of rope, went to the river, and dove in. He swam across the torrents, shook himself dry, walked to the nearest farmstead, and knocked on the door. Four men looked out.

"I need workers for my wall," Svein said. "You'll do. Come out and we'll discuss it."

The farmhands ran out, swords swinging, but Svein knocked them senseless with the cudgel, tied them up, swam them back across the river, and put them to work.

He got two dozen men this way, and soon the walls were finished nicely.

THREE DAYS PASSED. On the morning of the third day, word came to Ulfar Arnesson that the Hakonssons had given up their manhunt across his lands and were returning to their House. Their patrols upon the central valley road were likewise disbanded. It was said that Hord Hakonsson's brow was black as he rode for home; few of his men dared approach him and no one spoke loudly in his presence.

When darkness fell the people of Arne's House gathered in their hall for the evening meal. The paths around the House grew quiet, thick with shadow. Nothing stirred. All at once there was a movement in the black interior of the old hay barn. A muttered curse, the slap of a hand on a horse's rump. Out from the barn came a short, cowled figure riding a short, plump pony. The figure took a lingering look toward the gleaming windows of the House, then flicked the reins vigorously. The pony sped up not one whit, but with exactly the same leisurely rolling gait proceeded across the road and down a sidetrack into the trees.

During his time in the barn Halli's physical fortunes had dramatically improved. Each day Aud had brought him food and water to wash with; each day his injuries had healed and he had grown a little in strength. His old clothes were taken by Aud and thrown to the pigs; in their place Halli now wore a gray twill servant's tunic, with the plum sleeve slash that denoted the House of Arne. He had little resemblance now to the ragged fugitive who had fled from Hakon's lands.

Even so he proceeded up-valley with all due care. He traveled mainly in early morning and late evening, holing up during the populous portions of the day in roadside woods. On nights when the moon was full he traveled by its light. He was careful to avoid those regions where his face or figure might be remembered, took circuitous routes where necessary, and stopped for supplies only at the more remote farms. His caution paid off. Almost to his surprise he arrived in the wastes below the cataracts without being tarred, feathered, hung, or shot at, and with no one greatly conscious of his passing.

Neither Halli nor the pony, which Aud had stolen from a paddock of ancient, worn-out beasts, was in shape to climb the gorge at speed. Their ascent took three full days. During that time Halli passed several travelers descending: three wool traders from Gest's House, leading a train of horses laden with bulging sacks; a messenger hurrying from Rurik's House to Thord's; and last, close below the scree-slopes of the Snag, a young musician with his harp. Each man spoke pleasantly; no one tried to stab him. Still, Halli was beset by unsettling memories, particularly when he passed the little circular glade with the ash circle in its center. He did not camp there, but perched for the night on a narrow ledge a little higher up, listening to the crashing of the falls.

When he awoke at dawn, his cloak and hair stiff with

frost, he glanced up at the cliffs to the north, and saw, beyond the highest pines, a row of distant cairns. They seemed arrayed in silent challenge.

Aud's proposal, startling though it was, did not alarm him as once it might have done. In fact, when the first surprise wore off, Halli's objections quickly faded; it seemed that the more Aud talked, the sounder her theories about the Trows became. In part this was because her skepticism concerning the legends awoke questions that he had always harbored, in part because the flattery that she occasionally bestowed on him helped rebuild his battered confidence. In part it was because she sat so close, eyes sparkling in the half-light. But above all the adventure she proposed—dangerous and reckless as it was—went a long way to filling the hole inside him, the hollowness that his experiences had left behind. The strength of her desire was infectious, their shared confidences heady and alluring. Exploring the forbidden hills, risking the existence of the Trows, gave him a thrill of anticipation that made him feel alive. It contrasted utterly with the despondency he felt returning home.

When he had set off from Svein's House on his mission of vengeance, he had not thought much about what would happen when he got back. But deep down his hope then had been clear and simple: to be hailed a hero, an accomplisher of great deeds. Now all that was dust upon the wind, for his encounter with Olaf had transformed him utterly. His certainties had vanished and he no longer trusted the impulse that had driven him to act. All he knew for sure was that he neither wanted nor deserved acknowledgment for his actions. No one at his House needed to know where he had been and what had happened. He would keep quiet, make up some story, accept the inevitable punishments, and get back to normal. At least, until Aud came.

Above the cataracts, autumn was far advanced, and winter fast approaching. The trees were leafed with red and orange and snow hung low upon the hills. As on the outward journey mists shrouded the hanging saddle of the valley and the burial mounds beside the road. Looking neither right nor left Halli urged the pony on.

At Snorri's hut no light shone in the window and no one answered when he knocked upon the door. Presumably the old man was off somewhere in his fields, lopping beets with Arnkel's knife. Halli sighed. Yet another misdeed to be accounted for when he got home.

It was scarcely four weeks since he had last walked across Svein's lands, but the familiar fields seemed strange to him. He went without haste, allowing the pony to plod its weary way. There was no one on the road.

Dusk had fallen when he reached the House. As always the North Gate hung open. Descending from the pony, he led it through the gate and up past the workers' cottages to the little yard. Some people saw him then—he glimpsed Kugi gawping from the sty and Brusi frozen by the well; he heard the sound of his name rippling away along the side alleys and in and out of buildings, where pots boiled over on hearths, and men and women left their evening work to come and stare, so that before he reached the hall the whole House knew, even the goat girl, Gudrun, in her little hut beyond the midden. Halli took no notice of any of this. He led the pony up to the yard and tethered it, then, shouldering his pack a final time, walked under the porch and into the hall, where the early evening lights were burning.

His family was at the table. Old Eyjolf saw him first and cried out in astonishment and alarm. Then his mother came rushing, and his father also, and there was Katla bawling her eyes out by the fire, and his sister and brother looking furious and joyful all at once, and then he was enveloped by them all, and the self-imposed silence of his journey was filled with sudden clamor, even as the breath was almost driven from his body.

Halli's homecoming spread pleasure throughout the House and not a person there was untouched by the joy and relief felt by his family. This was for the first five minutes; thereafter things quickly became more complicated as bewilderment and anger set in.

It had been widely assumed, following Katla's account of their last meeting, that Halli, in grief at his uncle's death, had gone up the hill on the day of the funeral, perhaps to observe from a distance. When he did not return, searchers scoured the crags and quarries as high as was safe, until, after several days—when no trace of him had been discovered—the answer was reluctantly accepted by all. Halli, whether by accident or on purpose, had crossed beyond the cairns and would not be seen again.

In the gloom that followed, collective memories of Halli became encompassed by a hazy warming light; his zest and love of life were fondly recalled, his escapades chuckled over, his vanished promise affirmed beside the ale kegs. Now that he had suddenly reappeared, thinner about the face but evidently entirely well, the hazy light snuffed promptly out, and everyone vied with each other to recall anew his many faults and the irritations that he so regularly caused.

Halli cared little enough for most people's opinions, but the distress of his family affected him more than he had expected. He told them the story that he had prepared during his journey home and then fell silent, submitting to their outrage.

"You went to explore the valley?" Arnkel roared. "Just that? Without my leave?"

"You begged at the porches of the down-valley Houses?" Astrid cried, tearing at her hair. "Do you understand the *shame* you have brought upon your family?"

"You, a son of Svein, went about the land in a servant's tunic?" Leif shouted. "Then, when that was rags, took that of a servant of *another* House? Where is your pride?"

"You left us weeping," Gudny said simply. "Your mother

has not smiled from that day to this. What do you say to *that*, brat?"

To all of which, when he got a word in edgewise, Halli gave brief responses:

"I was grieving for Brodir. I could not be here a moment longer.

"I saw to it that no one knew my name.

"I did not feel worthy to wear our colors.

"I know the sorrow I have caused you, and I am sorry. But now I am back."

Whether any of his replies were heard amid the hubbub was unclear; even if they had been, it was doubtful anyone would have considered them satisfactory. The interrogation continued, on and off, for several days, as did the ebb and flow of relief and rage. Halli was shouted at, hugged, ignored, and wept at in bewildering rotation. He was beaten by Arnkel too—not once, but whenever a new slant on his wickedness came to his father's attention, which was often.

Halli made no protest. It was just punishment and he knew it.

What disconcerted him most was Katla's response. In contrast to his family, the old nurse fell silent and kept her distance from him.

"Come on, Katla. Talk to me."

"For weeks I've wept for little Halli. He is dead and gone."

"But no—look, here I am! I'm back—"

"The boy *I* knew would never have been so callous, so selfish as you have been. Go away and let me grieve."

Try as he might, she would not be comforted.

Despite the wonder of his return, preparations for winter were fully underway, and people had little time to spare for a wastrel second son. The clouds over Svein's House grew lower with each day. The livestock was driven nearer and nearer to the Trow walls; food was stockpiled, repairs made to the roofs and walls of the animal sheds. Halli took his place among the workers and set to quietly, and it was soon noticed that he was stronger and quicker than before, his face leaner, his eyes harder and more steely. Those who resented his escapade bit back their gibes when they saw this, and many people looked at him sidelong.

One day Halli was summoned to his parents' room. Arnkel, who had become rather gaunt during the autumn, and who was troubled by a recurring cough, sat awkwardly in his chair, staring up at nothing. His mother stood alongside, her gaze, as usual, piercing.

Arnkel glanced at Halli with the tail of his eye, then looked away.

"Still here?" he said. "Haven't run off again?"

"Father, I've said I'm sorry—"

"Your apologies were threadbare before; do not wear them out further. Enough of this. Your mother and I have a question for you. Kar Gestsson passed by this House yesterday, peddling the last of his mangy fleeces. I took two just to be hospitable, but that is by the by. Kar brought news from far down-valley. He says—and I have always found him truthful, if incoherent through lack of teeth—he says"—all at once Arnkel's eyes were full on Halli, watching his face closely—"that Olaf Hakonsson is dead, and his hall burned down. What do you know of this?"

Halli's stomach knotted, but he kept his face calm. "Dead? How, Father?"

"It is not yet clear. Foul play, apparently."

Halli's mother said: "There are rumors of a lone intruder . . ."

Rubbing his chin, as if in deep thought, Halli said: "This is startling news. I did see smoke on the air once, drifting from the east. Perhaps that was the hall."

"So you did not go to Hakon's House during your wanderings?"

"No, Father."

"You did not, in fact, kill Olaf?"

"No, Father!" Halli laughed uproariously. "Me?"

His laughter faded. He flicked his eyes from parent to parent. Both were stony-faced; they contemplated their son a long while without speaking. "Certainly the idea *seems* ridiculous," Arnkel said at last. "And yet . . . well, if it was not so, it was not so. We have asked, and you have answered, and the matter is closed between us." He sighed, stretching out his long limbs before him. His arms seemed thinner than Halli remembered, the great bones showing knobbly under flesh. "Speaking between men," his father went on, "I am glad that my brother's murderer is dead and I praise his killer whoever he may be. Your mother is more fearful. Next week we go before the Council to claim damages over Brodir's death, and she frets that our suit will be somehow affected by this news. That does not worry me. *Provided*," he added pointedly, "provided that we had no part in Olaf's death and that it *cannot be proved otherwise*. Then indeed we shall fear nothing."

Whether it was Arnkel's frailty, or something in the way in which he spoke to him, Halli felt a sudden eagerness to respond correctly, to please his father with his words. "I suspect," he said slowly, "that the killer will have left no clue to his identity. No doubt Olaf had many enemies. Many men will have wished him dead and there will be a host of suspects. It need not concern us. Father, are you quite well?"

"Oh yes, it is just the winter coming. I have never liked the season. My son, rein in your energies and you will be a credit to our House. In two years you shall have a fine farm of your own, if you apply yourself and work hard. Will you do this? Good."

Halli's mother had her hand upon Arnkel's shoulder. There was anxiety in her face; her expression, as she looked on Halli, was still hard. At last she said, "I hope for all our sakes that you are correct in what you say. It is of paramount importance that you present our case adequately before the Lawgivers."

"I will bear good witness, Mother."

"Very well. You may leave."

"One final thing," Arnkel called, as Halli neared the door. "You haven't seen my knife, have you, my finest one?"

Halli bent his head. "Father, I took it . . . I lost it."

Arnkel sighed, coughed. "I should beat you again, but you've already worn my strap out. Go away, boy, and do not tell anyone of this conversation."

Halli departed through the hall, where Svein's treasures hung, gray with dust. The box that had contained the silver belt still sat as he had left it. Halli, who had planned to return the belt, had not yet done so. It now lay concealed beside the fake Trow claw within the mattress of his bed. He would put it back when he had time, when people had forgotten his disappearance and no longer paid any attention to him.

Unfortunately for Halli, the traders who had brought news of events down-valley to Arnkel and Astrid had spoken to others in Svein's House too. Interest in Halli's activities was speedily rekindled, and conclusions drawn.

"They say," Grim the smith said, wiping ale froth from his beard, "that Olaf Hakonsson was dragged from his bed and had his throat cut, just like *that*. And then, as added insult, his corpse was set alight for his kin to find!"

"Olaf was no weakling, we all know that," Eyjolf whispered. "It would have taken great strength to carry out that killing."

"You'd never think it of the boy, would you?"

"No. So small, so short . . ."

Bolli the bread maker shook his head wisely. "Ah, but have you seen him working on the sheep sheds? The way he wields a hammer? You can sense his inner violence with each blow. In a way it's worse as he's so small. If he was a big man you'd understand it, it'd be more natural. Ah, it makes my skin crawl. I'd never cross him."

"Remember his great-uncle, Onund?" Unn the tanner said. "He was the same, the stories tell. Feeble enough most of the time, but when the rage flared in him—well, watch out! Snap your neck with his bare hands, he would, soon as look at you."

"I want to know how the lad broke into the House! You've seen those walls! Must've climbed them like some kind of bat."

"It's hardly natural, is it?"

"*I'd* never cross him."

It wasn't long before Halli noticed the way people fell silent as he passed them, the quick glances cast as he turned his back, the whispers on the fringes of his hearing. To his stupefaction adults began treating him with awkward, even fearful deference, while knots of the youngest children followed him about, goggling from behind posts and bushes as he went about his business.

"What's *wrong* with them all?" he exclaimed to Leif and Gudny in the hall one morning. "I've just had three urchins peering in at me while I was sitting on the privy! When I looked up, they giggled and ran away. The whole House is mad."

"Why should *you* worry?" Leif said shortly. Since the rumors had spread, Leif had begun treating Halli with a certain resentful caution. He was often seen at the ale-keg, brooding over his cup. "It's what you always wanted, isn't it?"

"What is?"

His brother laughed bitterly. "Your notoriety! Don't play the innocent with me."

Halli scowled. "I'm not. But this is—"

"No false modesty please, Halli," Gudny said. She too had become slightly more civil in the last few days. It was as if she truly noticed him for the first time. "Olaf had it coming. We're all agreed on that."

"Who's mourning him?" Leif grunted. "Not me, for one."

"Nor me," Gudny said. "Nor poor Father. We're glad you killed him."

"But—"

"How did you do it?" Leif said. "Father's knife, I suppose?"

"No. I—"

"Garrotte, then? I assume you crept up on him. He was too strong for you."

"*I* heard he was burned to death," Gudny said. "I think that's rather horrid, don't you, Leif? Even though he *was* a Hakonsson."

"Well, what else do you expect when killers settle their accounts?"

Halli rolled his eyes and clawed at the air. "Listen, what happened was—"

Leif held up a hand. "We don't really want to know *how* you went about it. It's rather distasteful, when all's said and done. Just make sure you don't foul up the trial next week. That's the important thing. We need that extra land."

A few days later a deputation departed for the trial by Council, at which Brodir's killers would be judged. It was to take place at a neutral venue, Rurik's House, across the valley from Svein's. Halli, relieved to be rid of the oppressive atmosphere at home, rode with his mother and brother, and a group of five men from the House. His father did not attend; his cough had worsened and he had taken to his bed with fever.

The journey took little more than three hours. Rurik's House was a pleasant midsized settlement set among green fields, not far from the rushing river. Like Arne's it had no Trow walls remaining, but was surrounded by orchards studded with hives—the source of the honey for which the

House was famous. The hall, taller and squatter than most in the valley, with a rather conical roof, was alive with activity; through crystal windows they could see the green livery of the Ruriksson attendants mingling with brightly attired dignitaries from across the valley.

They dismounted, and readied themselves in the yard, Halli standing quietly, looking at the doves fluttering above the roofs. Rather to his surprise, he felt no great anxiety at the prospect of meeting the Hakonssons again, only a dull resolve to get the business over with swiftly. All his hatred had evaporated in the heat of Olaf's fire, and since no one had seen him leave the burning hall, he had no fear of exposure now. Enough of such valley squabbles! When Aud came to stay, they would turn their attention to greater things; he raised his eyes to the ridgetops above the House.

Somewhere up there . . . A way of escape from all this . . .

Perhaps Aud would be present today. Her father Ulfar certainly would, in his capacity as a Lawgiver. Halli's heart beat a little faster at the thought. He scanned the courtyard for her, whistling to himself.

A shadow at his shoulder. His mother caught him by the ear and drew him to one side.

Astrid's voice was grim. "Listen to me clearly, Halli; pay attention with every sinew of your body. We now contest our case before the Council of Lawgivers—my equals along the valley. You will give an account of what happened to your uncle, and you will do so clearly, politely, and concisely, for much depends upon it. Address the Lawgivers only, and above all do not have any interaction with the Hakonssons, who will also be present. They may seek to put you off or pour scorn upon your story. Do not rise to their goading! *No interaction whatsoever*—do you understand?"

Halli spoke stiffly. "A hasty man might infer you did not trust me, Mother."

"Hasty or not, he would be a perceptive fellow, since I trust you less far than I could spit you. Hord and Ragnar will be five feet away. Avoid displays of open hostility or contempt, foul looks, exchanges of insults, abuse or impertinent hand gestures, and above all refrain from physical assault of any kind. Is the matter clear?"

"You could have been a little more specific in the details, but yes, I suppose so."

"Good. Then let us go in."

18

WHEN RURIK LEARNED how Svein had kidnapped his tenants, he went purple with rage. He took a group of men across the river to Svein's lands and killed the first group of farmers he could find.

Svein shook his head at the news. "It's dangerous for a man to start something he can't finish," he said. With that he crossed the river with his men and torched the nearest settlement, but he had scarcely got home when he learned that Rurik had carried out another raid as a reprisal.

All year the feud went on. At last Svein said, "Rurik's persistent, but let's see if he can do it on an empty stomach." So he set fire to Rurik's granaries and drew back to see what happened. It proved a decisive blow. When winter came Rurik was forced to come on his knees before Svein's gate, pleading for food to save his people. Svein let him crawl awhile, then doled out grain.

THE HALL, WHEN THEY ENTERED, was abuzz with noise: with whispers, laughter, shouted greetings, the camaraderie of important people jostling for status. It had been cleared of its usual furniture; ten chairs were arrayed in a semicircle at one end, with two other sets of chairs—for plaintiffs and defendants—facing one another along the longer edges of the hall. Most seats were filled; attentive servants flitted about, refilling ale cups and presenting platters of food to the ten presiding Lawgivers. Of these ten, eight were women. The remaining two (Ulfar Arnesson and another man whom Halli did not know) were Arbiters whose wives had died and who had taken the Lawgiving role themselves. Only the two Houses engaged in the action—Svein and Hakon—were unrepresented; otherwise the entire variety of valley life was there: the pink faces, fair heads, broad bellies, and splaying buttocks of the lower Houses; from up-valley, slighter, wirier frames, persons dark-haired and olive-eyed. Each Council member wore their House colors, each spoke volubly to the members on either side. It was an august and noisily intimidating circle.

Halli, Astrid, and Leif sat on the plaintiffs' side. The five men from Svein's House lined up behind them against the wall.

The chairs opposite were as yet vacant. Onlookers from Rurik's House and attendants to the various Lawgivers were filing in to stand in the margins of the hall. Halli looked hard among this number, but could not see Aud.

Now white-bearded Ulfar Arnesson left his place among the Council and bustled over, taking Astrid's hand with unctuous familiarity. "Well, well, cousin, it has come to this. I am sad my mediations bore no fruit! But I am sure all will be settled admirably today."

Astrid gave a wan smile. "So we hope too. How is young Aud? We are looking forward to enjoying her company this winter."

A flicker passed across Ulfar's smooth features; his expression grew a little cold. "Ah, yes, I had forgotten we made that arrangement! Forgive me, I have changed my plans. Ragnar Hakonsson has invited her to stay with *him* during the fever months, and of course I accepted his offer gladly. Sea air is healthy, you know. Besides it is not nearly so far for the girl to travel, and perhaps just a *little* more comfortable for her also? Hakon's is, after all, a splendid House." He was glancing away to the door as he spoke, as if in anticipation of the defendants' arrival.

Halli's mother flushed at the thinly veiled insult. Halli, who at the news felt as if his stomach had been punched, smiled pleasantly. "Is it *still* so splendid? I heard rumors the place had half burned down."

Ulfar's pink tongue wetted the fringes of his beard. "The damage was confined to a small portion of the hall. What would *you* know of it, young—I'm sorry, I forget your name."

"Halli Sveinsson. I shall be giving evidence today."

"Ah, yes." Ulfar regarded Halli vaguely. "You are the witness. I remember. If you will excuse me." With this he stalked back to his seat.

Astrid made a face. "No prizes which side *he* will take

this afternoon. He gravitates always to wealth and power, which is why his daughter overwinters with the Hakonssons. There will be a wedding there next year, if Ulfar gets his way. Are you all right, Halli? You look a trifle pale."

Halli hardly heard her. Aud would not be coming after all. She would stay with Ragnar Hakonsson instead. As in a dream he recalled Hord and Ragnar's discussion in the hall, their talk of arranging an advantageous marriage. . . .

Leif interlinked his hands and cracked the knuckles of his fingers one by one. "I did not like your insolence to Ulfar, Halli," he said. "If you cannot restrain yourself, we are lost."

With difficulty Halli battened down his distress. "Be sure that I shall treat everyone with the greatest respect," he said faintly. "Incidentally, Mother, I've been wondering—why is that dumpy serving woman sitting among the dignitaries? Surely someone should move her on?"

"That is in fact the eminent Lawgiver Helga of Thord's House, who is leader of the Council this year."

"Oh."

At the end of the hall there came a flurry of movement. Even without looking, Halli felt his shoulders stiffen, he sensed enmity suddenly in the room. He turned his head with careful calm, saw Hord and Ragnar Hakonsson stalking up the aisle, leading a group of men from Hakon's House. Both wore great furred capes, both had hair tied back and fixed with jeweled grips. Hord unclasped his cape and with a flourish draped it on his seat. He sat, clapped hands expansively on knees, and stared about with lofty condescension. His men arranged themselves against the wall. Ragnar, trotting behind, had difficulty unfastening his cape, and was still fiddling with it when Helga of Thord's House stood to open proceedings. He sat hastily as she turned her frown upon him.

Helga of Thord's House cleared her throat. She was a broad, powerful woman, with a voice that loosened earwax at a dozen paces. All listened attentively when she spoke. "The Council," she said, "meets today to hear the case brought by Svein's House against Hakon's House. Three men, Hord, Olaf, and Ragnar, are accused of the murder of Brodir Sveinsson shortly after the Gathering last year. Let us proceed with dignity and peaceful restraint in the great tradition of our valley! So, to begin. Astrid of Svein's House shall summarize."

Halli's mother stood and gave the bare facts soberly, without emotion. "My son Halli was witness to it all," she said. "May he be allowed to speak?"

"If you please."

All eyes now fixed on Halli. With a deep breath he stood and, turning to the Council, bowed politely. "I swear that I speak truth on this. Early on the morning of my uncle's death—"

The Lawgiver from Gest's House, an ancient woman, rheumy-eyed and wrinkled like a crabbed pear, banged her stick loudly upon the floor. "Why does that urchin speak from the far side of the room?"

Ulfar Arnesson leaned in close. "He is not distant, merely short."

"Continue, Halli Sveinsson," Helga of Thord's House said.

Halli gave his account as his mother had requested: succinctly, soberly, and without excess emotional coloring, while retaining all the details of the horror in the stables. At no time did he so much as look across at the Hakonssons. When he had finished, he answered one or two questions about specifics, then was told to sit. His mother patted him on the knee.

The Chief Lawgiver, Helga of Thord's House, nodded. "Thank you. Now, we must hear from the defendants. Hord Hakonsson, what do you have to say?"

"*This* will be interesting," Halli's mother whispered. "I do not think he can deny it; the evidence stacks up too high."

Hord rose, coughed, bowed low to the Council. He spoke in quiet tones, clearly designed to express humility. Rather to Halli's surprise, his version of events was more or less truthful. "But my late brother's action must be seen in context," he said. "Do not forget that this drunken lout, who insulted our honor so gravely, was the selfsame man who committed an outrage in our House, and escaped unpunished."

Astrid stood angrily. "Hardly unpunished! That matter was judged and our House lost good land because of it!"

Helga of Thord's House waved for her to sit down. "Astrid speaks truth there, Hord. Your actions and words imply that this can be justified as an ongoing honor-feud, not a question of simple murder. Feuding is forbidden, as you well know. It has been since the heroes' time. We have moved beyond such primitive responses now."

Cords tightened beneath Hord's cheeks, but he bowed respectfully. "As you say."

Various other statements were taken, but the discussion was soon over. "The details are clear enough," Helga of Thord's House said. "We shall consider our verdict presently. First, I would like to hear what compensation the plaintiffs require, should they win the case." She looked at Halli's mother inquiringly.

Halli's mother stood and bowed toward the Council. "For us this is a matter of principle, not material gain. We have lost a beloved uncle, a brother, a friend. . . . We'll take twelve thousand acres and not a tussock less."

As proceedings had gone on, Halli had slumped ever lower in his seat. Here then was the nub of the matter, the real reason why the trial was taking place. Politics and land! For all that his old ideas of vengeance had proved treacherous and corrupting, he disliked this bickering for advantage even more. This was not about his uncle, but about power. Where was the honor in this? Where was the bond between kin? Where, indeed, was love? Aud was right—there was nothing for him in the valley anymore.

The Council were asking Astrid and Hord detailed questions about compensation; as he sat waiting, Halli thought of Aud again, of her dreams of escape, of her fear of marriage . . . He imagined how she would be suffering now, with a winter—and perhaps a life—of Ragnar Hakonsson to look forward to. The idea made blood rise to his face, made his breath come fast. His eyes shifted; he found himself staring across at Ragnar Hakonsson, and saw Ragnar staring back, his face hardened with lines of hate. Halli did not look away. Their eyes locked; their gazes met midway across the floor and wrestled silently, unnoticed amid the crowded hall. Beside them their parents bartered in businesslike tones, discussing the merits of specific fields and flocks, with the Council members joining in, making suggestions, quoting precedents. It was a legal tangle to be legally resolved. Soon the matter of Brodir's killing would be over; the issue settled between the Houses. . . . But Ragnar and Halli sat motionless, staring at each other, their wills moving together like stags, first one backing, then the other, neither giving ground.

Helga of Thord's House allowed her voice to rise a little, rattling the ale cups on tables across the hall. "Well, that much is done. Now we shall discuss our verdict."

"A moment, please!" It was Ragnar Hakonsson who spoke. Without taking his eyes off Halli, he stood abruptly in his chair and walked a little way into the center of the hall. "Before the worshipful Council makes its decision, I believe we are allowed to bring to your attention other matters pertaining to the case, if such there be. Is this correct?"

The Chief Lawgiver nodded. "That is so."

Hord Hakonsson sat forward urgently in his seat. "Ragnar, what is this?"

"Wait, Father, and you shall hear. I wish to bring a countercharge of murder, which—at the very least—will negate and nullify any wrong done to the Sveinssons. I talk of my uncle Olaf's recent death. Prepare yourselves for a shock, but I have no doubt of it." He stared at Halli, eyes glittering. "His murderer sits here in this room."

At Ragnar's words, several of the Lawgivers audibly sucked in their breath and seats creaked as bottoms were adjusted into postures of fresh attention. Hord Hakonsson looked as surprised as anyone; he made frantic gestures at Ragnar that were ignored.

The Chief Lawgiver's voice was stern. "This is a grave statement that needs justification."

"I can give it." Ragnar bowed to the Council, then strode into the center of the hall. Now he spoke to Halli, sitting pale and frozen in his place. "My father," Ragnar said softly, "runs slower than I do. It took him time to cross the hall, to get to the window. So *he* saw nothing. But *I* saw. And *I* know."

"From a legal viewpoint your words are ever so slightly

opaque," Ulfar Arnesson called. "Also, could you speak up a little? This is most exciting."

Ragnar's smile was thin. "I think Halli Sveinsson understands me well enough."

Halli, recalling his mother's stern injunction, sat still and said nothing.

Ragnar wheeled away across the hall. "See! He is struck dumb with guilt! It is as if my uncle's shade had risen from the ground and placed his gory hand upon his toadlike shoulder. One can easily see that—"

Ignoring his mother's warning grasp upon his arm, Halli stood promptly. It seemed to him now was not the time for silence. "Pardon me," he said, "but I was silent in raw puzzlement. Setting inane riddles may, along with cow kissing and bog rolling, be a favored pastime among Hakon's people, but I do not indulge in it myself. Make yourself clear, please, or make yourself scarce."

Several of the Lawgivers frowned, but most nodded in agreement. "Enough theatrics!" the crone from Gest's House called. "Let us hear the meat of the matter."

Ragnar nodded. "Very well. Not long ago, when my uncle died by fire, an intruder was seen fleeing from the House. He was pursued for miles, but ultimately escaped. This is common knowledge throughout the valley."

"Quite," Ulfar called, "but the identity of the scoundrel—"

"Is known by me. Halli Sveinsson did the deed."

Sensation in the hall. Hord Hakonsson rose from his chair, several of the Lawgivers likewise. All turned their heads to stare at Halli, except for the lady from Gest's House, who was looking the wrong way. Beside him, Halli sensed his mother stiffen, and his brother Leif curse under his breath. Inwardly, it was as if his guts had knotted and the knot was drawing tight; but he kept his face impassive, his expression nonchalant as he could. He stepped confidently forward. "Does Ragnar have proof to back up these absurdities?" He smiled. "I fear not. This is a blatant attempt to avoid paying the fine for Brodir's killing—a typical Hakonsson trick!"

Ragnar's riposte was drowned out by shouts from Hord, from Astrid and Leif, and the attendants of both Houses; also from several of the Council members, who were growing wildly excited by events. The old crone from Gest's House had risen and was swinging her stick dangerously around her head, while Helga of Thord's House bellowed for silence in the manner of a bull. At last, through sheer lung capacity, she overcame all other sounds. "*Quiet*, everyone! All of you sit down! This must be dealt with appropriately and calmly! No—not a word more, Halli Sveinsson, until I say! Ragnar—what exactly is your accusation?"

"That Halli Sveinsson murdered my poor sick uncle foully by setting him alight. His purpose? To avenge his own uncle's death. How do I know it? Because when I came to the window through the burning hall, I looked down upon the parapet of the wall below and saw him there, just before he leaped into the moat! I saw him, clear as day!"

Helga said: "Halli, do you deny this?"

Halli spoke carefully. "I did not kill Olaf."

"Astrid of Svein's House—what do you say?"

Halli's mother stood. "It is a ridiculous assertion! Halli is a child, and not a very big one at that—how could *he* kill Olaf, a grown warrior?"

"It is unlikely, but presumably possible. . . ." Helga tapped her fingers on an ample knee. "Did he—or any of your household—go down-valley last autumn?"

"None of us, least of all little Halli! He was with us every day, helping in the fields, like the good dear boy he is!"

"You *lie*," Ragnar shouted. "You, a Lawgiver yourself, lying through your teeth to protect your son! Ah, this is a vile sight!"

At this Leif Sveinsson jumped up and made aggressive motions toward Ragnar, while the men from Svein's House bayed and gestured. On the opposite side Hord Hakonsson and his men leaped forward. Several local men from Rurik's House, each with biceps bigger than a pig's haunch, started forward from the edges of the hall, though whether to make peace or join the fracas was not entirely clear.

Helga of Thord's House gave a bray of outrage, which sent the rafters ringing and even the biggest men scurrying back to their places. She glowered round the company in awful silence. "This is *not* a hero tale," she cried. "This is *not* a place of violence. We do things differently here, and have done for a dozen generations! Shame on both sides for this disturbance! We must talk, we must debate, we must discuss; at the end, we must abide peaceably by the judgment of the Council. Is that accepted, or are you going to cut each other's throats for the sake of honor? Think hard! Every act will be accounted for!"

There was much coughing and mumbling into beards. Helga nodded grimly. "Very well."

Ulfar Arnesson held up a hand. "I have a question. Ragnar is a noble young man, we all know this, but I don't understand why he has delayed charging Halli, why he has kept even his father in ignorance!"

Ragnar shrugged: "No one but me saw Halli there; no one but me knows his guilt. I decided not to take the matter further, since I had no other proof. Besides I know my father wished to end these troubles swiftly, not drag them out still further. But today, when I saw Halli's horrid face gloating at me opposite, I could keep silent no longer. Whatever the verdict, I have said the truth."

Ulfar nodded. "That is well spoken. I am inclined to believe this story."

"Just as you incline toward the Hakonssons always!" Astrid called. "How is your poor daughter today, cousin? Locked away ready for her marriage to Ragnar here?"

Ulfar gave a hoot of rage and danced to his feet. As Helga hushed him, Halli said, "It's clear to me that Ragnar is talking through his leggings. Let me ask him this. The mysterious figure on the parapet. Did it turn toward you?"

Ragnar shook his head. "No."

"So you did not actually see this person's face?"

"No."

Halli smiled over at the Council. "In other words it might have been anyone."

Now Ragnar was on his feet. "Who *else* has your repulsive proportions?" he cried. "I did not *need* to see your face! Your curiously squat outline was enough, illuminated for a moment by the flames."

Halli shrugged. "The figure was down low and you were up high. It would have appeared foreshortened."

"Nothing could be *that* foreshortened. It was you."

Halli bared his teeth. "Is that so? I remind everyone that this is the first anyone has heard of this charge. I submit that it is pure invention, spurred on by hatred to my House. Last time I saw Ragnar, remember, he was treading on my neck."

Ragnar laughed shrilly. "Yes, the odor lingers on my boot sole even now."

"What more evidence does anyone need?" Halli said. "Why pick on me, Ragnar? Go accost someone with a more obviously criminal appearance. Your father, for instance."

Ragnar drew in an audible breath. He had been white-skinned before; now he was whiter. Over on the far bench,

Hord leaped up in outrage, veins popping.

Helga Thordsson gave a bellow. "Hord, return to your seat! Let us keep order here! Halli Sveinsson, restrain your comments."

Halli bowed. "Your pardon. I spoke in the heat of the moment; it is a way I have. But at least I do not knife people at such times, like old Hord over there." Once more Hord leaped forward, arms swinging like a bear, but Halli skipped back out of reach. "Why not stab me now?" he shouted. "Get some friends to hold me down securely first—but wait, would I even *then* be helpless enough? Fix a knife to a long pole so you can kill me from the next room and so avoid any possible danger to yourself."

Even as he spoke he knew he had gone too far. The tendons on Hord's neck stood out like tent ropes; his face was purpled, his eyes unseeing. With arm drawn back and fingers clenching, he lurched forward toward Halli, who darted nimbly away, only to knock hard into his chair and fall sideways against his mother's lap.

Hord loomed over them, fist raised. Astrid screamed; Halli held up an ineffectual hand, shielding his mother and himself—

A shadow moved from left to right. At its point of farthest reach, Hord's head snapped back as if a hammer had connected with his chin. He staggered, eyes woozily staring, but did not quite fall.

Leif, lowering his hand, rubbing chafed knuckles, said,

"*That* is why it is sensible to wear your beard long. He hadn't any cushioning."

A moment's silence; then—bedlam all around.

Several of the Lawgivers uttered piercing shrieks; onlookers cried out in alarm. From left and right the men of Svein's and Hakon's House came running: some vaulted chairs, others hurled them aside in their efforts to reach their enemies. The Ruriksson attendants sprinted in with equal speed—all across the center of the hall came multiple collisions as men met and grappled with each other, grabbing beards, exchanging blows, kicking, punching, biting with unleashed zest.

Halli, rising, attempted to pull his mother from her chair. Now, from behind the teetering Hord came Ragnar; eyes staring, mouth agape, he flung his arm round Halli's neck.

Over by the Council, Helga of Thord's House stood on tiptoe, roaring orders nobody could hear. A number of Lawgivers rushed past her, among them the lady from Gest's House, swinging her stick with alarming, if unfocused, skill.

Hord's fingers rubbed his jaw; now his eyes had cleared. He straightened his back, staring hard about him—and was knocked to his knees as the Gest's House crone brought her stick down hard between his shoulder blades.

Halli reared back with Ragnar's fingers on his throat. He thrashed from side to side, jabbing his elbows behind him to no avail.

Astrid swiped, her fingers clawing. Ragnar jerked back, his cheek streaming blood, letting Halli go.

Now from the Law Seats Ulfar Arnesson came, hurrying to the Hakonssons' aid. He directed several wild punches at Leif's back and midriff, all of which went quite unnoticed; Leif and Halli helped their mother over several toppled chairs, toward a clear space in the hall.

A number of onlookers from Rurik's House, finding themselves without anyone obvious to fight, stood uncertainly on the sidelines, then set to fighting each other. They blocked the way; Halli and Leif turned, uncertain of where to go.

Ulfar Arnesson kicked Leif hard upon his backside; Leif, registering dim awareness, turned and punched once, sending Ulfar spinning like a top across the room, to connect neatly against the flailing stick of the crone from Gest's House and ricochet across into the ample skirts of the largest, loudest Lawgiver. Her chair collapsed under them.

Leif and Astrid made tentatively across the center of the room, between little knots of fighting men. Halli, following at their heels, looked back. He saw Hord Hakonsson rising slowly to his feet, saw him looking about befuddled, then with renewed understanding. He saw Hord look up and see them; saw him reach inside his jerkin, draw out a hunting knife. . . .

Halli pointed, cried out, but his voice was lost amid the din.

Hord started forward, his knife held ready.

Halli backed away, jostled, knocked, impeded by the chaos all around.

Closer, closer came Hord.

Helga of Thord's House, finding her cries inaudible, got with stately menace to her feet and, picking up her chair in one hand, strode swiftly forward. With the ease of one who habitually carries lame sheep down from high pasture, she swung the chair in a lively arc and dashed it down neatly on Hord's head.

Hord toppled like a stunned ox and crashed to the ground. The knife spun away from his grasp, out across the floor, and came to a halt, still spinning. As it spun, it glinted.

As if it had made a great concussion, everyone's eyes locked on to it; men let go of each other's beards, noses, ears, and pigtails, and stood in silence up and down the hall. Halli, Astrid, Leif, Ragnar, the crone from Gest's House, Ulfar Arnesson still entangled with the kirtle of the Lawgiver from Orm's House: everyone stopped dead still and watched the spinning knife.

The knife's rotation slowed, slowed. . . . Now it had halted.

Helga of Thord's House, still holding her chair in one hand, raised the other to her face and brushed the hair back from her forehead. She was sweating mildly. "I think we can stop right *there*," she said, and this time she did not have to shout. "We are all shamed," Helga said, "that such a disgraceful exhibition has taken place at our sacred Council. To see violence break out in place of calm words and careful negotiations makes my blood boil, makes my arms itch to batter the sense into all of you. But I am just as much to blame." She flung the chair aside; it clattered briefly. "None of us are absolved," Helga went on. "We are all still tainted. It seems that no matter how many years pass, no matter how our families link and interlink by marriage, the old madness that afflicted the heroes lingers in our blood. How swift we are to rise up against each other, every one of us—old and young, man and woman—alike. Yes, we are all tainted. But only one side," Helga said, with a hardening of tone, "has dared draw steel—has dared draw it *again* I should say, since it is that very crime that we were supposed to hold in judgment today. Hord Hakonsson, we have all witnessed your intentions here, and there is no reason to doubt the evidence we have heard concerning Brodir Sveinsson's death. You shall be fined for that, and fined severely. You shall also be fined for producing that knife in sight of all. The many fields you lose shall, I hope, be sufficient lesson for the rest of us to hold our uglier passions back, to fight only to keep them under control. Now we must clear this mess up."

Hord lay flat upon the floor, blinking, puffing his cheeks in and out like a stranded fish. But now Ragnar, a handkerchief pressed upon his cheek, set up a clamor. "What of Halli?" he croaked. "What of his wickedness? Where is *his* punishment?"

The eye Helga bestowed upon Ragnar was cool, contemptuous. "You have no evidence whatsoever for your assertion, and the honor of your House has been so eroded that I see no reason to believe one word you say. If it is mentioned again in our Council, I will press further sanctions upon your House."

Ragnar stared dumbly at Helga, then toward Halli, who winked cheerily from the sidelines. Ragnar, expressionless, bent to help his father. Now Hord had risen to his knees; he moved stiffly, and seemed to be having trouble standing. His nose was red and swollen from where it had hit the floor; his eyes stared in various directions. But when he spoke his voice was steady. All in the hall heard him.

"It is well known that the judgments of the Council are often womanly, driven more by concern for easy peace than the dictates of justice," he said. "But Helga's statement sets a new low in this regard. See, there—my brother's killer walking off scot-free, while I must bow and scrape to enrich his House! Well, I do not accept this verdict. Know that I shall not deliver one single clod of earth to the Sveinssons. Know that if anyone seeks to impose this judgment upon my House we will resist them with force of arms. Know also that I shall have my vengeance upon the House of Svein, and in particular upon that runtish scoundrel grinning at me there, before a year is passed. Until he is in his cairn there shall be no peace in this valley, and I invoke the name of Hakon, greatest of the heroes, to endorse this vow. Now, I depart this hall, and I advise none to try to stop me. I thank the Rurikssons for their hospitality."

All heard him. All stood silent as, helped by his son, he rose painfully to his feet. All drew back, feet shuffling on the boards as, with hesitant steps, the Hakonssons progressed toward the doors. Hord's back was bowed, his nose protuberant. Ragnar's cheek was scratched and bleeding. They reached the doors, they swung them wide. Now they were gone, and bright daylight spilled into the room.

In Rurik's hall the silence held. Then there was a general exhaling.

Leif and Astrid stood staring at each other. As one they turned to gaze at Halli.

Halli clapped his hands together cheerfully. "So," he said. "That went well."

19

It wasn't long before Svein's House grew rich and splendid, and Svein himself likewise. He took to wearing jeweled brooches, torques, and rings, and intricately patterned cloaks made far down-valley. The traders who brought such delicacies were welcomed in his hall, but other visitors—beggars and wastrels drawn by wealth—aroused his irritation.

Svein had boundary posts erected at the margins of his land; within this area his word was law. He had a special chair carved and placed upon a dais in his hall, and from this Law Seat uttered judgments on thieves, loafers, and other miscreants. His edicts were firm and not many disregarded them; a gallows in the yard helped keep his rules fresh in the memory.

For some time after the Hakonssons' departure, Rurik's hall remained a place of intense activity. While servants hurried to drag away smashed furniture, and others retired to bathe black eyes and minor wounds, the Lawgivers of the valley, Astrid included, huddled together discussing the situation. It was an unheard of trouble; not since the early days after the Battle of the Rock, when several old feuds were still being pursued by the heroes' followers, had one House declared itself free of valley law. Opinion was divided about what action to take. One or two of the more warlike Lawgivers (the crone from Gest's House among them) wished to organize a punitive expedition against Hord and his family. Others pointed out that no one had any swords, and that anyway this would further destroy the careful peace the valley had long enjoyed. The majority view was that Hord would soon regret his hasty words, and retract them; all trade with Hakon's House would in the meantime be withheld, the better to encourage him in this regard.

"The snows are coming," the Chief Lawgiver, Helga, said. "Hord's anger will cool. He will have the winter to reflect on his intemperance, and in the spring we'll approach him again. Doubtless you will get your lands next year, Astrid."

"I hope you are right," Halli's mother said. "But what if Hord carries out his threats? What if he seeks to attack us?"

"He would not dream of it! Think of the sanctions we'd impose! Between you and me, I view this as a positive development. It is good to rein Hord back a little."

"Even so, I fear the consequences for my House and people." Astrid's face was grim, she spoke almost reluctantly: "And also for my son . . ."

Helga nodded. "Ah, yes. Halli. I was going to mention him. He was a *little* outspoken in the debate, was he not? Not entirely diplomatic on occasion? I think that might have contributed somewhat to Hord's overwhelming wrath. I wonder if you might educate him during the winter on the merits of restraint?"

"Oh, don't worry," Astrid said shortly. "I shall."

"Why blame *me*?" Halli roared, rubbing his throbbing ear. "I did not strike a single blow!"

"You did not *need* to," his mother cried. "Your tongue did the job of a dozen brawling men. Time and again you baited Hord until he lost control."

Halli folded his arms. "I thought you'd be pleased, since you got more land out of the affair, which is all that's important to you."

"We have got *nothing* yet, except for threats of vengeance—and may I remind you, you vile, stocky serpent of a son, that all this stems from *your* wickedness. Ragnar spoke the truth about what he saw, did he not?"

Halli looked away. "He did indeed. But it so happens I did not kill Olaf."

His mother gave a wrathful cry. "Do not lie to me!"

"Is lying suddenly such a crime, Mother? I notice you lied to the Council too, and did so rather fluently."

Astrid raised her hand to strike him, but Leif stepped quickly forward. "Mother, this demeans you."

Halli gave a curt nod. "Thanks, Leif—Ow!"

"It does not, however, demean me."

Astrid's face was bone white, her eyes staring. "May a Trow take you, Halli, for the harm you've done this House."

"A Trow?" Halli laughed in her face. "Big deal! I believe in *them* even less than I do in your doctrine of valley peace, which is nothing but blatant self-interest! Pull down the cairns! Let the Trows come for me! I don't care. I'm sick of all this."

Both Leif and Astrid made instinctive wards against ill luck. Leif's eyes were bulging. "Brother, I believe you're mad."

"On your horse, this instant," Astrid said. "And not another word. We must bring these hard tidings to the House."

News that the hoped for settlement had been postponed was greeted with muted despondency by the people of Svein's House. But Hord's threats caused a much wider ripple of anxiety. Old tales of massacres and burnings were aired and analyzed, and there was great resentment at Halli's role in the affair. Although still treated with extreme caution as befitted a dangerous killer, he was now, by common consent, more or less ignored, kept at the margins in the field and hall.

Halli kept up a dogged show of unconcern, but his isolation preyed upon his spirits. More than ever he regretted coming back to Svein's House, to its atmosphere of hostility, envy, and petty fears. Of all the Houses he had seen in his travels it was certainly the smallest and most decrepit; the glorious claims of the old tales now seemed laughable to him. He could not abide the company of his family, nor they his, but there was no escape now that winter was setting in. The cairns upon the ridge were seldom visible behind its shroud of mists and cloud.

Two things only relieved his mood. One was the fact that Katla was suddenly disposed to talk with him again. The magnitude of his misdeeds seemed to have softened her displeasure, and she took to bringing soup while he sat in his room alone.

"Thank you, Katla. I'm glad *you* don't see me as a criminal and outlaw."

"On the contrary, I believe you are truly cursed, and fated for a dismal and early death. Such is the fate of a Midwinter's child, as I have always said, and events are bearing me out. But there you go. You have my pity and—while you're still with us—you can have my soup as well. Tell me of Olaf. How exactly *did* you slay him?"

The other, more substantial, compensation for Halli was Aud's imminent arrival. With the Hakonssons' star suddenly eclipsed and the Sveinssons the objects of sympathy among the Lawgivers of the valley, Ulfar Arnesson had lost no time in swinging like a weather vane and changing plans for his daughter. Before anyone had left Rurik's hall, he had gathered himself up and run to Astrid to renew arrangements for Aud's visit. She was expected within days.

Light snows settled in the fields; soon the road past the cataracts would be impassable with drifts and ice. A week after the skirmish three riders appeared at the north gate. Two of them, burly men of Arne's House, immediately spurred their horses and headed back down-valley; the third, Aud Ulfar's-daughter, came smiling into the hall.

A feast was held to celebrate her arrival; most of the House attended, except for Arnkel, who remained sick in his rooms. Word of his condition was not promising, and the atmosphere in the hall was jittery and febrile.

Aud was dressed in official finery, her hair scraped into an adequate dragon's tail. With quick, elegant steps, she passed around, greeting the notables of the House. Halli, watching from the sidelines, noted how her graceful figure won favor with almost everyone. Only Gudny seemed reserved, and held back from the throng.

At last Aud drew near, with Leif following close at hand. Halli gave a formal bow. "It is good to see you again."

"And you, Halli Sveinsson. It has been *such* a long time." Her eyes were laughing. "What have you been up to?"

"Oh, not much."

Leif stepped between them. "Miss Aud, you have better things to do than talk to this felon. Come, let me show you great Svein's weapons. I can tell you many tales. . . ."

Aud, allowing herself to be led away, grinned back at Halli over her shoulder.

The following morning the snow clouds hung so low that the roof of the hall itself was swallowed, but the expected blizzard did not break. Its imminence hung heavy on the House. The last few animals were brought inside the walls to cluster hot and steaming in the sheds.

Astrid and Leif took up much of Aud's time that day and Halli seldom had a chance to talk with her. Observing from afar he noticed that she was capable of many subtle adjustments of personality. Whereas he knew her to be outspoken and skeptical, with Leif she was wide-eyed and playful, verging on coquettish; with his mother, she was altogether quieter, a modest young girl eager for instruction.

They met at last by chance in the passage behind the hall.

"Where have *you* been?" Aud said. "If I hear Leif's yawnsome stories of Svein once more I shall stab him with my hairpin. I keep waiting for you to rescue me."

"Sorry." He smiled at her awkwardly. "So . . . I'm glad you got here in the end. There was talk you were going to be spending the winter down at Hakon's."

Aud rolled her eyes. "Yes. My revolting father had it all planned out. He'd pretty much made the deal with Hord, I think. Can you *imagine*? A marriage to Ragnar? He's so insipid and weak-kneed! I'd have run away if they'd tried to foist it on me, or slit my throat, or drowned myself. Thank

Arne there was that rumpus at Rurik's House." She stretched out a finger and poked Halli's arm. "I believe I've *you* to thank for that, haven't I?"

"Well, strictly speaking it was Ragnar who—"

"Saw you when you burned his hall down. Yes. Credit where it's due, Halli. You've got a real talent for spreading happiness and light between the Houses. But in this case, it's worked out well—at least for me."

Halli sighed. "You're the only one who's celebrating. Hord's vowed vengeance on me, while everyone here thinks I'm a cold-blooded killer and treats me with varying mixtures of fear and dislike. You'll soon see."

"Oh, Leif's already warned me off you three times." She chuckled. "I just think he's jealous. And don't worry about Hord. He's a braggart, all mouth."

"I don't know. He's a man who's not afraid of action." Halli drew Aud aside as Eyjolf and a servant bustled along the passage; he noticed Eyjolf regarding them closely as he passed by. "But I don't much care," he went on quietly. "Hord can do what he likes next year, because by then we'll be beyond his reach."

Aud's eyes glinted. "So you've warmed to my idea about the boundary, have you? Not scared of Trows?"

"I'd rather a Trow ate me than spend the rest of my life here. I'm sick of Svein's House and everyone in it. The whole valley, come to that. What about you?"

"Father plans to marry me off to *someone* next summer,

come what may. If not Ragnar, there'll be some other dribbling dullard to take his place. Of *course* I'm still up for it.
I'd go today if we could, but the weather—"

"It's impossible now; the weather's turned. We've got to
wait for the thaw." He grinned at her. "But don't worry. It
gives you plenty of time to get to know everything about
our House and hero. No doubt Leif will make you an
expert before long."

Aud groaned. "It's going to be a long winter."

That night the storm broke. The House was buffeted by
winds that set the shutters rattling and blew candles out in
the deepest regions of the hall. The corridors echoed
through the howling night. In the morning the light was
white and sickly, the yard knee-deep in snow. The fields
below the walls were featureless as floodwater.

From then on there was no respite. The blizzards began.
People were penned in their houses like the herds. Peat fires
burned high in every hearth; smoke trails laced the rafters of
the hall. Each day men worked to clear passages among the
snow between the buildings; when they returned indoors ice
crystals hung glimmering in their beards.

Aud soon fell in with the House routine; she wove, she
helped in the kitchens, she carried meal to the animals and
seed to the chickens. In the afternoons, she sat with Gudny
listening as Astrid recited the histories. But she had free
time also, and it was noticed by many that she chose to

spend this in Halli's company. They were regularly seen in close consultation, laughing and talking avidly.

Shortly after Midwinter the storms reached a height of ferocity. No one went out. The atmosphere in the hall became fetid with smoke, stale ale, and sweat; tempers grew frayed, and mealtimes became arenas of heightened tension, where the slightest incident triggered sudden rage. It was always this way in winter, but this year was worse than any other. The threat from the Hakonssons still preyed on people's minds; also, it was becoming clear that Arnkel was very ill. He never left his bed.

Halli, bound up with dreams of exploration in the heights, kept his head down as best he could and sought respite in the company of Aud.

One morning he was working with his mother, bottling cloudberries in a corner of the kitchen. Astrid's hair was tied and concealed within a rough hemp scarf. Her sleeves were rolled up and her forearms stained red from pressing and stirring. She was gray-faced from her vigil at her husband's bed the night before. She supervised Halli as he ladled hot berries into heavy clay jars, pausing occasionally to shout orders across the tables at the girls preparing lunch.

Aud had been in briefly to get a jug of watered ale for the women in the weaving room. After she left, Astrid remarked: "She is a pleasant girl, Aud."

Halli nodded. "Yes, mother."

"Clever enough, and good-looking in her way. That's

full; now seal the jar with the cheesecloth. I'll tie the string round. I see you get on with her well."

"With Aud? Yes, mother."

"Pull it tighter. That's it. So, do you want to lie with her? Oh, see—now you've torn the cloth. You don't know your strength, Halli, and for Svein's sake do not flush so! I am your mother; I can ask these questions. There, *I'll* hold the cloth; you tie it round. Now cut it with the knife. Just so. Well, if the idea embarrasses you that is all well and good, because at fifteen you are not yet a man. But your brother Leif is a full four years older, Halli, and I must find him a wife. I have told him to talk with Aud, see what he makes of her. Reach me that next pot, the one over there. Of course, Arne's House is *not* one of the better ones, but she is an only child, and that means a great deal. We would unite the Houses by that marriage. Why are you not ladling?"

Halli resumed his work mechanically. His mother paused to consult with a serving girl who was taking broth to Arnkel's room. When he had her attention once more, Halli said: "Perhaps Aud does not yet want marriage."

"She will be sixteen in the spring. I met your father at that age. Of *course* it will be on her mind. I want you to leave the poor girl alone for a while, Halli—give Leif his opportunity. He is not the most expressive of boys; the last thing he needs is you scowling like a stoat in the corner of his vision while he tries to press his suit."

"Mother, Leif needs no sabotage from me. If he

manages two sentences without tripping over his trailing knuckles he will have exceeded my expectations."

His mother rapped him on the head with her ladle. "Such remarks are *exactly* why you must be elsewhere. I expect Aud's tired of you by now in any case. She seems a gentle, rather sensitive child. You are a violent killer. I doubt she will have much use for you."

Following his mother's confidences Halli urgently wished to talk with Aud, but found himself singled out by Eyjolf for long, complicated tasks in obscure portions of the hall. When at mealtimes he emerged, begrimed, he found Aud always inaccessible, sitting with Astrid and Leif, smiling and laughing at their conversation.

Halli sat glumly at a distance, often joined by Gudny, who seemed equally irritable at the attention Aud was getting.

"They won't get anywhere with *her*," she remarked at last.

Halli grunted. "She seems to be enjoying it."

"*Seems* to, Halli, that's the key. The girl's a vicious flirt. She wears a dozen faces, molds people to her will. Look there at Leif, see how he gawps and grins like a half-wit, with his sleeve trailing in his soup. If she asked him to jump from a crag this moment, he would do it at a run. What has she got *you* doing?"

Halli started. "What?"

"You're in her power too, don't deny it. I've watched you

for weeks. If anything, you're more addle-headed than Leif, craning your neck round after her like an owl. Keep clear of her, is my advice. She'll lead you into trouble, not that you need any help with that."

Halli didn't have much to say to this. He went back to his work.

•

20

EVERYTHING AROUND US belongs to Svein. Not just this hall, this House, its wall and fields, but the landscape beneath them too. There isn't a stream, forest, or crag round here that doesn't attest to it. Listen to their names: Svein's Leap, where he jumped the gorge to catch the Deepdale boar; Skafti's Boulder, which he threw upon the thief who tried to steal his belt; the great pit at Trow Delving, dug by Svein in a single day to unearth three Trows and burn them with the sun; as well as all the rest of the meadows, tracks and trails that he mapped out, so that our lives might be a little easier on our way toward the cairns.

"This is my land, and you are my people," Svein was fond of saying. "Obey me and my laws and I'll always protect you."

FOR EVERYONE IN THE HOUSE the winter was long and difficult. The snows fell deep as the Trow walls; a minor outbreak of dank mottle lay several children low. Supplies of salted meat and fish were gradually depleted. The well was ice-bound and even the pails brought into the hall froze solid unless stored near the fires.

Little by little the weather quieted and the nights grew marginally less long. It was possible on some days to see across the valley to Rurik's ridge. Ordinarily such improvements signaled a time of hope and expectation for the coming spring, but that year shadows lay upon the inhabitants of Svein's House. The Arbiter, Arnkel Sveinsson, seventeenth in line from the Founder, lay dying in his bed. The canker that had grown within him secretly had taken final hold; as the winter ended, his strength drained steadily with it. The flesh on his frame fell in; the bones pressed jaggedly up beneath his skin like crags and outcrops on the hills. His face was a jutting ridge, each cheek a tumbling escarpment; the blood in his veins ran cold like mountain streams.

Members of his family took turns to sit with him as he slumbered, his breath bubbling with intermittent coughs and rasps. He seldom woke, and when he did his conversation was hard to understand. He ate and drank with a messy lack of control, dribbling like a child.

Halli did not find it easy to be in his father's presence and his vigils were spent in tense, unhappy silence, dreading that Arnkel might stir before he'd left the room. He kept his thoughts as far from the sick bed as he could, letting them roam the moors, searching out the old path the settlers had taken. For hours he watched the tumbling snow beyond the window, willing it to stop, dreaming of escape.

Soon, sometime soon, the thaw would come. When it

did, that would be the end of his ties to the House. He and Aud would be gone, first chance they had.

Despite the disapproving scrutiny of his sister, Halli had continued to spend much time with Aud throughout the winter. It may have been that Astrid would have done more to separate them, but she had grown increasingly preoccupied with her husband's condition, and was not interested in Leif's shrill complaints.

"She excused herself from my table claiming a headache!" Leif roared. "What should I see soon after? Aud closeted in Halli's room, fresh-faced and giggling and obviously in the best of health! What is the matter with the girl?"

It wasn't long, however, before Leif himself became too preoccupied to give much thought to Aud. With Arnkel fading and Astrid distracted, he had to assume leadership of the House. From the beginning this did not go well. By turns hesitant and overbearing, Leif struggled to impose his authority. At meetings in the hall, when pent-up emotions frequently spilled out into bitter argument and, occasionally, drunken tussling, he was unable to keep control.

A frequent question put to him concerned the danger posed by the Hakonssons, to which Leif always replied the same way. "There is nothing to fear! Even if Hord persists in his aggression, the Council will defuse the issue long before he can come up-valley. With the thaw comes the great melt; the torrents will be impassable. By the time the roads are cleared, the Council will have acted, and Hord will have seen sense. It will come to nothing. Don't worry your silly heads about it!"

So spoke Leif, but not everyone was convinced and they told him so. His confidence battered, he sought frequent solace in the ale keg, and this made him even less effective than before.

Halli, meanwhile, prepared for his expedition beyond the valley. He and Aud gathered fleeces and extra woolens against the cold and stored them in secret beneath his bed. Halli also located a number of old tools that might double up as weapons.

"What's the point in *that*?" Aud scoffed. "They'll weigh us down."

"I know, but if we're wrong, and the Trows—"

"Oh, please. Even if they do exist—which they don't— they'll be tucked up underground. It'll be daylight, remember? The first time we go up we won't stay long. A quick look round—then back before dark."

"It's best to be prepared."

"Well, *you're* carrying them."

In the late evenings, when the House was quiet, they talked long with Katla, mining her for details about the lands beyond the boundary. The old nurse approved of Aud, and was garrulous and cheerful, particularly with a hot posset of wine and milk in her ample lap. She would sit close by the hearth, her wrinkled face shining, bright eyes flicking from Aud to Halli and back again.

"Of course," she'd say, "I knew Halli when he was even smaller than he is now. When he was nothing but a chubby fat babe, squalling naked by the fire! Ah, you should have seen his little bottom, smiling up from the rug! All pink and dimpled, it was. I'd pat it dry with—"

"Oh, I don't think Aud wants to hear all *that*," Halli said hastily. "Tell us one of your old tales, why don't you? About Svein or the Trows or something."

"Yes, tell me, dear Katla," Aud said. She was sitting below Katla in a posture of utmost familiarity, nestling close against her knees; Halli, who was in a chair opposite, was mildly irritated by the sight. "Tell me of the founding of the House again," Aud went on. "It is *such* a fascinating story."

Outside the winter storm shook against the doors and windows. The fire leaped in the grate. The old nurse simpered. "How can I resist your pretty face? Well, they say that when Svein was but a babe—rather less chubby than Halli, I don't doubt—his parents brought him over the mountains. A good many other settlers were with them. The valley was heavily forested then. They arrived in a pleasant glade, where—"

Halli snorted. "Oh, this is the old one about Svein and the snake."

Katla scowled at him across the hearth. "If you know it so well, tell it yourself!"

"Oh, but he's terrible at storytelling," Aud said, "so tedious it's impossible to believe. We'd be asleep in moments. *Please*, Katla."

But Katla was affronted, her face corrugated with annoyance. She took a long drink from her cup and wiped a milky moustache from her upper lip with a vigorous hand. "No, no. Halli might be bored. We wouldn't want that."

Halli gave a shrug. "Why mind me? Repetition's never stopped you before."

"You wouldn't *think* he was a killer, would you?" Katla remarked to Aud. "He seems so inconsequential."

With a glare at Halli, Aud said, *"Don't* be so cross, dear Katla. If you don't want to tell it, that's all right. But I was wondering about one thing. When you told me the story the other night, you said this was the very first House to be settled in the valley."

A curt nod, a sip of posset. "Yes, yes, that's true."

"All the other settlers dispersed after Svein's parents chose this site?"

"So the story goes, as Halli will remember, since he's heard it so *very* often."

Aud wriggled coyly where she sat. "Oh, forget about Halli; he's just a churl. How I love these old tales! So that means that the way the settlers came across the mountains must be somewhere close, above this House."

The old nurse cocked her head. "It must be so. The details have been forgotten long ago. It's said great Svein discouraged talk of the old days before his time. He liked tales to be about himself—and who can blame him, when he was so above the ordinary? *His* story began here in the valley and we're his people, so that's where our story begins too."

"Even so, I wonder if there's still a path up there," Aud said smilingly. "A high pass, a way to the world beyond. I wonder where it might go, what's over there . . . ?"

But now Katla's features had darkened. "What an odd fancy, sweetness. What makes you ask such foolish things?"

Aud's smile faltered. "Um . . . Halli was talking about it the other day, and I just wondered. But setting his stupidity aside, it's funny to think there might be a path up there that we'll never see. Would you like some more wine, Katla?"

"Fill it up and fill it high. Well, you can thank your lucky stars, girl, that you'll never see that path. If you did, it would be while running for your life with a big fat Trow slavering at your heels. Ah, what they'd do to an innocent like you . . ." The old woman broke off wistfully for a few moments. "No, it's not a pretty thought. Good thing Svein's up there with his sword, warding them off. *That's* what they're scared of—that matchless sword. With that in hand, and his silver belt around his waist, Svein never lost a battle. *Not* for him a sly garroting or a treacherous stab in the back, like *some* people we could mention." She winked across at Halli, who scowled. "No, if you displeased him, he'd lop your head off in an honest, straightforward manner. Harsh, perhaps, but you knew where you were with him. Ah . . . those were the days."

"His sword was forged before the settlement, the tales say," Halli ventured. "Impossibly hard and sharp; could cut through anything."

Katla nodded. "Yes, it's a pity we haven't swords like that now, for when Hord Hakonsson comes a-calling. Who in the kitchen's fault is *that*, I wonder? Not yours, sweetness," Katla said, ruffling Aud's fair hair. "Not mine, either."

Spurred on by a surge of indignation, and perhaps by the posset in his cup, Halli leaned forward in his chair. "Say what you like about the Trows, Katla," he said, "but they just come out at night, don't they? So why shouldn't people go beyond the cairns by day? Like Svein and the heroes did."

Katla gave a hoot of mirth. "I should think the Trows would be enough deterrent for anyone. Even the heroes were careful of their claws! But if that's not enough for you, breaking Svein's boundary brings disaster on your House— *and* on your person, more's the point."

"What kind of disaster?" Halli persisted. "What if a foolish, headstrong girl, say, should step beyond the cairns?"

Katla's expression became one of dark satisfaction. "Such a girl would go barren that same instant. She'd be a husk, as arid as a poor old maid like me."

"Well now," Halli said, glancing at Aud. "What sensible girl would risk that?"

Aud grinned lazily back. "What if the miscreant was a boy, dear Katla?"

"A boy? Oh, for *him* the consequences would be even more fearful. But I don't know as I like to mention the details in such delicate company."

"Oh, Halli can take it."

"No, dear, I couldn't possibly say."

"Oh, go o——"

"Well, if you *must* know," Katla went on, almost in the same breath, "if you force me to mention it, for a man the curse would work as follows. First his privy parts would suffer a sudden dramatic dwindling; then they'd curl up like a dying wood louse; then all at once they'd fall off, plop." The old woman drank deep from her posset and smacked her lips. "So who in their right mind would *dare*?"

"Who indeed?" Aud stepped near the fire and took down the jug. "Another drop, Halli? Your mouth looks rather dry."

Little by little the winter waned. Snow stopped falling; the weather improved. Beyond the Trow walls the old snow was piled across the fields in undulating waves of crisp, etched dunes, sculpted and scoured by winds. One morning, with wan sunlight breaking through the cloud banks, Halli noticed that the dunes seemed a little lower. Next day their crests began to sag and gape. When he stood on the porch he could hear the stir of water moving; the air swelled with the rush of dripping, the sound of the coming thaw.

"Good," Aud said. "Shall we head off?"

"Not till we see grass all the way to the top."

A week passed. Men went out into the block-hard fields. With each day the snow on the ridge behind the House retreated farther into hollows, pits, and shaded strips in the lee of walls. The slopes were patterned with dirty white streaks. Green stripes stretched to the cairns.

"All right," Halli said. "Let's go."

The morning was still young, the pale sun clambering through the southeastern sky, in and out of wisps of cloud. The wind that tumbled down from the heights held more than a trace of winter, but it was already the warmest day of the thaw so far. Sweat stippled their foreheads as they climbed.

They were halfway up the ridge.

Halli, somewhat out of breath, turned to look back. The House was still just visible away to the right beyond the hill's fold. Svein's road showed beyond like a length of dark cord, winding off amid the mess of snow-sodden fields. One or two people worked there breaking earth, striking it with soundless strokes; they seemed very far away.

His gaze rested on the steepled roof of the hall that his father would never leave again until—very soon now—his final journey to his cairn. For a moment a pain pierced him, but he shook it off, drawing sharp air into his lungs. He adjusted his pack then, feeling the muscles in his calves and buttocks jar and tingle as he resumed his climb. It felt good to be alive and active again after so long. With a quick movement he scanned the sky.

"Think it'll stay fine?" he said.

"Yes. Not scared are you? Holding back?" Aud was braced against the slope of the hill above him, looking down. Her hair was tucked back in her hood, and this, together with the tunic and leggings Halli had lent her, gave her an oddly masculine appearance. She was finding the climb easier than Halli; several times she had sat ostentatiously on a stone while he struggled to catch up.

"Not in the slightest." He drew level with three plowing strides. "It's a bit steep, that's all."

"Well, you *would* go this way. Why not there, where the track is?" She pointed east along the curve of the hill. "That's much more gentle."

"Also more exposed to the House," Halli said. "We'll be out of sight of it soon. Just in case someone looks up, not that they ever do."

"Do you want me to take the pack for a bit?"

Halli pursed his lips indignantly. "No, thank you."

"Just because I'm a girl? Fine by me. You deserve to carry it, anyway. It's your fault it's so heavy."

He shifted the pack upon his shoulders. "We might need them."

"No, we won't. It's daytime. Well, come on, then. Where's this broken wall of yours?"

"Not much farther. We'll see it when we clear that brow."

The summer before, when he had spent time in the high pasture, the grass had been threaded with blue and yellow flowers; bees had hummed amid the drifting grasses, and the proximity of the boundary had—by day at least—been easy to ignore. Now, however, as they cleared the brow and found the little plateau before them, still half choked with weathered, crispy snow, the sight was altogether drearier. The hut hunched like a beggar against the slope of the hill; wind fretted against its stones. Beyond lay a ragged, undulating line—the broken sheep-wall running between little spars of rock projecting from the snow. Still farther off, and higher, crimping the blank horizon beneath the gray-white sky, rose the line of cairns.

All of a sudden they were very close.

Both Halli's and Aud's pace slowed a little, though the ground was almost flat. Neither one looked at the other.

The cairns were gray-backed, moss-flecked, their stones interlaced with snow. Most were widely spaced apart, but some leaned close toward each other as if in secret confidence.

Halli and Aud stood quite still. Wind blew against their faces. There was no other sound.

The cairns were right on the ridge crest and the moors

could not be seen. To glimpse them, it would be necessary to walk right up among the cairns.

It was easy enough. Twenty steps or so, thirty maximum. All they had to do was walk.

They didn't move.

Halli said, "So, nothing's stopping us, is it?"

"No."

"So we should do it, then."

"That's right."

"We've been talking about it long enough, haven't we? Why wait another moment?"

"Exactly."

"Exactly . . ." Halli blew out his cheeks, took a deep breath. "Do you want a snack or something? We could sit in the hut, have a breather, think about how—"

"I think," Aud said, cutting over him, "we should run at it, not walk. Get it over with quickly. Do you know what I mean? Halli?"

Halli, who had been remembering the fate of his ewe the summer before, and also Katla's tale of the half-eaten boy, shook his mind clear. "What? Oh, yes. Run. All right, we can do that. And we should carry this too." He shrugged off his pack, reached inside and brought out a hedger's bill-hook, wooden-handled with a thick, curved blade. The metal was spotted with rust and broken at the tip, but the edge was sharp. He hefted it in his right hand. "Just in case. You want one?"

"No! Like I've said a thousand times, nothing's going to happen. The Trows *do not exist*, Halli. Stories and lies. That's all."

"I hope you're right."

"Well, if you want me to go alone," she said tartly, "you can scurry home. I'm going on."

"Who said I was going back? Let's get on with it." In anger, he slung his pack over his shoulders and seized her hand. It was colder than his and (he thought) shaking a little. "Together, then?"

"Together."

Then they turned their heads toward the sky and ran straight up toward the line of cairns.

21

UNDER SVEIN'S RULE the outlaws, thieves, foot-
pads, and brigands that had once plagued the land
were driven down-valley or left to kick their heels
upon the gallows in the yard. But the menace of
the Trows persisted and, despite Svein's training,
most men were reluctant to fight them. Their
claws were sharp enough to slice through flesh and
bone and pierce the strongest armor; their teeth
were like needles; their skin was hard enough to
resist puncturing by all but the finest swords. At
night, provided they kept to the soft earth, they had
an eerie strength in their thin, thin arms; only
when drawn onto rock or wood did this power
grow brittle and a chance come for their victim to
break free. While the sun was up they hid in holes
or in the Trow-king's hall high on the moors; at
night they scurried forth, seeking human blood.

SNOW FLEW HIGH against their faces; grass
threshed their shins. Faster, ever faster up the slope
they went. *Eight steps, nine* . . . They leaped across the
old sheep wall. Halli's pack clinked and jarred upon his

back. *Eighteen, nineteen* . . . Up the final rise. He saw in his mind the fragments of the ewe, the scattered pieces of flesh among the stones . . . But it was too late to draw back; he could not have halted even had he wished to. *Twenty-three steps, twenty-four,* and before them now, the nearest cairns, low-slung, ancient, tilted, farther apart than they seemed from below. They jerked and jumped in his vision as if they were alive.

Thirty-one steps, thirty-two . . .

Aud gripped him tight; he felt her nails against his skin. On either side of the first cairn they went, and their linked hands passed over the top of it. Three steps more, stumbling on the bumpy ground, Halli's mouth open in a soundless shout, fingers holding Aud's hard as he could, her nails digging into him.

They ran, ran, and then the second cairn was passed on Halli's side and they were through, over the ridge crest and down a little way, out onto the forbidden moors, still running.

"Halli—" A tug came on his arm. "Halli, we can—we can stop now."

He glanced at her, wild-eyed. Yes. Yes, it was done. He forced his body to ease, and slowed, halting at last in unison with Aud. A final step . . . Stillness. Their hands remained linked for a moment before dropping free.

It was very silent. Their chests rose and fell. Aud was half-doubled over, palms on thighs. Halli still had the billhook raised; little by little he lowered it to his side.

They stood in a broad sea of grass and melting snow. A great green-white expanse stretched out on either side. Scattered here and there were strange black outcrops, sheer crags of rock rising like buildings; otherwise the moor was lonely, desolate, gently undulating. Ahead it dropped away, before rising again to a little conical hill in the middle distance. Beyond the hill was a gulf, then—seemingly no nearer than he had always known them—the familiar gray-white mass of the mountains.

Halli looked back. The cairns seemed lower than they had done, a double line of dark gray shrugs on the lip of the slope, guarding a bluish vagueness—the valley that they had suddenly, and so easily, left behind them.

Aud, straightening, gave her little barking laugh. "Done it!" she said, gulping with relief. "Oh, Halli! What were we afraid of?"

The grass by her feet erupted; something dark rose up. Aud screamed.

A small dun bird rose into the sky and with a high, piping cry, looped away across the hill.

Halli had jumped back, billhook raised; now he was laughing. "Corncrake," he said. "Just a corncrake. Don't worry, if she'd pecked your nose I'd have rescued you."

"I notice you jumped *away*," Aud said, when she'd finished swearing.

"Sorry, sorry." He was still laughing, conscious of a

mild hysteria; he felt light-headed, thrown out of kilter by their sudden act. He knew he was grinning foolishly. "I never thought," he said, "it would be so simple. I thought——"

"You thought a great big Trow would leap out from the ground and get you. Like this——!" Shoulders high, fingers bent like claws, a hideous expression on her face, she leaped at him, swiping left and right. He ducked away, grinning. "It's nonsense, Halli, the whole thing. Where do we explore first, then? I vote for that little hill. We'd get a view of the moors there; it's not too far."

But Halli had noticed something else. "In a moment," he said. "Come and look at this."

He set off, snow flicking from his boot caps, following the line of the boundary. Not far away rose a great mound. It was set amid a cluster of cairns, many tall and grandiose, yet all cowering in its shadow. It was sow-backed, humped, and tapering east-west, and was positioned right upon the hill crest so that it could be seen far off across the valley. Where the sun had lingered, green grass showed under the snow.

Aud caught up with Halli as he stood beside the mound, his face suddenly still.

"This is——?"

"Svein's. Of course. Look there, though. There's been a collapse."

Not far from them, halfway along the southern flank of the mound, the soil had fallen away, exposing the bare stones of the cairn beneath. Some of these had shifted too, fallen from their old position. The snow below was humped with scattered stones, and the rocks in the gash looked precariously balanced.

Halli's eyes were wide. "Look at the *size* of the thing. It's almost like a hall."

"Why are we whispering?" Aud said. She scuffed in the snow, located a fleck of stone and tossed it irreverently at the gash in the mound, where it chinked against a rock and lay still.

"Don't," Halli said. He was thinking of all the old tales, of the legends of the hero, how he sat somewhere inside, sword ready, looking out across the moor.

"Come *on*." Aud was tugging at his arm. "We're hunting for a path, remember?"

Their walk across the moors was slow, monotonous, and silent, under the lowering sky. The hill was farther than they had guessed, and the land between pockmarked with dips and depressions hidden in the snow. More than once Halli disappeared waist-deep and had to accept Aud's help to struggle free. They saw no sign of life and nothing of interest or consequence, save the jutting outcrops of black rock, some of which rose high as the roof on the hall below.

"No Trows here," Aud said after a time. "Unless they're very small." She was still grinning.

Time passed; the low lying hill got closer. "There's a

story about Svein," Halli said. "He went to a hill like that. Found a door. The way to the Trow-king's halls."

"I know it. Arne went too, on *our* side of the valley. Just a story, Halli."

"You were happy enough to believe Katla's one," he remarked, "about Svein's being the first place settled when the people crossed the mountains."

"It's just I never heard it before. It got me thinking."

Halli shrugged. "Well, we'll see what's over this bump."

The hill, when they reached it, was higher than they expected, and by the time they gained its summit both were sweating and breathing hard. The top was studded with boulders and still thick with snow. Ice crusted in sheltered hollows.

"Go carefully," Halli advised as they came out on the summit. "It'd be easy to slip here. Oh—look at the *view*."

Ahead of them the landscape contorted with new harshness: blank folds of heather, a tangle of ice-bound streams winding among them, a stepped recession of cliffs and straggling grass, thin white waterfalls hung about with icicles, tumbled pyramids of broken rock beneath gullies scoured in the foothills of the mountains. It was cold, barren, an inhospitable waste, but its wildness and grandeur took Halli's breath away.

But Aud was scowling. "So much for a *path*," she said finally.

"Well, it's not going to come up and shake us by the

hand, is it? We need to look about, that's all. . . ." His voice trailed off. "What's *that*, Aud?" he said, pointing.

She frowned. "What? Not a path, I know that much."

"Stop moaning and look. See down there, that little spur where the sun's shining right now. In the crook of it; is that a cave in those rocks, or just shadow?"

Aud squinted under her hand. "Might be shadow . . ." she said slowly. "Only one way to find out."

The southern slopes of the hill lacked the snow and ice of the northern flank, but the ground grew increasingly waterlogged as they neared the cluster of rocks nestling near its base. Both of them had slipped frequently, and their leggings were sodden, the wool heavy, chafing their skin. Neither gave the discomfort a thought. They had come to a standstill, silent, gazing.

Ahead, amid a jumble of great split stones, a fissure opened, narrow at the top, wider at the base. It hung like a jagged teardrop in the rock. Cool, damp air radiated from it; it held the smell of darkness and old quiet. Halli felt the hairs on the back of his neck stir at the implications. He said, in rather a small voice: "Aud . . ."

She was brisk, decisive. "It's just a cave. Not the Trow-king's front door."

"Well, yes, you *say* that, but——"

"Oh, I'll prove it to you. I'll take a quick look."

"No, Aud. I don't think——"

"If we had a light, it would be better, but I bet I can see

in a little way. . . ." Now she was hopping over the litter of rocks, scrambling down to the entrance of the fissure.

Halli said, "I really don't think this is a good idea. Take the billhook, at least."

"I don't *want* the bloody billhook." She came to a standstill on flat, wet rock. "Now then; I won't go more than a few feet in. If I see a Trow, I'm going to run, all right?" She chuckled briefly, stepping forward. "It goes a long way," her voice came whispering back. "Really we need a lantern." He watched her slender form grow gray and indistinct, framed by cold rock. Now it was amorphous, scarcely visible; now it was gone. He heard her feet crunching on loose pebbles.

Halli waited. The top of the fissure, where it narrowed swiftly, was made of smooth stone, billowing out like frozen drapes. It reminded him a little of the curtains at the end of their hall back home, leading to the private rooms where his father lay. He saw then in his mind's eye the slow, unchanging, rise and fall of his father's chest beneath the quilt; felt again the sense of entrapment that had stifled him so long. . . . It occurred to him that he could no longer hear Aud's footsteps.

"Aud?" he called. "Aud?" In the silence his pulse hammered against his ear. "Aud?" he called again; louder this time. "Oh, *great Svein* . . ." Sweat broke out on his palms; he started forward, slipping down among the tumbled rocks.

Almost immediately he heard her, very faint, as if from far away. "Halli . . ."

"Where are you?"

"Come here. . . ."

There was fear in the voice. He cursed again, fumbling in his pack for the billhook as he dropped down onto the flat stones of the cave mouth and, without hesitation, stepped out of the light. For several heartbeats he was entirely blind, shuffling forward, hands still rummaging in the pack. . . .

"Ah!" He had collided with something; he heard Aud's squeal, felt the rasp of her fleece against his frantic hand. "You *idiot*, Aud," he snarled, "what's the *matter* with you? If I'd had the hook out I might have—"

"*Look*, Halli. Look."

At first he saw nothing; his eyes struggled with the dimness. But little by little faint shapes swam into view: Aud's face, ghostlike, floating; a tilted slab of rock, hanging hazily beyond her, reflecting the meager light that drifted from the opening behind them. And, at their feet: a scattering of pale things that gleamed a dull soft white. Some were long and thin, others slighter, curved. Still others were little more than fragments, bright shards scattered on the dark, dirt floor.

"Aud . . ." Halli whispered. "I think they're—"

"I know what they *are*, for Arne's sake!" Her voice was taut as a drum.

"Good, good, then you'll know we need to get *out*. . . ."

He located her arm, pulled savagely, heading back toward

the light. She struggled, but without conviction. Moments later they spilled into brightness, blinking, breathless, out under the gray sky and the arching mountains.

Aud's hood had fallen back, and her hair had tumbled loosely over one side of her face. She pawed angrily at Halli's clutching hand. "Let *go*."

"Gladly."

"*Why* are you panicking? It isn't necessarily what you think."

"No? What alternatives can you suggest? And if you talk about wolves and eagles again, I'm going to kick you."

She stamped a foot. "Kick away. It *might* be wolves, or bears—"

"They weren't animal bones, Aud! I saw thigh bones for sure, and ribs, and—"

"Even so, wolves might be to blame. Or . . . or . . . they might have been outlaws or criminals who went beyond the cairns. Yes! Long ago . . . They're not new bones, Halli. They might have been outcasts, who went there for shelter, and, and died of cold."

"Oh, so you don't think we might possibly have found the Trow-king's hall?" he cried. "You know, the one in the stories you don't believe? The one all hung about with men's bones?"

"No, actually, I don't." She had her hands on hips, glaring at him now. He stood at a distance, tense with anger and agitation, knuckles gripping white upon his pack strap. She shook her head again. "Halli—whatever was in that cave, it died a long while ago. Hundreds of years, maybe. The bones were ancient. We shouldn't panic."

He moistened his lips, rubbed at the side of his face. "Maybe."

"I'm right, you know. Would Svein or Arne have run in fear because of a few old bones?"

Halli exhaled slowly. "We need to talk about this. Let's get away from the cave."

During their climb back up the little hill, the argument continued, neither giving any ground, yet neither perhaps wholly sure of their own position. For his part, Halli was torn between his natural caution and a deep reluctance to appear more fearful than Aud. This tension made him sharp-tongued; Aud likewise was jittery and scathing. By the time they reached the summit, the atmosphere was sour. Even so, hunger drove them to sit upon a stone for lunch. From the position of the sun they realized it was already early afternoon.

For a while neither of them spoke. Then Halli said, "We should go back soon."

Aud was tearing on a strip of smoked meat. She spat a piece of gristle into the grass. "No. We've got hours yet."

"To do what? Where shall we look?" He gestured at the immensity around them. "We won't find the path today. We'll need to come back another time, look again."

"You're just scared of a few old bones."

"Oh, shut up."

Aud hurled her meat aside. "If I have any more of this, I swear I'll vomit. All winter there's been nothing else." She put her hands in the pack, rummaging among the weapons. "Surely you packed some cheese or something. . . . What's this?"

Frowningly, she drew out an odd black object, sickle-shaped, knife-thin, its lumpy, rounded base shapeless as a pig's-knuckle. Light gleamed on the serration of the inner, shorter edge and the vicious curvature of the blade.

"It's that Trow claw I was telling you of," Halli said. "The one the trader tried to kill me with. Careful with it."

"Why? It's fake, isn't it? Why did you bring—*Ah*, Arne's blood, it's sharp!"

She jerked her hand away and sat back, sucking the side of one finger with an expression of shock. After a moment she took the finger out and held it up; dark blood dripped down it and ran like water across the back of her hand. It pooled in the hollow between her fingers and fell in thick droplets onto the ground.

"You *idiot*, Aud." Halli took the claw by the lumpen base and dropped it in his pack. He snatched up her hand quickly, drew it to him, and folded it in the loose fabric of his tunic, squeezing it tight, staunching the flow. "What were you doing, grabbing at it like that? Why do you think he tried to kill me with it? It's sharp. That's why I brought it."

Aud's face had gone white; her shoulders shuddered. "I feel quite sick," she said in a shaky voice. "And now I'm ruining your tunic. Look at all the blood."

"You'll be all right. What were you playing at, grabbing at—?"

"Don't snap at me. Shut up about it."

"Well, it's your stupid fault. Will you just keep *still*?"

They sat in silence, Aud rigid, staring; Halli gazing gloomily off across the waste, still holding her finger tight. His eyes wandered. For a time he focused on nothing, then his attention was caught by something halfway up a distant slope, amid an otherwise unbroken line of cliffs and crags. A narrow band of grass, scarcely visible under the snow, rose diagonally toward a little notch upon the skyline. Halli squinted, frowned. It was very distant; he could not be sure. . . . But it was just possible to think it a passable way onward, out of the moors, onto the high mountains. . . .

He made this observation to Aud, who had tentatively withdrawn her hand and was examining her bleeding finger.

"Let's go and see, then," she said curtly. "That's what we're here for."

"Well, we obviously can't do it *now*," Halli said. "It's late, and you're injured, and after what we found. . . ."

"Oh, what is *wrong* with you?" She rose abruptly to her feet, stony-faced. "When are we going to get the chance again? My father will send for me any day, and that will be that."

"No, he won't! The torrents will start soon. He won't come up-valley for weeks."

"I'm not risking it." Whether it was the pain of her wound, or the shock of the discovery in the cave, there was a brittleness in her voice he had not heard before; she did not look at him. "You stay here, or go back," she snapped. "*I* don't care. I'm going to look."

"Oh, don't be so pig-headed." He had sprung to his feet now. "You'll never get there on your own."

"Just watch me." And she was striding down the slope, hand wrapped in her fleece, face imperious, lips set.

Halli gave a snort of rage. Stepping close, he snatched at her hood to pull her back. Aud squealed, pulled herself free, dashed his hand away; she gave a little run to get clear of him, slipped upon a patch of ice, stumbled, and caught her boot in a hole between stones. She lost her balance and fell heavily into the grass, twisting her leg awkwardly.

The cry she gave made Halli's heart lurch. He hurried over, anger dissolving into anxiety. "What happened? Are you all right?"

"No thanks to you. Ankle hurts a bit." She flexed her foot experimentally. "It's all right. For a moment there . . . Help me up."

"Sorry," he said, helping.

She breathed hard. "Me too. It's just—" She was standing upright now, resting her weight cautiously upon her leg. "It's just I can't bear the thought of going home. You don't know what it's like with my father. He drives me mad."

"I wasn't *saying* we should give up," he said. "Just stop for today. That gap in the cliff is promising. We'll come back soon and find a route to it, I promise. But now——"

Aud cried out. She had tried to walk away, back up the slope, and her ankle had almost collapsed under her. He grasped her arm, stopping her from falling.

Halli's eyes were round. "You can't walk, can you?"

She nodded, wincing. "Don't worry, it's a little sore, that's all. It'll be fine soon."

He looked at her. "You think?"

"Oh, yes."

"So you're not going to have any trouble getting back to the boundary?" he asked. "Before nightfall, for instance?"

Aud gave a slightly high-pitched laugh. "No, no, of course not! How unlucky would *that* be?"

22

On moonlit nights, when Svein grew tired of sitting on the Law Seat and dictating business to his people, he took up his belt and sword, and climbed to the ridge to hunt for Trows. They were not so numerous down by the House, being cautious of his presence, but on the moors were plentiful still. One by one they came, gray shadows clambering from the ground or sidling through the gorse, and he fought with them under the cold moon, and took their heads and skins to decorate his hall.

Even Svein often came back bruised and torn from these adventures, and he forbade his people to climb upon the moors under any circumstances. "The Trows are too strong up here," he said, "and you'd be too far from help. Stay close to the home I made you."

AFTERNOON BECAME EVENING; in the east the sky merged with the land; light bled away into the west. The snowy moor grew dim and purple, its folds and depressions filled with pools of dusk. Here and there the rocky outcrops rose like great black nails rammed into the earth.

A flock of geese flew high above them, beneath the first bright stars.

They were still a long way from the cairns.

Halli said brightly, "It's a good thing we don't believe in the Trows, isn't it?"

"Very." They shuffled on a few more steps. His arm was tight around Aud's waist, keeping her from falling; her arm hung heavy across his shoulders. She swung herself forward by little hops and jerks, her bad foot raised above the grass. In such a way, they had already negotiated the slope of the little hill, and more than half the moorland. But the going was dismally slow.

Periodically Halli attempted light conversation, which he found almost as tricky as the physical exertion. It was hard talking of favorite meals and invented gossip when his mind kept returning to images of Trows stirring beneath the earth. He scanned the landscape around them; even as he watched, it faded. He could not see the boundary.

They had just passed under the shadows of one of the great protruding crags and were setting out again amid the emptiness when Aud glanced up, scanning the flat gray half-light. "Halli," she said, "what was that noise?"

He hesitated. "I didn't hear anything."

"No? Perhaps I didn't either. I thought that—No, but it's hard with this wind."

"Exactly. Let's not halt and discuss it, eh? Let's keep going."

"Good idea."

They pressed on amid the gathering dark. The little light remaining hung pale and faint above the western mountains; the nearby crags protruding from the moor grew hazy and indistinct. There was still no sign of the cairns ahead.

Snow crunched beneath their stumbling feet; the air was growing cold. Aud leaned heavily against Halli, gasping whenever her foot brushed ground.

A thought occurred to Halli. "You've got your hand bound up, haven't you?" he asked. "I mean, you're not leaving a trail of blood behind us or anything?"

"Of course I'm not. Shut up."

"Just checking." Halli was quiet for a few paces, then began whistling a jaunty, raspy, intensely repetitive tune between his teeth. He kept this up for a long while. Finally Aud gave an angry cry.

"Will you just *shut up*? If I hear that dirge one more time I swear I'll slap you."

"I was trying to keep our spirits up."

"By showing how scared you are? Great idea."

"Me scared? Look at my face; look at it—is that the face of someone scared?"

"I don't know, Halli. I can't honestly tell. Why? Because it's dark and I can't see a thing. It's *dark*, Halli. And we're still not over the boundary, thanks to you!"

"Thanks to *me*? You're the one who fell over!"

"You practically pushed me."

"Oh, *this* is rich," Halli cried. "First off, I thought you didn't care a bent pin about the boundary or the Trows. Secondly, might I remind you that if you hadn't got so stroppy, we wouldn't be in this mess right now and *you* wouldn't be panicking."

Aud uttered a whoop of rage. "Me? I'm perfectly relaxed!"

"Sorry, I didn't quite catch that—your voice was a little too shrill."

There was a brief whistling sound. Halli said: "What was that?"

"Me trying to slap you. I missed."

"No, not that. Something farther away."

They stood in the darkness and listened to the movement of the winds across the blank surface of the moor. Aud said in a small voice: "I can't . . . I don't . . . I don't *think* there's anything. . . . Are you scratching yourself?"

"What? No. What kind of question is that? *Am I scratching myself.* That's the noise I *heard*, Aud. Where's it coming from?"

They listened, eyes staring blindly at the dark. No doubt about it: faintly, carried on the wind, scarcely audible above its howling, but separate from it, there came a low scrabbling sound. Several times it broke off, only to start

346

again almost immediately; it rose and fell, but even when it diminished almost to nothing it was still there—a thin persistence on the edge of their hearing. Where it came from was impossible to say.

Halli felt something grasp his arm. "I hope that's your hand, Aud."

"Of course it is. What *is* that sound, Halli?"

"Well . . ." He tried to seem cheerful. "I don't think it's wolves."

"I *know* it's not wolves, Halli. What *is* it?"

"It's . . . the wind on the stones."

"Oh. Really? What do you mean exactly?"

"Erm . . . Let's keep going. I'll tell you as we walk." Grappling each other close, they continued through the snow. Every now and then they halted and listened hopefully, but the noise remained. At last Halli, who had been thinking hard, said: "Here's how it works. The wind blows little pebbles down the crags and cairns. They skitter and slide down natural gullies, causing the sound we hear. I hope this is the right direction."

"Of course it is. We haven't turned, have we? The boundary's straight ahead." She was panting a little; they were hobbling rather faster than before. "So, pebbles in gullies, you think it is? You don't think it's more like a kind of *burrowing*, like claws coming up through earth?"

"Well . . . it could be that too."

"Oh, great."

347

"But, Aud, remember. Those bones were old. So you don't believe that Trows—"

"No. That's right. I don't. And nor do you. Ah, this ankle—I *wish* I could run on it. Even a little." She reached up, squeezed his hand. "Thanks for being reassuring."

"All part of the servi—*Svein's ghost!* What's that?" Halli lurched sideways, clutching at Aud, who stumbled and almost fell.

Aud had stifled a scream. *"What?"*

"There! Where I'm pointing."

"But where the hell's that? It's dark. How could you see—"

"I sensed something. Big. Very big, there to our left."

They clung together, staring. In the western sky the faintest paleness lingered after the vanished sun. Against this glow it was possible to sense, by looking indirectly at it, a hulking outline of darkest black. Aud forced out a pent-up breath. "That's just one of the *crags*, you fool. Probably the last one before the cairns. Great Arne, Halli; I nearly *died*."

An embarrassed laugh in the dark beside her. "Sorry. False alarm."

"So will you let go of me now?"

With a flurry of manly coughs and brusque adjustments of clothing, Halli drew away. There was a brief silence.

"Come on," Aud said. "We must almost be there now."

"And did you notice?" Halli put in. "That weird noise has stopped too."

"Thank Arne for th—"

Somewhere in the blackness, not too distant, there sounded the gentle crack and scrape of shifting rocks. It ceased abruptly.

Halli and Aud froze as motionless as stones embedded in the moor. Every nerve and sinew strained against the dark.

Now there was nothing. But this fresh silence did not greatly reassure them.

Halli ventured a whisper. "You know what I think that was? I think the wind dislodged a biggish stone, which tumbled abruptly down a cairn, giving the uncanny illusion of a sinister and stealthy footstep."

"You don't think that at all, do you?"

"No. How fast can you hop?"

"Let's see."

Onward together, Aud lurching, Halli supporting her as best she could. His pack bounced roughly on his back; her breath came in frantic gasps. Twice they nearly tumbled; once Aud floundered in a snow filled hollow. The darkness flowed against them like a river in spate, and still they had not reached the cairns.

All at once, close by: an odd swift skittering, something hard moving upon rock.

They drew up short. Halli put his mouth against Aud's

ear. "I'm going to open the pack, get out the weapons."

"You do that."

With Aud leaning on him, Halli flung off the backpack, plumped it down onto the snow, and set to untying the knotted string. As the night was black, his fingers numb with cold and his hands shaking with fear, it was not as straightforward a task as he might have wished. Also, the knot had slipped.

From somewhere close came a curiously unpleasant creaking, then a loud, thin crack, as if brittle stone had snapped under sudden weight.

"Halli," Aud hissed. "Come *on*. . . ."

"It's this bloody knot."

Now, from just a little closer: the surreptitious, delicate crunch of trodden snow.

"What do you mean, *the knot?* You tied it, didn't you? Get it undone!"

"Stop hassling me—There . . . Oh, no—it slipped again."

"Halli . . ."

Another sound, this time behind them: crisp snow broken, knocked aside. It held the suggestion of slightly faster movement, a growing eagerness. . . .

"Curse it, now I've snagged a nail."

Aud pressed close beside him. "Please tell me that the bag's now open."

"Yes, finally. What do you want? The billhook or the turnip knife?"

"I don't care!—anything with a blade. Quick." Fumbles of cloth, a clink of metal.

"Here." Halli held a weapon out, handle first; he sensed Aud's hands patting the air frantically, connecting with the wood, closing on the hasp. She wrenched it away from him and gave a cry of pain.

"Ah, my *hand!*"

"Hold it in your left, then." He had the billhook now; he rose from his crouch, feeling its weight, swishing it briefly side to side. Away to his right, but not too far, he heard a hurried noise in the snow. "Put your back against mine," he said. "I'll help support you. And be very quiet. We'll hear when it comes in."

"What then?"

"Swipe. Hard as you can."

Her back, narrow, slender, pressed firmly against his. He drove his legs deep into the snow, scrubbing his boot soles against the grass beneath, seeking better purchase. He closed his eyes, listened, trying to concentrate. Shuffling steps, odd creaking sounds . . . Now they were on his left, now straight ahead of him. . . . Something was going quickly, circling them, moving inward all the time. It didn't seem to be at all slowed by the utter dark. Halli knew that it could see them.

All at once the pattering drew back, faded. He could hear nothing.

Halli ventured a whisper. "You all right, Aud?"

"Oh, I'm very well. You?"

"Not so ba—" A sudden confusion of noise: snow threshed outward at a run, grass crushing, Aud sucking in a scream. Her back jarred against his; even through the padding of their clothes he felt her shoulder blade wrench violently round—she had swung her arm out, slashing with the knife. Then a concussion, something somewhere connecting hard: the impact jolted through her, through him, so that his legs almost buckled under him. There was a spattering of snow on either side, and a horrid snarling. Steps receded into darkness.

Silence. Aud's head rolled back against his shoulder.

Halli reached up a frantic hand, touching her hair and hood. "Aud—"

A small voice: "I hit it, but I lost the knife."

"Did it hurt you? Aud, *listen* to me—are you hurt?"

"No, no. I felt so cold when it grabbed me. I struck it, but I dropped the knife."

"It doesn't matter. Maybe you've driven it off." He was staring this way, that way, eyes darting vainly all about. Meaningless lights and swirls distracted him. Wait, what had Svein done on the Rock when the moon was covered? He'd closed his eyes. Halli forced himself to do the same. Better. The lights had gone. When he listened he couldn't hear anything but Aud's gasping breaths. Her back shook against his.

"We're going to have to make a move for the cairns, Aud," he said softly, patting his hand against her hood. "Can you do that, you think?"

"Of course. Don't patronize me!" Her sudden anger reassured him. "I don't know *where* the knife's gone."

"Forget it. Take mine." He half turned, fumbling for her arm. "Quickly."

"But what'll you——?"

"I'll use the claw." He bent to the pack, pushed careful fingers to the bottom. They closed swiftly on the solid, knuckle-thick base of Bjorn the trader's Trow claw. He straightened. It was probably sharper than the billhook anyway, though harder to hold. Might give the thing a shock, if it saw it—might think it was a real one. "Ready?" he said.

They went on, step by step, arm in arm, Aud leaning on him as before. Every few yards they stopped and listened. All was quiet, save for the wind, their breathing, and the blood drumming in their heads.

Halli's hopes began to rise. He said, "I think we're almost there. Aud?"

She stirred. "Mm?"

"We're almost at the cairns. See there, that little light?" A speck of yellow, floating, dancing in the dark. "I think that's one of Rurik's farms on the far side of the valley. To see that we must be close to the crest of the ridge. A few more steps, Aud. Then we'll be safe." He waited, but she didn't answer. "Aud?"

"What?"

"It didn't hurt you, did it? You'd tell me."

"I'm fine." But her voice was small again, drifting. Halli scowled into the dark and strove to increase the pace.

The attack, which came a moment later, was almost without warning, unheralded by the slightest noise. But he felt the sudden rush of cold, foul air upon his face and, by instinct more than conscious thought, lurched to his left, pushing Aud aside in the opposite direction. He landed on one knee, skidding in the snow, feeling something forceful pass at speed. The taint that struck his nostrils made him gasp; nearby he heard Aud choking.

He got to his feet, whirled round and slashed out vainly with the claw—a speculative act, as he could not tell where the enemy might be. Then Aud screamed, loud this time, followed by the odd, discordant ring of metal breaking. Teeth bared, Halli started toward the sounds, only to collide with something backing on to him, bringing with it such a stench of earth and deep, foul rotten things that his gums ached and his teeth felt loose in his jaw. The thing was cold too, piercingly so; his skin grew stiff upon his face and his fingers numb. He almost dropped the claw, but steeling himself thrust it out regardless, catching the unseen creature even as it spun round at him.

Harsh noises, as of teeth being gnashed together.

A weight struck the side of his face. Halli, crying out, staggered back, but remained standing.

Sharp things caught him by the throat, digging at his flesh. His head grew numb, his knees began to give way. Far off he heard Aud crying; the sound suppressed the spreading chill. He brought the Trow claw abruptly up in front of him, with a hard, sharp, chopping stroke. Instantly the grasp upon his throat was broken. There was a cry of pain and bitter desolation. Halli was struck in the chest by an unknown force, hurled backward into snow; he rolled head over heels, sprawling in a drift.

Lights tumbled before his eyes; he struggled upright, blowing snow from his mouth and nose. He was still holding the claw.

What could he hear?

The wind, a distant clattering of stones, Aud weeping in the darkness.

Halli moved forward, following the sobs. He went cautiously, step by careful step, but knocked into Aud all the same. By feel he established she was sitting on the ground.

"I struck it again," she said. "But the impact broke my knife."

"I hurt it too, I think. It's fled, but it'll be back, bring others. Get up, Aud. Come on."

He helped her rise. Without further words they stumbled on and almost immediately brushed their hands against the stones of a cairn: they had been right beside the boundary without realizing. Then, bad leg or no, they broke into a run, careering helplessly over the hill crest, half colliding with first one cairn, then another, until they knew they'd passed them by; and then fell tumbling together, gasping, safe, in a snowy mass of unseen heather, with the distant yellow lights of Svein's House glittering far below.

SVEIN WAS KEEN TO VISIT the Trow-king's hall again, but his wife was doubtful.

"They'll be expecting a third visit," she said. "And believe me, they'll catch you this time. What happens then? Your flesh will bubble in their pot."

Svein said: "Don't worry. They won't catch me. I'm too quick for them. Put my supper on at sundown; I'll be back to enjoy it." Then he went up to the ridge.

Into the Trows' hall he went, past the hanging bones and the burning fire, past the holes where the Trows curled sleeping. Taking a burning torch, he went to the staircase leading into the earth. He looked back at the distant entrance, where the light of day was slowly dimming. Did he have time? Surely!

Down the stairs he went, slowly, slowly, on and on, until he came out in a great round room with fires burning and a pile of treasure in the center. Beside the treasure was a golden throne, and in that throne sat the Trow-king, vast and terrible. But also sound asleep and snoring.

"This'll be easy enough," thought Svein. He popped some gold into a bag, then stole forward toward the throne, sword raised. But at that moment, above the earth, the winter sun went behind the ridge. And the Trow-king opened his great red eyes.

When he saw Svein creeping up, sword in hand, he let out a roar that woke the other Trows, and they all came rushing, intent on tearing him limb from limb. But Svein sprang away, down a tunnel he saw in the rock beside the chair. He ran, ran, but here came the Trow-king, slashing with his long arms and roaring with his great, great mouth. And behind *him* came all the other Trows, screaming out Svein's name.

Svein ran, ran, holding out the brand before him to light his way. And every few paces the tunnel divided and he had to choose one way or the other, and sometimes the tunnel went up, and sometimes down, until he was hopelessly lost. "This is no good," he thought. "I might as well stop and sell my life as dearly as I can." But just then, from along a narrow passage up ahead, he smelled something delicious, savory, familiar. "That's my supper cooking!" he cried, "I'd know that anywhere." And he plunged on down the passage, with the Trow-king swiping at his heels.

All along the twisting tunnels Svein followed the smell of stew until ahead of him he saw the faintest chink of evening light. He cut the earth away with his sword and sprang up—out into Low Field just above his House! But Svein didn't waste time celebrating; he watched the hole. Out popped the Trow-king's head. Down came Svein's sword. The head went bouncing in the grass. Svein picked it up, with the jaws still snapping, and went home. *Thump*, he tossed it on the table. "Present for you," he told his wife. "Oh, and here's a bit of treasure. You saved my bacon today."

And that was Svein's last visit to the Trow-king's hall.

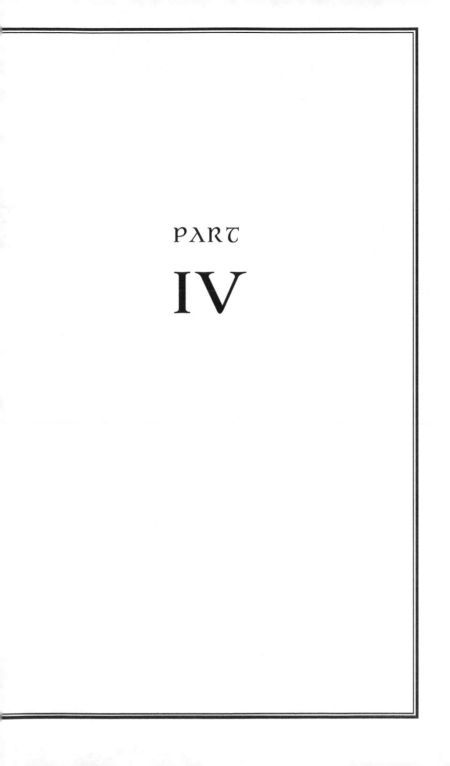

PART

IV

23

AFTER THE TROW-KING'S death, and with Svein growing older, he didn't leave his hall so often. True, he led new raids against Rurik's and Ketil's Houses, but despite intensive fighting, the outcome of each expedition was inconclusive. It is not said whether it was this or his age that blackened his mood, but in his later years Svein's character grew darker than before, and his judgments in hall harshly predictable. He took to wearing his sword even on the Law Seat, and many of those he convicted never made it to the gallows in the yard.

Some thought Svein had become impatient with life in his House and sought another great deed to accomplish. At last, one summer, he sent messengers to the other heroes, requesting a truce and a conference to discuss the question of the Trows.

THE WINDOWS IN SVEIN'S hall were tall slabs of darkness. Outside, wind stirred against the panes. Fire burned low in the braziers hanging from the walls, and the hearth light crept like a living thing, red and many armed, across the flagstones in the floor.

Aud and Halli huddled close beside the hearth. They did not speak.

Halli had strong wine in his cup; he drank it quickly. With every sip he stole a sideways glance at Aud, staring uncomprehendingly at her white face and matted hair. Her fleece had been slashed across the chest, the wool sliced almost through. One hand was newly bandaged, one ankle clearly swollen beneath its fresh, clean strapping. She held her cup as if it was the only thing in the world she could be sure of. Above the clenched knuckles, her eyes were blank, unseeing.

Halli drank his wine. He, by contrast, had got off lightly. True, his fleece was torn about the collar, and his neck ached to the touch—he could still feel the points where the Trow's claws had grazed him. But aside from that and the chill in his bones from his hours upon the hill, he was outwardly unharmed.

When they had at last drawn near the House, after a long and cumbersome descent, they had been met by searchers bearing torches, out scouring the fields for them. The general reaction was relief and concern for Aud's injuries; she had been promptly whisked away by Katla while Halli explained to Leif, Eyjolf, and an assembled throng how, during their walk among the higher pastures, Aud had slipped and fallen from a crag, following which he had slowly, carefully, helped her home. After expressing predictable indignation that he should so jeopardize the health of their guest, the rest of the household retired to bed. To Halli's surprise no one thought to challenge his story. His lies were swallowed without question.

Halli drank his wine and stared into the fire. Stories and lies . . .

The problem was, of course, the stories had turned out to be *true*.

The Trows were up there. They were up beyond the boundary. It kept them at bay just like the tales said. There was no other explanation. Which meant, in turn, that Svein and the other heroes *had* beaten them back at the Battle of the Rock so very long ago—the heroes *had* existed, and had performed that final feat. It meant their cairns *did* still keep the valley safe. It meant the Trows were up there, penned and waiting on the heights.

It meant there was no way out.

Halli watched the darting upward movements of the flames, how they leaped, flared brightly, and vanished without trace. Was that the way of it, then? After their one brief attempt at escape, after daring to do what no one had done for generations, after glimpsing that far-off notch upon the skyline, a possible route up into the mountains—after all of *that*, would he and Aud just fall back now, their hopes snuffed out, to drift quietly through life toward the dark anonymity of a cairn?

That was what everyone else did.

Far off behind closed doors, he heard a ragged sound. His father coughing.

Partly to block it out, partly to channel the dull anger that flared suddenly inside him, Halli said roughly, "That tear on your fleece. Didn't go through, did it?"

Aud looked up. She cleared her throat; it had been a long while since she'd spoken. "No. I'm bruised, not cut."

"Good."

There was a silence. "Your neck looks bad," Aud said finally.

"Does it? Feels fine."

"There're five red marks on it."

Halli shuddered, but he said only: "Well, the touch was very cold."

"I know. I couldn't breathe when it struck my chest." She stared down at her swollen ankle, then at the fire again. "I'm sorry, Halli."

"That's all right." He took a sip of wine. "For what, exactly? Just to be clear."

"For taking us up there. For everything I said—about the—about the stories, you know; I'm sorry I denied it all, Halli. It's just I never thought—"

"Nor I."

"Is there any more wine?"

"Not here. I'll get some from the kitchen." But he didn't move.

"You don't think," Aud said, after a silence, "the Trow

might follow us down here? Because we crossed the boundary, I mean?"

"It would have caught us long ago, if so. We took ages getting down. The boundary still holds."

Aud hunched deeper in her chair. "You didn't see it, did you?" she said.

"No. Just smelled it, heard it, felt it. . . ." He rubbed irritably at his eyes.

"What fools we were. It's true, everything the stories say . . ."

Halli noticed that her voice was small and shook a little. He stirred in his seat, making what effort he could. "Well, not *all* the stories," he said. "Katla's one about the curse, for instance."

"What curse?"

"It hasn't happened. . . ." He attempted a grin. *"You know."*

Her look was blank. "How do you mean?"

"The curse affecting men . . . men who cross the boundary . . ." He blew out his cheeks. "Oh, never mind."

"I see. . . . You're still all there? Right. That's good."

There was a silence.

"But a Trow nearly *killed* us, Halli!" Aud cried out. "That's *not* so good!"

"Well, we lived through it, didn't we? We survived."

"Yes, but what's the use of that? We're stuck here! In the valley, in our Houses. We're trapped, just like the stories say."

The fact that this statement exactly mirrored his own thoughts made Halli's anger swell. He could suppress it no longer. "I don't accept that at all," he growled. "I'm going back up there."

"What? *What?* Don't be a complete—"

"Two of us, Aud. Two of us, with a couple of rusty farm tools and a lousy old fake claw." He leaned forward, flourishing his wine cup. "We held off that Trow in pitch blackness. What if the moon was shining? What if we had burning brands to see with? What if there were more of us? We'd have killed it easily."

Aud made an incoherent noise midway between a snort and a sneer. "One Trow, Halli! That's the point! Just one! There'll be hundreds of them up there. Remember those bones? You want to end up scattered in that cave? Go right back up that hill."

"We didn't even have a proper weapon!" he said, plowing on regardless. "Look at this thing—" He flicked his jerkin aside to reveal the sickle-shaped Trow claw tucked inside his belt. "Yes, it's sharp, but it's nothing special. Bjorn the trader probably carved it himself in half an hour. Yet it hurt the Trow—it drove it away. Now, if we had a *sword*, a proper one, made in the old ways . . . Well—what would happen then?"

"We haven't got any swords, Halli."

"I know."

"The only swords are in the heroes' cairns."

"I know."

He looked at her. She looked at him. A gust of wind reverberated against the windows. Aud said, "If you're even thinking what I think you're thinking, don't think it. And certainly don't say it. It's madness."

"Why? It could be done."

"No, Halli, it couldn't. The stories are very clear. It's the swords that keep the Trows at bay."

"Exactly! With one of those, we——"

"That's why everyone's given a little sword when they're carried to their cairns. To reinforce the boundary."

"——we could make it across the moors, get to the mountains . . ."

"But it's the *heroes* that keep the boundary strong, Halli. Their swords; the memory of what they did. Who knows *why* it works, but it *does*——as you and I now know! Arne protects his lands. Svein protects his. They keep everything the same."

"There was a hole in his mound, Aud."

"If you took it, Halli, if you broke the boundary that way, what would stop the Trows coming down into the valley?"

Halli's laugh sounded harsh even to his own ears. "Who cares about that? *We'd* be gone."

Aud got up from her seat. Firelight spilled against her, but the gashes in her clothes gaped black. She limped forward to stand before Halli. "Look at me," she said. *"Look at me.*" He did so then, mouth clamped, eyes sullen. "Do you *want* this to happen to your family and your people?" she asked. "Do you *really* want them to suffer like this? Because that's what would happen if you take the sword and the Trows come down from the hills. If it's what you're happy with, fine. Just say so, and I'll leave your House this moment; I'd never want to see you again. I want to escape just as much as you do, Halli Sveinsson, but no matter how much I hate my family, I could never do something like that."

She had not raised her voice; her fury was penned back in her eyes. But as she turned away she left Halli white-faced in his chair.

He waited until she'd sat again, then said, "I'm sorry. I was being stupid. I'm just angry, that's all."

"I know. Me too."

"I don't *hate* them."

"I know you don't."

Silence fell.

Halli looked toward the dark windows. "My father's dying," he said.

"Halli . . ."

"You haven't been in there! You don't know what it's like to see it! I can't talk with him, Aud! Svein knows, I can't even *look* at him—" His voice was cracked and uncontrolled; he stopped short, took a deep breath, let the pressure in his heart slowly subside. At last he said: "Still, you're right. I wouldn't want anything to happen the way you said. Svein's sword stays where it is. But I *am* going to find a way out of the valley. Trows or not, there'll be something we can do. We just need to think a bit, that's all. We need a little time."

There was a sudden frantic banging on the closed hall door.

Aud gave a little scream. Halli dropped his cup; firelight danced along its contours as it rolled upon the floor.

"The Trows!" Aud whispered. "They've come for us!"

Halli shook his head testily. "They wouldn't *knock*, would they?" Even so, there was a catch in his voice and he did not get up from his chair.

Once again, a thump, thump, thumping on the door.

Far away, his mother called out fearfully: "Who is that? What is that?"

"Who'll answer it?" Aud asked. "Eyjolf?"

"Deaf."

"Leif?"

"Drunk."

Bang, bang, bang went the door again.

Halli said heavily, "I'll do it."

Leaving the table, he walked slowly across the hall toward the passageway and the door that opened on to the porch. As he went he eased his right hand beneath his jerkin to where the Trow claw hung. He gripped it firmly. His other hand stole to the latch.

Bang, bang, bang upon the door.

Halli flicked the latch and swung the door wide.

A great black shape surged forward. Halli jumped back. There was a clopping of hooves, the smell of horse, and a wet blast of breath upon his face, then the animal had brushed past him as it was ridden under the low beams of the passage and out into the firelit hall.

Over by the hearth, Aud rose from her chair in terror. Halli had the Trow claw in his hand. He ran after the horse and rider, reaching for the bridle.

"Stop!" he shouted. "No farther! State your business! Are you friend or foe?"

The rider's cowl hung low about his head; his face could not be seen. Only his hands protruded from the cloak— aged, veined, liver-spotted hands, with long curved nails like talons. At his side hung a great dark bag, heavy, bulging. Something about the rounded shape of those bulges, about the leaden way the bag swung as the horse came to a stand-still, made Halli's skin crawl. He waved the Trow claw so that it shone darkly in the light.

"I ask once more! Are you friend or—"

With a sudden flourish, the rider flung back his cloak. Light gleamed palely on a long knife suspended in his belt. It was a knife that looked familiar.

Halli stepped back, mouth open. "Snorri . . . ?"

The ancient hands threw back the cowl, to reveal the wildly tufted eyebrows, the staring eyes, the gaunt and weathered face of the old man from the roadside hovel. He stared at Halli grimly, then cast his implacable gaze around the hall—at Aud standing wide-eyed by the fire, at Gudny peering through the drapes, at one or two servants clustering at the door. His eyes narrowed; he seemed to hunt for instant evidence of atrocity or corruption. At last, finding nothing obvious, he deigned to look on Halli once more.

"I have come," the old man said, tapping Arnkel's knife in his belt, "as I said I would. To do you a good turn. To return your favor, to return the kindness you showed me many months ago."

Halli blinked, nodded. "Erm, thank you. Wouldn't you like to get down?"

"Two things!" Snorri cried, in a voice that roused echoes along the hall and made Halli flinch back. "Two things I bring you! *This* is the first." Half turning, he loosened a cord that tied the great dark bag to the saddle; it fell with a solid thud upon the floor. Large, heavy, rounded shapes rolled within the red-stained sacking.

Halli swallowed audibly. "What, what *is* that . . . ?"

"A bag of beets. I have more than I know what to do with. A gift of greeting."

"Well, that's very nice—"

"Wait!" Snorri cried. "The second thing I bring is news! Terrible news! Hord Hakonsson and his men have scaled the ice-choked gorge! They are already in the upper valley.

Tomorrow night, when you are sleeping, they will be at your gates! They seek to burn your House and take your lands!" He scratched his nose, cocked a bony leg and began to dismount. "Oh yes," he added, pausing, "and kill you all."

24

BEFORE DEPARTING for his meeting with the heroes, Svein summoned his wife before him. "I intend to rid our valley of the Trows once and for all," he said, "and it may be that I'll meet my death in doing so. If I don't come back, here are my instructions. I've no son, but my men are good fighters. Go out on raids, and whoever acquits himself best, make him your Arbiter. After that, respect my boundaries and my laws. If someone in my House is killed, his enemy must be killed in turn. If one of the other Houses threatens us, their hall must be burned down. Keep our wells clean and our blood pure. Remember that you are the greatest people of the valley. As for me, build my cairn on the ridge above the House so that I may watch over you always; and those of you who obey my laws shall join me on the hill."

THEY HAD BEEN COMING in twos and threes since before dawn, and now the people of Svein's House filled the hall. The noise they made carried down the little corridor to Arnkel and Astrid's room; it resonated distantly like the crashing of the falls.

Halli stood before the bed, waiting for his mother to speak. Her chair was at the margins of the candlelight; she sat straight-backed and motionless, hands folded in her lap, her face cast in shadow by the bright, sharp edge of her long fair hair.

Close by her, Halli's father slept quietly in the center of the bed.

"This comes of your deeds," Astrid said finally.

"I know."

"Have you woken Leif?"

"Yes. Well, I tried. He was befuddled with drink. Eyjolf took him to the trough."

His mother made a sharp noise between her teeth. Halli waited. As he waited, his eyes drifted slowly across the bed to where his father lay. The candle on the table cast soft light upon the ravaged face. Arnkel was sleeping more peacefully than in many months, his white hair spread out upon the pillow behind his head. Halli watched his father sleep. It struck him that Arnkel's beard had grown long and vigorous during the illness—that it must have been that way all winter. He had not noticed it before.

"Halli?" His mother had been speaking to him. "Did you hear what I said?"

"No."

"I asked if you had slept at all."

"A little, Mother. A few hours. I needed to."

"Good. Come here." She sat as still and upright as if in her Law Seat rather than a bedside chair. Halli, approaching slowly, felt as diffident as if she judged him in a trial. He came to a halt before her, eyes lowered at the floor.

"Mother—"

"Look at me." Her expression, pale and somber, did not change, but her hand reached out to touch the side of his face. "Whatever has passed between us is forgotten now," she said. "You are my son, and I know the qualities you have. You need to use those qualities now, Halli Sveinsson. Use them for the good of your House. Go to the hall. Help Leif as best you can. Your father would wish it so."

Her hand brushed his cheek and was removed. Halli said thickly, "Please, come with me. You know they will want to hear from you."

She turned her head away; the hair fell forward to obscure her face. "No. I cannot leave Arnkel. Not now. It is too close. Go on, Halli."

Outside, he paused in the darkness of the passage. From beyond the drapes the roar of the crowd thrummed against his ear. Weariness rose in him; his eyes were hot. He closed them, leaned back against the wall—and saw an image of the southern mountains as he had seen them from the moor-top hill: clear, stark, terrible, inviting—a world awaiting exploration.

He opened his eyes abruptly. No. That was nothing but a dream.

Meeting the Trow had altered everything for Halli. Above all, it had corroborated the tales of Svein. The hero's luster, which over recent weeks had been all but extinguished, shone for him once more—if not as bright as it had once been, at least bright enough.

What had Svein done? He had roamed the moors just as Halli had; he too had fought the Trows up there. But in the end he had turned his back on the lands beyond, and died protecting his House and valley. Halli had no desire to emulate the harsher aspects of Svein's rule, but the message that the stories gave was clear. It was his House, his family, and he knew what he had to do.

Halli looked toward the drapes. He took a deep breath.

He pushed the drapes aside and went into the hall.

From dais to porch, from hearth to wall, almost everyone from the House had gathered there in the dawn half-light, and every person, by shared, unspoken instinct, carried an item of defense. There were men with mattocks and scythes, billhooks and flails, women with hoes, rakes, and sharp, curved sickles. Older children held spades, forks, and shovels; younger ones had cudgels made from wood scraps found in carpenters' workshops. Sturla and Ketil each had long oak staves, Kugi the sty-boy a menacing dung-rake, and even Gudrun the goat girl, watching timorously from near the door, held a rusty shard of metal, perhaps from some ancient plowshare.

The noise of the crowd rose and fell like a living thing. Everyone looked to the dais, where the Law Seats stood. They waited for the Founder's Family to emerge.

In the shadows beside the dais, Halli discovered Gudny and Snorri. Aud was not there; her hand and ankle were being redressed in Katla's room.

Snorri, who had finished his third helping of breakfast, and was still chewing on a heel of bread, acknowledged Halli's arrival with a nod. He gestured around the hall. "It is the same as ever with the warlike Sveinssons! See their weapons bristling like nettles after rain!"

"They're scared, that's all!" Gudny said indignantly. "We are a peaceable folk."

"Tell that to the dead men in the mounds beside my hut! Look at those infants with their little knives—I shan't bend to tie my boots lest they cut my throat!"

Halli's emergence had been noticed by the crowd; silence fell like a cloak. One or two people coughed, otherwise all was still.

Gudny glanced at the drapes, lips white with tension. "*Where* is Leif?"

Halli shrugged. "Still dousing his head in the trough, most likely."

"That's all we need! Halli, go up and talk to them."

"*Me?* They hate me! There'll be a riot."

"Well, we can't wait any—"

With sudden violence the drapes were cast aside. From the darkness of the passage strode Leif, his face flushed pink, his eyes red-rimmed. His hair, still dripping from the trough, hung lank upon his brow. Blinking a little at the brightness stealing through the windows he took brief stock of the multitude in the hall. Uttering a curse beneath his breath, he passed Halli and Gudny without a word, bounded up the steps, and loped across the dais to the Law Seats, where he sat in Arnkel's chair.

Leif smoothed back his hair with a flick of the wrist and jutted his chin assertively. He cleared his throat and, chest swelling, opened his mouth to speak.

A voice from the crowd: "You're not Arbiter yet! Get up from there!"

"Arnkel still lives!" cried another. "You bring bad luck upon us!"

"Where is Arnkel? Let *him* speak! Where is Astrid?"

"Get up from there!"

At first Leif remained defiantly where he was, but as the protest swelled, and his attempts at speaking went unheard, he thrust himself up from the chair and stalked to the front of the dais, to stand glowering at the people. Gradually the tumult quieted.

Leif shook his head contemptuously. "Thank you! I'll remind you that I am acting Arbiter, as my father is so ill, and you would do well to be deferential to your leader, especially in such troubled times. Now, I know why you're here: odd rumors have spread during the night and it is time we looked into them. But I'm sure we shall have no need of any of *that*." He waved his hand at the motley assortment of weaponry arrayed before him. "So, where is the man who started all this? A stranger, I believe . . . Ah, you? Come here."

Slowly, hesitantly, and with one or two prods from Halli, Snorri shuffled onto the platform, still gnawing on his bread. In daylight, and without the shielding cloak, his clothes were revealed as little more than rags held together by grime and habit; in places the holes outnumbered the shreds of cloth. Without haste or ceremony, the old man came to a diffident halt beside Leif, who stood arms-folded, resplendent in his official tunic of silver-black.

"Your name?" Leif said.

A chew of bread, a final swallow. "Snorri."

"Of which House?"

"None."

Leif's mouth curled. "So you are a beggar then?"

Snorri's eyebrows jutted indignantly. "Not at all! I have my beets, my hovel, my little strip of land. I bother no one and hold allegiance to myself alone."

"Well, well," Leif said. "I am sorry for you. Now—"

"Why? I am content in my poverty. Better that than to be an arrogant popinjay who smells of ale, and who, if the reputation of the Sveinssons is correct, gargles daily with his own—"

From the side of the platform Halli came hurrying. "Enough of these pleasantries! Let us concentrate on the essentials! We haven't got much time!"

A few hisses had risen from the crowd at Halli's appearance; weapons were flourished in the air. Raising a heavy hand to subdue the noise, Leif said, "Yes, enough from *you*, Halli—we don't need your interference. All right, old man, tell us your story, but I warn you, if you breathe one word of a lie, I'll whip you from here to the Snag. Go on."

Snorri was silent a moment, but when he spoke his voice was clear and calm. "How graciously put that was, the words of a true leader. I'm sorely tempted to leave you all to be murdered in your beds, but I owe Halli Sveinsson here a favor. He did me a kindness once and showed me courtesy too. So regardless of this shambling clod beside me, I'll repeat myself once more: the Hakonssons are coming and will be here this very night. Well, that's it. Good-bye and good luck to you."

He turned to go, but was restrained by Leif's grasp upon his collar. "A little more detail, if you please," Leif growled. "How do you *know* this? How is it possible? The gorge is blocked with snow. No one can climb from the Lower Valley yet!"

"Nonetheless, twenty men have done so. I saw them all."

"Impossible!"

"Well, you seem to know far more about it than I do,"

Snorri said. "Don't forget to be similarly assertive when Hord is hanging you in the yard."

Leif's face grew black with rage; still holding the old man by the collar, he shook him vigorously. "You cur! Speak plainly, or I swear *you'll* be the one hanging."

Halli leaped forward. "Get your hands off him! He's a guest in this House!"

"Yes, and if you shake any harder all my rags will fall off," Snorri added. "Do you *want* my bony nakedness displayed? There are women and children here."

With an oath, Leif loosened his fingers and drew away. "Well, get on with it!"

Halli said, "Please, Snorri. It is important that they all hear what you've told me."

Fingering his throat, Snorri spoke resentfully. "Will I get another hot meal?"

"One, two—as many as you wish!"

"Will that sweet old woman serve it? The one who dressed my wounds?"

"What sweet old—? Oh, you mean Katla? Great Svein. Yes! I'm sure she will, now please—"

"Very well." Snorri looked out across the hall at the attentive throng. "For Halli's sake, I'll tell you. Two days ago, in the waning of the afternoon, when the mists rose up from the grave mounds by the road, I was out burying rats in the corner of my plot. There is still much snow upon the fields down there. As I scraped and patted, I saw dark shapes approaching in the mists, strange shadows, helmeted, with swords hanging at their sides. I thought it was ghosts from the grave mound, come to steal my beets; of course I drew my knife—the one young Halli gave me—and stood firm, ready to sell my life. To my astonishment out from the mist stepped mortal men, weary, rime-caked, with ice upon their whiskers and their pigtails frozen hard. Each wore a helmet, not unlike that one behind me—" He pointed a withered finger at Svein's battered helm hanging on the wall above the Seats. As one the crowd raised their heads to look; as one they gasped.

"Their helmets were newly forged," Snorri went on, "their tunics covered with coats of mail. I could see the links were fine and strong, though thickly crusted with ice. At their belts, each had a sword; over their shoulders, light packs hung frozen. Their tunics showed scarlet beneath their jerkins—it was the red of Hakon's House!"

Whether it was the old man's words or the emotion with which he uttered them, the people in Svein's hall stood rapt; not a murmur could be heard.

Snorri drew his rags across his spindly chest, rested a hand upon his knife and continued. "I could not withstand twenty warriors, sturdy as I am. They bound me and took me to my hut, which they commandeered. At first the leader—Hord Hakonsson, as I know him now—believed I was of your House; he was tempted to run me through. Only when I protested my fervent dislike of all your many vices did he let me go. I was made to prepare good food, while the men huddled near my fire. I kept quiet, listened to their words. I gathered they had scaled the gorge, alone, without horses, clambering up endless shelves of thick blue ice above the frozen falls. It took them four days, and nearly cost them their lives; Hord himself had almost plummeted into the abyss on one occasion, but his son had grasped his arm, clung on, and pulled him out. None of the men were lost and only three were injured. By the sounds of it, their ascent was a great feat, worthy of the old heroes. Certainly their morale is high."

Leif, who had been listening with bulging eyes, could restrain himself no longer. "They're mad!" he cried. "It is an insane act! *Why* should they do this?"

"To catch us and the other Houses napping," Halli said, his eyes shining darkly. "No one thought they would act so soon! By the time the thaw and torrents are done, and the Council stir themselves for spring, it will all be over. Our House will be taken or destroyed, and Hord and Ragnar left in charge of all our lands; they will be even less inclined to listen to the other Houses than before. Well, it is an audacious adventure, more than I thought they were capable of. Finish your story, Snorri."

Leif gave an angry cry. "Wait! Who's in charge here!"

Halli shrugged. "I forgot. Please—"

"Finish your story, old man," Leif said.

"That night the twenty men slept in my hut, with one

on guard at all times. The next morning ten went off to Rurik's House to get horses. They returned—"

"Hold on," Halli said, "you mean they *stole* the steeds?"

Snorri clicked his tongue. "From what they said I rather believe the men of Rurik's House had the horses ready for their use."

At this many of the people in the hall cried out in alarm and fury, and dashed the hilts of their weapons on the floor. Leif's face was ashen. "So Hord is in league with our neighbors? I can't believe it!"

"Why? For generations the Rurikssons have considered you an arrogant, warlike House," Snorri said. "Whereas, watching you waving agricultural tools around your heads I can see that that's an utter fallacy. Anyhow, they came back with twenty horses. Hord wished to attack last night, but his men were weary; they voted to wait until today. The Rurikssons had given them ale; they drank and grew merry. I saw my chance, and when all were asleep, stole a horse and made my way here."

"They'll know we're warned," Halli said.

"No. I rode east as if I fled toward the gorge, leaving prints as I went. Four miles farther on I turned and looped up here. I hope you consider my debt paid back now, Halli Sveinsson."

"I do, and more so. Thank you, Snorri. We owe you our lives."

They clasped hands, smiling. From the audience came a

plaintive cry. "That's lovely, but oughtn't we to *do* something? Tonight we're going to die."

"You're right." Leif cleared his throat. "Halli, get off the stage—and you, old man. People of Svein's House, listen well. The Hakonssons won't arrive till nightfall. That gives us time. We'll be gone long before they show. This morning we pack whatever we can carry. Everything else we spoil or burn. We'll take as much livestock as it's possible to drive along with us and cut the throats of the rest, so they don't fall in to Hord's hands. At noon we'll set off on the western track, heading for Deepdale and the edge of Gest's lands. Some outriders can go ahead to warn Kar Gestsson. He'll have to put us up in his hall until things settle down. It'll be a squash, and some of you may have to bed down in the stables, but we can't help that. It'll only be for a month or two. When the torrents are over, we can send word to the Council. They'll look dimly on Hord's aggression and he'll have to sue for peace. We'll get our lands back and more besides. In the end, justice will be done. Right!" Leif clapped his hands. "Let's get to work!"

He stopped and looked about the hall.

Once or twice during his speech, Leif's oratory had faltered as he sensed the void into which his words dropped and vanished. It was not that any of his listeners made hostile sounds or movements; indeed it was their very stillness, their utter silence that was unnerving. When he had finished, this silence did not break, but was indefinitely expended, like a thread of spider's silk being gently pulled, pulled, pulled. . . . Its elasticity was remarkable, but soon it was going to snap.

Leif knew it; for a few moments he withstood the tension, then, face suffused with anger, gave in. "Don't just *stand* there, you fools!" he shouted. "Our enemies are coming! We must flee or die! What is the *matter* with you all?"

In the center of the hall, Grim the smith, burly, tousle-bearded, slowly raised his hand. It had a mallet in it. "Why do we run?"

Leif smoothed back his hair with both palms. "Did you not hear what the old beggar man said, Grim? Hord and his men have forged *swords*. We have no swords."

"I have this hammer."

Kugi the sty-boy gave a cry. "I have this dung-rake!"

Shouting over numerous similar announcements, Leif called for calm. "Yes, yes, all this is true, but we know the old tales, do we not? Did Svein wield a dung-rake? No. He used a sword. Why? Because swords are the finest weapons and can easily cut a man in two. Listen to me—we will not be able to withstand this attack. We have no option but a tactical retreat!"

At these words many of the onlookers made noises of muted agreement, but others gave shouts of derision. "You ask us to flee our House!"

"To leave it unprotected!"

"What leadership is this?"

"This is cowardice, Leif Sveinsson!"

The tumult in the hall rose to fever pitch; on the dais Leif stood speechless. From beneath the swell of sound came a rhythmic banging that quickly imposed itself; one by one the people fell silent. The old manservant Eyjolf, gaunt, emaciated, standing in the center of the crowd, continued striking the shaft of his hoe upon the flagstones until all around was still. Finally he stopped and said, "It is clear Leif means well, and what he says has merit. Certainly there is no point staying here to be slaughtered."

Leif held up his arms, exasperated. "At last! Some sense! Thank you, Eyjolf."

"*However,*" Eyjolf went on, "it is not clear to me that such slaughter is inevitable, and like most of us I believe that it would be a great wickedness to abandon our House. Before we do so, we must examine the other option. Perhaps we *can* defend it. I suggest—" Here he had to wait while certain persons, Leif included, attempted to interrupt and were shouted down. "I suggest," Eyjolf went on, "we listen to the views of the one person among us who has active and practical experience of violence and feuding—Halli Sveinsson."

At this there was silence. On the steps of the dais, where he had loitered, Halli stood irresolute, uncertain what to do.

Leif made a wild, indignant gesture. "*Halli?* He is the *cause* of all this trouble!"

"He is a scurrilous individual, granted," Eyjolf said. "But who of the rest of us have actually killed a man?"

"Which of us has burned a hall?" shouted another.

"Yes, Halli broke into their House!" a woman cried. "He must have killed dozens of men to get to Olaf. He can lead us now!"

"At the least let us hear him!"

"Have him step up before us!"

"Halli!"

"Halli! Step up here!"

The hall now echoed to the sounds of implements being banged upon the floor. On the stage, Leif stood slack-jawed, dumbfounded. Still Halli hesitated. Glancing aside he saw Gudny and Snorri watching him, and also—by the drapes, from which they had evidently just emerged—old Katla and Aud. He couldn't quite see the expression on Aud's face.

Slowly Halli climbed onto the stage. The noise in the hall reached a crescendo, then swiftly died away. More than fifty faces stared up at him, tense, unsmiling, waiting for his words.

Halli stood in the center of the dais, looking steadily around him, meeting the eyes of the people of his House. At last he spoke. "Some of you have called Leif a coward," he said. "This is not so. During the fight at Rurik's Hall, when Hord attacked our mother, Leif struck him down. He fought valiantly throughout the skirmish. He is as brave as any of us here."

He paused. Silence in the hall. "As for me," Halli

went on, "I am held to blame by many of you for these troubles. In part this is true. I *did* travel to Hakon's House to avenge the murder of my uncle Brodir. Because of my actions Olaf died and his hall was burned, events which Hord now uses as excuses for his feud with us. But I will say this. When I lay concealed in Hakon's hall, before going to Olaf's room, I overheard Hord and Ragnar talking of just such a raid as this. Hord spoke of his contempt for the Council, his impatience with its rules, and his desire to expand his lands. He also referred to work his smiths were undertaking—work I now believe were the swords and armor Snorri has mentioned he saw. In other words, my friends, Hord has been planning this a long while. Perhaps Svein's House was not always his intended victim, and it may be *I* am to blame for that, but this means it falls to us to thwart the Hakonssons now, just as our great Founder defeated Hakon so many times. I believe this is not an ordeal but an honor, not a time for fear but a time for pride. I believe that we can face our assailants, and with ingenuity and valor, we can win."

He halted; he let his words drift amid the smoke above the people in the hall. The ensuing silence was of a different order to that which followed Leif's speech; it was a ruminative one, a silence of digestion, as everything he said was considered, weighed, and judged. He saw one or two people—Grim the smith among them—nodding slowly, heard a gradual murmur of agreement swelling in a score of throats.

Leif said thickly, "All well and good, but pride alone will not save our skins."

"We must not be frightened," Halli said. He glanced toward Aud. "Svein knows there are worse things to face than mortal men. And there are many strategies we can use. What is the weather, for instance? I have not been out today."

Unn the tanner raised a great brown hand. "There is a mist. It lingers."

"Good. If it holds we can use it to our advantage. We know the land."

"There'll be a full moon tonight," a woman called.

"That too we might use," Halli said.

"Wait!" Only by the shaking of one hand did Leif display his agitation. His voice, though strained, was relatively calm. "We have not yet decided," he said softly. "Are we to leave or fight? In my view all Halli's pretty words will not forge us a single sword. I say again: we have to flee."

"I say we fight," Halli said.

"And *I* say," said a voice from the corner of the hall, "that you should follow Halli's leadership." As one, all looked: all saw, standing in the shadows of the drapes, the tall, slim form of Astrid, Lawgiver of the House. Her face was pale as moon cast, her hair spilling like willow fronds about her shoulders; her kirtle glowed white like snow. She had not been seen in public for many weeks. "Your Arbiter," she said, "is dying now. Today perhaps, tonight, tomorrow—it will happen soon, and it will happen *here*. I do not choose that he dies out on the road, a fugitive from his own House. You may leave if you wish, but if you do, Arnkel and I will not go with you. My sons have both offered valid choices; it is up to you whose advice you take. I only say this—what would Svein have done? Now I am going back to my husband. Gudny, dear—we need fresh water; can you bring it, please?"

The drapes fluttered; Astrid was gone.

Leif took a deep breath. He looked at Halli. "All right, brother," he said. "What do you say we do?"

25

THE HEROES MET on a meadow midway along the valley, and to begin with there was much bristling of beards and flexing of shoulders, and every hand was on its sword hilt.

But Svein said: "Friends, it's no secret we've had our differences in the past. But today I propose a truce. These Trows are getting out of hand. I suggest we stand together and drive them from the valley. What about it?"

At last Egil stepped forward. "Svein," said he, "I'll stand with you." And one by one, the others did likewise.

Then Thord said, "That's all very well, but what's in it for us?"

Svein said, "If we vow to protect the valley, it henceforth belongs to us twelve forevermore. How's that sound?"

The others said that would do very nicely.

Then Orm said, "Where shall we make our stand?"

MIDMORNING, AND THE MISTS had withdrawn only a little from around the House. The dark wedges of the nearest fields showed faintly, receding into whiteness. Solitary trees were dim gray outlines, encased in silence. Nothing moved on the road; distant bird flocks twisted briefly and were gone.

At Svein's House all such stillness ended. Here was constant movement, never ceasing, never slackening, remarkable for its intensity of purpose and extreme variety. Even during preparations for the Gathering the year before, nothing like it had been seen.

Among the reeds and grasses of the old dry moat a host of people bent and scrabbled, gathering stones fallen from the walls. Women and children scooped up the smaller pieces, while men carried bigger ones up to the road and in at the gate. The very largest rocks were hauled by horses or manhandled bodily by straining groups of three or four. Inside the gates, other teams assessed the stones and distributed them to various portions of the tumbled walls, which were slowly taking renewed shape.

Inside the House, at the workshops abutting the central yard, another process was in full swing. A great pile of logs, removed from dry storage, had been stacked here. Men came, chose logs, and rolled them into the workshops; from within came the rhythmic chopping of the ax and the rasp of saws.

Close by, in Grim's forge, red light glowed strongly.

Grim's voice rose above his hammer strikes, bellowing orders to his sons.

Away beyond the far side of the House, near the South Gate, where the wall had entirely fallen, a small group of youths worked with spades and mattocks, digging the soft ground.

Meanwhile, from every cottage, women hurried with baskets, boxes, kegs, and churns, bringing them to the hall. Livestock was led from the sties and stables beyond the wall, up through the gates and into the yard; pigs, chickens and geese roamed free among the bustling throng.

And in the center of it all, in the middle of the yard, stood Halli Sveinsson, watching, listening, giving orders to all who came.

Here waddled Bolli the bread maker, red-faced, sweating. "The loaves are almost risen. Where shall they be stored?"

"Gudny is organizing the kitchens; she will tell you where to take them."

Here was Unn, emerging from the tannery. "I have four vats prepared. Who wants them?"

"One for each side. Get Brusi to roll them down."

Here strode Grim, a glowing poker in his hand. "I need more pails or buckets. How many of these things are we making?"

"As many as there are logs. It is a long wall."

Grim paused, wiping a burly forearm across his brow. "You think this will work?"

"It worked for Svein, didn't it? Kol was completely fooled."

"Well, I have sixteen completed already and they are cluttering up my forge. Someone will need to take them."

"I will ask Leif to do so. He is commander of the wall."

Grim departed. In the interlude that followed, Halli took stock. All was in order, so far as he could see. No one was idle; everyone worked for the desired outcome. This was not to say that they were happy doing so. Some at least were visibly skeptical, some downright hostile—his brother Leif among them. But from the first faltering moment when he began outlining his suggestions, no one had challenged him. Suggestions had become orders; caution had given way to confidence. With increasing vigor he had outlined his ideas; his people had absorbed his plan—and something of his energy too.

"Halli." He looked up, startled; the voice jolted him from the novelties of the present situation; he felt suddenly smaller, back to normal.

"Aud!" A wave of guilt rose in him. He hadn't spoken to her since early morning, when Katla had whisked her off and he had gone to rouse the House. In the hall she had been an isolated figure on the fringe of the debate. He had not had time to consider how she was feeling. "I'm so sorry," he said. "I should have—"

Aud waved her hand; it was lightly bandaged. "That's all right. You've had things to do. I'm better. Almost." She grinned at him. Her eyes were clear; the terror and anger of the night before had gone from them.

Her ankle was bound with new strapping. "Looks less swollen," Halli said.

"Katla made a paste this morning and smeared it on. A black, foul-smelling gunk. I dread to think what's in it."

Halli winced. "I know the stuff. Did she cackle as she mashed it in a mortar?"

"Yes. Still, it's working wonders. I'm sore, but I can walk again. I've been down at the wall, shifting rocks with the others. The bit by the gate's looking good now."

"That's fine—oh, wait." Halli raised a hand and hailed a passing girl. "Ingirid, could you run to the North Gate, check that Leif's getting the hinges fixed? I forgot to remind him before. Thanks." He turned to Aud. "Sorry—it's just you reminded me—"

"Like I said, it's all right." She looked at him. "I know it's hard to think about, with all this going on, but . . . how are you feeling about . . . last night? I can't get it out of my head. When I close my eyes I'm back in the darkness, with that—"

Halli reached for her hand and squeezed it. "Me too. It's there always. But Aud, listen—we survived it, and it's made us stronger."

"You reckon? How's that, exactly?"

"Are you truly afraid of Hord Hakonsson after what we've seen?"

She sighed, without replying. At last she said: "I listened in the hall this morning. You did well there, Halli." She gestured round at various hurrying forms. "The people believed your words; they're acting on them."

Halli shrugged, watching two anxious men, bent-backed, rolling barrels to the porch from outside stores. They glanced at him, and he waved them on. "That's as may be. My father would have done the same, and they'd have loved him for it. They're no fonder of me than before—they just need someone to tell them what to do."

"Tell *me* something," Aud said.

"Mm?"

"Is it going to work? Your idea?"

Halli didn't answer for a moment. "It *might*," he said. "It might in part. I think we *will* take Hord by surprise, maybe do enough damage to send him packing, but . . . He's not someone easily dissuaded. Setbacks anger him, Aud, as they do me. And he does have swords." Halli hesitated. "Which brings me on to a different matter. I've been wanting to talk to you about this. Now that you're in one piece, I think you should leave."

Aud looked at him. "What?"

"Take your horse; go by the west track to Gest's House. You'll be able to follow the field walls even in mist. Get them to take you in. I'd rather you were safe, and—"

"Have you quite finished?" Aud said.

"Well, no, actually, I was in the middle of a sent—"

"Then shut up." She stepped close to avoid a convoy of pigs that trotted across the yard, driven by a small boy with a switch. "You think I'd just run away like that?" she said. "Like Leif was going to?"

"I'm not saying run away. But you're a guest here. It's not your—"

"It is," Aud said. "Of *course* it is. It's as much my fight as yours."

Halli folded his arms. "And how do you work *that* out precisely?"

Aud folded hers. "Hord threatens all of us. Nowhere in the valley will be safe if he wins the battle here. Is that, or is that not, so?"

Halli wrinkled his nose. "Technically 'so,' I suppose."

"Hence it's my job to foil him too. So I stay." She grinned triumphantly.

Halli chuckled. "Good. Are you done? That argument would just about hold water if you were a big, bearded fellow with muscles like iron and a fine line in swinging a stake mallet. As it is, you'll be less than useless if it comes to fighting, and will be slaughtered in seconds. If you want to stay in the hall with Gudny and the women, that's fine. There'll be babies needing changing, I don't doubt. Or, as I advise, you can get on your horse and g—Ow! Great Svein! Don't kick me in front of everyone! Think of their morale. And that was your bad foot and all."

Aud was white, her voice a furious whisper. "How *dare*

you speak like that to *me*? You forget I am a daughter of a hero's line! More to the point I could at least hope to carry a sword at my belt without it tripping me up every time I moved my little pudgy legs."

Halli's eyes bulged. "Now stop just there—"

"You think *you* could fight in battle?" Aud hissed. "The most to say of you is that an average sword-swing would sail harmlessly above your head! Oh, and perhaps in aiming for your heart, an enemy might cut his own toes off and topple over. Otherwise the outlook for you is not so hot."

Halli boiled with rage. "Is that right? Is that right? Who saved you on the ridge?"

"Oh, I *know* you saved me," Aud hissed. "But as I recall we faced that Trow together. Did I flinch then? Did I flee? Did I let you down then? Well? *Did I?*"

Halli bit his lip. "No, you didn't, but—"

"Do you think perhaps I'd fail you here?"

"No! But—"

"So what are you saying then?"

"I'm saying—"

"Well?"

"I'm saying I don't want you hurt."

"Because?"

"Because . . ." Halli waved his hands wildly about. "Because then your father will get mad and there'll be *another* diplomatic incident, which my House can ill afford."

"That's the reason, is it?" Aud said.

"That's the reason."

"I see. Well, that's very considerate of you. I'm sure my father would be most grateful." Her voice was cold and distant.

"I'm glad to hear it." Halli turned aside from her just as Ketil arrived to ask a question about grass netting. Then came Leif to sullenly consult about the defending of the walls, and Grim roaring for more pails, and by the time Halli had finished with them and a number of other queries, and looked about for Aud again, she was nowhere to be seen.

Late afternoon, and the mists were drawing in once more. Like wisps of wool they stole across the fields, threading through trees, muffling the dying sun. The meadows below the House were gone now; so too the road beyond the moat.

Halli stood on the wall top, staring out at nothing.

He breathed in the air, absorbing its stillness and the imminence of danger. Hord was close now—he knew it as surely as if he crouched beside him in the fields; he was hunkered down with the little company of men that he had led successfully up the ice-bound gorge. Hunkered down, waiting for the dark.

Halli narrowed his eyes. Where? Where would *he* have gone if their positions were reversed? He'd have ridden as far as the old wood, yes, to tether the horses. Then gone cross-country, avoiding the main road, to come out . . . where? On the northeast side, maybe, above the orchard, by that copse that fringed a little hollow. . . .

He scrambled along the wall top, peered off into the swirling murk.

Yes, in the distance, scarcely visible, a faint gray mass of trees. . . .

Halli grinned thinly. That was it. Right there.

Scouts might be closer, of course, circling the House, looking for the weak points on the wall. Good—those should be obvious even in the mist. With luck they would make the obvious assumptions.

He glanced at the sky. Not long till dusk. It was time to get his people ready.

The final meeting in the hall was difficult, for with the waning of the light, tension had heightened and nerves were strained. The atmosphere was thick with fear and fresh beet soup. Everyone clustered around the tables where Gudny, Katla, and other women doled out provisions. Snorri stood helping Katla, at every moment casting sly winks and side-smiles at her, so that she blushed and twittered. There too was Aud—demurely ladling soup for all. Halli narrowed his eyes; Aud's passivity seemed out of character. He would have liked to talk with her, but there was no time now. With an effort he pushed her from his mind.

Halli clambered on the dais. His first act was to order the removal of an ale cask that Leif had broached. "Time for celebrations in the morning," he said, over the chorus of complaints. "Hord will not be drinking now, you can be sure of that."

When the soup had been drunk and everyone was silent, Halli raised his hands in a broad-armed gesture he had often seen his father use. "People of Svein's House," he said, "we must go to our posts. Dusk is upon us. I do not think that Hord will move till night has fully fallen, but we should be ready even so. Mothers, children, the weak, and infirm will remain here in the hall under Gudny's authority and the doors will be barred after the warriors leave. Do not drink all the ale while we are gone, please—we'll need it on our return!" He chuckled briefly into utter silence and struck his hands together with the relish of one going to the feasting table. "Fond tales will be told of this night by our sons and daughters yet unborn, but the widows of Hakon's House will curse it! Come, friends, let us go."

So saying, Halli gave a virile bound from the dais, landed with an impact that jarred his teeth, smoothed back his hair, and marched from the hall. The crowd parted. In his wake trooped the defenders of Svein's House, the able-bodied adults, youths, and older children. Straggling knots of women and infants watched them leave; near the door a baby set up a thin, high wailing.

Now the mist was thick and the air cold. The gleam of the forge and the lanterns in the cottage windows showed more strongly than the last light in the sky. There was a smell of moisture and the dank earth of the fields, and a waiting silence.

Into the yard the defenders came and the door of the hall was closed behind them. They heard the bar being drawn on the other side.

"Everyone to your posts," Halli said. "You too, Leif. I'll come round to visit you all, check you're all right."

Shadows dispersed across the yard toward all four corners of the House. No one spoke; boots were light on stones. Halli waited a moment, his eyes flitting toward a low flame burning behind shutters in a corner of the hall. His parents' room . . .

Afterward, he would go there, tell his father of the victory won on his behalf. Afterward, when all was well . . .

Halli laughed softly. The chances of either his father or he being alive at the end of the night were fairly remote, for rather different reasons.

The yard was empty now, the House in silence. Halli took up a lantern from several flickering ready on the porch. There was a small range of weapons there too, those rejected by the defenders. Halli selected a long, thin butcher's knife and tucked it in his belt, beside the curved, black claw. Then he set off on his inspection. He pattered down to the North Gate, tested the bolts and hinges, found all secure.

Up on either side, where the day's activities had increased the wall's height a little, he saw the first two mock sentries. Each was little more than a pine log, roughly shaped to give the vaguest outline of a head, neck, and shoulders. Onto each, Grim had fixed a "helmet"—one a milk pail, one a slops bucket, each well-hammered to remove its telltale contours. Both were positioned at the top of the wall, wedged within stones so that just the helmet and head sections were visible from outside. Lanterns below them ensured they would not be missed, even in darkness.

Halli nodded with satisfaction. It was Svein's old trick, the one he'd used to fool Kol Kin-killer. In the half-light, and with the mists, this section of wall would appear well defended. Keeping his lantern low, he slipped behind the nearest cottage to the left, following the line of wall. Before long it fell away, almost to nothing. Along this first low section three more softly illuminated log defenders had been erected, two close together, one isolated, just peeping from behind a tumbled stack of stone. Each had a length of hazel wood nailed at their side—long, thin, pointed, reminiscent of a spear. Halli examined them critically, adjusted the angle of one helmet, which seemed a trifle rakish, and continued on his way.

For a brief period the wall rose high again, then tumbled down low to the section behind Unn's tannery, where Leif had once fallen into the midden. It was a place of piled refuse, stacks of pottery, old tools, and plowshares. This too was a vulnerable defensive spot, but no fake defenders were on display. All was silent, empty; above the mists a full moon was just rising above the southern mountains.

Halli went cautiously now, craning his neck from side to side. "Kugi? Sturla?"

Six armed men leaped from behind assorted mounds of refuse and bore down on Halli from all sides. He let out a hoarse whisper of alarm. "Stop, you fools, it's me!"

Kugi halted his dung-rake inches from Halli's head. Sturla lowered his scythe. Various other cudgels and bludgeons were reluctantly put away. The air was thick with muted apologies. Halli pushed them all aside and clambered to his feet. "I suppose I should congratulate you for being ready," he said grudgingly. "Remember though, Kugi, the attack is likely to come from *outside* the House."

"Oh, right. Yes."

"This is one of three likely attack points," Halli said. "From what I've seen, you'll defend it admirably. Whistle for help, though, and we'll come running."

The defenders melted away to their posts; rubbing various bruises Halli continued his patrol of the wall. Round to the southern side of the House, facing the ridge; more tumbled stretches, more weak points guarded entirely by mannequins. Then, near the South Gate: another open stretch, seemingly defenseless, where the wall was scarcely higher than his knee. Here he located Eyjolf and a number of the older persons of the House squatting silently in a byre.

Halli had approached with care, lest he was again

molested, only to find the defenders asleep and snoring. He rapped Eyjolf on his bony head. "Wake up! You should not be dozing! Our lives depend on you."

The old man jerked awake. "It was a strategic interlude."

"Let's have no more of them. You've got the stones ready?"

"A great pile, knobbly and jagged."

"Excellent." Halli gazed through the byre slats at the fragments of wall and, beyond, the open meadow stretching away into the mists. "This is a certain point of attack. Whistle when you need us."

On he went, past further mannequins, following the tumbledown wall. By the time he reached the west side of the House, night had truly fallen, and the mists rising from the ground shone bright and colorless in the light of the moon. He could not see the trees of the orchard below, though it was very near. The wall here was little more than a ramp of grassy rubble. Any attacker could stroll up it and—as he and Aud had done on the morning they first met—hop down through a narrow, bending alley between cottages, and so into the central yard.

Halli did not think to walk along that alley. After glancing up it, noting its bland, inviting emptiness, he doubled back and, leaving the wall behind him, approached the alley by way of the yard. Even here he went slowly, swinging his lantern so as to be easily observed.

"Leif?"

A voice in the blackness. "Yes?"

"It's me, Halli."

"I know. Otherwise you'd be dead."

"Oh. That's good. Are you all set?"

"We're ready."

"You'll whistle for help when—?"

"It won't be needed. You can clear off now."

Halli pursed his lips, but without response drew back grimly into the night. The fact that Leif tolerated his authority at all was miracle enough.

Back in the yard he slowed and stopped. So. That was everything.

Except—

He had almost forgotten. Hurrying across to the stables, he entered, and ignoring the fidgets of the horses in the stalls, went to the nearest deserted corner. Crouching, he scrabbled in the straw.

"Putting your lucky belt on?"

He stood abruptly, the hero's belt glittering in the lantern light. The figure in the doorway was invisible to him, but he knew the voice and was not surprised.

"I *thought* ladling soup might bore you before long," he said, brushing straw away from silver. "How d'you get out?"

"Window in my room. Going to order me back in?"

"No." He removed his jerkin swiftly, draping the belt across his shoulder and fixing it diagonally across his chest. The familiar weight pleased him. He put his jerkin back on and picked up the lantern. As he walked to the door, her shape became visible, outlined against the mist.

"Sorry about before," he said. "You must do whatever you think's right."

"I can help better out here—"

"Fine." He was close to her now, looking beyond her into the mist, at the glow of red light from Grim's forge. "The only thing I ask," he said quietly, "is—keep away from me. Hord wants to take the House, he wants to humiliate us—but *I'm* what he wants most of all."

"You don't know that."

"I do. That's how I felt when Brodir died. That's what Hord's feeling now. He's living by the old rules. Vengeance is the key. If he gets me, he'll be satisfied. Listen, Aud—no, shut up a minute and listen. You asked before if my plan's going to work and I still don't know. But if it doesn't— if the defenses don't hold, I mean—I won't let them break in here. I'd rather go out to Hord myself than see that happen."

"What? Leave the House?" He heard her bafflement and alarm. "He'll kill you."

"He'll try."

"Yes, if by 'try' you mean 'tear me to pieces,' you're spot on. Don't be a fool."

He spoke irritably, but still didn't look at her. "I'm not going to stand still and let him, am I?"

"*Halli.*" She took firm hold of his arm. "You *can't* fight

408

him. We've talked about this. Even if it was just you and Hord, he'd have a sword, while you"—she gestured at the long knife in his belt—"you'd have that pig-tickler there. You'd be rubbish."

Halli ground his teeth and leaned in close. "I'm *not* planning on fighting him myself. Why should I when there are *other things* that might do that for me? You know what I mean." He pulled away gently. "Listen—I've got to go over to the forge, check Grim and the rest are ready."

There was a silence. Aud had not released his arm.

"Aud—"

"You mean . . ." Her voice rose in sudden indignation. "Well, how the hell are you going to get him up there?"

"He wants revenge on me, doesn't he? I reckon I could lead him up. If the mist persists, he'll never know where he is until it's too late. Anyway, I don't want to talk about it. I've got to—"

"Halli," Aud said, still grasping his sleeve, "this is the worst scheme I ever heard. What would *you* do when you got up there?"

"There are those crags. I could get off the ground. Trows are weak when—"

"Yes, not that weak. They killed the heroes, remember?"

"It's not a perfect plan."

"You can say that again. There are a thousand reasons why it won't work."

"Well, let's hope it doesn't come to it, shall we?" Halli

snapped. "Now, leave me alone. I'm going to the forge. You can come or not, as you choose."

They stomped in silence across the yard, Halli first, Aud some way behind him. In Grim's forge the light burned red. Grim, Unn, and twenty other men and women of the House stood or sat like a huddled congregation of fiends, surrounded by their weapons of choice. Grim's great hammer was flat upon his lap. Unn had a narrow, curved knife, normally employed for scraping fat from skins.

As Halli entered, everyone stirred, shuffled, and moved their shoulders into attitudes of new alertness.

Halli nodded round at them. "Everything's ready. Now we just have to——"

Even as he spoke, a short sharp whistle sounded, far off, shrill in the night. Then another—of a different, deeper tone. Almost at the exact same time came shouts, screams, and other incoherent noises.

"Hord's early," Halli said.

Across the forge hands snatched up weapons; twenty men and women sprang to their feet, their shadows black upon the bloodred surface of the walls.

Halli was already back out of the door. Whistles blew in three locations. Halli ran, Aud ran; the defenders ran. In moments they had dispersed across the cobbles of the yard.

26

AND ALL AT ONCE, the sound of digging rose
from a hum to a mutter to a roar, and all along the
base of the tilted rock the Trows burst forth, spattering the men with soil and reaching with their
clasping fingers. Svein and the rest stepped back
again, a little way up the rock, for they knew that
Trows are weakened when they no longer touch
the earth. And soon they heard the claws clicking
on the stone.

Then—blinded as they were—they swung their
swords mightily and had the satisfaction of hearing
several heads go bouncing down upon the rock. But
as the dead Trows fell, new ones erupted from the
churned muck of the field, and still more came
pressing behind them, snapping their teeth and
stretching out their thin, thin arms.

THE LOUDEST NOISES came from the eastern
side, where Leif's ambush had lain in wait. Halli
took the lead, Grim and four others running alongside. A single glance showed that Aud was not among them:
she had gone a different way.

Across the yard, through floating fingers of mist, toward the alley. Halli's lantern swung wildly in his hand, but the light was useless, weakly spinning over swirling whiteness. He tossed the thing aside.

Ahead came dull, repeated impacts and the cries of men in pain.

Halli reached for the long knife in his belt.

The mists parted; they were there.

At the end of the narrow alley a net—ordinarily used for catching hares and rabbits in the fields—had been dropped with weighted corners, so that it hung taut from the roof ends, blocking the exit into the yard. Grim's son, Ketil, stood there with a knobbed stave in his hand, watching confused and desperate movements in the dark beyond. Even as Halli ran up, an unfamiliar bearded face, red lips apart, appeared briefly at the net. Fingers wrenched at the knotted threads, sought to rip them; Ketil struck the face with his club, so that it groaned and fell away.

Halli stepped back, surveying the rooftops above the alley. On either side, he saw Leif's men, risen from concealment. They hurled rocks into the alley below, thrust down with forks and mattocks, and beat zealously with flails. The contents of Unn's vats was poured in noxious torrents. Anguished cries came from the darkness.

"How many here, Ketil?" Halli said.

"Six or seven only. We've dropped a net at the other end so they can't get out." Ketil's face was lively, grinning. His eyes flashed with grim merriment. "Don't think they'll much enjoy *this* welcome."

Ketil stepped back to the net, squinting to see through. A sword blade stabbed through the net and into the side of his chest, catching him beneath the arm. With a gargling cry he lurched clear, dark blood gouting on his tunic. Halli cursed, caught him as he fell forward, stumbling back with the youth's face pressed against his neck. He felt hot wetness on his left hand.

A howl of rage and grief. Grim the smith thrust Halli aside and took Ketil in his arms. He lowered his son slowly, first to his knees, then leaned him back so that he sat slumped against the nearby wall. There was blood at Ketil's mouth.

Halli's other companions were clustered at the net now; they stabbed through it viciously with hoes and fish spears, screaming as they did so. Halli stepped close, dragged two of them back. "Stop! You'll tear the net to pieces! Gisli, Bolli—you two wait here and guard it. No one gets through. You others come with me."

Back across the yard they went, through the curling mists. Sounds of combat came from southern and western sides. Halli's face was set hard, the corners of his mouth clamped downward. Ketil's blood felt cold upon his palm.

With a swing of the hand he led the two men with him toward the House's southern edge. They passed Eyjolf's byre, now empty, leaped upon the tumbled wall, and halted, looking down into the meadow.

A little way off, like hunching birds of prey, a group of defenders stood silently around two black squared holes in the earth. Eyjolf and another man held torches; light flickered against the wisps of mist and the harshness of their faces. Several of the party held rocks in their hands, but it seemed that the use for these was past. There was a groaning coming from one of the holes. Fragments of branches, turf squares, and pieces of grass netting that had been used to camouflage the pits lay scattered beneath the defenders' boots.

Halli called, "All well, Eyjolf?"

The torch moved, the old man stepped nearer, his face an inhuman mask floating redly in the mist. "We have three beauties here. Three others evaded the trap and ran away when we came charging."

"Are your captives dead?"

"Most are wriggling. We have just been discussing how to kill them."

Halli thought of the dull weight of Ketil's face pressing upon his neck. Then came memories of Brodir, Olaf, the hulking form of Bjorn the trader. . . . He said quietly, "Discuss all you like within their hearing, so that their fear for their lives is raw and intimate, but do not kill them. Just make sure they don't get out."

Eyjolf said peevishly, "Svein would have buried them alive."

"Well, I am not Svein. Do what I say, old man." He spoke then to the two men with him. "Seven to the east and six here. There'll be seven more to the west, fighting Kugi and Sturla's group. That's not good odds."

One man said, "Unn and several others went that way at the first alarm."

"Even so, they'll be hard-pressed. Come on."

Back through the yard. In the east, where Leif's net trap held, the sounds of battle were diminishing, but to the west the noises had intensified. Past Unn's tannery they ran, along a narrow lane toward the midden. The way was dark; ahead, between the houses, beyond the tumbled wall, Halli saw the light of the full moon shining on the mists that billowed on the fields. Silhouetted black against this, men were fighting in twos and threes, sword against scythe, sword against mattock.

The two defenders accompanying Halli sprinted past him on longer legs and threw themselves into the fray.

With his knife raised, Halli accelerated too, and immediately tripped on a body lying face up on the stones. He sprawled across it, scraping the palms of his hands on the ground. He rose, looked. Moonlight had broken through the mists; it splashed on a dislodged helmet, fair hair, a short cropped beard, a ruddy, open face. It was the face of Einar, the man of Hakon's House who had befriended Halli the year before. Einar's eyes stared fixedly at the sky; his open mouth grimaced like a smile.

Halli stumbled back. Looking wildly about, he saw all around a confusion of wrestling bodies and bursts of violent movement. Men gasped for breath, metal splintered wood; dark blood fell on stones.

The Hakonssons were clear enough to see: they wore long chain mail-coats, which clinked dully as they moved. Their rounded helmets, with long nose guards and curling cheek plates, hid their heads entirely. Their eyes were black slashes, without form or light. Moving quickly, swinging their blades with brutal speed, they seemed something scarcely human, creatures from an ancient tale.

The defenders of Svein's House had no such armor—their heads were open, unprotected—but in the livid whirl of mist and moonlight, in the mess of flurried action, with the screams and howls they uttered, it was growing hard to recognize them too.

Something glittered at Halli's feet: a sword, lying by Einar's curled, stilled hand.

Halli shoved his knife into his belt, bent and scooped up the sword, instantly aware of its cumbersome, unfamiliar weight.

There was movement straight ahead of him. A small form collapsed against the Trow wall, a broken dung-rake clattering on the rocks.

"Kugi—" Halli started forward, but the sword was heavy, his movements sluggish. Out of the night swooped a savage figure, dark hair flying, great arms slashing with a skinning knife: Unn the tanner, coming to Kugi's rescue, driving an armed and helmeted Hakonsson back over the wall.

Now, to Halli's right, another tall invader stepped, his sword held casually out and to the side, pursuing a cowering youth, who crouched back against the flagstones. The youth was Brusi, Unn's son, the shaft of his scythe sliced pitifully in two.

With some effort Halli swung his blade around, leaped forward—

From the opposite side a figure limped from the darkness and swung a metal bar at the Hakonsson's sword arm. A wail of pain—a clattering as the sword fell. The man leaped back, clutching his arm; as Halli lurched close, he ducked away, threw himself over the wall, and fell heavily to the midden below.

His departure seemed to trigger a general retreat. Two other helmeted warriors suddenly drew back, jumped from the wall, and disappeared into the mists. All along the tumbled wall, movement suddenly slowed; weary men and women lowered their weapons.

Halli took this in obliquely through the tail of his eye. He was staring wordlessly at the person with the metal bar.

"Hello, Halli," Aud said, panting.

He didn't answer: the other survivors were silently congregating around him in the narrow yard, and he knew

417

he had to address himself to them. With the exception of Unn, who was helping Brusi to his feet, they were a bedraggled sight. Most bore wounds on their arms and bodies; many had lost their weapons, or held them shattered in their hands. There were several bodies lying on the ground.

Unn's knife was dark and wet. There was triumph in her doughy face. "Easy work, this, Halli! Svein would be proud of us! We'll celebrate long tonight!"

"I hope so," Halli said. "Sturla, Brusi, if you're both uninjured, I want you to do something for me. Go round the walls quickly and remove the log mannequins. Just get them out of sight. If they're still there when the Hakonssons look back, they'll know they're fake. Do that quickly."

The young men flitted away into the dark. Halli said to Unn and the men and women round them, "You have all fought well. How many were there? How many have we lost?"

"Seven came over the wall," Unn said. "Four fled. As for us—it is as you see."

Halli took a lantern and inspected the bodies on the ground. Three Hakonssons were dead. One was the man that Halli knew. Neither of the others was Hord or Ragnar.

Five people of Svein's House lay among them, three—a man and two women—dead from sword wounds. Kugi the sty-boy was one of the injured, his arm and chest both badly slashed.

Halli knelt beside him. Kugi's face was a dull gray-green and his eyes gleamed wild and bright. Halli said, "Well done, Kugi. You're a hero of this House. We'll get you to the hall now."

Kugi's voice was faint but sure. "Have we won, then, Halli?"

"We've beaten them back on all three sides. At least half are dead or captured. I must speak with Leif now." He squeezed Kugi's shoulder and stood. Looking around, he saw the remaining defenders crouched beside the fallen; some of them were weeping. The sight made him sick at heart, but his face stayed calm. "Aud," he said loudly, "can you marshal everyone, get the wounded back to the hall? Those who can still fight wait here and guard this point. I'll ask Gudny to send food and ale out to you at once. The first attack has been repulsed, but we must not yet weaken."

With the wounded going ahead, Halli hurried toward the hall with Aud alongside him. As they went they inspected the workmanship of the sword he'd taken. Three other swords had been left with the defenders of the wall.

The hilt was crudely fashioned, a cumbrous wedge of metal, softened with wrapped cloth. The blade, a little longer than the entirety of Halli's arm, seemed rather uneven, and was notched and pitted in places.

Aud said: "It's a bit blunt, though the point's keen enough. Not quite a hero's sword."

Halli grunted. "Hord's smiths haven't mastered the old techniques yet. You can have it if you want. I can't use it, anyway—as you predicted. It's too long for me." His tone was listless, absent: memories from the skirmish bore down upon him—the cries of the wounded, the faces of the dead. He could hear Aud talking again, speaking hopefully of the battle and their success so far, but his mind was elsewhere. Out in the mists, Hord would be regrouping, gathering his men together, taking stock of losses. What would he do now? Flee? Hardly. It would be a stain upon his honor. . . . So—what then? It depended how many survivors Hord had.

"We've got prisoners," Aud said, suddenly. "Look."

Outside the hall porch a large group was gathering in the lantern light. At its center Halli's brother, Leif, stood, talking loudly, making ornate gestures. He had a sword in his hand. Around him clustered five or six of the defenders from the eastern alley, the wounded arrivals from the western side, and one or two from Eyjolf's group. They were considering two dejected Hakonsson men, bleeding, disarmed, and helmetless, whose hands were being tied roughly behind their backs.

One of the defenders—Bolli the bread maker, whose tunic was bloodied at the shoulder—kicked out at a captive's shin, causing him to stumble back in pain. Leif and many of the others laughed. Someone struck the other prisoner from behind; a fist flew; blood flecked the ground. The crowd bucked and surged round its prey like a living thing.

Halli strode close. "Stop that, Bolli," he snapped. "And you, Runolf!"

White faces, twisted, hateful, gazed at him. "They killed Ketil and Grim," a voice said.

"Even so. Leave them be." Halli became aware that both his hands grasped the sword hilt; he stared round at the suddenly silent crowd. "Touch them again and I'll deal with you myself. Leif—speak up. What's happened here?"

His brother's head was lowered; he regarded Halli from underneath his brows, his chest rising and falling heavily. "We held them trapped with the nets," he said at last. "Seven all told. Hord and Ragnar were there. They fought furiously, though the odds were hard against them. Several of us were wounded, but I killed a man myself, and Thorli here struck the head from another. Then Ketil was slain beside the net and Grim—who witnessed it—could not contain his grief. He leaped from the roof into the alley and set about his son's murderers with his hammer. He slew one, but then Hord came, fighting like a demon, and Grim was killed. He was a brave man." Murmurs of assent came from the crowd. Leif nodded. "And all that being the case," he went on, "I do not see why we should give these dogs a scrap of mercy now."

He did not speak loudly, but it was a challenge nevertheless; and the crowd was with him. Several men shouted out at Halli, but he ignored them. "You haven't finished your report, Leif," he said. "Where are Hord and Ragnar?"

Leif shrugged. "They cut through the outer net and escaped. These two were too badly injured to follow them. The battle is over. We've won and can do as we like. *I* say we kill them."

"No," Halli said. "We lock them in the granary. Bolli, you're nearest. Go and do it."

In the silence that followed, the crowd held back, irresolute. Their hostility was clear, but muted; they looked to Leif to articulate it for them. Leif stared at his feet, then swiftly round at the group. He took strength from their willing silence. "They're enemies of our House, Halli," he said savagely. "They've broken valley laws and killed people of our blood. We all know what they deserve—and that's death."

The crowd roared agreement. Halli showed his teeth. One hand still held the sword; the other drifted to his belt and the hilt of his knife. "Leif," he said, "I should not need to tell you this. We spare these men for two reasons. First, because it is dishonorable to kill a helpless man, and second, because the night is not yet over. There are still nine men out there: Hord will return, and hostages will be useful if we need to parley. Any man who denies this is a fool. Now, for the second time, Bolli"—he did not look at the fat man, but kept his eyes fixed levelly on Leif—"go and take the prisoners to the granary."

Everyone watched Leif again; for a moment he did not move. All at once he gave the slightest nod. A stir ran round the company. But no one spoke out and the captives were quietly removed.

"Good," Halli said. "Now, we must quickly get men watching each side of the House. If Hord tries—"

"It seems to me, brother," Leif said huskily, "that you can stop there with your ordering us about. Yes, your plan's worked nicely; none of us deny it. And perhaps it's best to keep our hostages safe, as you say. But things have changed now. We've broken the attack, and the Hakonssons are hardly likely to threaten us any further with only nine men. So maybe we no longer need your talent for violence; maybe it's time to remember it was *your* actions that brought this tragedy upon us in the first place." He glanced round; mutterings of approval rippled through the crowd.

Aud gave an angry cry. "It's Hord Hakonsson who you should blame, not Halli! Don't be an idiot, Leif—"

Halli touched her with his hand. "Now is not the time to argue about this," he said. "We must watch for Hord—"

But the noise of the crowd had intensified. "You see?" Leif cried. "The people know I'm right. You're a bringer of troubles, Halli, always have been. How many of us are dead now, because of you? How many wounded? You shame this House, brother, and if Mother wasn't out of her mind with grief, she'd have made that clear to you today."

Halli breathed in sharply. "Is that so, brother?"

"It's so. Best now if you are silent and let me take charge of things."

"Halli—" Aud put her hand upon his arm.

"It's all right." He shrugged her off. As he did so, his jerkin parted, revealing to all a flash of silver.

Leif's eyes widened. "What is that? What is *that* you're wearing?"

All followed his gaze; all noticed the silver belt beneath the jerkin. There were assorted gasps of horror and dismay. During the argument the aggression of the crowd had washed restlessly back and forth, seeking focus. Suddenly it found one.

Leif spoke in disbelief: "Svein's silver belt!"

"He's taken it," someone gasped. "He wears it for his own!"

Far off across the yard, unnoticed, a figure came running through the mist.

"He has stolen the luck of the House!" a woman said.

"No wonder we suffer so!"

Halli said evenly, "Yes, it's Svein's belt, with which he never lost a battle. Anyone care to challenge my right to wear it? You, Leif? You, Runolf?" He waited.

Amid the mist, the figure ran. His voice was faint and breathless. "Halli!"

No one in the crowd had spoken. Halli smiled, shrugging. "Well, then—"

"Halli!"

Aud said: "Look, there—"

Out of the mist came Sturla, who had been sent round the wall to remove the mannequins. He careered toward them from the direction of the North Gate, his face a mask of terror. "Halli! Halli! Hord is here! He has archers—with arrows of fire! They want you brought forth, or they will burn the House! They will torch us all!"

No one spoke. All, as one, stared out into the mists. All saw an orange-yellow dot emerge beyond the wall. It soared into the sky, arcing upward, scarcely bigger than the stars through which it crept, hovered for a moment like a hunting bird, then fell toward them, growing, flaring with life, trailing a yellow tail. There was no time to speak or move.

With a whistling scream a bolt of fire exploded against the flagstones a few yards from Aud and Halli. A ring of orange flame flickered briefly against their sides, their clothes rippled, their hair blew back. They didn't move. The crowd of defenders screamed and scattered. Leif dived to the ground, he and others rolled about in utter disarray.

High overhead drifted other fiery lights; with fizzing sounds they dropped from the dark sky, becoming balls of flame. One hit midway up the hall roof, one in the middle of Grim's forge. There were muffled impacts: fire rose instantly from the turf. Another shattered on the stones beside the flagpole. Shouts came from within the hall; the yard was suddenly alive with panicked forms.

Halli looked at Aud. She looked at him. "It's time," he said.

"No. Halli—"

"Here, you have this." He placed the sword in her hand,

closed her fingers fast upon it. "It'll only slow me down where I'm going. Leif"—this to his brother, staggering to his feet—"you're in charge. Better do something about the fires."

Leif's face was waxy, his eyes flickering to and fro. "You—?"

"I'm going out to save the House." He turned to Aud and smiled at her a final time. "Good-bye." Then he was running: away from her, away from all of them; past the milling people of Svein's House, past the wounded and the stricken, those who hated him and those who didn't; down the alley between the cottages, where weapons lay, and helmets, and the bodies of the dead; past torn nets and dark pooling blood, over rocks and scattered debris, to where the Trow wall rose before him.

He scrambled up, paused only a moment, then leaped down the bank and was gone, a small, broad, bandy-legged figure, swallowed in an instant by the mist.

27

AFTER THE BATTLE of the Rock Svein's body was brought home and a cairn built for him on his boundary. They sat him in it on his best stone chair, facing the moors, still clasping his bloodied sword. Set all about were the things he liked best in life: his drinking cup, brimful of ale; his silver plate, piled high with meats and bread; his favorite horse and hunting dogs, strangled by his grave and lain out at his feet. Many thought his wife should go with him too, so as to serve him during his watch, but she argued strenuously against this and by two votes won her case. Much gold and silver, won in battle with Trows and neighbors, was scattered round him, but his silver belt was unbuckled from his waist and taken to the hall, to bring his people luck. Then the cairn was sealed and the hero left upon the hill to keep the Trows away.

IT WAS NOT DIFFICULT in the end. Halli was relieved at that. He had feared that when the moment came he would not see it in the confusion of the siege, and so miss the opportunity to act. Worse still, he had feared that he *would* see the moment all too well, but simply draw back afraid. Yet when Sturla came running, and the fiery arrows began to fall, all doubt and anxiety passed from him like the dropping of a cloak and he knew what he must do.

His clarity of purpose startled him, but as he left the House and leaped down into the long wet grasses of the moat, he realized that deep inside he had always expected such an outcome. Ingenious as his defenses had been and successful as they had proved—by his reckoning around half the invaders had been killed or captured—the enemy's advantages in equipment and training were just too great, the hatred with which Hord Hakonsson pursued Halli too strong. It had never been likely the battle would be won simply with the advantage of surprise.

But there was a deeper reason too, why Halli had to finish it alone. It was a reason that stretched back far into his past, to his early childhood and Katla's admonitions on his character and prospects. Was he not a Midwinter's child, with a doom upon him? He was fated to bring disaster down upon all those in his life. He was a male of Svein's line too, as Brodir had noted—a likely recipient of an early death. Such predictions were coming to pass with outstanding swiftness. But Halli was not dismayed.

Once he would have railed against his destiny, lamented its injustice. No longer. He had done too much, and seen the consequences of his actions. By avenging Brodir he had helped sustain a feud. By seeking to escape the valley, by breaking the hero's boundary—perhaps by even wearing the hero's belt—he had brought down Svein knew what misfortunes on his House. Whatever he tried had failed or gone wrong; tighter and tighter the doom pressed in. Yet Halli accepted responsibility for it all, and that very acceptance now helped free him.

He was trapped by the enmity of Hord, by the hostility and incomprehension of his House, by the Trows waiting for him on the hill. So complete was the malign circle about him that Halli was utterly empowered. He had nothing left to lose.

Saving the House by leaving it was the first step. The moment he jumped from the wall he walked with a lighter tread.

So Hord wanted Halli to come out, did he? Well, he would get his wish and the House might be spared. But Halli did not intend to give himself up without at least trying the plan he had told Aud. She was right that it held little chance of success, and his chances of survival were smaller still, but Halli thought he would attempt it anyway. To seek to lure Hord beyond the cairns was something akin to madness, but its heroic futility rather added to its appeal. It gave him the sensation he had always had when listening to the story of Svein's last battle, with the heroes lining up on the Rock in darkness, waiting for the Trows. He felt that same fatal recklessness inside him, an exultant sense of death approaching. . . . In the meantime, if he was going to bring disaster and destruction on someone, Hord Hakonsson would do as well as any.

White mist bloomed about him. He wormed his way quickly among the reeds and grasses of the moat, following the Trow wall's edge. Somewhere overhead the moon was shining, but its light bled opaquely through the swirling whiteness and Halli could see little. Moving by instinct along familiar childhood paths he drew close to the North Gate. Dimly he heard the twang of bows, heard sporadic shouts and screams beyond the wall. Hunching low, placing each foot as soundlessly as he could, he went more slowly, staring this way and that in the direction of the road.

A faint yellow-orange smudge caught his eye, a shifting blur hanging at an unknown distance. As he drew closer, he heard its noise: the little spits and crackles as the bonfire burned.

Dark shadows clustered round it, bending, straightening. Bright gobbets of fire were drawn out, lifted, sent shooting away into the air.

Halli, crouching in the moat ditch, hidden by mist and reeds, bit his lip in anger. He counted the shadows swiftly: five, maybe six. . . . Where were the others? At least nine men had successfully fled the walls. And where, above all, was—

Not far away from Halli, closer to him than the fire, a portion of mist moved.

The figure had been so still that Halli had not noticed him, had not realized how close he had come to the earth bank that formed the roadway up to the Gate. The bank was raised a little above the moat; it seemed now that something shifted in midair, a black and solid shape warping and congealing from the threads of mist. Halli, lurking below, recognized that shape immediately. The moon's light, diffused and weakened as it was, picked out the broad shoulders, the bearlike bulk. A long sword hung ready at his belt; mail glinted at his arms and waist. There Hord stood—a great helmed warrior, legs planted firmly apart, hands jammed implacably on hips. He stared up toward the walls in a posture of supreme confidence; it was as if a hero of old had been reborn.

Crouching in the mud, his bottom damp with dew, Halli's hands drifted uneasily to his own small weapons—the butcher's knife and Trow claw, tucked beneath his jerkin. He had no armor, no helmet, no bow or sword. . . . He breathed in deeply, suppressing his fear. This is how it had to be: he wanted nothing to weigh him down.

Except Svein's belt, of course. He patted the cold metal strip that spanned his chest. It had served him well enough so far. He needed its luck one final time.

Up on the earth bank, Hord's outline shifted; Halli heard a barked command. The shadows by the bonfire grew still. No further arrows were fired above the wall.

Then Hord cried out, his voice so loud that Halli, despite himself, shrank back amid the reeds. "People of Svein's House," Hord shouted, "do you not hear me? Cast out Halli Sveinsson from your gate and we will cease this burning! Cast him out and we shall depart, never to return! Or roast in your own hall!"

He waited. The smell of smoke drifted in the air; high overhead, the mist was black with it. No answer came from beyond the wall.

Hord grunted irritably, and turned to motion his men to continue their work.

Halli rose from the reed bed, hands hooked nonchalantly at his belt. "Hello, Hord!"

His voice echoed, died. The ensuing silence was different in quality from that which preceded it; suddenly the night was aware of him. He saw the figure on the earth bank stiffen. The archers at the bonfire froze, tar arrows burning at the bows.

Halli chuckled. "Why so scared? I have come out!"

Again a silence. He noted Hord's outline twist and swivel as if uncertain where to look. Hord's voice was eager, hesitant all at once. "Halli Sveinsson? Is that you?"

Halli spoke with casual confidence. "It is I."

"Where are you?"

"Here, close by. Down in the moat."

Hord turned and stared toward him, his black silhouette floating in the mist. Halli smiled back grimly; he stood in full heroic posture, feet broadly spread, arms folded, the picture of defiant disregard.

Hord's helmet cocked doubtfully. "All I can see are reeds."

"Oh, for Svein's sake." Halli hopped sideways away from the thickest patch of reeds, which were, admittedly, slightly taller than his head. "There, can you see me now?"

The great head nodded. "I see something lurking like a rat in a hole." In the depths of the helm Hord laughed, a hollow reverberation. "So they actually cast you out?"

"Not precisely," Halli said. "I came of my choosing."

"May I ask why?"

"Isn't it obvious? Your demands have been made: if I emerge, you stop your wicked attack on Svein's House. Correct?"

Up on the bank Hord nodded slowly. "Of course. I have given my word of honor. It shall be so."

"Good. Please instruct your men."

Hord looked across toward the shadows beside the bonfire. "Extinguish the arrows; pull apart the fire! The House will burn no more. Frankly, Halli Sveinsson," he said, turning back to Halli, "this is not what I expected. I thought you'd not come willingly, so that they'd either toss you out, trussed and helpless, like a fat little parcel, or let you remain inside. If you'd stayed in we would have done much damage to your hall, but in the end our arrows would have run out, and you would have lived. I confess I don't quite understand. . . ."

Halli noted that as Hord spoke to him, one of his hands—the one nearest the fire—made certain minute gestures, finger flicks and twitches, that might be subtle signs.

Speaking calmly, keeping his eyes fixed on the mists around him, Halli said, "I only do what you would have done in my place, surely. It would have been dishonorable to remain inside while my people suffered. Your quarrel is with me, not them. They joined with me to foil your first attack, yes, but that was to save the House. The remainder of our disagreement must be settled here, between men."

"My feeling exactly," Hord said. "Come up here. We can settle it soon enough."

"I'll stay below for the moment, thanks." Halli squinted into the mist. Its drifts and eddies moved unceasingly, filled with weird, imaginary forms; the incoherent whiteness hurt his eyes. But he thought to detect other movement—solid, purposeful figures flitting away from the dying fire, spreading out stealthily so as to come behind him.

Hord said heartily, "I must compliment you on your tactics earlier. It was you, I suppose, who came up with those tricks—not that fool brother of yours. It put paid to my first plan, which was to take the House by surprise. Cost me eleven good men, too—and three others who now lie wounded yonder beneath a tree."

"All our captives are still alive," Halli said. "So I'll bargain with you, if you like. Finish your feud with me and, on my honor, you can have your surviving warriors back, unharmed." He spoke loudly enough for his voice to carry to Hord's men as they stalked through the mists toward him.

If Hord hesitated, it was imperceptible. "My men follow

me without question, just as Hakon's men followed him. Whatever their fate they meet it without complaint. To give up my vengeance on their behalf would dishonor us all."

Halli heard the crunch of pebbles, a whisper of fabric moving against grass. His skin crawled. But he did not react; not yet; he wanted them close when the chase began.

"In that case," he said, "I suppose it's no good me suing for peace now? No good me suggesting that we end this feud before things get further out of hand? Too many men have died already—and for what? What has anyone gained? Let us put old hostilities aside; why shouldn't we work together to spread harmony between our Houses? Would that not honor us more than killing?"

The hulking figure on the earth bank stepped forward menacingly and a mailed fist clamped fast upon its sword hilt. A growl emerged from the darkness of the helm. "Ah, Halli! You have a nerve! You, who killed my brother, who burned my hall . . . to ask for peace! I shall twist your head onto a pole and fix it before Svein's gate!"

"Right. So I suppose there's no point saying I'm sorry?"

"No point at all."

"No chance me winning you over with fair words?" He heard boots slipping, sliding down the moat bank beside him, heard the clink of metal very near. He tensed his muscles, ready to move.

Hord's snarl was scarcely intelligible. "Halli, the time for fair words is past."

"Fine," Halli said, "In that case you're a beet-faced, pear-bottomed oaf, a part-time glutton and full-time coward, a man whose women differ from upland cattle only in altitude and breadth of haunch." He was turning as he spoke. "Oh, and a stubble-chinned murderer of his own men, whose brother died dishonorably, and whose people will invent new jigs of merriment to celebrate when you drop d—"

Out from the mists on Halli's right, with sudden appalling clarity, a warrior leaped, helmeted and mailed. Halli caught a flash of Ragnar's pale face, teeth bared in a grimace. His sword swung at Halli's head; Halli ducked, heard the blade whistle close above his scalp and, with his enemy momentarily unbalanced, kicked out viciously with the side of his boot, knocking Ragnar bodily into the reeds.

Up on the earth bank, Hord's roar of fury shook the night; he sprang into the moat, a dark, malignant form, sword looping upward in his outstretched hand.

Halli had already turned and was scampering into the long reeds. To his left, another figure rose, his bow strung taut, an arrow notched. The arrow point swung round, tracking Halli as he passed.

Halli ducked low. The arrow cracked on the wall beyond his head.

Along the moat, through the mist, back the way he had come along the old familiar trail. The pursuers, close behind him, found the going harder, the twists and turns more unexpected. Seemingly from all around came crashes, footfalls, vegetation brushed aside. Again he heard an arrow's whiz, Hord's distant cries of rage.

He broke from the moat near the orchard, close to the place where he had left the House. He glimpsed the torn net hanging between walls, saw a man's body sprawled, arched and stiff, upon the tumbled stones. Sounds of pursuit were near at hand. Halli darted to the left, over the turf wall into the orchard. Mist clung about the trunks, and silvered moonlight shone through branches. Halli crossed the orchard swiftly; at the far end, where a turf wall gave on to the field and the ground began its long, steady rise toward the ridge, he looked behind him.

Nothing: the orchard was empty. Halli cursed to himself, chest rising and falling in savage strokes. What were the fools doing? Could they not even chase him properly? Would he have to go back, try to pick them—

Away among the avenues of trees dark figures burst from the mist. Six of them, or seven: glints of moonlight shone on helms and naked blades.

Halli's heart leaped in dark elation. Very good—the pursuit was on!

Now he just had to get them to the ridge.

Out onto the field he ran, away from House and trees, away from all perceptible forms. The field was fallow, grassy, and wet with mud; sheep had grazed here after being let out from the pens. Night mist hung close above the ground, congregating in hollows and pockets; in other places fading almost to nothing. Halli ran, hard as he could. At times he broke into open air, and glimpsed the livid moon, a silvered disc bright enough to blind him; then he plunged back into the mist's cold thickness, and could scarcely see the ground beneath his bounding feet. The grass was very uneven, choked with humps and tussocks, and many times he nearly fell.

Behind him came the drumming of boots, the rhythmic clink of metal. They had him in sight, or almost so. This was important. It would be no good losing them.

His idea depended on two essential things; three, if he wanted to survive.

First he must get them to the ridge—keeping them close, but not so close they caught him. Strong as they were, and faster than he, they wore heavy mail and carried swords. Halli, whose legs already ached, devoutly hoped that the effort of climbing would sorely tax them.

Second, he relied utterly upon the mist. If it broke or thinned before the ridge crest, his plan would come to nothing. The cairns would be clearly visible under the moon, and he would never lure them over. If it stayed thick, however . . . if he could draw them up beyond the hut, where the cairns were few and far between . . .

Halli grimaced as he ran, cold dread flooding through him at the thought—if he got them up there, it was likely Hord and his men would get a bleak surprise. Halli, though, would have to find high shelter, far away from the soft, dark earth, or the chances were he would share their fate.

On he ran, and now the field was steepening sharply. Somewhere ahead, concealed in mist, a stone wall marked its boundary; beyond was the track that wound up to the high pastures. The going would be smoother there, better than the field. Halli broke out of a plume of mist; moonlight bathed him. Far off, to his right, he saw the hoped-for wall. Changing tack slightly, he angled for it, forcing his limbs on.

Behind came a shout, a yelled command.

With sudden instinct, Halli zigzagged to the side. He took three paces farther.

Something struck hard against his shoulder blade, making him swivel, lose his balance, and fall heavily against the ground. He felt a dull, persistent pain. Struggling to his feet, he felt his shoulder, found an arrow shaft protruding there. Grimacing with anger, he pulled at it, crying out as it came away. Warm blood ran between his fingers.

Out of the mist, twenty yards distant, a warrior plunged, bathed in sudden silver. His sword was a narrow shaft of white. Seeing Halli, he gave a yell, increased his pace—

Stumbling, tripping, Halli ran for the wall. One hand grappled for his knife, sought to wrest it from his belt. Pain flared in his shoulder. He knew already that he would not reach the wall, that the enemy behind would catch him; in sudden hopelessness he knew that he would never reach the ridge.

Ahead, a low dark shape: the field wall blocking off escape. The harsh breathing of his pursuer took on a sudden new intensity—he too sensed the end was near.

If Halli had been taller, if he had been less tired, perhaps he could have vaulted the wall and bought himself more time. He did not even try. Half falling against the stones, he tore the butcher's knife from his belt and flung himself round to face his foe.

And the warrior was upon him, running full pelt, sword outflung to the side.

Halli raised the knife, spitting defiance.

He saw the pale face, the familiar squared jaw.

With a cry of triumph, Ragnar Hakonsson swung the sword at Halli's head.

It didn't connect. There was a clash of metal, a violent impact that sent white sparks flickering against Halli's face. He had ducked to the side, expecting the fatal blow; now, from the corner of his eyes, he saw another sword blade wedged against Ragnar's, locked against it, straining.

Halli lunged forward with his knife, stabbing Ragnar in the upper arm.

A wail of pain. Ragnar leaped backward, dropping his sword. In the dark holes of his helmet, his eyes were wide with shock. He cried out into the mist: "Father!"

Close by came answering shouts.

"Get his sword," a voice said tersely.

Halli turned. His gaze followed the sword's length

back to the wall above him, where Aud crouched, long hair whipping in the wind.

"Well, get a move on," she snapped. "We've got a hill to climb."

28

WITH THE HEROES DEAD and the Trows driven back, things became quieter in the valley. People were tired of the old ways and wished for a calmer, more peaceable time. No sooner had the heroes' cairns been raised upon the heights than their widows came together to discuss the situation. This was the first Council of Lawgivers, which established the laws we follow today. Feuding was forbidden, trade promoted, and the seasonal Gatherings begun.

To further promote peace along the valley, marriages took place between the twelve young widows and certain eligible men from other Houses, who became the new Arbiters. What Svein and the other heroes would have thought about this innovation is not entirely clear, but the system worked well enough. Within two generations the last feuds were finished and swords were outlawed in the valley.

I T WAS THE WORK of a moment to snatch up the sword; the work of another to scramble over the wall and fall down upon the hard dirt track. The mist clung thick about them; off in the field Ragnar's voice could be heard lamenting shrilly, accompanied by deeper, angrier exclamations. They began to climb the track, following its steady gradient. They did not go fast: Halli was light-headed from his pursuit, and somewhat out of breath, Aud limped a little as she jogged beside him.

"What," Halli gasped, "are you doing?"

"Save it."

"Go—go back."

"Shut up."

"It's not right for you, for you to do this. I told you to—to stay—"

"Stay with Leif and all those other brutes and fools, with you out alone here, trying to save our skin? No thanks." Her voice was scathing. "I'd rather die than live with that."

"But the Trows—"

"I'll chance it."

"Your leg—"

"Will hold."

Halli bit his lip. The recklessness that ruled him paid little heed to his own survival, but he could not extend such disregard to Aud. He would have stopped then and there to argue, but he could hear wall stones being scuffled, chain mail clinking, boots dropping hard onto the track behind.

He only said, "Please, Aud. *I've* got to do this, but *you* don't have to." He waited. Aud said nothing. "Don't you understand?" Halli said again, a slight catch in his voice. "I should do this alone. I'm fated."

A rude snort sounded in the darkness.

"I don't want you with me when the Trows come."

"Tough."

"I—I don't want you dying with me."

Fingers gripped his arm, not gently. Her voice was a ferocious hiss. "Well, you'd better make sure we *both* live—hadn't you?"

They clambered up in murky whiteness. All at once the shimmering light that illuminated the mists went out. The moon had been swallowed by the clouds. They crossed to the edge of the track and kept on climbing, feeling their way by touch along the wall. The mist's chill wetness drifted on their skin.

"How did you find me?" Halli panted.

"Knew you'd head for the track; it's the quickest way. I sneaked out by the South Gate, guessed where you'd be. I was too high at first, but then I heard your gasps and wheezes, got down to meet you just in time. Oh—listen to that."

A little way below them on the hill, a voice like a wolf's howl echoed in the night: "Halli! My son's blood is on your hands! I will follow you forever!"

"Not forever," Halli said, under his breath. "But a little longer would be nice."

"To think I might have married Ragnar," Aud growled. "His sword strike was like a woman's. D'you think you killed him?"

"Pricked him a little, that's all."

His left arm bloodied, weak, and numb, Ragnar Hakonsson trudged up the track in his father's wake, with three warriors beside him. The moon was gone; the blackness of the mist was absolute; they climbed like blind men, driven by their leader's fury. Ragnar held his long knife outstretched, fearful of the dark; the others tapped the ground with swords. Every few moments, at Hord's growled command, they froze and listened. Always they heard the scuffling of their quarries' boots not far above.

The men at Ragnar's side cursed and muttered as they went. One said: "Don't know where they think they're going. Any higher and they'll reach the cairns."

"Then we'll have them, won't we?" Ragnar said savagely. "Shut up and climb."

Small drops of blood fell from his sleeve, leaving a trail behind him on the earth.

Onward, upward, for an unknown time; for Halli it began to seem as if the ascent had gone on for ever, that he had been born to it and would die still climbing. Existence boiled down to certain dull sensations: darkness swirling at his eyes; the repetitious rasping of his boots on stone; the corresponding noises behind them on the track. He heard Aud's breathing near at hand, and felt the pulsing pain within his shoulder. The sword he carried weighed his good arm down. He began to grow sickened by the strain.

With each step his fear rose in him too; subtly at first, concealed amid the physical effort of the climb. Little by little it grew and strengthened, washing through his leaden limbs, clasping tight at the back of his throat. The marks on his neck flared and itched; his eyes stared blankly at the dark. Somewhere close, the cairns were standing; somewhere beyond, a terror waited in the earth. Halli listened to the silence of the mists, every sense straining with anticipation. This was surely how Svein had felt standing on the Rock that fateful night, hearing nothing, but knowing an attack would come.

In their wake he heard Hord shouting, cursing bloody vengeance on their heads. Such clamor meant nothing.

Halli listened to the silence up ahead.

He and Aud climbed on.

Hord Hakonsson was scarcely out of breath—the climb had angered, rather than exerted him. One of his warriors kept pace alongside; the rest—his misbegotten son included—trailed in his wake. Their weakness was another irritation. He followed the unseen wall as swiftly as he could, pausing every dozen paces to listen.

Whenever he stood still, hearing Halli's footsteps close

above him on the path, he rubbed the chain mail of his sword arm, feeling the place where the blacksmith's hammer had struck. Sore, but it would heal. So too the other knocks from the fight between the nets. Hord ignored them all. Great Hakon had frequently suffered injuries and fought on unconcerned—he had trailed his enemies for days with a colorful variety of wounds! As always Hord would do as Hakon did, though he anticipated this particular chase would not take quite so long.

Halli was weary, Halli was wounded. Neither he nor his accomplice could run forever. They would come to the boundary in the end, and turn at bay. And then—

Hord's lips parted at the thought—he would bring the matter to its end.

High overhead, the moon emerged from behind the mass of cloud, shone for a dozen heartbeats, and was gone. Gray-white mist blossomed, darkened, faded into black.

Halli said softly, "I saw the hut, I think. Over to the right."

"So soon?"

"Can't you feel the track's gone? We're on grass. We're at the upper pasture."

"The cairns will be just ahead, then."

He took her hand. "That's what we want. Let's go."

As they shuffled along disconsolately, Ragnar and his companions almost collided with his father, standing motionless, staring into the dark. Ragnar spoke with a touch of petulance. "What are you doing? You startled me."

"Be quiet. I'm trying to hear."

"They're onto grass now," a warrior said.

Ragnar sniffed. "We'll never find them."

"Be *silent*."

Wind from the high moors rolled over them, six men standing in the mountain mist.

From some way off: a sudden wail, a desperate cry of pain.

They listened.

Trailed on the wind came a sad lament. "Ah! Ah! My leg . . ."

Ragnar said: "That's Halli."

Hord's voice was gleeful. "Injured, maybe. Come on."

They had crossed onto the moors now; they knew it even without sight. The ground had risen sharply, then leveled at the boundary. To their relief they had not stumbled into a cairn.

"What if Hord realizes?" Aud whispered. "What if the moon comes out?"

"The mist'll still block his view. He'll follow us across as long as he doesn't stop to think. Shall I shout again?"

"Not yet. Let's go a little farther, find a crag."

"All right." He hesitated. "Aud."

"Yes?"

"Keep listening."

"Careful, Father," Ragnar said. "There's a pile of stones here; some old wall."

"Ground's rising," a warrior remarked.

Another said: "Hord, we must be very near the tops."

"What if we are?" He spoke from up ahead again. They heard him plowing onward.

"The cairns . . ."

"We must be sure to . . ."

"There! I *hear* him!" Hord's frantic whisper cut across them like a knife. The men fell silent. Out in the darkness, just as before, they heard the fugitive's mournful wail.

Hord laughed. "He's lamed himself, the fool. This is good; we're close behind. A final push, my lads, and we shall have him."

One by one, with varying degrees of doubt and hesitation, six men pressed onward through the mist and darkness. One by one, with equal blindness, they passed within an arm's length of a cairn.

Halli said: "They're right behind us, speeding up."

Aud said: "Arne's blood, *where's* the crag?"

"It'll be here somewhere. . . ."

"If only the moon would . . . We might see it then, despite the mist."

"It's somewhere close, but——" He stopped.

"Halli . . ." Aud said.

"I know."

"I think, I think I heard . . ."

"Don't. Don't think anything." His voice was high and stretched. "Thinking about things is bad right now. We mustn't stop. Keep going."

"Stop, all of you," Hord hissed, "and listen."

Ragnar and the others halted. A warrior said, "I hear scraping."

"Scratching."

"Like he's climbing on a rock."

"Almost like he's digging."

"Yes, but *where?*" Hord snapped. "That's the point. I can't make it out. To the left, you think?"

"Yes . . ."

"No—I hear it to the right. There!"

A crack of stone on stone.

"I'd swear it's to the *left* as well," someone muttered. "How——"

"Well, there are *two* of them, aren't there?" Ragnar snapped. "They've split up."

As he spoke the darkness flickered into life. Black clouds, silver rimmed, moved suddenly aside; the moon's cold radiance shone down. Their six gray shadows stood in conference within the drifting mist. One by one, they drew their swords.

450

"Ragnar," Hord said, "you take Bork and Olvir, and go that way. You others come with me. Hurry—while there's light. Whoever you find, you kill, and bring their head to me."

Halli and Aud walked on, hand in hand. All about them the white mist churned, carrying sinister subtleties of sound, the shift and sigh of moving earth.

Aud looked over her shoulder and for an instant saw a creeping shape, moving at angles to their route. Mist plumed over it; the figure was gone.

Hord strode swiftly through the mist, eyes glaring. The persistent scratching noise grew louder. It seemed to come from more than one direction.

Halli squeezed Aud's hand. A slab of solid darkness rose before them, blocking out the moon. Silently they increased their pace, hurrying toward the crag.

The sounds that Ragnar's party followed—the brittle clinks and snaps of stone—had ceased just as they drew near. Ragnar motioned to his men for silence: the movement caused fresh blood to drip down from his arm.

The outcrop of squared black rock jutted from the grass and rose to unknown height within the mist. The near side

451

was sheer and tilted; looking up, they noticed an overhanging ledge, just wide enough to grasp.

Halli looked at Aud and mouthed his invitation. *After you.*

Hord stopped; his men stopped with him.

"Saw one," he whispered. "Moving this way."

"Halli?"

"No." Too tall and thin. "His friend."

Time for the first killing. Hord gripped his sword and bared his teeth. Moonlight gleamed on his mail coat, his shining helm.

He strode into the mists. His men strode with him.

At their backs came dark, eager, hurrying forms, congregating from all sides.

Aud tucked her sword in her belt, jumped up, seized the overhanging ledge of stone in both hands. Her feet dangled in midair.

Ragnar smiled very slightly. He pointed.

Just visible within the mist: a low-slung shadow, coiled and crouching, as if it sought to conceal itself from view.

Ragnar's men moved outward, stepping carefully across fresh drifts of earth. He waited, wrinkling his nose at a rank and bitter smell blowing from somewhere near.

Now they had the dark, hunched shape encircled.

Ragnar raised his knife. He snapped his fingers, gave a cry.

All three of them ran in.

Aud had swung her feet to a crevice, and was levering herself up onto the ledge when the screams began. The shock made her lose her grip and she almost fell.

Halli spun round to stare into the mist. He saw nothing, heard much: shouts, screams (loud at first, then gone), varied impacts (some metallic, some dull and heavy), the rasp of sundered mail, the cracking of teeth, odd scrapes and draggings upon the ground, rustles of torn clothing, and assorted creaks and shuffling steps that were familiar to him from the night before. . . .

He pressed his back against the cold, damp stone.

"Halli . . ." The voice awoke him from his terror. He looked up, saw that Aud had disappeared.

"Hurry," she called. "Climb up."

Slowly, slowly, Halli moved away from the crag; with great difficulty, he turned his back on the swirling mist and its vivid array of sounds. Like Aud had done, he tucked his sword into his belt; like Aud he ran, jumped up—and utterly failed to reach the overhanging stone. He jumped again, fell back to earth. No good—it was just a little too high for him; his fingers brushed the base of the ledge, but could get no purchase.

Halli wet his lips, which were a little dry. His shoulder throbbed. Suppressing his surging panic, he felt around for alternative cracks or crevices below the ledge, but in vain. He cursed under his breath.

A whisper from on high. "Halli . . . what's the problem?"

He flashed a glance over his shoulder—swirling mist—and whispered: "Can't get up."

"What?"

His croak was just a little louder. "Can't—get—up."

"Oh, great Arne!"

"Are you at the top? Shall I go round? Where's the best way to climb?"

Silence. Halli spun slowly round; the noises were quieting now. No one was screaming anymore.

Aud's voice: "The other sides look hard too. But the top's above the mist; it's flat enough—we could defend it. Halli, you've *got* to get up. The Trows—"

"You think I don't know? I'll go round, I'll find another way."

Keeping close to the rock, he set off, but had gone only four paces when Aud's voice came again, only louder. "Don't go round."

"Why not?"

"I can see them in the mist, Halli . . . they're coming from the other side."

"Svein's blood, how many?"

"Can't tell . . . they're too hazy; the moon's too bright and they keep so low, like they're bent double, crawling."

Halli stepped back a few paces, gave a little run up, and sprang with all his vigor at the ledge. Missing it completely, he collided with the rock and fell in a sprawling heap. His shoulder was a blaze of agony; his blood splashed on the ground.

"Halli?"

"What now?"

"There are more coming from behind you. *Jump*, for Arne's sake! How short can your legs be?"

Halli made no answer; he was busy hopping and jumping and bounding against the black surface of the crag, hands scrabbling desperately at the rock. He became aware of shuffling noises drawing close from all around.

"Come *on*, Halli . . ."

Halli stopped jumping. He came to a decision. He turned, and drew the sword that he had taken from Ragnar. He weighed it in his hand, looked down its length at the nicks and dents left from the fighting at the House. He considered the solid metal hilt, wrapped with cloth. The hand guard was wide and sturdy.

Halli held the sword ready. Somewhere above, Aud was shouting at him, but he no longer heard her; blood pounded in his ears with an intensity that was oddly calming.

The mist flickered, dimmed: dark shapes moved within it, came toward him. Their forms were slabs of shadow; it seemed to Halli they were roughly human height, but appallingly thin, their legs almost swallowed by the meager moonlight, their arms like broken rushes, stretched toward him.

Halli took a deep and measured breath. He raised the sword.

The figures moved in with sudden speed.

Spinning round, Halli reversed the blade and rammed it into the soft earth at his feet—deep, deep as it would go: half the blade was gone. He hopped back—ignoring the rapid sounds behind—and jumped.

His boot landed on the sword hilt, pushing it down, propelling him up.

His outstretched hands landed on the ledge; he had his elbows on it.

He wriggled his legs, pushed with his elbows, levered his weight onto the ledge. Something collided with the sole of his boot.

His feet swung up amid a mass of noise and movement, of clicking, shuffling, and gnashing of teeth; of things bumping and scrabbling at the steep walls of the rock.

Moving without pause or conscious thought, ignoring his flaring shoulder, he clawed, tugged, and swung from handhold to handhold, clambering up the crag, as far and as fast as he could. Fear gave him strength. The mist grew thin; moments later he saw Aud waiting just above, her head framed dark against the moon.

* * *

The summit of the crag was a broad, irregular slab of stone, of uneven gradient, but for the most part flat enough to walk on. It was as long as three men lying end to end and almost as wide as two. At one side the rock had weathered into jagged, brittle spurs that cracked beneath the feet; the other edges seemed fairly sound. In all directions the summit ended abruptly above steep shelves of rock. Halli and Aud, investigating hurriedly, thought that two areas in particular seemed vulnerable to attack: the place they had ascended, and a narrow protruding wedge a little way off where the slope was not so sheer.

The crag was an island in the mist. Away to the north, the crest of Rurik's ridge was visible, but the valley in between was hidden by a silver sea of mist, flat and silent, unbroken save for two twisting cords of smoke that rose from Svein's House in the depths. To the east the top of the Snag poked clear; to the south they could just make out the little hill where Aud had fallen. Near at hand a few other crags protruded; far off, the mountains shimmered. They were alone under the moon.

The edge of the mist sea lapped against the rock a few yards below their feet. The surface was calm, but dark things could be glimpsed beneath it, pushing and pressing against the bottom of the crag. It was the same on every side. Muffled a little, but clear enough, came rustlings and cracking sounds.

Aud and Halli sat side by side, close to the edge. Aud held her sword, Halli his butcher's knife.

Halli said: "I've been thinking. Suppose we don't manage to keep them off till dawn. If they get up here and we can't escape . . . I think . . ." He looked at her. "I think we should use the sword."

"Yes."

"I don't mean to fight. I mean—"

"I understand you," Aud said. "And the answer is: yes."

"At least we've got the moon," Halli said, after a long pause.

"Like it came out for Arne and Svein when they fought upon their rock."

"Exactly. A bit of light to fight by."

"Did you *see* the Trows?" Aud said suddenly. "Down there. Did you see them? What were they like?"

Halli was turning his knife so that it flashed in the light. He cleared his throat. "Not really. I just saw their outlines. Thin, really thin . . ."

Aud brushed hair from her face. "Like the stories say."

"Maybe." Halli turned the knife. "Do the stories say the Trows wear clothes?"

"Clothes?"

"Not proper clothes: just rags, and tatters. . . . I don't know, I only caught a glimpse. I never thought they did, somehow. What the hell are they *doing* down there?"

From the base of the crag came a shrill scratching, as of claws on rock.

"I should think they're climbing up," Aud remarked.

"That's good," Halli said. "I was getting bored."

"Arne's line," Aud said.

"No, it was Svein's."

Aud got swiftly to her feet. Her hands shook, her teeth chattered together, but she kept her voice calm. "They're following the way we took," she said. "Where else . . . ?" She pattered over to the protruding wedge of rock, peered over, listened. "Yes, here too. I'll take this side. Do you want the sword, Halli?"

"No. You have it."

"I don't know how—"

"That makes two of us. Just hack at anything you see."

Each turned to face their chosen side. Above, the moon was a fierce white disc, the sky veined silver and black. Halli waited half-crouched, knife raised ready, watching the edge.

So it must have been for Svein and the other heroes on the Rock. The final moment before the Trows appeared. It was not an ignoble way to die.

The noises grew louder; the mist below seemed to boil and heave.

Halli tensed, ready to strike—

Behind his back, Aud squealed.

Turning, he saw her swing the sword down at a dark head rising above the stone; he saw it slice through the neck with a short, sharp snick. The head fell away; he heard it thud distantly on the ground. Two clawing hands remained upon the parapet; with a furious whimper Aud kicked out a boot, once, twice, cuffed them both from view. A heavy impact followed. From the mist came much rustling and agitated clicks of teeth.

Halli blew out his cheeks. It had all happened so quickly that he had not quite had time to register the Trow's face. True, it had been bent, shrouded from the moon, but even so, he'd thought—

No. No! It couldn't be.

A little sound. A furtive shuffling at his back.

Halli swiveled hurriedly to face his side of the crag— and found someone there beside him. He was squatting on his haunches, teeth grinning beneath the knotted hair of his tangled, spreading beard. The face had shrunk and changed; its skull-tight flesh had all but vanished, the holes where the eyes had been gaped deep and black, like fissures in the earth. On the chest, where the white shift hung loose, the thin knife hole had spread and darkened; it seemed to Halli that the skin had burst and come away.

Uncle Brodir held out a callused, clawing hand to him. "Halli—come close. Let me hold you, boy."

29

"AS FOR ME, build my cairn on the ridge above the House so that I may watch over you always; and those of you who obey my laws shall join me on the hill."

HALLI JERKED AWAY, screaming. He lashed out a leg, striking the figure in its bony midriff. It toppled backward, white grave-shift flapping once like a seabird's wings in moonlight, and vanished over the edge of the crag. There was a brittle crashing of foliage, a bump, a moment's stillness.

Halli too had fallen back. His eyes protruded, his mouth hung open. He heard himself breathing like a panting dog. He sat up painfully, then crawled toward the edge. He craned his head over.

Below him the rock face fell away, disappearing into mist. Deep below the surface he could just make out the ledge on which he'd rested, and beneath this a restless, complex movement, a host of figures jostling at the crag's base. Amid the clicks and shuffles and the scratching of claws on rock, he heard now peculiar gulps and hisses that stopped, started, rose, and fell—not words so much as reproachful echoes of past speech, whispers heard from far away.

Up the side of the crag something now crawled on hands and knees, proceeding like a spider in little rapid darts. Its head protruded from the mist—he saw the curled gray hair, the long, thin neck. . . . It hung in shadow, but he sensed it looking up at him.

"*That* wasn't a very nice welcome for your poor old uncle," the voice said.

Halli's hair stood up on his neck and scalp. His lips were dry; he pulled them back, panting, baring his teeth and gums.

"Oh, smile *now*, why don't you?" the voice continued, "but I've got to climb up again, a fearful job with a body so stiff as mine. Come down to me instead."

Fear had tightened Halli's throat so that his breath wheezed and whistled. "You're not what you seem to be," he whispered.

"Oh, but I am. And you are a very audacious boy, whose crimes have now caught up with you. Do you not remember me telling you most clearly that it was ruin to pass the cairns? Yet here you are, disobedient to the last. Never mind, I forgive you, seeing as it's so nice to be together again. If you *do* make me climb, the whole business will take ages, Halli."

"I don't believe it!" Halli croaked. "This is Trow magic—an illusion designed to drive me mad."

"Child, what do I know of Trows? Listen to my voice. Am I not your uncle?"

"No! You sound quite different."

"That is because the wind snatches at my words. Also because my tongue and palate have half rotted away, which makes forming consonants taxing."

Halli gave a cry. "What kind of an excuse is that? Anyone might use it."

"Halli, Halli, you *know* it's me."

Halli said: "Uncle Brodir—if, if that is who you truly are—try to remember: we buried you not six months past! All the appropriate sacrifices were made. You—you had a full and vigorous life and . . . and were well loved by us all. You should be taking well-earned rest, not walking the cold hills in that threadbare shift, with those poor bare feet. . . ." He trailed off. The figure below was scrabbling at the slope, seeking to climb; he glimpsed a bony knee out-flung, a gristly elbow bending as it hung upon the surface. Something gave way, with a screech of nails, the shape skittered down the rock.

The voice gave a gentle cry of frustration. "See what you put me to, dear Halli! Every time I slip I lose more flesh!" It paused in its attempts; he knew it was looking up again. "I was sleeping soundly in my little house, shielded from this horrid, hollow sky, and now I am drawn out once more. . . . Because of you, Halli. Because of *you*." A feral, gargling growl drifted upward. "I don't mind saying I resent it."

"But Uncle, the House is under attack—I had no choice. I lured our enemies up here so that the Trows could deal with them, and—"

Teeth clicked irritably. "*Why* do you persist in this? I know nothing of Trows."

"It's just we thought—"

We. Aud! He had entirely forgotten her, defending the other way up the crag! Halli flashed a glance behind, and to his unutterable relief saw her still crouching at the rock edge, sword in hand. As he watched she made frantic stabbing motions downward out of view.

When he looked back down *his* side of the crag, Halli was disconcerted to discover that the white-robed figure had suddenly and silently progressed more than halfway up the rock face. He saw the gray grave-hair whipping in the wind, the gaping eye sockets staring; and, behind the ragged, ruined beard, the cavernous toothy mouth.

Halli shuddered. "You tricksy thing." He held out his knife, twisting it so its edge flashed in the moonlight. The figure paused its frenzied ascent. "Ghost or figment," Halli said, "come any closer and I will slice you in two. After that I'll watch with interest your next attempt at moving—up, down or any which way. What do you say to this?"

A low desolate moan spilled from the open mouth. "Nephew, you are cruel! Surely you would prefer the fingers of me—who loves you—to press upon your throat than any other's. Throw away that silly thing."

"One inch farther and your head will spin into that cloudberry bush down there."

"But I dandled you in my arms as a babe—"

"Poke anything above the rock, I'll lop it off."

"I gave you ale and friendship—"

"So then," Halli snarled, "why try to kill me now?"

"It is not *my* doing," the form on the rock face whispered. "Do not blame me, or any of your other ancestors who wait below for you with open arms. It is not our choice. *We* do not choose to be here. We wish to sleep." Regret hung heavy in the ragged voice. "You can help us sleep, Halli Sveinsson. You can help us. Come down and let us punish you, as we must. Then he will let us sleep again—you and the girl as well. I will take you to my cairn."

Halli's gorge rose; his body shook so hard he almost dropped the knife. "You're very kind, but—No."

"If you delay," the voice said peevishly, "he'll come. None of us want that."

Instinctive panic surged through Halli; he sprang upright on the summit of the crag, looking left and right, over the valley, up toward the mountains. "I don't know who you're talking about," he whispered. "I don't know who you mean."

"He's already calling you," the voice said. "Do you not hear him?"

"I hear nothing."

A shudder, a sigh. "He speaks clearly enough to me."

The moon was covered for an instant by a spur of cloud

and Halli was blinded. He heard a scuttering below him; when he could see again he looked sharply at the figure hanging off the rock.

"You've come closer, haven't you?"

"No."

"You have. Your arms have changed position."

"I was weary. I adjusted myself."

"High time I adjusted you farther." Halli bent low, with knife upraised.

There was a scream, a shout behind him. "Halli, I can't—" A clasp upon his wrist; Aud was there, backing away from the edge she guarded. Over the rock's lip, rising up with eager haste, came outstretched arms and grinning heads. Moonlight shone on drifting strands of gray—white hair, on skull domes, grave shawls, tattered rags, and hints of bone. Long clawlike nails clasped the stone; teeth snapped together; whispers echoed in gaping throats.

A hop, a skip, a flurry of white; Brodir sprang up the rock face, dodged beneath Halli's flailing knife, and came to a crouching halt just out of range. He shook his head sadly. "Now, nephew. This gives me no pleasure, but it must be done."

Aud grasped Halli's hand. They backed away along the crag top, surrounded on three sides. With a series of flops and scuttles, the residents of the cairns closed in.

Aud flourished her sword. Halli jabbed his knife to ward off a lunging bony arm.

Brodir said: "Ah, your gestures are brave, but your bodies are weak and fearful. See, girl, how your sword shudders like a dandelion in a breeze; feel, Halli, how your teeth clatter like bone dice."

"At least we have our bodies still," Halli gasped. "More than can be said for you."

"A cheap shot," Brodir said. "Unworthy. Halli, Halli, do you not see that this is *your* doing? Why did you disobey his laws? Why did you break the boundary—not once, but twice? Why—above all—did you steal his precious treasure?"

Halli's voice was a croak. "I don't know who you mean."

"Oh, but you do."

Back toward the crag's edge; little by little, step by step. The moon went in and out of cloud; the stone of the summit dimmed and flared, flared and dimmed. The dark throng all around pressed closer, arms raised stiffly, bone knees shuffling on the rock. A thing of rags and teeth sprang from the pack; Aud swiped with the sword, striking it in midair, cleaving it in two. The top half fell beyond her, over the edge and away into the mist; the bottom half struck Halli with a hollow clatter. Cursing wildly he grasped a protruding leg bone and hurled it away.

Brodir made a disapproving sound. "Poor Uncle Onund! That is not respectful behavior to your ancestor."

Halli hacked and slashed with his knife, fended off a dozen clasping hands. "How about some respect for *us*?"

"We have no choice. We are his people. We must obey his will."

Aud struck out wildly left and right. Bone cracked, rags tore. Halli's knife grew tangled in a knot of grave cloth; he felt it wrenched away. In desperate fury he kicked and punched, only to have his arms snared, his leg grappled and pulled from under him. Falling back upon the stone, he found himself dragged forward; dark shapes swept over him, bringing a deathly chill. There was an icy grip upon his throat; he choked and gasped for breath, but the air was filled with foulness—

The grip lessened abruptly, the shapes withdrew. Halli stared up at the stars.

In a flurry of horror, he rolled, bent, got to his feet. Aud stood beside him, chest heaving, clothes torn, hand blood-ied, sword still in hand. All around, with an urgent rustling and clicking of bony joints, the ancestors were drawing back, retreating to the crag edges, lowering themselves down in awkward lurches. Skulls gleamed, teeth glittered; they vanished from view.

Only Brodir remained, crouched at the far end of the crag. He shifted fretfully from side to side.

Halli and Aud clung close to each other. The moon shone bright upon the surface of the crag.

The noises on the crag sides faded; all was still.

Somewhere away beneath the mists came a great noise, a crashing and clattering of rocks. It ended. At the same time the moon's light flickered and went out.

Brodir's voice said: *"Now* you've done it."

Long moments passed; neither Halli nor Aud spoke or could have spoken. Then, through the dark they heard, very faintly at first, but growing ever stronger, the steps of something approaching over the moor. Little by little the sound increased, and with it came the rhythmic clink of a chain-mail coat. A heavy tread, a mail coat clinking: louder and louder, until the crag and the mists and the very mountains that ringed the valley took up the echo; nearer and nearer . . . It reached the foot of the crag.

Silence.

In the darkness they heard Brodir's nervous scuffling.

Bang! An impact on the rock. *Bang!* Another. *Bang!* Something clambering up, with each hand- and foothold striking the stone with such force that the whole crag shook. Halli and Aud pressed close; each put an arm around the other. Still the moon was smothered by the clouds.

"Oh," came Brodir's whisper. "You've *really* done it now."

Bang! Right below the edge. And then came a rattling of mail and the rasp of leather; sounds of swift movement; a great weight landing on the summit of the crag.

In the silence that followed the clouds grew ragged in the sky; bright slashes of moon shone through. Weak light illuminated the summit.

It outlined the figure of a man.

His stature was a giant's: taller by far than Hord or

Arnkel, or any other leaders of a House; broader in chest and arm even than Grim the smith. A great helmet swathed the head. Light gleamed dully on its crest and side, but the face was shadowed and could not be seen. Faint glints across the body revealed the long mail coat, the armored sleeves, the metal greaves below the knee. The legs were braced apart, straddling the crag top; the arms hung motionless, one hand resting at a hip, the other silhouetted on the hilt of a dark and slender sword.

Power radiated from the shape, a power unbridled: the kind of power that tore rocks from the earth, split trees, withstood the river's torrents, sent its enemies wailing into the dark. Halli and Aud stood stricken; strength ebbed from their limbs. The force of the figure's presence beat against them like a tide.

It seemed to affect Uncle Brodir too: he skulked, cringing, by the crag's edge, as if eager, but unable, to depart. Now, suddenly, he stirred.

"Do you not hear him?" he croaked. "He speaks to you."

Halli shook his head, his voice the faintest whisper. "I hear nothing."

"He orders you to bow down before him—"

Again Halli shook his head, but he could not summon words. His knees trembled; he felt a strong desire to quell the shaking, to bend down, kneel. . . .

"He orders you to—"

Aud's voice was faint, but firm: "Know that we are of Svein's and Arne's Houses, of noble and ancient stock. We bow to no nameless creature of a cairn." She gripped Halli to her as she spoke; some of her strength passed to him. He drew himself up.

The great figure stood motionless; thin light drifted on its helm. Brodir said: "Halli Sveinsson, he talks to *you*, not her. Why do you not kneel? You *know* his name."

Halli sought to shake his head once more, but the effort was beyond him.

Light faded; all was almost dark; only the faintest gleams of armor showed. Brodir said heavily: "You know his name, Halli Sveinsson. You know who he is. He is the rocks and trees, the fields and streams. He is the stones of your hall, the timber of the bed you slept in. He is your bones and blood. He is the Founder of your House and the Father of you and all your kin, and he *dislikes* being disobeyed."

Until that moment Halli's dread had overwhelmed him. Now, suddenly, he felt a spark of anger too. "Why can he not tell me so himself?" he asked softly. "Let me see his face."

Brodir's wail was shrill, despairing. "Do not question him! He is terrible!"

Halli said: "That may well be. But in one matter you are certainly wrong. *My* father's name is Arnkel. He lies in his bed down there. This thing is no kin of mine."

Metal clashed, chain mail rang: the silent shape stepped nearer in the darkness.

"Arnkel?" Brodir cried. "Arnkel, who is weak and woman led? Arnkel, who dies without ever having struck a man? He shall not be part of our company when he is carried up the hill."

Halli bared his teeth. "That is not my uncle speaking. He loved his brother." He glared into the dark. "What thing are you that needs to use a dead man's tongue? I say again: let me see your face!"

Even as he spoke the moon broke out from behind the clouds and shone harshly down upon the silent form. Halli and Aud cried out; they flinched away.

The figure was bathed in silver light. Its armor shone gloriously, pitilessly—the crested helmet, inscribed with ornate tracery, with loops and patterns; the chain-mail coat, gleaming with the seamless intricacy of fish scales. . . . The sight was brilliant, painfully beautiful—it almost blinded them.

But beneath it was nothing but squalor and decay. Inside the helm: a moldering skull with broken teeth and sagging jaw. Within the shimmering mail: a gaping hollowness. Ribs poked through rents in the armor; where the mail coat ended, tattered fabric gave onto gristle, knotted kneecaps, yellowed leg strips. . . . The silver greaves swung loose on fleshless shins; the feet inside the rotting boots were nests of little bones.

Brodir gave a howl. "Great Svein is our Founder! We are his children, and must follow him after death!"

Halli shook his head. His fear was quite forgotten now, its place taken by a quiet, icy fury. It was an anger born of grief and indignation—at the deaths that he and Aud would shortly suffer; at the piteous state of his uncle Brodir, summoned from his cairn against his will; and, deeper down, but most bitterly, at the final shattering of the heroic dreams that had sustained him as a child. Like the glittering armor before him, those ideals were now proved utterly false and hollow. Where had they come from? Where, in the end, did they lead? The answer was the same. To the silent, voiceless, rotting thing that stood upon the crag top, radiating arrogance and brutal pride.

"Long ago I dreamed of being a hero in your company," Halli said huskily. "I'm sorry to say your reality disappoints me."

Brodir's head lolled as if he listened to faint sounds. His mouth opened. "Silence! He orders you not to speak. You—who have wasted the qualities he cherishes, who has grown soft and tractable under the influence of women, who is weak, without stomach for a fight—*you* may not speak to him. You are no follower of Svein."

"No?" Halli said. "When I always sought to maintain the honor of our House? When I sought vengeance for my uncle? When I protected the hall when the Hakonssons came? How have I offended him?"

The giant figure stepped closer, bone fingers cracking fast about the sword hilt. "Do not speak!" Brodir cried. "How have you offended? The list is long. Each time you had a chance to kill a man, you drew back. You let this girl fight your battles for you. You consort with her, when she is of another House. Worse than this, you break the boundary; you seek to leave the lands he made for you. Worst of all, you dare to wear his belt!"

The last words were a livid scream; with a shriek of metal, the sword was drawn. A bone hand held it, shimmering and delicate. A winding serpent pattern ran along the blade. It was twice the length of the clumsy, stubby one Aud had.

Aud whispered: "Halli—take my sword."

Halli, ignoring Aud, speaking to the silent shape, said: "You are nothing but a dead thing in a cairn. You can have no use for belts or anything else, for that matter. So what if I leave your lands? Your time is past. The people of your House consort with who they will. My mother is from Erlend's House; we are all of mingled blood. Aud Ulfar's-daughter has just helped defend your House against the Hakonssons—"

"None of his children are worthy of him!" Brodir whimpered. "They do not live by the old rules."

"I know someone who did," Halli said savagely. "Hord Hakonsson. He killed Brodir here. He burned your hall."

Brodir moaned, clutched his skull with both hands.

"Hord Hakonsson *was* worthy," he whispered. "He would have walked among Hakon's company forever, had he not been so stupid as to cross the boundary with you."

To hear such words forced from Brodir's mouth made Halli's anger flare. "Since when," he cried, "did the hero Svein care for Hakon's kin? You loathed him and all his House."

Once more Brodir listened; once more he relayed the things he heard. "In life the heroes were divided," he said. "But at the Battle of the Rock, they joined together in death, bound by their vow. Their sacrifice saved the valley. They stood against the Trows. They slew a hundred of the beasts in a single night, so that their corpses were piled stinking on the earth of Eirik's field. They drove them to the moors, so they never dared return, but died at last in the wilderness beyond. They cleansed the valley. It is theirs. It is theirs by right—and they exert that right *forever*." At this the armored figure stepped closer; in the shadow of the helm, bone glinted, bare teeth grinned. "Take off the belt," Brodir intoned, "and bare your neck."

"The Trows died in the wilderness. . . ." Halli said.

"Then that cave," Aud whispered. "It wasn't *human* remains at all, but—"

Halli's voice was small and wondering. "The bones of Trows . . ."

"Take off the belt," Brodir said. "Your master commands it."

Halli looked up abruptly. "The time is past when I cared a straw for what the dead might want. Get lost, Svein. I keep the belt."

For an instant there was silence on the crag.

Then Brodir's body contorted violently, his hands pressed against its head, as if deafened by some unimaginable roar of rage. And the armored figure sprang forward. Bony legs took rapid strides. Rags flapped and spun on decaying threads; chain-mail twisted; the terrible sword was out-flung wide.

"*Please* take my sword, Halli," Aud said, thrusting it into his hands.

Halli had scarcely time to grasp it when the glittering, shining shape was upon him. Moonlight gleamed on the serpent in the metal; the sword swung down. Halli lifted his in desperate defense.

The falling sword sliced clean through Halli's blade, was deflected slightly, and struck deep into the surface of the rock beside his feet. The force of the blow sent Halli to his knees; he struggled to rise, but with vicious speed the hero's sword was raised again, drawn back and driven forward, point-first into Halli's chest.

His mouth opened in a scream, but no sound came out; the pain engulfed him. He fell forward onto his face, fingers clawing at his chest.

Aud gave a cry; she flung herself upon the giant figure, grappling the arm that held the sword. Chain mail shifted, the arm jerked to the side, hurling Aud away across the crag. She landed heavily at the edge of the summit, head overhanging the precipice behind, hair dangling brightly in a thin cascade.

Raising her head stiffly, Aud saw a dark, bent form come scuttling near.

Brodir. Holding Halli's discarded knife.

At the far end of the crag the remnants of the hero Svein stood over Halli's limp and lifeless body. Its skull stared down. Deliberately, contemptuously, it drew back a leg and kicked him hard. Once, twice . . .

Halli gave a groan, and rolled suddenly aside. The hero Svein stepped away in stark surprise.

Halli got rapidly, painfully to his feet. He turned to face the hero. The center of his jerkin was slashed right through. Beneath it was no blood, no wound. Only—glinting merrily, unbroken despite the sword blow's force—the silver belt.

"Still lucky, you see?" Halli gasped. "Don't you wish you had one of these?" Still winded, breathing fitfully, he patted at his waist for weapons.

No sword; no knife. Nothing. Except—

Bjorn the trader's Trow claw, tucked forgotten in his belt.

With fumbling fingers, he pulled it clear: a little sickle-shaped curl of blackness.

"Come on, then," he said.

Black sockets stared beneath the shining helmet. The sword was lifted; the hulking shape stepped forward to strike the final blow.

A thin, bright line flashed at Svein's back, striking the neck bones just below the helm. Vertebrae cracked, shards of bone went flying. The skull skewed sideways within the helmet, tilting so that moonlight shone into the sockets and the hollow place between the jaws. The interior was filled with cobwebs.

Aud pulled the butcher's knife back: she struck again. This time she hit the chain mail on the nape and had no effect.

But now Halli was moving too. As the figure flailed and spun, seeking, with its free hand, to readjust the skull's position, Halli ducked in close, dodging the wildly swinging blade, and with the Trow claw struck down hard upon the arm that held the sword.

The claw cut through the bone as if through butter: the wrist shattered. The hand and sword both fell away. They landed on the rock.

Bone cracked to powder; the sword clanged once and lay still.

The maimed arm swung furiously over Halli's head; the hero pitched, kicked, clawed with its remaining hand. Still skewed inside its helmet, the skull stared blind and helpless at the moon.

Halli and Aud danced back and forth around the giant,

darting, feinting, keeping out of reach of its flailing limbs.

Aud shouted: "Halli—the neck!"

It seemed to Halli, for a moment, that he heard something: the faintest noise inside his head, a little voice piping as if from far away.

Stop! I am your Father, the Founder of your—

Halli dived low, came up at the figure's back. "Oh, we've been through all that. You're nothing but bones and air."

He jumped high, swiped with the claw with as much force as he could muster, feeling his shoulder wound tear as he did so. The claw bit through the weakened vertebrae, parting them with the driest of cracks and coming out the other side so that the moon's light sparkled bright upon it.

Halli swung the claw back, striking the neck again, spinning the head round even as it knocked it sideways.

Helm over skull, skull over helm, the head flashed through the air, cracked upon the rock, lost its jaw, bounced, rolled, and came to a halt upside down halfway along the crag top, with the teeth grinning up at the moon.

Then it shattered.

An empty helmet rocked gently to and fro.

The rest of the body took two steps backward, the remaining hand slapping ineffectually at the air. A third step—into space. Over the edge of the crag it went. It toppled away; the mists enveloped it. It was gone.

Silence on the crag. Silence in the mist. Silence in the valley and the ridge.

Halli turned: he saw Aud standing on the crag with knife in hand. She was alone. Bare rock and darkness surrounded her, nothing more.

He walked over to her, passing without a second glance a rusted sword and helm that lay discarded on the stone.

They looked at each other without speaking.

"Bloody hell," Aud said finally. "Your relations."

Dawn was near. Bruised, cut, shivering with cold, they huddled together on the center of the crag and waited.

"What I'm wondering now," Halli said, indicating the Trow claw that lay on the stone in front of him, "is if perhaps this thing isn't *quite* as fake as I once thought."

He looked at her. Aud's shoulders were slumped, her legs outstretched before her. It reminded him of her posture when she'd fallen from the apple tree. She wore the same expression of faint surprise. She shrugged at him, smiled, said nothing.

"Here's another thing I'm wondering," Halli said. "Where'd you get my knife? I'd lost it. They took it from me."

Aud said: "Ah, there's a story there. Your uncle Brodir gave it to me. At least, one moment he was near me, carrying it, the next he'd skipped away—and the knife was left lying on the rock."

Halli stared at her. "You really think—?"

"I do think so."

Halli thought for a time. "Good," he said, at last. "I'm glad."

Below the crag the mists grew ever more faint and lace-like, until the moor could once again be seen, empty, barren, nothing but grass and gorse rolling to the higher ground. Little by little the moon's power faded too; it drew back, sickly and afflicted, as a pale, golden light advanced upon the eastern sky. The distant sea was lit first, then the snowy tops of the southern mountains.

With the valley still in darkness, Aud and Halli sat watching the light gather on the far-off places, the places they had not yet been.

Not long afterward, birds began singing among the cairns.

Listen then, girl, and I'll tell you again of Halli Sveinsson, hall burner, Trow-tamer, great Halli Short-leg, who won the Battle of Svein's House in your grandmother's time, and so made us the richest people of the valley.

Here's how his story ended.

When the fighting was at its hardest, Halli and Aud, she-wolf of Arne's House, lured the enemy away under cover of mist and led them beyond the cairns. No living person saw what happened then, but awful screams echoed from on high. Some people thought that Halli had summoned the Trows to kill the Hakonssons; others that great Svein himself had come to help Halli in his hour of need. . . . Only one thing's sure. Not one of the Hakonssons came back down the hill.

Neither Halli nor Aud spoke of that night, except perhaps to Arnkel Sveinsson, whom they visited on their return to the House. He died a day later, and afterward Halli helped bury his father in a cairn atop the ridge. Then Leif, the new Arbiter, together with his mother, Astrid the Lawgiver, went down-valley to the great Gathering at Orm's House, where the Council awarded them the lands that make us so powerful today. But Halli and Aud stayed quietly here, and spoke little to anyone.

And it was not long after that, with the first green flush upon the trees, and the days grown newly warm, that Halli and Aud vanished from the House. It's said they left Svein's silver belt lying on the Law Seat, together with an ancient helmet and a rusted sword, which hang upon the wall of treasures to this day. Only Halli's old nurse spied them go: she came hobbling after, and they embraced beyond the wall, down where Halli's Gate is now. Then she watched them as they went across Long Meadow and straight up the ridge, past Svein's Mound and away over the hill, and that was the last anyone ever saw of Halli Sveinsson.

Now, *some* say they crossed the mountains and came to another valley and are living there still, but *I* say the Trows got them. That's much more likely.

No—of course no one else went over the hill. Who would want to, when we have so many fields to work and cows to milk and crying mouths to feed? We've more than enough to keep us busy here.

So. Take that dreamy look off your face and snuggle down. You pay too much attention to these silly tales. If you need to go, the pot's below the bed, but hop back sharp or the Trows will get you. Till morning then, my dear, Svein keep you safe.

Sleep tight.